LAST OF THE STRAWBERRIES

June Pettitt

authorHOUSE®

AuthorHouse™ UK Ltd.
500 Avebury Boulevard
Central Milton Keynes, MK9 2BE
www.authorhouse.co.uk
Phone: 08001974150

First published by AuthorHouse   16/1/2011

ISBN: 978-1-4567-7201-7

In memory of my son Mitchell who was sadly taken from me,
and to my beautiful granddaughter Tayla-Ann who he left behind.

For James, in appreciation of his help and encouragement
in making this book possible.

Preface

The small southern Ireland town of Kilcullen has roots in ancient history. 'The Annals of the Four Masters' tells of terrible Danish attacks in 936 and 944 AD, and probably led to the construction of the Round Tower. Located on the River Liffey in County Kildare, some thirty miles from Dublin, Kilcullen grew around the site of a 15th Century Franciscan Monastery. During the reign of Henry VIII the Protestant Archbishop of Dublin asked Cromwell, then Lord Privy Seal, to assign 'New Abbey' as a country home for himself. Remains of a church, the tower and three carved stone columns still adorn the fields near the early settlement. However, the building of a bridge across the River Liffey in 1319 saw the village relocate around this focal point. A rebellion against British rule dominated the county in the latter years of the eighteenth century, and in 1798 Kilcullen scored the only significant victory for the rebels. British troops were held off for over two weeks, but eventually the local heroes surrendered to the trained soldiers under the command of General Dundas.

It was now 1860. The population of one thousand mainly agricultural workers and their families had survived the ravages of the Irish potato blight.

CHAPTER 1
The Beginning

'Holy Mother of God, it's hot,' thought Michael Rafferty as he wiped the beads of perspiration from his brow. The fierce July sun penetrated his old brown trilby, causing his blue-black curly hair to stick to his forehead.

Farms in Kilcullen usually prospered on the plentiful supply of cheap labour, but it had been a hot, dry summer, and the fields, predictably a lush emerald green, were yellow and covered with dust from the shrivelled earth. With not a cloud marring the cerulean blue sky there was no promise of rain.

The all-round stillness was punctuated only by the occasional flick of Danny's tail which sent a welcome breeze towards Michael, perched on the cart's hard seat. The rhythmical clip-clop of the horse's hooves lulled Michael into a daydream. He dreamed of Siobhan, the same Siobhan whose beautiful face haunted him day and night. Would he get her to acknowledge him today? Could he get her to smile? What had got into him, Michael Rafferty, chief potato collector at O'Neill's farm? He could have any girl of his choice, and had, but since noticing Siobhan he had lost interest in other girls. 'If it's hot for me, Danny, what's it like for those pickers, poor buggers?' said Michael as he approached the potato field.

Toiling from dawn to dusk, picking was hard work for anyone, but especially for women and children. Their ankle length dark serge dresses carried a deep apron pocket into which the potatoes were dropped, then transferred at intervals to a sack. Their pay depended on how many sacks were filled. Babies were strapped to their mother's backs until their size made this impractical, after which they were laid in a makeshift oil-cloth tent to shield them from the weather. With the flaps folded back on fine days a breeze was allowed to blow through. By four years of age a child was expected to look after younger siblings, but soon they would start helping their mother. The picking season was short and money earned had to last them through the winter. Their men-folk were frequently out of work, but rarely did they pick potatoes - a question of dignity, as this was women's work. If a husband was lucky enough to be employed she could opt for fruit picking - the work was much lighter, but the job was not so well paid.

He went through the wooden gateway, the gate having long ago fallen victim to the ravages of the climate. The call went up. 'It's Michael! Michael's here!' This adoration always pleased him. He knew he was good-looking, six foot tall, twenty years of age, and in his prime. He had flawless tanned skin and twinkling forget-me-not blue eyes fringed with thick black lashes. His mouth was generous, and his smile showed a perfect set of even white teeth.

'Hi! It's your Michael, girls. Now don't all rush at once. I can only deal with you one at a time,' he said smiling.

'I wish you would deal with me, Mikey,' shouted Maureen O'Rourke.

'Yea,' he thought. 'I could have the pick of any of them.'

As always, his eyes searched the field for Siobhan. Even at a distance she stood out from the rest of the pickers, displaying a quality that he could not define. Even under all the grime, her white, flawless porcelain skin shone through. Close up it was her eyes that captivated Michael - large pools of sapphire blue, fringed like his own with thick, black lashes. Her nose was small, slightly tilted, and beneath, perfect rosebud lips. If he had ever seen her smile he would have seen an array of small pearl-like teeth. Her heart-shaped face appeared even smaller because of her thick black hair tied back with a single piece of string. 'Last as usual,' thought Michael. Her sack was too heavy for her frail arms to drag. Michael longed to help her, but he did not dare. He was the collector, and as a collector he had a certain status to uphold.

'Here Mikey, here's me sack.' The fat freckled arm of Maureen O'Rourke handed him her potatoes, grabbing his hand at the same time. 'Wouldn't mind getting in the sack with you, me luv,' she said with a raucous laugh, joined by the other pickers. 'Give us a kiss,' she said, pouting her thick cracked lips. Michael inwardly shuddered.

'Kiss that, never!' He thought Maureen O'Rourke's nature was as obnoxious as her looks. She was big and fat, with massive breasts that seem to have a life of their own. She had bright red hair, a red spotty face with permanent cold sores around her mouth. Her eyes reminded Michael of a snake's, small yellowy-green, darting from side to side in case they missed something. She was the cock of the field who terrorised the rest of the pickers. Michael had long suspected that she bullied the other girls into filling her own and her gang's sacks.

At last Siobhan came to the cart. She tried to lift her sack up, but it was too heavy. Michael smiled at her brave effort, and before he realised he was breaking his own rules he found himself saying, 'Come here, let me help you. Jesus, that sack is as big as you are!'

He felt himself blush as, without looking up, she whispered, 'Thank you.'

'What is the matter with me?' he thought. 'I'm acting like a love-sick schoolboy.'

Maureen's snake eyes didn't miss this. Her sore mouth shouted, 'What's so special about her that you have to help her?'

Michael didn't answer Maureen, but whispered to Siobhan, 'You are special, very special to me.' Siobhan thought she'd misheard - he couldn't have said she was special. She didn't want to be special, she wanted to be no one - a nobody.   Siobhan gazed up at Michael, fear mirrored in her eyes. He realised by his remark this fragile creature would now receive the brunt of Maureen's cruel jealous tongue. Quickly he shouted, 'Maureen O'Rourke, you ought to know there's only one special girl in this field, and that's you.' Laughter filled the air as Maureen, appeased, fluffed up her chest and strutted like a peacock. Siobhan scurried from the field unnoticed, except by Michael. He watched the beautiful, frail girl limp bare-foot down the track, back towards the hovel where she lived. 'Oh! Siobhan! Siobhan! What awaits you back home?' he said to himself. That, too, was what she was wondering, just as she did every time she entered her home. Would her father be there? If so, what mood would he be in?

Everyone in the village knew about the Dohertys. They thought of the family as scum, and were to be avoided. Jim Doherty was a drunken blaggard who would pick a fight at the least provocation. He abused his wife and his sixteen living children. It was hard to tell which were his wife's children, and which were those of his own daughters. How many more had been stillborn, aborted or murdered was anyone's guess.

The priest, pressurised by the villagers, paid a visit to the Dohertys to try to make Jim see the error of his ways. A bloody nose and a black eye was his reward - he never went back.

Siobhan crept in as quietly as possible, hoping not to be noticed. The house was quiet. Her mother leaned over the sink peeling potatoes, the children's main food - boiled, mashed, baked - even the skins were made into a broth with the leftovers from Jim Doherty's meat dinners.

The money the children earned was handed over to their father - a small amount was given to Mrs. Doherty, the rest was spent on potcheen to be pissed against the wall.

Jane Doherty did not look up. She had long ago lost her maternal instincts - they had died with her continual pregnancies and abuse. She was almost grateful her husband now satisfied his passion with his daughters.

CHAPTER 2
Jane Doherty

Twenty five years ago Jane Doherty had been a beautiful girl of sixteen. The only child of Kathleen and Thomas O'Shea she was loved and over-protected, leaving her immature and innocent of worldly matters. The O'Sheas were comfortably off, but Jane had no idea what her father did for a living. If the truth were really known, neither did Mrs. O'Shea. It was sufficient for her to say he was 'in business'. Jane had no need to work, and the few friends she had were daughters from her parent's social circle.

Jane was befriended by one girl in particular. Maria O'Brien did not particularly like Jane, it was just that Jane hung onto every word she uttered, and faithfully believed everything Maria told her. Although Maria's life was equally dull, she would concoct stories making believe she was having a wonderful time. Her four older brothers had given her a better insight into the desires and aspirations of the adult world.

It was at the monthly dance at the village hall that Maria first met Jim Doherty. He was tall and handsome in a swarthy way. The other lads were wary of him because of his reputation for having a fiery temper. No-one knew where Doherty came from, only that he hung around with the tinkers, and, despite not having a job, was never short of money. To the girls of the village Doherty held a wicked fascination, especially to Maria who would stand gazing at him on the occasions he came to the dance. One night she could not believe her luck when he strolled over and asked her to dance. He whisked her round the floor, holding her particularly tight against him. Doherty was a man alright, the feel of his taut manliness sent shivers through Maria's body. When the music stopped he continued to hold her for what seemed an eternity. 'Fancy a drink?' he asked, returning her gaze. He was not particularly attracted to her, but felt she would suffice for tonight. The local cider was not very strong, but after two drinks it went straight to Maria's head.

'Whoops! My legs are giving way,' she said, giggling.

'Ya need some air,' said Doherty, taking her outside. 'Ya not drunk, are ya?' She shook her head, her eyes sparkling with excitement. He lowered his head to her lips, making her feel faint and out of control. His tongue slipped into her mouth exploring all its innocence. Never having been kissed like that before she started to gag. Worse still, the drink eventually got the better of her and she was physically sick over Doherty's jacket.

'Holy Jeasus! What you doing girl?' he said, walking away in disgust.

'Wait!' she cried out, 'Wait.'

'Forget it,' he said looking back before disappearing into the tin shed that served as a gent's toilet. A sobbing Maria turned and walked home, having missed her chance with the appealing Jim Doherty.

Maria related the story to Jane, or at least a glamourised version of it. She conveniently omitted the part about being sick, and of Doherty walking off.

'Will you be seeing him at the next dance?' Jane asked, wide eyed.

'I expect so. He seemed really keen on me,' lied Maria.

'I've never been to a dance. I wish I could come,' said Jane.

'It's your seventeenth birthday next month. Why don't you ask your parents if you can come? I'll look after you,' said Maria, not having thought through the consequences of having Jane with her when she next met Doherty.

After much consideration, Mr. & Mrs. O'Shea agreed she could go on the condition that Maria looked after her and got her home by 10 o'clock.

On the day of the dance Jane was so excited she could hardly eat. She had never been to a real dance. Of course, she had danced with other girls at the 'School for Young Ladies', but never with boys. When Maria came to collect her, her face dropped. Jane's dress was not at all suitable. It was childish - pretty, but childish. Still, it was too late to do anything about it now. Jane herself looked lovely, even beautiful in an innocent sort of way, thought Maria.

Outside the hall Maria pulled Jane to one side. 'Let me take that ribbon from your hair and comb out those silly ringlets,' Maria said forcefully.

'Why?' asked Jane, frowning.

'Girls at dances don't do their hair that way,' advised Maria. 'And these frills,' she said, pulling at the adornments on the neckline of Jane's dress.

'Don't,' said Jane putting her hands across her chest trying to conceal her now enhanced cleavage.

'Don't worry. You can sew them back on before your mother sees it,' said Maria, just a trifle unconvincingly for Jane's liking.

Walking into the hall with Jane was better than entering alone to face Doherty. It was fairly crowded and they slipped in without anyone noticing. Jane held Maria's hand nervously, hoping they would not get separated. Looking at the other girls, Jane could see what Maria had meant about her dress and hair. Maria's eyes searched the hall, but Doherty was nowhere to be seen. Disappointed, she walked over to talk to her friends, thankful that their nonchalant manner confirmed they knew nothing of the previous dance's encounter. Jane stood alone, happy enough to watch the dancers and listen to the music. Suddenly, she felt a hand on her shoulder. 'Want to dance, darlin'?' said a voice close to her ear.

Without looking round she said instinctively, 'I can't dance.'

'With me you'll be able to dance,' the voice said. Doherty took her hand and pulled her onto the dance floor. He held her tight as if they were one as they glided round the room. Jane was reticent to even raise her head to see what this stranger looked like. He smelled strange, not unlike the smell of horses mixed with musk and perfumed oil. It was not unpleasant, but somehow she found it disturbing. When the music stopped suddenly he continued to hold her, right in the centre of the dance floor.

'Doing well, your friend is,' said one of Maria's group, nodding towards Jane and Doherty.

'Well, would you believe it?' Maria said, looking on in amazement.

After what seemed to Jane like an age the music started up again. She and Doherty danced around the floor, oblivious of other couples and onlookers. With growing confidence Jane slyly stole a look at her partner. She saw what other women had seen - a dark man who, although handsome, had the look of the devil about him. Seeing her glance, his face broke into a wide smile. His features seemed to change significantly as deep dimples appeared in his cheeks. Doherty's perfect teeth gleamed white against the dark colour of his skin. 'You must be hot. I know I am. If you go outside I'll bring a drink out to you,' said Doherty, leading her off the dance floor.

Maria, who hadn't taken her eyes off Jane, followed her outside, grabbing Jane by the shoulders. 'What in the name of Mary do you think you are doing,' yelled Maria. 'Don't you know that's Doherty?'

'I..... I didn't know,' stuttered Jane in surprise.

'Didn't know? Well you know now. Come on.' She started to pull Jane further away from the entrance. 'Anyway, where's he gone?'

'He's gone to get me a drink. He told me to wait here,' replied Jane.

'I bet he did. And do you know what sort of drink he'll be bringing you,' said Maria. 'He wants to get you drunk so he can have his way with you, as he does with all the girls,' continued Maria, conveniently stopping short of relating her own recent experience. 'Come on. We're going home.'

'Won't he wonder where I am?' asked Jane, not sure she was doing the right thing.

'Oh! He'll wonder alright. Let him!' said Maria, seething with anger. As she dragged Jane along, Maria's mind was turning fast. 'This little nobody getting all the attention from Doherty,' she thought. Hissing the words through her clenched teeth she said, 'It'll be the last time I bring you to the dance'. With spite in her voice she added, 'I hope your parents see their little girl with her hair down and her cleavage on show for everyone to see.'

Bewildered, Jane crept quietly into the house, thankful that her parents had fallen asleep whilst waiting for her. That night Jane went over in her mind what Maria had said. 'Have his way with her? What way?' She would ask Maria next time she saw her.

Doherty was none too pleased to find the girl had gone. He asked around the hall, but nobody seemed to know who she was. By chance, one of the girls remembered she had arrived at the same time as Maria, and was not seen again after Maria had left. Maria! Of course, now everything became clear to Doherty. For some reason the girl had got under his skin. She was not really beautiful, but had the fresh demeanour of innocence about her.

It did not take long for Doherty to find out where she lived. He hung around the bridge in the centre of the village day after day until his uncommon patience was rewarded. Jane appeared some distance away with a basket over her arm. Her direction and briskness of her walk suggested she must be heading for the market. Jane stopped to examine the display on the haberdashery stall. Suddenly a sun-tanned arm appeared alongside her and picked up a red ribbon. 'Holy Mary! Wouldn't this be looking well in your lovely hair,' said the voice from behind her. She turned to look who it was. Tingles went through her body as she recognised the man standing there.

'You! How?' she said awkwardly.

'Why did you run off?' Doherty asked.

'I didn't. It was Maria,' she answered rather weakly.

'Aw, Maria. I see. Well, Maria isn't here now, so let me get you that drink I promised,' he said. Taking her arm he led her to the drinks stall and handed her a glass of lemonade. Jane was shaking inside. Her throat had constricted so she could not swallow. 'By all the saints, you're a nervous little thing and no mistake,' Doherty said laughing.

'I had better go now,' said Jane after finishing her drink. 'My ma will be worried.'

'Aw, we can't have your Mommy worried, can we? Come on, I'll walk you home,' he said, gulping down his drink.

'No thank you,' said Jane, shaking her head, 'Ma would not like it.' Doherty did not press the point. He knew she could not be hurried, but he could wait. After all, he had all the time in the world.

'Do you come to the market every Tuesday?' he asked.

'Most Tuesdays,' she said, a little disappointed that he had not been more insistent on walking her home. 'I walk on the heath most Sunday afternoons,' she added bravely.

Meetings in the market, walks on the heath. The courtship had begun. Doherty took his time. In a way he found it a refreshing change and a boost to his ego. Jane listened to him, mesmerised by the tales he told of how he had been abandoned by his mother, how the gypsies had found him and brought him up. Some tales were true, others were fantasies. Doherty wondered when he should make the first advances towards her. Already he was having to work hard to suppress his sexual feelings.

The opportunity arose one Sunday afternoon. They were caught in a very heavy shower, soaking them both to the skin. Seeing an abandoned shepherd's hut they ran for shelter. 'I'll light a fire,' said Doherty. 'We must dry these wet clothes or to be sure we'll catch pneumonia.' Doherty removed his shirt and trousers. Embarrassed, Jane looked away and made no attempt to remove any of her clothing. 'Aren't yo taking your blouse and skirt off?' he said, looking at her. She didn't answer. Doherty continued, 'Alright, have it your own way.' Before long Jane started to shiver. Doherty pulled her close to him and put his arm around her shoulders. 'Look, be sensible. You must dry these clothes.' he said. Gently, he unbuttoned her blouse, removed her skirt, and put them by the fire to dry. 'Come on now, lie by me on this hay and keep warm,' Doherty said encouragingly. 'I won't hurt you. Come on,' he said, holding out his hand.

Until now, Doherty had suppressed his sexual desires for her, but having her half naked body against his was as much as his feelings could contain. He increased his hold, and before she could object he was kissing her. He kissed her passionately on the lips so she was neither able to struggle free nor speak out. He moved his kissing down to her throat, her neck, and then to her firm breasts. Doherty used all of his sexual repertoire to get her aroused. Soon she was responding with as much passion as he. At first he made love to her gently, knowing that she was a virgin. Jane had never before experienced such inner feelings. It was like an all consuming fire which she did not wish to end. Doherty, caught up in her unexpected responses, made love to her over and over again. Finally exhausted, they lay quiet until Doherty became conscious of Jane shivering in his arms, the fire having reduced itself to an inadequate pile of embers. His movement aroused Jane from her blissful rest. However, now awake, she was overcome with embarrassment. She reached out for her clothes and clumsily started to dress. Doherty watched with amusement as she fumbled over such a simple task. 'You're not sorry, are you Jane?' he asked. When she did not respond he cupped her face in his hands and looked into her tearful eyes. 'I love you and you love me. This is a natural thing that people in love do,' said Doherty.

From that day, every other Sunday was spent the same way. Somewhat inevitably, it wasn't long before Jane fell pregnant. She was not aware what was happening to her body, only that she had missed two periods. Eventually her morning sickness did not escape the attention of her mother, who had no choice but to discuss the matter with her husband. 'But, my dear, she can't be pregnant. She hardly ever goes out,' said O'Shea, dismissively.

'There's her Sunday afternoon walks,' suggested Mrs. O'Shea. 'I have noticed that she appears very flushed when she returns. And her clothes are sometimes in such a mess. I put it down to the windy heath,' she continued.

Mrs. O'Shea stood uncomfortably outside the bathroom door listening to Jane heaving. There was no alternative but to confront her daughter. Jane was surprised to see her waiting there as she came out, but did not argue when she was told to go into the parlour. Her father was standing in front of the fire, his hands clasped firmly behind his back, a stance Jane knew from experience was the one he adopted when very angry. 'Sit down, Jane,' he started in a firm tone. 'Your mother and I have a few questions to ask you. And don't lie, because we will get at the truth.' Jane continued to stare down at her shoes. 'What I, that is, we, want to know is what you have been up to,' said O'Shea, his reddening face belying an attempt to keep his self control.

Fearing her husband's temper would get the better of him, Mrs. O'Shea intervened in what she hoped was a gentle tone. 'Now, my dear, we are not going to be angry with you, but sooner or later you will have to tell us,' she started. 'Are you with child?'

Jane looked up, tears rolling profusely down her cheeks. 'Yes, yes, I am,' she blurted out.

O'Shea sprung forward intent on striking his daughter. Half anticipating this reaction his wife deflected the descending arm. 'That will get us nowhere,' she said with as much reticence as she could muster.

'Who is this man? Did he attack you?' O'Shea demanded, Jane's body now partly shielded from her father's wrath. 'He must have. Never would you have let a man defile you in this way,' he reasoned with himself. 'We've always watched over you, sheltered you from the outside world. I can't see how this could happen. You must have been attacked.' Without waiting for an answer O'Shea began to pace rapidly up and down the hearth rug. 'I'll kill the bastard,' he said in an instinctive rage.

'No, father! I wasn't attacked,' cried Jane, hysterically. 'He loves me and I love him.'

'Love! What do you know about love?' asked her father rhetorically. O'Shea side stepped his wife and grabbed Jane by the shoulders. 'What is the man's name?' he demanded.

'I won't tell you his name until you promise not to hurt him,' screamed Jane, now losing her own control.

Having been thwarted the first time, O'Shea now successfully landed the intended slap across Jane's face. 'Hurt him? Hurt him? I intend to kill him!' he exploded, reiterating his earlier threat.

Mrs. O'Shea reached out for Jane's arm and pulled her away from the immediate striking range of her father. 'Get to your room and stay there whilst we decide what's to be done,' she said, pushing Jane towards the door.

In her room Jane's mind raced from one emotion to another. What was the best thing to do? She would tell Jim? He would know what to do, after all, he had said that he loved her. Leaving her outer coat on display in the hallway, Jane slipped silently out of the house heading for where she knew the gypsies were camped. They would know where Jim was.

Her arrival at the encampment was met with a stony stare from a few residents attending to outside chores. The gypsies were a law unto themselves, and no-one went there uninvited. Jane felt frightened, but found courage to speak up. 'Do you know where Jim Doherty is?' asked Jane, directing her question to nobody in particular.

'What's he been up to then?' said a rough voice to her left. 'Bit young, aren't you? You're not his usual type.'

A girl with a mass of long dark hair appeared from one of the caravans. 'Who's asking for Doherty?' she asked.

'I am,' said Jane in a frightened tone.

'Well he ain't here, but you can wait inside if you want,' said the girl, stepping back to allow Jane to squeeze by. 'I'd be more than interested in what you want with him.' Jane sat down and began to shiver, partly through her unease, and partly through her inadequate attire. Feeling that Jane seemed distressed the girl made her a cup of tea, hoping to find out what she wanted. 'Here, get that down you. You look as though you need it.'

It seemed an age before Jim Doherty entered the caravan. He displayed a mixture of surprise and anger at seeing Jane sat there. He had not mentioned in the camp that he was seeing Jane, not wanting everyone knowing his business. Doherty turned towards the gypsy girl and gestured her to leave. 'Well, what do you want?' said Doherty, somewhat abruptly. 'It had better be something important.'

Jane started to cry, her trembling lips barely able to form words. 'I'm having a baby,' she managed to say at last. 'My parents have gone mad. Dadda says he's going to kill you.'

'You mean you told him it's me,' yelled Doherty.

'No, I haven't told him. I sneaked out of the house before they could beat it out of me,' she said, now shaking even more.

'Has he hit you?' said Doherty, his tone suddenly and inexplicably softer.

'No, only slapped my face,' she said, 'but he's threatened to.'

'He'll hit no girl of mine,' said Doherty, reverting temporarily to his former tone.

'Am I your girl, Jim?' said Jane with a glimmer of hope in her voice.

'Of course you are, me darlin',' he said. 'We were going to get married, it's just going to be sooner than I intended. Come on, we will go and see your father together.'

He took Jane's arm and they walked in silence to the O'Shea house. Jim Doherty's mind was working quickly. In less than an hour he was contemplating the change from a free man to the ties of a wife and child. On the other hand, O'Shea would pay him a decent sum of money to marry his deflowered daughter. Yes, he could be set up for life. It was about time he settled down, and after all, Jane was not a bad looking girl. Once established, there would be no-one to stop him seeing other women, if he so fancied. He walked towards the O'Shea house with a new-found air of confidence.

'Why, you're nothing but a good-for-nothing gypsy,' was the opening gambit of Thomas O'Shea as he disgustedly surveyed the man before him. Directing his conversation towards Jane he added, 'If you had to choose a man without our consent, you could have picked someone better than him.'

Doherty felt his temper rising, but managed to hold himself in check. After all, he would gain nothing if he were to lose control at this stage. He summoned his most charming voice. 'Look, Mr. O'Shea, I came here in good faith. Any other man would have disappeared when he heard a girl was pregnant,' he reasoned. 'I am prepared to marry your daughter - at a price.'

'What do you mean, at a price? I ought to flog you to within an inch of your life,' said O'Shea, raising his hand to strike Doherty.

Doherty grabbed his wrist in a vice-like grip. 'Now that will get us nowhere,' he said. 'Do you want it known that you are the grandfather of a bastard?'

Mrs. O'Shea began to sob. 'Oh, the shame of it all,' she managed to say. 'We won't dare show our faces in the street. Thomas, you've got to do something.'

O'Shea went to comfort his wife. He had not cast an eye in the direction of Jane for some time. She had been with this vermin, and now he felt only disgust towards her. 'Right! You marry my daughter and I will give you a sum of money,' he began, almost as though he had rehearsed it often. 'Enough to buy you a small house, and a bit extra to get you established. But there is one condition,' O'Shea said with authority. 'After the wedding you go away from here, and I don't want to see either of you again - or the child.'

Jane ran towards her father. 'Oh, father, don't say that,' she said crying. 'I love you both so very much. It will break my heart not to see you.'

'You should have thought of that when you were cavorting with this fellow,' said O'Shea in a way that Jane knew was final.

So it was agreed. The next time Jane saw Doherty was at their wedding in a quiet church several villages away. Only Mr. and Mrs. O'Shea were in attendance. 'We are only here to see that you go through with the ceremony,' said O'Shea to Doherty at an opportune moment. 'When the two of you are legally married, only then will I arrange for the release of the funds, not a minute before.'

Jane had mixed emotions. She was happy to be marrying Doherty, but heartbroken that she may never see her parents again. She went through the service in a daze. In just a few months her whole life had been turned upside down. Only one thing was crystal clear in her mind - she really loved Jim Doherty with all her heart.

At the end of the service O'Shea took his wife's arm, and, without looking back, walked out of their daughter's life forever.

Jane and her new husband set up home in a little cottage several miles away. Doherty vowed he would get a job and that they would live happily ever after. He was as good as his word on the former and got a job on a local farm. Jane did her best to keep the cottage neat and tidy with the limited resources at her disposal.

It was a very difficult labour, but memory of the pain soon faded as she and Jim enthused about Cairan, their newborn son and heir. Doherty felt there was no prouder man in the whole of Ireland.

Jane was still sore from the birth on the evening when Doherty made the first moves to restore sexual relations with his wife. An argument ensued which culminated in Doherty storming out of the cottage. He intended to go to the local tavern, and he intended to get drunk, very drunk.

Still very handsome, Doherty always caught the eye of unattached women. Since the wedding he had ignored their advances, but that night he did not come home. His eventual return to the cottage was met with a barrage of questions from Jane. Doherty did not answer, but slapped her hard across the face. That was the first time he had hit his wife, but it was to be the first of many.

Reflecting later, Jane saw this event as the turning point in their relationship. She never refused his sexual advances again, but the passion she once felt was no longer there. The magic had gone. Doherty sensed this, and his love-making degenerated to an exercise in lustful relief. Sometimes it was just a mechanical routine, other times it was accompanied by an aggression that frightened Jane. She began to dread the night. She was relieved when Doherty did not come home from the tavern, better still when he did not come home for days at a time.

It was on one of Doherty's absences that Cairan developed a fever. Jane knew that she had to keep the baby cool, but the more she tried the more intense the fever became. She feared the child was not well enough to take him to the surgery. Eventually, Doherty returned home to find the child dead in Jane's arms. He blamed her for neglecting the boy. She said it was his fault for not being there. Out of guilt he launched himself at Jane and beat her to a state of unconsciousness.

From that night their relationship went from bad to worse. Doherty lost his job because of his drinking binges. He owed money on all fronts until they were forced to sell the cottage to settle their debts. They moved on a few miles and were offered the use of a small crofter's cottage on condition that Doherty worked on the farm. Jane became pregnant again, and for a while Doherty seemed to regain some of the charm that first attracted her. Unfortunately, the baby boy only lived a few hours and Doherty returned to his old ways. After that Jane seemed to be perpetually pregnant. Sometimes she mis-carried, sometimes a child was stillborn. It seemed to her that it was the unfortunate ones who lived.

During one of their many arguments Jane said she was leaving and would beg her father to take her back. Doherty laughed. 'You could try,' he sneered, 'but they both died in the first year we were married.'

'Holy Mother! How do you know? Why didn't you tell me,' she screamed, tears pouring down her face.

'Why should I?' he said, still laughing. 'They didn't want to see you again. I found out through a friend that they had left all their money to a local hospital, with instructions that you should receive nothing. Anyway, if anyone should leave it's me.'

Jane restrained herself from uttering her next thought. 'And where would you go? Who would have you?' Time had not been kind to his formally handsome looks. He was now decidedly chubby, and his incessant drinking showed on his stomach. The villagers knew how he treated his wife and despised him for it. The farmer became increasingly annoyed by the little productive work that Doherty was doing on the farm, and he had no alternative but to turn them out of the cottage. He could not help but feel sorry for Jane and the children, and said they could have use of the hut in the top field. With their few belongings the pitiful procession trudged to their new home. Home! - a four walled hovel built of large rough stones held together with mud. There was a hole in the brushwood roof to let out the smoke from the open fire. Small apertures in the walls served as windows, across which a previous incumbent had secured dried sheep skins. Some old planks of wood had been shaped to form an inadequate door.

From that moment Jane became conscious of losing control of her mental faculties. She reflected on the death of her mother and father, the countless unborn children and Doherty's constant abuse. In a perverse sort of way her subdued state came as a blessed relief.

CHAPTER 3
Leaving

Jane Doherty was on her knees by the fire grate. Siobhan looked at her mother's boney frame, twisted with arthritis brought on by her many broken bones. She felt no love for her mother, and none for her brothers and sisters. The only emotion she felt was fear - fear of her father. Fear that he would notice her and it would be her turn for 'the big bogey thing', as her sisters called it. She would listen to the older girls describing what their father had done to them. She did not quite understand - she only knew it hurt and often caused them to bleed. After a while their stomachs would swell, and a new Doherty would be added to the brood.

Silently the older children started to drift in, subdued, until they realised their father was not in the house, then they started to chatter, even laugh. Eventually they heard the dreaded footsteps. 'He's a comin',' one of them shouted. The little ones ran and hid in terror, the older ones bowed their heads in silence. The door was kicked open and Jim Doherty's huge frame filled the doorway.

'What's the bloody matter?' he shouted. No one answered. 'It ain't a bloody funeral parlour. Is there no greeting for your father?' Jim Doherty was in a good mood. He laughed as he threw a bag full of food on the table. 'Get that down ya. Ya father's had a bit of luck.' Greedily the children snatched at the pasties and sweetmeats, cramming what they could into their mouths before it was taken away.

That night there was singing and laughter. Not only was there food, but potcheen as well. Encouraged by Doherty the children took it in turns to sip at the lethal brew from the stone bottle. The older children became drunk and the little ones were physically sick. 'Can't take it like your

17

father, eh?' said Doherty, exercising his weird sense of humour. Tonight there would be no beatings and no 'big bogey thing'. Tonight they would be safe.

The children slept on the floor, the bigger ones on sheep skins, the less fortunate on whatever rags they could gather up. They slept fully clothed and snuggled up to each other for warmth. A thin blanket hung down from the ceiling, separating them from their parent's makeshift bed constructed from a couple of old pallets, but it did not keep out the sounds of their father's regular abuse of his wife's body.

In the middle of the night Siobhan was awakened by Little Betty wanting the toilet. She watched as the girl went into the back yard. Coming back, the child fell over an empty bucket, causing a clatter. 'What the bloody hell's going on?' came a roar from within the dark of the cottage. Jim Doherty stumbled naked from behind the partition. He went through the door looking for the source of the noise. As the moon came from behind a cloud, lighting up the yard, Doherty saw Little Betty lying on the ground. 'What are you doing here child?' he said softly. Tenderly he picked her up, but Doherty felt her stiffen with fright. Still half drunk he shouted, 'You're not bloody frightened of your father, are you?' Betty's failure to answer infuriated Jim Doherty. 'I'll give you something to be scared of,' he snarled. Siobhan didn't want to look, but she couldn't turn her eyes away.

'Please, God, not Little Betty,' she prayed. He ripped the thin shift from Betty's body. The child stood naked, shivering.

'Bend over,' he shouted. Betty did as she was told. In a state of shock, she made no sound as he beat her bare buttocks, which enraged Jim Doherty even more. 'Not hurting enough, hey, you little cow? I'll give you this,' he said, grasping his penis in his hand. 'Perhaps this will make you yell,' he snarled. He thrust it into her small body. One scream after another pierced the night, then Little Betty's body went silent. Blinded with drink and lust he didn't notice. He pushed himself harder and harder into the child.

Next morning Little Betty had disappeared, presumably buried with the others in the field beyond. The day progressed as usual with no mention of the night's events. Jane Doherty reflected that there was one less to feed. The other children were glad it wasn't them.

Siobhan dragged herself to the potato fields, the already warm morning promising another scorching hot day. After last night's happenings she felt tired and sick. 'When was it all going to end? Why couldn't they live like normal families? No wonder the villagers scorned them, they were no better than animals. On second thoughts, animals wouldn't do to their young what their father did to them.'

Her thoughts were broken by Mary O'Rourke's shrill voice. 'Here she comes! Slow coach. Don't you ever wash? Lie in the dirt and we wouldn't notice you, would we, girls?'

Laughter and more abuse rang in Siobhan's ears, although she was normally immune to the name calling she had endured all her life. Today, feeling very vulnerable, tears started to fill her eyes. 'It isn't fair. It isn't fair,' she whispered as the tears ran down her cheeks, leaving white streaks in the grime.

Michael couldn't wait to get to the field where Siobhan worked. She'd been on his mind all night. He'd felt troubled. Something would surely happen to the girl if he didn't get her away from Jim Doherty. He wondered if she'd already been abused. 'No,' he told himself. 'Her eyes were those of a virgin.'

'Michael, Michael, want some strawberries?' a voice shouted as he passed the strawberry fields. A pretty, dark-haired girl came running up to him with a basket of ripe strawberries.

'Here, Michael. This will be the last.' She handed them to him.

'Why, thanks,' he said, reaching out.

'Not before payment,' she said, pulling back the basket.

'And what payment might that be?' laughed Michael.

'A kiss, a real smackeroo,' said the girl, smiling provocatively. Michael got off the cart and took the girl in his arms, and, much to the delight of others, kissed her passionately.

'The last of the strawberries!' he thought. 'Another picking season nearly over. How many more years will I still be driving this cart?' He had planned to go to England like his friend, Patrick, but sunny days and pretty girls kept getting in his way. Michael was in deep thought as Danny plodded on.

'Day-dreamin', Michael?' Maureen O'Rourke's voice brought him back to reality.

'Ay, day-dreaming Maureen,' he answered, his eyes searching the field for Siobhan. He spotted her. She seemed smaller than ever today. He wondered how old she was - fourteen, fifteen? He bet she didn't even know herself.

Eventually she came up, slower than usual. He could see the white tear streaks on her cheeks. Without thinking, he reached for the basket of strawberries and handed them to her. 'Here, me darlin', strawberries to match the redness of your lips,' he said, smiling. She hesitated, looking puzzled. He nodded and pushed them towards her, encouraging her to take them.

Maureen O'Rourke's voice boomed out, 'Strawberries, red strawberries. It'll be red strawberries to match your red arse when your Dadda finds out.'

Trembling, Siobhan started to shake her head saying, 'No! No! Don't tell me father. Here,' she said, thrusting the strawberries at Maureen. Terrified, Soibhan thought, 'God in heaven help me if me father found out. It would be a beating, or even worse - the bogey thing! What was Michael Rafferty doing causing trouble? Strawberries! Maureen O'Rourke! There'd be trouble, big trouble. God help me!'

Maureen ran off laughing, stuffing the strawberries into her mouth and singing, 'Strawberries to match me lips.'

As Siobhan looked up at Michael their eyes met. 'Come on,' he said, holding out his hand. Without hesitation she took it and jumped on the cart beside him. They sat in silence as the cart went as fast as Danny could manage through the fields. The pickers looked on open-mouthed. He didn't stop until he reached the cottage which was his home. It was only then that he wondered what on earth he was going to do with her. He knew she couldn't stay at the cottage - there was hardly enough room for the rest of his family. Anyway, he knew Jim Doherty would soon come looking for Siobhan when he heard what had happened. Not that Doherty cared for the girl, but it would be an excuse for a fight.

Surprised, Michael's mother came rushing out of the cottage. 'What's happened, Michael? What's going on? Who's the girl?'

'Calm down, Mother, one question at a time,' he said as he helped Siobhan down from the cart. 'Get the girl a drink, she's had a shock,' he said, sitting Siobhan down. He proceeded to tell his Mother what had happened. She knew all about the Dohertys, and agreed with Michael that Jim Doherty would come looking for her.

'But why did you get involved? You and your girls, you'll see where it'll get you,' she said as she handed Siobhan a drink. 'And what are you going to do with her now, I'd like to know?'

What was he going to do with her? The thoughts went around Michael's head again. Suddenly he shouted, 'I've got it, we'll go to England. I've always said I'd go, well, now I have a reason.'

'What!' shouted his mother in disbelief.

'I've got enough saved, and like Patrick, I'll be seeking me fortune,' he said, laughing.

'And the girl? What about the girl?' His mother looked at the frail creature.

'Ma, I said "we". I'll take her with me. I mean to marry her, mother.'

His mother could see he meant it. She'd heard him calling out in the night. 'So this is Siobhan, is it?' she said quietly.

Siobhan sat there, not really taking it all in. She was in shock, odd words floating around her brain. 'England! Marry!' It all meant nothing to her, none of it made sense.

'You'll have to clean her up and no mistake. She's filthy. I'll see if I can find some of our girls' clothes that will fit her - hers are only fit for burnin'.' Looking at her with pity, Michael's mother took Siobhan's hand, saying, 'Come on, child. Let's get you cleaned up.'

Mrs. Rafferty took Siobhan to the yard pump. At first the cold water was a shock to Siobhan's skin, but on such a hot day it soon became pleasant. She had been reluctant to remove her ragged shift, but was assured that there was no-one around to see her. Mrs. Rafferty was shocked to see how thin her poor little body was. 'Here, luv, let me help you get soaped up,' said Mrs. Rafferty. The carbolic soap worked a treat, washing away years of accumulated grime. 'Holy Mother, you've thick hair,' she continued, washing and re-washing Siobhan's matted hair. With the filth and knots combed out it hung like a black cloak over her shoulders. For the first time in her life Siobhan felt what it was like to be really clean. Michael had been secretly watching from the kitchen window, and could not believe his eyes. He always thought Siobhan beautiful, but now, cleaned up and in half decent clothes, she was breathtaking. Even his mother uttered, 'You're a pretty lass, and no mistake.'

Michael's few possessions were hurriedly packed. He was eager to get away before Doherty came looking for them. He kissed his mother and thanked her for the parcel of food she had given them. He should have refused for he knew they could ill afford to spare it, but Siobhan would find the journey hard enough without having to cope with hunger. 'I wish I could give you some money, son, but we have little enough as it is,' said Mrs. Rafferty with tears in her eyes.

'Don't get cryin', Ma. When I've made me fortune you'll have more money than you've ever dreamed of,' said Michael with a cheerfulness he could barely muster. He felt uneasy about leaving his mother, but knew his brothers and sisters would do their best for her. Michael could hardly remember his father who had died in a stable accident when he was a child. His main memories were of his mother's struggle to keep the family together.

Goodbyes were said and off they set to make their fortune. With Siobhan beside him he loosened the tension on the reins. The horse, hesitant at first, gently pulled the cart into motion. 'Well, me darlin', we're on our way. London, here we come!' said Michael to a silent Siobhan. He felt he had a world of experiences behind him, but in reality he knew his world was limited to Kilcullen and the surrounding villages. Dublin was less than thirty miles away, but Michael had never been there. He had heard tales of tall brick buildings, of thieving, drunkenness and even murder. Nevertheless, it was just another town like he supposed London must be, and could not help but feel excited. Because of Siobhan he had been forced to do what he'd always intended to do.

Throughout the journey Siobhan's state of shock stifled any sound she wanted to make. Her life had changed so quickly. One minute she was in a field dreading her home situation, next she was on a cart heading for…… She had no idea, but anything would be better than the hovel. If Michael had difficulty imagining a city then what chance had she. She only knew the name Dublin from snatches of conversation she had overheard as a child.

Michael chose to follow the country lanes, avoiding for as long as possible the main arteries into the city. Siobhan held her breath at the sight of the Blessington Lakes. Never had she dreamed of such an expanse of water. 'Is that the sea, Michael?' she exclaimed, free from shyness, and breaking her fast of silence.

'No, me darlin',' he laughed. 'That's only a lake. The sea is a million times bigger.' A warm feeling flowed through Michael's body, not just because Siobhan had spoken at last, but it was the first time she had used his name when not directly calling him.

As they neared the city the country lanes unavoidably gave way to metalled roads flanked by brick houses, all standing together in continuous rows. And the people, hundreds of them, hurrying about their daily business. Siobhan was overawed and clung to Michael's arm, her ears unaccustomed to the incessant noise of city life. 'It all right, me darlin', now don't be scared. Your Michael's here,' he said with an air of uneasy courage.

The noise and activity of Dublin docks amplified the degree of hopelessness in which they found themselves. He had naively imagined securing the horse and cart before getting a message back home for farmer O'Neill to collect it, but they had little money and there were no fields to leave the horse. He reasoned that the only alternative was to sell the horse and cart. He knew the true value of a reliable healthy steed, but this was a buyer's market. Many other emigrants were in the same predicament and only a pittance was raised. 'It's not really stealing, Siobhan,' Michael began to say out of guilt. 'I'm just borrowing. I'll send the money to farmer O'Neill when I've made me fortune.'

Since the famine thousands of Irish emigrants were on the move to the industrial parts of the mainland. The poorest adopted 'step migration', taking cheap steamers to Liverpool or Glasgow in search of casual labour that would give them enough money to buy a passage to America or Canada.

Siobhan's eyes were wide with amazement at the sight of the crowded dockside with its colourful steamers and sailing ships. Her ears buzzed with all the different sounds - people shouting, ships' captains screaming for business. She had little time to reflect on what Michael had planned. Planned! If only it were so.

Michael searched the docks to find the cheapest passage to any destination. Eventually, he bought two tickets for an old steamer that would at least get them across to Liverpool. 'It'll be standing all the way,' said Michael, counting what was left of his money. 'But the sea's calm so it shouldn't be too uncomfortable.'

Colourful steamers there may have been, but they were both taken aback by the state of the old ship at the far end of the gang plank. It was barely sea-worthy and already crowded. Still, it had probably made the journey many times before, and for them it had only to make one more.

True to Michael's prediction the water was calm. Siobhan looked in amazement. 'When we get to the end of the sea, Michael,' she began in a frightened voice, 'won't we drop off?'

'No, me darlin',' said Michael, comforting her. 'The world is round. Don't you know that?' Siobhan blushed. How could she know? After all, she had never been taught to read and write.

Though even bigger and busier than Dublin, the noise and bustle of Liverpool was this time less daunting for Siobhan. They stood on the quay side with all the other immigrants, some apprehensive, some bewildered, but all with an uncertain future ahead of them. 'Now, Michael Rafferty,' he addressed himself. 'Pull yourself together and find a place to sleep for the night. Tomorrow you'll find work to pay for the journey to London.'

Michael took Siobhan's hand and led her away from the crowds. The smell of food made Michael realise he was hungry. 'Fancy something to eat, me darlin'?' Siobhan nodded. They sat outside the tavern eating hot pies and drinking ale. Siobhan had never tasted anything so wonderful in her life. The ale made her feel quite giddy and, for the first time in her miserable life, she felt happy.

At the end of the meal Michael pulled Siobhan to her feet. 'Come on. We can't leave it until it gets dark,' he said. 'We must find a bed for the night.'

It was easier said than done. They tried several boarding houses, but the moment the landlords heard their Irish brogue, doors were slammed in their face. Suddenly, Michael didn't feel so happy. 'Why do they hate us?' he said, more to himself than to Siobhan. Weary with constant rejection they spent the night by the fires of the homeless tramps on the wharf. Exhaustion soon overcame them both and they drifted off to sleep.

Michael suddenly awoke, shivering. The rain was pouring down, the fires had succumbed to the downpour and the tramps had disappeared. Siobhan, probably more accustomed to adverse conditions, needed a little encouragement from Michael to wake. 'Come on, me darlin',' said Michael with a false air of cheerfulness. 'Another day, another way.' He saw her start to shiver and added, 'What we need is a warm drink.'

Michael tramped from lodging house to lodging house but with no result. He could not think of getting work until Siobhan was settled. It rained all day, and another night was spent sheltering on the wharf. Disillusioned and bored, Michael snapped. 'I didn't think it would be like this,' he said. 'I wish I'd stayed where I was.' He saw Siobhan stiffen and immediately apologised. After all, it was not her fault. 'Look, tomorrow we'll start our journey to London.' He saw the look of fear in her eyes. 'Just a few miles a day,' he added. 'That's alright, isn't it?' Siobhan nodded. He had no idea how far London was, but knew it would not be too difficult on his own. He could easily tramp down to London, but with Siobhan in tow it would be a very different matter.

Over the next few days they made their way along the roads adjacent to the Mersey estuary, then inland towards Nantwich. Michael was worried that his money had almost gone. After all, his aspirations of a couple of years, however inadequate, had not included an allowance for a second person.

Michael was in a pensive mood as they approached the village of Kemberton. Suddenly, his thoughts were broken by the clatter of hooves on the cobbled street. A horse and carriage came thundering around the corner, a woman hanging out of the window of the coach, screaming. 'Help! Help!' cried a shrill voice. The horse had bolted, throwing its driver. Quick as a flash Michael took off his jacket and waved it in front of the horse as he had done many times on the farm. The horse reared, its hooves grappling at the air.

'Hey ya, hey ya,' Michael shouted, still waving his jacket. The hooves came down. Michael stepped aside and grabbed the reins. 'Whoa, whoa. Come here, boy. Come on, come on. There, there, no need to be afraid, no need, no need.' The latter words tapered to a whisper. The horse's nostrils flared, its eyes ablaze. Michael began whispering in its ear, and, slowly, the horse responded to the lilting Irish voice. 'No need to be afraid, no need, me darlin'.' Michael continued to lull the horse until, as if hypnotised, it was calm.

The screaming lady got out, her hands raised above her head. 'Thank the Lord. Thank the Lord,' she said repeatedly.

Another voice joined in as the Reverend Parker emerged from the coach, his dog-collar on the twist, and his wig of office almost covering his eyes. 'Well, my boy! You saved our lives. With the Lord's help, you saved our lives,' he said as he dusted himself down.   By this time a crowd had gathered, so Reverend Parker seized the opportunity to address the public, hoping it would help to fill his half-empty church the following Sunday. 'The Lord in His wisdom sent you to us. The Lord is merciful, the Lord is good. In what way can I reward you, boy?'

Michael knew this was their salvation and said, in mock reverence, 'The Lord is good; the Lord sent me to you. He sent you to me. We've come over from Ireland to find work. So far we've been out of luck, so I reckon the Lord sent you to us in our hour of need to give us work and lodgings. The Lord be praised.' Michael finished by putting his hands together in prayer.

This wasn't what Reverend Parker had in mind at all, but with the crowd watching, he couldn't see how he could get out of it. 'The Lord sent you to the right person, my boy.' Then addressing the crowd, he said, 'The Lord has also sent you good people to me. He's reminding you that I am His servant. I am His word. He's showing you the way to His church on Sunday. I hope you all have heard His word. Praise be to the Lord. Amen.'

The crowd, filled with the excitement they had witnessed, repeated, 'Amen.'

By now a battered and bruised coachman had made his way from where he had been thrown to the front of the gathered onlookers, his respectful apology to his master being totally ignored. Dutifully, Michael turned his attention back to the horse for a final word of comfort. He and Siobhan then climbed into the coach to the applause of the crowd.

The rhythmic clip-clopping of the hooves soon sent Michael first into a doze, then into a deep sleep as some of the troubles of the previous nights were now, however temporarily, less critical. Siobhan, on the other hand, was awake, her mind racing with the events of the last few days. Was she being missed at home? She guessed not, as it would be one less mouth to feed. She thought of Michael whisking her away, the boat trip to England, and now they were in a coach with these fine people. It was all too much for her weary mind to take in. Slowly, her eyes began to close. Mrs. Parker had never been more awake, her face grim with anger. What situation had the Reverend got them into now? Why, these two looked like scruffs, and they were Irish. She had heard all about these Irish immigrants - thieves, drunkards - they could be murdered in their beds! At the vicarage it would all have to be sorted out. She pulled her cloak tight around her, in the hope of protecting herself from unspecified contaminants.

With a jolt that awakened its occupants the coach came to a sudden stop in the village of Little Chester. 'We are home, Mrs. Parker, home,' said Reverend Parker stepping out of the coach to be welcomed by Sally, their serving maid.

'What on earth.....,' exclaimed Sally on seeing the dishevelled appearance of the unexpected visitors.

Mrs. Parker clutched Sally's arm for support, saying, 'Don't ask! Don't ask! Just make a pot of tea and bring it to my room. I've one of my headaches coming on.'

Michael and Siobhan stood there forgotten. 'What about us, Sir? Where shall we go?' Michael shouted up. For the first time, Sally heard their Irish accent.

'What the devil!' she said in surprise.

The Reverend chose to overlook the reference to the devil. 'Oh! These two will be working here for a while. Take them to the kitchen and give them something to eat. I'm going to the study.'

Sally gazed on in amazement. 'Had the Reverend taken leave of his senses?' she thought to herself. 'Why, they were nothing but gypsies.'

CHAPTER 4
The Vicarage

Reverend Parker was fifty years of age, his wife ten years older. They were united twenty three years previously as a marriage of convenience for both parties. Dorothy Parker was no beauty, being short and dumpy with a rounded chubby face. Her small blue eyes were almost hidden by the encroachment of surrounding fatty tissue. Her redeeming feature was her hair - long, thick and deep auburn in colour. She had given up all hope of marriage until the day a penniless Arthur Parker had come to the village church to complete his training as a vicar. He had little education, but, as the church was short of men wanting to be ordained, this short-coming was overlooked as long as they had enough money to buy into a parish. Arthur had somehow got this far on trust, and hoped something would occur before his predicament was put to the test.

Dorothy's mother and father had died in a coach accident, leaving her a substantial sum of money. Arthur began by providing comfort in her time of grief, but this led to them becoming close friends. His proposal of marriage was happily accepted. Dorothy's money bought him into the parish where they had lived for the last twenty-odd years. The marriage was not blessed with children, an occurrence not helped by the few times that intercourse had taken place without desire or passion. Both now sought sexual comfort elsewhere.

Reverend Parker, now retired to his study to think things over, had given instructions to the cook to feed Michael and Siobhan. What on earth was he going to do with these two? He could hardly turn them away, not after so many of his parishioners had witnessed the incident with the coach. Collecting his thoughts, he sent for his unscheduled guests. 'Well boy,' he began with a voice that was friendly, but at the same time firm. 'I'll keep my promise. I'll find you work to do, but it will only be for a short while.' He paused. 'Now tell me about yourself and your sister,' he continued with an unjustified assumption. This gave Michael the chance to exercise his imagination.

'I'm Michael Rafferty and this is me sister, Siobhan,' he began confidently. 'When our mother and father died there was nothing left for us in Ireland, so we've come to England to seek our fortune.' Michael felt that was sufficient, but then added, 'And the Lord sent us to you.'

'True boy, true,' interjected Parker. 'How old are you?' Before Michael could answer the Reverend remarked, 'Your sister looks too young and frail to work, and I'll not be keeping you for nothing.'

Siobhan suddenly spoke up for herself. 'I may be small, but I can work as good as the next,' she said.

'She can too,' confirmed Michael, before becoming aware of the sharpness in his voice. 'Oh, sorry if we've spoken out of turn,' he began deferentially, 'but we are both used to hard work and don't expect to be kept for nothing!' He felt he had resumed his place. 'To answer your question, I'm twenty and Siobhan here is fifteen.' Reverend Parker got up and lifted Siobhan's chin. He thought that she was small, even for fifteen, but she was pleasant enough looking. No, she was beautiful. He redressed himself for having such thoughts, after all, she was only a child.

It was agreed that Michael would sleep in the barn and Siobhan would share a room with Sally. Sally was none too pleased with this arrangement and told Mrs. Parker. 'Look, Sally,' said Dorothy Parker dismissively. 'There is nothing I can do about it tonight. All this upheaval is making my headache worse. Will you be a dear and see if you can ease it for me and I will see what I can do about those two tomorrow.' Mrs. Parker handed the maid a silver backed hair brush and Sally began to brush her employer's hair. Sally began humming to her rhythmic brush strokes. 'Wonderful, wonderful,' murmured Mrs. Parker, closing her eyes. 'You always know how to make me relax.'

'Isn't that what you pay me for, Ma'am,' responded Sally, then added to herself, 'And you'll go on paying if those two scruffs don't spoil things.'

'My shoulders now, Sally, please,' continued Mrs. Parker, ignoring the interjection.

'I'll just lock the door,' said Sally. 'We don't want any interruptions, do we?' She loosened the fastenings of her dressing robe, causing it to slip to her waist and exposing her melon-like breasts. With an air of expertise that came with experience Sally started to massage the fat shoulders before increasing the radius of her strokes to encompass the white mounds of Dorothy's breasts. She stopped short as her hands reached the already hardened nipples. 'I think you ought to lie down on the bed,' began Sally, pre-empting what she knew would be the inevitable consequence of Mrs. Parker's arousal, 'then I can massage you properly.' As if in a trance Dorothy was guided across the room and laid down. Sally gently opened up the rest of the loose dressing gown and let it fall down the sides of the bed. The fully relaxed Mrs. Parker soon fell into a deep sleep.

Her task completed, Sally tip toed from the room. 'Now to deal with the Reverend,' she thought as she tidied herself up and made her way to his study door.

'Come,' said a voice from within.

'I've just come to see if I can get you anything, Sir,' said Sally quietly.

'Have you got rid of Mrs. Parker's headache?' said Parker with an air of sarcasm in his voice. He had an idea of what went on in that bedroom, but as long as it kept his wife happy then he was happy.

'Yes Sir,' Sally began, 'but what I've come to see you about is those two gypsies. Mrs. Parker is most distressed - I mean, they could murder us in our beds...' She would have continued if the Reverend had not stopped her.

'Listen, I know Mrs. Parker does not like the situation – neither do I - but some of my best parishioners witnessed them saving our lives.' Parker began to explain. 'I wish I had just offered them some money, but in the confusion of the moment I foolishly asked what they wanted. Once everyone heard I had no choice but to promise to help them.'

'Saved your lives! What exactly did they do,' queried Sally, deciding to re-charge his brandy glass, 'I mean, I couldn't make sense of what Mrs. Parker told me, what with her headache and all.'

Reverend Parker took a deep breath and began to relate the sequence of events. 'Now you see why I cannot get rid of them for a while,' he said, holding out his brandy glass for another refill. He drank it down in one. 'Anyway, Sally, my servant, what the hell has it got to do with you? I think you take too many liberties, my girl. You know you must be punished, don't you?' Parker was already unbuckling his belt. Sally knew from experience what would come next.

'Oh,' she began to think, 'both of them in one day! Never mind girl, think of the extra money.' She dutifully turned to face the desk and, loosening the draw string, let her bloomers fall to the floor before leaning forward onto her elbows. The sight of her round, peach-like bottom excited him. After some fumbling he held the belt in one hand and his erect penis in the other. Parker brought the belt down on her, firmly, but more on the extremes of playfulness than violence. The sound of the belt, her body's instinctive recoil and the sight of the red wheal forming on her flesh brought him to a climax. Sally lay there for a few moments waiting for the Reverend to regain his composure before retrieving her bloomers and standing up.

'That will be all, Sally,' said Parker, breaking the silence. 'The matter of the two Irish will be dealt with in due course. In the meanwhile the girl will sleep in the room with you, the boy in the barn.' Pouring himself another brandy he coughed nervously and added, 'The money is in the usual place.'

Relieved that she had been spared the full force of his sexual pleasure, Sally took the sixpence out of the small drawer in the cabinet and quietly left the room. 'Yes, I'm on to a good thing here,' she smiled to herself, 'and nobody's going to spoil it.'

Sally went into the kitchen where Michael and Siobhan were seated at the scrubbed top pine table eating generous helpings of ham and vegetable broth. Michael didn't look up as Sally entered the room, too intent on filling his belly in case the whole episode turned sour. Siobhan had little experience of gobbling down food, and chose to slowly savour each mouthful of the unquestionably delicious morsels. 'I see they're making themselves at home,' Sally said to Mrs. Bunce, the part time cook, trying to apply the same sarcastic air that she had just heard her employer use.

'I'm just doing as I was instructed, you've no objections I hope,' said Mrs. Bunce in a tone that showed Sally did not have a monopoly on sarcasm. Sally let the comment pass.

'Girl,' Sally barked at Siobhan, 'When you've finished, get yourself washed. Use the pump in the yard. If you must stay in my room I want you clean - no fleas or lice. Understand? And he's sleeping in the barn,' she added to no-one in particular. She stormed out of the room, slamming the door and causing the hanging saucepans to rattle.

'Well I never,' said Mrs. Bunce quietly. 'Takes too much on herself, that one. Come on girl, you wash at the sink here. I'll boil the kettle. At least you'll have warm water.' She lifted the cast iron kettle onto the trivet and swung it over the fire in the black lead grate. 'Fleas, indeed,' she muttered.

Siobhan was shown to Sally's small room in the attic. 'You may have to sleep in my room, but it won't be in my bed,' snarled Sally, pointing to the corner of the room. 'It's the floor for you my girl.' A blanket and pillow were thrown in the direction indicated. 'And think yourself lucky I'm giving you these.'

Siobhan, too frightened to say anything, removed her dress and snuggled down. She wrapped the blanket tightly around her but could not sleep. Once again she thought about leaving home, the steam ship and Michael - the Michael she hardly knew. He was a potato collector who had singled her out and said she was special, but what was special about her? He had saved the lives of the Parkers, so he must be good and brave. And what of her own mother, her brothers and sisters? Was her father looking for her, and would he come over to England? She shivered at the thought. Of course he would not come. England was a big place and he could never hope to find her. She had prayed to the Holy Mother to help get her away from her father, and the Holy Mother had answered her prayers. With this comforting thought Siobhan finally dropped off to sleep.

'Come on. You can't sleep all day,' said Sally, shaking her by the shoulder. 'While you are staying here you'll earn your keep.'

In the kitchen Sally told her to clear the cinders from the cooking range, put fresh coal in the grate then polish the surround until it shone like black gold. 'Cook comes in at seven o'clock and she likes everything spick and span,' she began, enjoying giving the orders. 'The Parkers eat at eight o'clock, but I take Mrs. Parker a cup of tea at half past seven. Then I help her dress. The fat cow can dress herself, but she likes me to help her.' She brought herself up short. It was not right to make disrespectful remarks in front of a total stranger. 'When you've done the grate come to me. I'll be somewhere in the house, dusting and polishing. You can help me.' Sally reflected on the situation. Perhaps the girl could be quite useful after all.

The Parkers sat in silence, eating an ample breakfast. A good thing about the Parker household was a copious supply of food. Sally came bustling in with a fresh pot of tea. No mention had been made of Michael and Siobhan, so Sally resigned herself to the task of broaching the subject once more. 'Sir, what shall I tell the boy to do? What work is there for him?' she asked whilst pouring the Reverend his tea. The Reverend looked puzzled.

'The boy and the girl,' prompted Mrs. Parker. The Reverend started to chuckle.

'You know, my dear, I'd forgotten all about them.' He turned to Sally. 'You can find something for the girl to do. As for the boy, send him to my study after I have finished my breakfast.' Sally went back to the kitchen muttering about things always being left for her to do. She was the one to do the sorting out.

'Now, you know you wouldn't have it any other way,' said cook.

'Maybe,' started Sally before noticing Michael and Siobhan devouring a plate of bacon, sausage and eggs. 'What's going on here?' she shouted at cook.

'Them's entitled to a breakfast if they'm be working here,' she shouted back at Sally. 'Anyway, there's more than enough to go round.'

Michael just sat there eating and listening to the conversation around him. He, like Siobhan, had spent part of the night reflecting on their new situation. It was obvious that Sally was running the household, so he must keep on the right side of her. He took his first step in winning her round. Michael lifted his head and, with all the Irish charm he could muster, looked her straight in the eyes. 'I'm sorry, Miss, if I've overstepped the mark, but I didn't know the proper thing to do, well, not being used to grand people like yourselves.' His eyes sparkled as he added the last part. Sally did not seem to notice the mockery, only those blue eyes fringed with thick black lashes. The look sent shivers right through her body. She just stood there transfixed.

'It's... It's alright,' she eventually managed to stutter. 'And, yes, you are right, I do run the household. Master will see you in his study at nine o'clock.' With that she fled from the room.

'Well I never!' said cook. 'What's up with her?' Michael laughed. His charm had worked, and yes, he could have any girl of his choosing.

Promptly at nine o'clock Michael knocked on the door of the study. 'Enter.' Reverend Parker looked Michael up and down. He thought what a handsome youth he was, and well built. He could get done some of the tasks that had been let slip in recent years. 'Well, my boy, I'll keep my promise and find work for you and your sister for a few weeks.' He listed a number of jobs that needed doing around the vicarage.

Michael thanked the Reverend and started work on a broken fence close to the house. Sally watched him from the upstairs window. 'He's certainly good looking, and he's got a fine body on him,' she found herself thinking. 'Now what would he be like in bed. It would be nice to be made love to for once by a proper man, a man she was already falling in love with.'

Sally looked up at the sky. She watched the movement of the clouds as if they were jockeying for position in an imaginary race, and began to reminisce about her past life.

CHAPTER 5
Sally

All her life Sally had manipulated men to get what she wanted. Her mother, abandoned by her lover, had given birth to her in the workhouse, but died a week later. Like all workhouse orphan children they were reared and set to work as soon as they were strong enough. Some of the lucky ones were adopted by childless couples, others sold into virtual slavery as unpaid skivvies. The pretty ones were the least fortunate. They were bought by pimps to work as prostitutes, or for their new master's sexual gratification.

Sally was never beautiful, but had a certain attractiveness and a quick brain. As soon as she realised the fate of the chosen ones she set about maintaining a low profile to ensure no-one would select her. She was, however, always pleasant and agreeable to the house governor. He was a squat, tubby man with a ruddy complexion and sparse greasy black hair. He prided himself on being a fair man who meted out punishment only when fully justified. Provided his establishment ran smoothly he turned a blind eye to the activities of his staff, including the abuse of boys and girls in their care for their own personal gratification.

From an early age Sally played the role of 'devil's advocate'. She was happy to alert staff when the governor was on his rounds, but equally prepared to inform him of the indiscretions of his staff and inmates. Consequently, even at the age of thirteen, she was respected by members of staff and occasionally became a confidant of the governor. Sally made full use of her friendship with a few educated young ladies who, like her mother, had disgraced their families and been abandoned by their lovers. Having nowhere else to go, most of them lived in the workhouse doing manual tasks for their keep. With reluctance Sally would do some of the jobs assigned to her companions in exchange for being taught to read and write. Inwardly she felt no compassion for these girls. 'After all, they had been brought up not knowing hunger or poverty,' she reasoned with herself. 'If they had been stupid enough to let a man ruin every privilege they had, they deserved the consequences.' No man would ever do that to her.

In the early evening Sally would visit the governor's study, pour him a brandy then feign tidying up until he began to engage her in conversation. She would listen attentively whilst he rambled on about life's missed opportunities, how his poor eyesight had precluded him from joining the navy. He told how the love of his life had been lost to his cousin. Night after night she would make sympathetic responses, even though she had heard the tales so many times before.

Sally chose an evening when the governor was on his umpteenth glass of brandy and feeling particularly melancholy. She stood behind his chair and put her arms around his shoulders. 'Why, you poor dear,' she began in mock sympathy. 'Life has treated you really badly. You're all alone with no-one to care for you. It's a good job you've got me.' She began to stroke his hair and caress the nape of his neck. He looked back at her. His eyes began to fill with tears that soon rolled slowly down his fat cheeks. 'Now, now, no need to upset yourself. I'm here to look after you,' said Sally, undoing his cravat. She bent forward and gently kissed him on his thick lips. Her actions made her heave with disgust, but nevertheless she continued in the belief that it could be a passport to life outside this hell hole. She undid his shirt and loosened his trousers - instinctively she felt she should not undress him too far. He was well under the influence of the brandy, and with a bit of luck would not remember the next day whether or not they had been intimate. Sally had no intention of doing the final act. 'If I play it right,' Sally reasoned to herself, 'I might never have to give myself fully to him. My greatest asset is my virginity, and the right man would pay dearly to deflower me.' She was not going to waste a potential opportunity to a mere workhouse governor.

After that evening Sally felt inclined to keep away from the governor's study. If he was regretting the incident then she did not want to incur his wrath. If, on the other hand, he found pleasure in the tryst he would surely respond.

On the third day her patience was rewarded when the governor sent for her. 'Where have you been, Sally,' he said in a concerned manner, 'I've been lonely without you.'

'I didn't know whether you would want to see me again, Sir,' she began with coyly lowered eyes. 'I was afraid you may have thought I'd taken liberties,' she added, putting aside the reality that it was he who had taken the liberties.

'You come to my study tonight, my dear,' said the governor, ignoring her comments. 'I've a little something for you,' he said smiling.

Sally did go to the study that night, and for most nights afterwards. Each time she was rewarded with a small present or some money. It was the money she particularly liked, as this was to be the key to a life outside the workhouse. She was allowed to go out shopping for clothes, and he would get a thrill from watching her parade the new purchases seductively before him. Not that all of her clothes were new. He would never notice a degree of recycling of garments, so she could retain as much money as possible. She would let him partially undress her, to fondle her developing breasts, and even to touch the soft down of her vaginal hair. But that was as far as she would allow him to go. 'One day when I am old enough and feel ready,' she would say to him. With his relative sexual inexperience he seemed to accept the situation, content with his fanciful level of expectation.

That was how the relationship remained until the time of her fourteenth birthday. The governor started to become demonstrative, saying that since she had started 'the curse' she was now a woman, and it was time she gave herself fully to him. Sally wondered how long she could keep persuading him to wait a little longer. She had a small amount of money that should keep her until she found a job, but running away would surely result in the house beadles finding her and bringing her back. A possible solution arose on one of Sally's visits to the local market to buy provisions. She heard there was a position for a kitchen maid at Bromley Manor. A post like that would allow her the opportunity to work with the gentry, even if she did start at the lowliest of positions. There was, however, no way that she could seek employment whilst belonging to the workhouse. Unless....

That evening she was enduring the usual barrage of pestering from the governor. 'Alright, you can have me,' Sally began. 'But first I want a favour in return. There's a position of kitchen maid going at Bromley Manor. I want you to see that I get it.'

'But I won't see you if you get the position,' stammered the governor.

'Of course you will,' returned Sally. 'I'll come back here in secret on my day off, and sometimes at night. It may be for the best. I haven't said anything before, but the staff are starting to talk about us,' she continued. 'If it gets to the ears of your superiors we might both be looking for a job.'

The governor thought this over for a while. 'Are they really talking about me?' he asked, sounding a little worried.

'Yes, they are,' said Sally. 'Why do you think I have been looking for a job away from here? It's to protect you.'

'Alright,' said the governor. 'I'll go to the manor and see the cook in the morning. Now, Sally, you can give me what I've been waiting for so patiently.'

Sally started at the manor house a few days later with no intention of ever setting foot in the workhouse again. She readily agreed when cook informed her that, of course, she would have to live in. It took less than a week before she first wondered if she had done the right thing in coming to the manor. Sally was put to work from dawn until dusk doing all the dirty and unpleasant duties. No sooner was one task finished than another was lined up for her. With sheer determination she persevered in the hope that a more suitable position would manifest itself. It was not long before her patience was rewarded when an upstairs maid left suddenly. No-one knew why, but a rumour went around that it was something connected with the young Lord Peter.

'I know you haven't been here long,' said cook after breakfast, 'but, Sally, you are a good worker and always do as you are bid, so I'm sending you to the housekeeper.' Cook had something wrapped in brown paper. 'If she thinks you are suitable you'll get the job of upstairs maid,' she continued, handing her a smart navy dress with white apron and cap. 'You'll wear these to see the housekeeper. Mind, if you don't get the position you'll have to give them back.'

Sally did get the job working with two other maids to change the bed linen and towels and keep the upstairs neat and clean. With only Lady Anne residing there permanently it was not a particularly arduous task. That is, except when Lady Anne's son, the young Lord Peter Bromley was in residence. He would return home with a number of his friends and then it was partying every night. The cook employed extra staff and the housekeeper and footman were run off their feet. Just as suddenly as they had arrived the group would leave for another venue.

'Thank the Lord for that,' cook would exclaim as she sat by the fire range wiping her brow.

'Till the next time, eh, cook,' would be the standard retort from James, the footman.

'At least there's been no trouble this time, has there Mr. James?' asked cook.

'Not that I have been aware of,' James responded. 'Lord Peter kept himself in check.'

'Must be a worrying time for M'lady, though,' said cook. 'I mean, she never knows when the madness will come over him. In the past Lady Anne has had a lot to put up with, what with the master beating the daylights out of her and their son whenever he felt the urge.'

'Lord Peter may look like his mother with that mop of blonde hair and green eyes,' said James shaking his head, 'but he's inherited his father's nature and there's precious little he can do about it.'

Summer came and went, and soon the preparations had begun for the Annual Christmas Ball at Bromley Manor. Sally had enjoyed the year she had worked there. The workhouse governor had tried on numerous occasions to see her, but cook had been alerted to say she was too busy. After a few fruitless visits he had simply stopped trying to contact her.

An air of excitement filled the household. Decorations were constructed and hung around the walls, and wonderful aromas permeated from the kitchen as festive dishes were prepared.

The highlight of the year for the staff at the Manor was their own celebration held the day after Boxing Day. Lady Anne would come down to the kitchen at the height of the party and give to each member of staff a present and a financial bonus to thank them for the smooth running of the Manor in the previous year. Most of the female staff had made or bought a new dress for the occasion, and Sally was no exception. Her pretty green frock showed off her now clean light brown hair, and made her look sensuously attractive. Sally had experienced a few flirtations with male members of staff, but nothing serious. The one man she dreamed of making love with was Lord Peter! She knew it was only a pipe dream, but she could not help thinking what it would be like to be held in those wonderfully strong arms. 'He's so handsome isn't he?' Sally would say with a sigh whenever she caught a glimpse of him.

'Handsome he may be girl, but you keep away from him,' said cook dismissively.

On the night of the party everyone had more than their share of the drink, especially the punch, which tasted like cordial, but was very potent. The party was in full swing when Lord Peter, worse for drink, suddenly appeared in the doorway where the celebrations were taking place.

'Everyone having a good time, eh?' he said as he slowly walked over to the punchbowl and helped himself to a glass. Everyone went quiet, not sure what they should answer.

The footman, James, went up to him and gently tried to steer him out of the room. 'Come on Sir, I think you have had enough to drink for tonight and we don't want to spoil the staff's fun do we?' he said in a quiet voice.

'Take your bloody hands off me, James, I know when I have had enough to drink! Spoil what fun? I'm ready for fun! Now which one of you pretty girls will dance with me?' Fear of the Master resulted in no answer. 'Come on fiddler, start playing,' he said. He grabbed one of the serving girls and started to jig with her before swapping her for another girl, then for the cook. At the sight of the straight-laced cook jigging around with the Master, they relaxed and joined in. Sally stood there wishing he would grab her. Disillusioned, she started to leave, but felt herself being dragged back towards the dancing. 'Not going are you? Upset that I had not picked you?' Lord Bromley said, then whispered in her ear, 'Don't you know, girl, I always leave the best until the last?'

Her dreams had come true, she was in his arms. She felt her heart would burst with happiness. He held her tight as he whirled her around the floor. When the music finished he did not let go of her, but danced out of the room into the hallway. 'Where are we going?' Sally asked, giddy from the punch and the dancing.

'I thought you may like some champagne. Don't you know that all beautiful girls should be given champagne?'

'Oh!' Sally thought, 'He had called her beautiful!' She imagined herself being his mistress. He would spoil her, and dress her in magnificent gowns! She would probably have her own apartment in the town. Wild thoughts raced through her tipsy mind.

Before she realized it they were in his bedroom. She had cleaned it many times, but never in her wildest dreams did she think she would be here by invitation. Lord Bromley uncorked a bottle of champagne. 'I always have a bottle put on ice, just in case,' he said.

Sally gulped down the champagne thinking, 'I don't know why they go mad about it. Why, it's only like fizzy lemonade.' She was soon giggling and laughing - she didn't know why, just that she was happy.

Lord Peter was laughing as well, but his laughter held a note of hysteria. 'All gone,' he said, holding up the bottle, 'and now, my little virgin, it's time to play. I take it you are a virgin? I don't want second-hand goods you know?'

'Yes, my Lord, I ain't never been with a man.' To her, the Governor of the workhouse did not count. Lord Bromley started to unfasten her dress, but soon became impatient with the small pearl buttons and tore the dress open. Sally gave a squeal. 'Here, that is my best dress,' she said trying to pull the remnants together.

'Don't worry about this cheap rag,' he said, 'If you please me you will be wearing the finest silk. Now come on, let me see how you can please me. First of all I'll lie on the bed and you can undress me.'

Stepping out of the remains of her clothes she stood naked at the side of the bed, undressing him. When she removed his britches, her eyes widened at the size of his manhood. The Governor's had been a red limp little thing, but this one was long and fat. 'Cor, how the hell am I going to get that inside me,' she said, gingerly touching it. As she touched, Lord Bromley suddenly became alive, jumping up and grabbing her. A madness appeared in his eyes as he threw her on the bed.

'By God, I'll soon get this inside you, every damned inch of it, now open your legs you little whore.' Sally became frightened - she didn't like the tone of his voice. In her dreams it wasn't like this, and if she could have escaped she would have done so, but he was forcing her legs apart. Suddenly, a searing pain shot through her and she felt as if she was being torn in half. He started to thrust in and out, in and out. She tried to push him off, but his weight was suffocating and her every breath was being squeezed from her chest. She couldn't breath and slipped into unconsciousness. This did not please his Lordship - he liked his women alive, kicking and screaming. He slapped her hard across the face, bringing her back to life. 'Whore, little whore, fuck you, little whore,' he shouted. He grabbed her buttocks and slid her up and down his penis. It seemed to go on forever, with him riding on top of her like a stallion. As she thought she would surely die, he let out a piercing scream, shuddered and then fell limp on top of her. Hardly able to breathe, she waited until she thought he was asleep, then gently tried to ease herself from underneath him. 'What are you doing, whore?' he said suddenly as she was almost free.

'You are squashing me, Sir,' she whispered, terrified.

'I'll squash you right enough. In fact, I'll do more than squash you, the whoreing fly that you are!' He slid off her and walked across the room.

'Now is my chance,' thought Sally as she tried to get off the bed, but was in so much pain that she couldn't move her legs. Lord Bromley looked at her.

'That's right, move fly, try to fly away then I can have fun swatting you!' She saw the riding crop in his hand and feared the worst. He was going to beat her to death. They were right - he was mad!

'Please, God, help me!' she cried out. That was her last coherent utterance as she slipped in and out of consciousness. Beatingarhythm with the crop on Sally's bloody body, Lord Peter masturbated up and down, up and down. This time, when he climaxed, he gave a howl that sent shivers down the spine of anyone who heard it. Finally, Lord Peter stumbled across the room, knocking things over, pulling back the curtains and, as if in a trance, stood gazing at the moon.

Lady Anne heard the clatter and walked along the landing towards the noise. It seemed to emanate from her son's room, but just as she was about to open the door, James, the footman, came running up the stairs. 'Don't open the door, My Lady, I'll go in first and see if anything is amiss,' he said. He had heard the howl and knew instantly where it had come from. Gingerly, James opened the door, Lady Anne following. At first it seemed no one was in the room, but as their eyes became accustomed to the dark, they saw the naked figure of Lord Bromley silhouetted against the window. A cloud moved from the moon sending its shafts of light into the room. It was then they saw the broken body of Sally.

'Oh, my God, not again,' cried Lady Anne! She did not dare go over to her son or speak to him when he was in one of his states. He was not himself and was liable to turn on her as he had done in the past. James quietly went over to Sally, not daring to light the lamp in case the Master awakened from his trance. There was no knowing what he might do - at times like this he had the strength of ten men! The best he could do was to examine Sally and check if she was breathing. He discovered she was still alive, but only just. Without speaking, he motioned Lady Anne to help him put a blanket around her and pick her up. A scream of pain looked as though it was about to escape from her lips before James covered her mouth to prevent any more noise. As quietly as possible James carried Sally out of the room, unsure where to take her. He looked enquiringly at Lady Anne who indicated the room that had formerly been the nursery. Lady Anne took one of the oil lamps and led the way. Gently, James lay Sally down on one of the single beds. He was turning to go when Lady Anne's voice asked in astonishment, 'Where on earth are you going?' she said.

'To the Master - to see if he is alright - and lock him in,' said James. 'If he starts wandering around the house, heaven knows what might happen. We have, as usual, got to keep this as quiet as possible. I'll go to fetch Doctor Phillips, he'll know what to do.' 'And he will keep his mouth shut,' he thought!

Lady Anne looked at Sally, tears filling her eyes. Perhaps it would be better if the girl died! What ordeal had she been through? This time her son had gone too far, he would have to be sent away to an asylum if necessary. 'You poor girl,' she said, pulling the blanket carefully away from her body. Sally winced as parts of the blanket had stuck to her bleeding wounds.

'No more! No more please,' she whispered through cracked lips.

'No more, my dear. No more, ever again,' said Lady Anne shaking her head with a resolution.

James went back to Lord Peter's room. Not lighting any candles, he went to Lord Peter and gently took his hand. He knew from past experience that any sudden movement might start his Master's madness off again. He led him to the bed, gently laying him down. Lord Peter opened his eyes. All the madness had gone out of them like the gentle boy he once was. 'I'm so tired, James, so tired!' he said in a subdued voice. He closed his eyes and finally let the riding crop drop to the floor.

The Doctor's first action was to look in on Lord Peter. 'He'll sleep for a few days as usual, not remembering anything when he awakes' he said with disgust. 'He wants shooting! If he were a dog they would,' the Doctor said, looking at James. 'If it wasn't for Lady Anne I would report him to the authorities.'

'And the large fee she pays you?' James added sarcastically.

'Where's the girl?' said the doctor, ignoring the remark.

'Nursery,' James responded, and led the way along the landing.

The doctor examined Sally, wetting the blanket to ease it away from the deep wheals on her body. 'Lucky he didn't catch her face! The wheals should heal without leaving too many scars - it's the scars to her mind that will probably never heal,' he said as he attended to her wounds. 'She's lucky to be alive. It wouldn't be advisable to move her for a few weeks.' Shaking his head he added, 'There's not only the wounds you can see, but I've had to stitch her inside as well, if you get my meaning.' He didn't excuse himself for being blunt, it wasn't the time for niceties.

Lady Anne finally spoke up. 'Don't worry, the girl will stay here until she is strong enough to be moved. When my son is fit enough to travel I think it would be for the best if he went to a private sanatorium some distance away until he has been cured. We cannot have this thing happening again.' Lord Peter Bromley was duly sent up north to a sanatorium, hopefully to be treated for his madness.

Lady Anne and James nursed Sally back to health. No one mentioned what had happened. Sally was over-awed at being nursed by Lady Anne and glad to be alive, but was warned not to repeat what had happened. The staff whispered amongst themselves, saying she got what she deserved, dancing with Lord Peter - didn't they all know what he was like? James had warned them all that if he heard any gossip, not only would the culprit be sacked, but would most likely be put in prison for spreading false rumours.

In the village of Little Chester, the Vicar was asked to find employment for Sally as a live-in maid. In order to encourage him, a sum of money would be paid annually in return for employing the girl.

That was six years ago - a lifetime in Sally's mind. She had settled in quite well at the Vicarage and the Reverend and his wife were not too demanding. Mrs. Bunce and the other staff were aware that the Parkers were being paid to employ Sally, and that somehow Bromley Manor was involved. However, they did not know why this arrangement had been made, and, even if they had their suspicions, they dare not voice them. All they asked of Sally was that the vicarage was kept clean, and the washing and ironing done. Mrs. Bunce came in every day to cook the main meals and often gave Sally a hand with lifting the heavy steaming sheets from the boiler in the outhouse. In exchange Sally said nothing about cook taking home the left-over food. She found she could make extra money from comforting Mrs. Parker and being punished by the Reverend. Sally was content to see her savings grow. She saved every penny she could and there were always ways to earn a bit more. One day she hoped for a home of her own with a husband and children. These dreams kept her going through her mundane life.

CHAPTER 6
Miss Hazel

The sound of her name being called brought Sally back to reality. Answering her Mistress's call she went upstairs. 'Have they gone, those two?' said Mrs. Parker, getting out of bed.

'No m'am, Reverend Parker is finding work for the lad and I'm going to see if I can find work for his sister in the village.' There was an afterthought developing in Sally's mind. Get the girl out of the way, then she could start work on the brother.

Michael began by repairing rotting woodwork and various other jobs that had been neglected. Siobhan made herself busy cleaning and helping Mrs. Bunce. She had never cooked before, and, living on her diet of potatoes, she hadn't seen half of the ingredients. 'Dain't your mother ever cook, child?' said Mrs. Bunce, watching the fascinated Siobhan.

Siobhan blushed. 'Not really, we were too poor.' Cook felt uneasy. The girl was as thin as a lath. She may possibly have come from a poor family, but the brother seemed well built. Strange that.

Sally came back from the village where she had had no luck in finding a job for Siobhan. 'Why don't you ask at the Manor? They always want staff there,' suggested one of the villagers.

'Never,' thought Sally. She wouldn't wish that on her worst enemy, still having nightmares about what happened to her. Lord Bromley had come back to the manor after his mother's death and was said to be a changed man, but Sally doubted it.

A week went by and Sally began to give up all hope of finding employment for Siobhan. She had kept her busy giving her all the jobs that she herself hated doing in the Vicarage, but it wouldn't be long before

Reverend Parker would resent paying for food that the girl ate. That would mean Michael and his sister would be on the way to London, but Sally didn't want to lose Michael. The more she saw of him the more deeply she was falling in love.

Sally had been flirting with Michael, rubbing herself against him at every excuse. At first he had pulled away from her, unsure whether she meant it or not, but, like any man, he became aroused when she pressed her ample breasts against him. He often flirted back whenever she brought out a drink to him. England, too, was having a hot summer, and Michael usually worked stripped to the waist. Sally would touch his firm body, stroking his taut muscles. There were times when she could hardly contain herself from lying in the hay with him there and then.

The village shop was the centre for all the gossip, and Sally walked in when the topic was Miss Hazel, the retired village schoolteacher. 'Can't get about, crippled she is. Had a nasty fall,' the conversation went on.

Seizing the opportunity, Sally went to Miss Hazel's cottage. Was this the chance she had been waiting for? Maybe there would be a job for Siobhan. It seemed an age before the door was opened by Miss Hazel, struggling on two sticks. 'Well, what do you want?' asked Miss Hazel, annoyed at being disturbed. 'Hurry girl, can't you see I am in pain?'

'I've heard you'll be wanting a girl to help you after your fall,' blurted out Sally before the door could be slammed in her face.

'If I did, it would not be the likes of you,' said Miss Hazel, a grim look developing on her face.

'No, not me, but a girl Reverend Parker has taken in. He's found work for her brother, but with me and cook there's nothing for the girl to do,' said Sally, rapidly.

'A girl the Reverend has taken in, eh?' At the mention of the vicar Miss Hazel's tone changed. Now interested, Miss Hazel said, 'Come in, you make a pot of tea and tell me all about this girl.'

'Someone's happy,' Michael said looking up from his work.

'You and your sister will be happy too when I tell you I've found her a job,' said Sally, smiling in triumph.

The smile was soon wiped off her face when Michael said in a harsh tone, 'What job? What business is it of yours to find me sister a job?'

'Don't get nasty with me. You don't think the Reverend Parker could afford to keep her here with nothing in return? If it wasn't for me convincing the Reverend he needed you to do the repairs you'd be out on the road,' she said, walking off in a temper. Realizing his mistake Michael ran after her, catching her by the arm.

'Look me darlin', I'm sorry,' he said. 'It's just that she's so young and I promised me dear Mammy that I would look after her.' Then added to gain her sympathy, '....before she died!' These extra words had the desired effect on Sally.

'Now Michael, do you think I would get her a job where she would be unhappy? Miss Hazel is a lovely person, a real lady, a retired schoolteacher now crippled with arthritis. She just needs a girl to help out, and if Siobhan is suitable she can live in.'

'Live in?' said Michael, not liking the sound of that at all, but what choice did he have. The sooner he saved some money the sooner they would go together to London.

Siobhan was both happy and frightened at starting the job - happy to get away from Sally who gave her all the dirty jobs, and never missed a chance to put her down by criticizing her in front of cook and Michael. She had seen the way Sally flirted with Michael - not that it bothered her, but it made her feel very uncomfortable. 'Can't wait to bed him, that one, like a bitch on heat!' said Mrs. Bunce stirring the stew. 'I can't think what's got into the girl! Think she'd have learned her lesson.'

'What lesson?' Siobhan could not help but ask.

'Never you mind. Just warn your brother to be careful.'

There it was, mentioned again. Michael! Her brother! He had warned her not to deny it - it was better if they thought she was his sister. She did not like the lie, but if Michael said it was for the best then it must be.

Early next morning, Sally and a clean and tidy Siobhan set off for Miss Hazel's cottage. All the way Sally warned her to do as she was told, to be polite and not to speak until she was spoken to. She went on and on with 'don't do this', and 'don't do that'. After a while, Siobhan shut her mind to the monotonous drone. It was a fine morning. The sun was just rising with the promise of being another hot day. The birds were singing, joyful at the abundance of fruit the hot summer had brought forth. Wild flowers of every colour adorned the grass verges. She could not help but feel happy on such a wonderful day. With uplifted spirits she started to skip. They were not even dampened when Sally shouted, 'Here my girl, what do you think you're doing? It's off to work you're going, not to a party.' Sally looked at Siobhan and a stab of jealousy went through her. The girl was really beautiful! In the short time she had been at the Vicarage the ample food had begun to fill her out. The sun's rays danced on her thick curly hair and it gleamed like the blue black of a magpie's wing. There was a charming innocence about the girl. It wasn't fair thought Sally, I'd bet she has not known any trouble in her life, not with a brother like Michael to look after her.

Eventually, they arrived at Miss Hazel's cottage. At one time the overgrown garden would have been full of colour, now weeds grew between the stones of the path. The purple flowered wisteria had grown rampant, covering the front of the cottage, even over the windows. The cottage, once immaculate, looked shabby and neglected.

Being of an independent nature Miss Hazel got up early and, with great difficulty, washed and dressed herself. She doubted the girl would be suitable, but in spite of her misgivings, she was eager to see her. She hated to admit it, but she could not go on much longer without help, especially with winter just around the corner. Her arthritic hands would not be able to lift the coal bucket to keep a fire going. In years gone by they had been one of her best features, but the sight of them now made tears roll down her cheeks. Bertie had remarked how slender and elegant they were as he slipped the diamond engagement ring on her finger. How different her life would have been if he had not caught pneumonia and died. They would have been married, she would have had children. She shook herself. No point dwelling in the past - after all, there had been hundreds of children in her life, even if it was only to teach them.

A loud knock on the door shattered her train of thought. Before she could get to the door another loud knock sounded, accompanied by the voice of Sally. 'It's me, Miss Hazel,' she shouted, '- with the girl.'

Miss Hazel opened the door, saying in an angry voice, 'My girl, I may be crippled, but I am not deaf! Come in.' They followed her into the room which was a parlour and kitchen combined. It was a heartless place! There were some good quality pieces of furniture, but all dull from lack of polishing. No fire burned in the cast iron fire range, and Sally wondered how she cooked her food and made herself a hot drink.

'Your fire's gone out, has it?' remarked Sally, then without waiting for an answer added, 'Never mind, Siobhan here will soon get it going!'

'Taking a lot for granted aren't you? I may not find the girl suitable,' said Miss Hazel, looking Siobhan over. 'You're very thin. You don't look as if you are strong enough to do a full day's work.'

At that, Siobhan suddenly spoke up. 'I am so. I was strong enough to lift heavy sacks of potatoes. Ouch!' The pain from Sally's kick made her cry out.

'Oh! You have got a tongue then,' said Miss Hazel, smiling, and liking the girl for speaking up for herself. 'I'll give you a week's trial and if you suit me I will take you on permanently.' Siobhan and Sally were overjoyed.

'When does she start,' said Sally, eager to get rid of her.

'She can start straight away, and her first job is to get the fire going and make a pot of tea,' said Miss Hazel. Sally quickly said her goodbyes, eager to get back to Michael. Now she had him all to herself.

Siobhan soon cleaned out the old ashes and got the fire going. Thank goodness Mrs. Bunce had shown her how to light the kindling first, then gradually add small pieces of coal, then the larger pieces. Soon the kettle was boiling away and a pot of tea was made. Siobhan only put one spoonful of tea in the brown earthenware teapot - never having had the luxury of tea she was frightened of wasting it. 'Three more spoonfuls, girl,' shouted Miss Hazel, watching her. 'I like my tea so that you can taste it, not like coloured water.'

'I'm sorry,' apologised Siobhan, blushing.

'No need to be sorry girl, you weren't to know,' comforted Miss Hazel. 'Some folks like their tea weak. Come and sit down and have a cup of tea with me. You'll find the biscuits in the cupboard - that's all I've got for now. Later you can go into the village and get some groceries for me. I haven't been able to get about much since my fall.' Over the tea, Miss Hazel asked Siobhan about herself. Sally had told her a few things, but Hazel felt she could not be trusted to tell the truth. 'So your name is Siobhan Rafferty,' said Miss Hazel. Siobhan was about to say No, Doherty when she remembered Michael was passing her off as his sister. 'And you and your brother came over here from Ireland when you were orphaned?' Siobhan nodded. 'And how old are you Siobhan?' Siobhan didn't know what to say - she didn't really know how old she was. She took a guess.

'Fifteen, Ma'am.'

'You're small for fifteen,' said Miss Hazel, then seeing the disdainful look on Siobhan's face added, 'I dare say you will grow!'

That morning, Siobhan set out to prove she was a good worker by scrubbing and polishing until the place shone. 'You had better stop now or you won't have time to go to the village before you have to return to the Vicarage,' said Miss Hazel, writing out a list of things she wanted.

Siobhan hesitated as she was given a purse. Miss Hazel saw the hesitation and quickly realized that the girl had not been used to handling money. To save her any embarrassment, Miss Hazel wrote a note for the grocer. 'Just give Mr. Gibbs the purse,' she said, 'and he will take out what is needed.' She asked Siobhan to read the list, but all she heard were a few incoherent mutterings. Miss Hazel realized the girl couldn't read, but, not wanting to make her feel awkward, didn't pass comment. Perhaps they do things differently in Ireland, she thought, as she pointed the way to the village.

Siobhan entered the village shop and became aware of the different smells, some deliciously spicy and others sickly sweet. She had never been in a proper shop before - her eyes could not take in all the different things on the shelves, jars and bottles full of colour, sacks on the floor full of grain, nuts, coffee beans, and lots of other things that she could not identify. 'How ignorant I am,' she thought, her eyes wide with wonder. At first she didn't hear a voice talking to her.

'Yes, Miss, can I help you?' Mr. Gibbs, the grocer, was a fat red-faced jovial man, always pleasant to his customers, except when they asked for credit. Whatever the circumstances, he and his wife never allowed credit. 'Once you start, people take advantage and before you know it, you're out of business,' he would repeat over and over again. Mr. Gibb's face beamed when he saw Siobhan - 'What a beautiful girl,' he thought, 'now where's she from? Ain't seen her afore!' He paused, then said, 'Now what can I get you, pretty Miss?' Without a word she handed him Miss Hazel's note. 'Oh! You're the new girl working for Miss Hazel, are you?' he said as he filled the basket with the items on the list. 'There you are my girl, everything that's on the list except the sugar, fresh out of it I'm afraid. It's been a good summer for fruit, all the jam making you see,' he said as he packed the basket, 'and that will cost...' Siobhan was astonished at the sum. It sounded an awful lot of money, but if the man said that's what it all cost it must be right. She handed him the purse. He looked puzzled, but took out the money that was owed, writing down the amount on the paper as Miss Hazel had requested. Perhaps the girl was none too bright. Mind you, she didn't have to be bright with those looks, he thought reaching into the jar of toffee apples. 'Here you are, sweetheart, a present from me for you to eat on the way back.' He thrust the toffee apple at her, squeezing her hand. When she was more used to him, perhaps he'd get a kiss or more in return, he thought, licking his lips. She thanked him for the toffee apple.

Mr. Gibbs thoughts were broken by a voice bellowing from the back. 'Giving away the stock, are we? Better not let me catch you giving anything else away.' It was his wife.

Walking back to the cottage her thoughts went over what Mr. Gibbs had said, that she was pretty. Was she pretty? Michael said she was, even the Reverend had so remarked. Once again she felt happy and treasured the feeling. Very few times in her pitiful life had she felt this way. Please, Holy Mother, let it last - don't let anything spoil it now.

Miss Hazel had been waiting impatiently for Siobhan to return. She'd been wondering whether she had done the right thing in sending her with her purse to the village. Not that she thought the girl would steal her money, but she might get robbed or lose it. The girl seemed very immature for her age and very innocent, as though she had never lived in a proper home or seen kitchen utensils. Perhaps she and her brother had lived in one of those hovels she had read about. She had heard how poor the Irish were and that is why they were migrating to England or America. Well, it was not her worry. If the girl did her work, that's all she cared about. Eventually, the door opened and in came Siobhan laden down with the heavy basket. 'Come on girl, you've taken your time, and what is that around your mouth? It looks all sticky? You haven't been spending my money on toffees have you?' Siobhan became nervous, and instead of speaking slowly she lapsed into a thick Irish brogue. Miss Hazel could hardly distinguish what Siobhan was trying to say. 'Speak clearly, girl, I can't tell what you are saying. Still nervous, Siobhan began again.

'Holy Mother, Ma'am, I wouldn't be doing that, Mr. Gibbs gave me a toffee apple as a present,' said Siobhan wiping her mouth with the back of her hand.

'A present! A present? And what else did he do?' quickly interrupting herself with, 'Do not wipe your mouth with the back of our hand, use the cloth. Never, ever take anything else from anyone without paying for it. Remember, Siobhan, no one - especially a man - gives something without wanting something in return. You understand me?' Miss Hazel was furious. She had heard about the tricks Mr. Gibbs got up to behind his wife's back. Lots of her girl pupils had complained to her, how he had tried to kiss them and even touch their breasts. She ought to have warned the girl, but she did not think he would try anything with a stranger. Miss Hazel softened when she saw Siobhan cower as if waiting for a slap. 'Look, I am not going to hurt you child, but I am just letting you know for your own good, that men aren't to be trusted. Come on now, you have worked hard enough for one day, time to go back to the Vicarage.'

Miss Hazel explained the way back in case she had forgotten. 'Go straight to the Vicarage and do not stop or speak to anyone, and I'll see you early tomorrow.' Miss Hazel waved her off and shut the door. The girl had only been with her a day, but now the cottage seemed cold as if the life had gone out of it. She sat thinking that Siobhan was too beautiful for her own good!

Back at the Vicarage, Sally had taken every opportunity to be alone with Michael. He tried to keep away from her, but every way he turned there she was. He wasn't interested, his mind had been thinking of Siobhan and wondering how she was getting on. He hoped she had not let it be known that she wasn't his sister - he had warned what would happen if the vicar found out.

It was dusk when Siobhan reached the Vicarage. Michael was sitting on the gate waiting for her. He put his arm in hers. 'I thought you were never coming,' he said. She's not been working you too hard, has she?' Siobhan was aware of his arm through hers, and it felt warm and comforting.

'No, she didn't work me too hard, she's a bit sharp, but she's nice enough.' She told him about going shopping and that she felt embarrassed at not knowing how to count the money! She left out the part about Mr. Gibbs calling her pretty and about the toffee apple. After all, Miss Hazel had thought that was a bad thing to have happened.

'Well, my darlin', we can't have you embarrassed, can we?' Michael said. He put his hand in his trouser pocket and fetched out a few coins, arranging them on the table in an order that wasn't clear to Siobhan. He began to show her the coins in turn and explained their value. 'I haven't got a guinea or even a half guinea, but I doubt you will ever have to handle either.'

Silently, Sally watched from the kitchen doorway, dying to show off to Michael that she wasn't penniless. 'I've got a guinea,' she piped up, '..and an half'un. I'll go and get them.' She ran up the stairs and recovered the tin box from its hiding place. She smiled with pride as she opened the lid revealing a fair horde of cash. Oh, yes, she had accumulated a nice nest egg over the years, some from working, some from her 'personal services' and more than a little spirited away dishonestly. One day she would have enough to leave and buy a home of her own. And who knows what the future would hold now she has met Michael Rafferty.

The sight of the guinea and half guinea widened Michael's eyes. 'Now how has a servant girl like you come by this fortune?'

'Never you mind, now,' said Sally tapping her nose.

Michael gradually let Sally dominate the tutorial. He could impress Siobhan, but in truth he was not sufficiently familiar with the English coinage system to explain it in the presence of a 'local'. Siobhan tried to take it all in, but soon her eyelids grew heavy and her head started to droop. Michael saw the signs. 'Enough for tonight,' he said, 'Get yourself to bed - there's another early day for you tomorrow.' He helped her up from the chair and, without thinking, kissed her cheek. Sally watched intently and pursed her lips provocatively.

'Don't I get a kiss?' she asked.

'You're not my sister,' replied Michael, hoping his careless move had not been too damaging.

'Sister or not, it's not too much to ask, is it?' Before he could stop her, her lips were on his. He pushed her away.

'Mary, Mother of Jesus,' he said, 'You'll get me sent packing if anyone sees us.'

Sally just laughed. 'You would have to do a lot more than that before you're sent packing.' Michael left the room and walked towards the barn. A voice from the doorway behind him added, '.....but I can wait, you'll do well to remember who runs this household!'

The week went by very quickly for both Siobhan and Miss Hazel. By the third day she had made up her mind to let Siobhan live in, but waited until the week was up before informing her. Siobhan was over the moon with the thought of living at the cottage. Miss Hazel got crotchety at times and shouted at her, but it was only when she was in pain. Most of the time she was very gentle and kind. Michael didn't like it one bit when he was told the news. It was bad enough only seeing Siobhan a few hours in the evening, but the thought of only seeing her on a Sunday was unbearable.

'You promise, me darlin', that you will come and see me every Sunday,' he said as she left for Miss Hazel's cottage. 'I'm going to save hard, and before you know it we will be off to London to seek our fortune.' Sally, of course, was overjoyed. Now she would have Michael all to herself without attention being lavished on his sister.

The cottage had only two ground floor rooms and a washhouse, so Siobhan had to sleep in the attic - not that she minded. Anything was better than how she had slept in the hovel in Ireland. Funny, she reflected, she had barely spared a thought for her mother or siblings since coming to

England. But she would still lie awake in the middle of the night shaking, thinking she could hear her father. In truth, the room was nice and cosy - a straw mattress, pillow and blankets and a chair to drape her clothes on, plus an old oil lamp. To Siobhan, who had never had any space of her own, the little attic seemed like a palace.

Miss Hazel was unable to climb the steps to the attic. 'You can use one of the drawers in my chest for your clothes,' she shouted up. 'There's not room for one up there!' Then she thought back to Siobhan's arrival. The girl had not brought any clothes with her, nor any other belongings for that matter. 'Where is your change of clothes, dear?' asked Miss Hazel. 'Have you forgotten them?' Siobhan felt too ashamed to say she had only got the clothes she was wearing. She had washed them at every opportunity so that they would be as fresh as she could manage. Miss Hazel sensed her embarrassment. 'Look,' she said, 'I have lots of clothes I never wear. When you have done the cleaning we will get them out and have a look at them. They will be old fashioned but we can soon alter them. You do know how to sew, don't you girl?' said Hazel from the bottom of the attic ladder. Siobhan, ashamed, looked down and shook her head.

Good grief, Miss Hazel thought. What had the girl been doing all her life? Didn't her mother teach her anything? She couldn't count money, and it was doubtful if she could read or write. The girl wasn't an imbecile, and may even be moderately intelligent. Without thinking of Siobhan's feelings Miss Hazel decided there and then to find out about her and her brother's upbringing in Ireland. 'Let's sit down and have a cup of tea, I want to talk to you,' said Miss Hazel as Siobhan returned to the kitchen. She saw fear come into Siobhan's face. 'Don't be frightened, I'm not angry with you, but I just have to know whether you had any teaching at all in Ireland, and speak slowly so that I can understand you.'

It seemed an age before Siobhan answered. In her mind she was trying to find the right story to tell. Michael's words kept going around in her mind. 'You are my sister, we were orphaned. If people found out what really happened we will be turned out.' Siobhan started in a stammering voice. 'We were very poor. Father was ill and couldn't work and mother was busy looking after him and my younger brothers and sisters. I had to go out to work to earn money when I was old enough, so did the others. None of us had any schooling.'

'So you and your brother have never been to school?' Miss Hazel asked. Siobhan was silent for a while, thoughts going around in her head. If Miss Hazel ever met Michael she would know he had been taught.

She began again. 'Michael went to the village school when he was young before father was ill and we weren't so poor!'

'What work did you do?' asked Miss Hazel, looking at the thin frail girl.

'Potato pickin', or fruit pickin' in the summer, and in winter digging up sods!' Siobhan didn't dare look Miss Hazel in the face in case she could see part of the story wasn't true.

'What happened to your brothers and sisters when your parents died,' asked Miss Hazel, with concern.

'The older ones went their own way, the little ones went into an orphanage or were adopted. Michael took me with him and brought me to England.' It sounded so true Siobhan even started to believe it herself.

'You poor little thing,' said Miss Hazel, more to herself than Siobhan. She struggled up from her chair and said with determination, 'Well, from now on things are going to change for you my girl. Whenever we have the time, I'll teach you! I used to be a teacher, you know. I've still got all the books somewhere.' Muttering, she hobbled on her sticks into her bedroom. 'Yes! I will enjoy doing that.'

So the education of Siobhan began. The mornings in the cottage she spent doing the cleaning and washing, and in the afternoons Miss Hazel patiently taught Siobhan. She had to start from a very basic level, but Miss Hazel was amazed how comfortably she took to learning. Siobhan proved to be an intelligent girl. By the end of the first week she had learned the alphabet and to write her own name. They would sometimes work into the evenings, delaying eating until late. With this new stimulus Miss Hazel's health improved and she became more agile. She was so exhausted that, instead of lying awake in bed, she fell asleep the moment her head touched the pillow.

The week had gone by so quickly that it was Sunday before Siobhan realized. She didn't really want to leave Miss Hazel, but thought that if she didn't visit Michael and Sally she would appear ungrateful. The journey from Miss Hazel's cottage to the Vicarage was a pleasant walk along country lanes. The dry spell was still continuing, prematurely gold and russet leaves were appearing on the trees, ripe juicy blackberries shone like black pearls from the hedgerows, and the cob nuts were in abundance. Everything was still and quiet except for the occasional buzzing of a bee. Siobhan had never been so happy and once again she thanked the Holy Mother and Michael for rescuing her from her animal existence.

Against the advice of Sally, Michael walked to meet Siobhan. He had wanted to go to see how she was getting on during the week, but Sally had said Miss Hazel didn't want any visitors. He had been worried, feeling responsible for Siobhan as he had brought her over to England. She was such an immature girl, and so unworldly. Michael would ask himself what Miss Hazel was like - he should have met the woman. He should never have let Siobhan out of his sight - she was so beautiful, anything could happen to her. Bugger! Nothing was turning out the way he had planned, and that Sally was another matter! All week she had mothered him, giving him the best food, seeing to his every need. He had only got to turn around and she was there, watching like a big spider, tempting him into her web. If his heart had not already gone to Siobhan, he would have gladly taken Sally, as he had done with many others. Girls, women, they had all thrown themselves at him and he had taken them without a moment's regret. He never kidded them or himself that it was anything more than a bit of fun. Love had never entered into it. With Siobhan, however, he felt different. He was in love with her, but never once had he thought of making love to her. It would happen in time when she was a woman, until then he could wait.

The sight of Siobhan brought a lump to his throat. He saw how beautiful she was with the sun shining on her thick black curly hair. Taking in her every movement he waited until she reached him before greeting her. 'What's this?' he shouted, 'A new dress? My, you do look bonny.' She explained about the dress as they walked the rest of the way to the Vicarage. Enthusiastically, she told him what she had been doing and how Miss Hazel was teaching her to read and write. Michael couldn't help but feel jealous. He didn't want to share her with anyone and feared she could grow away - he really wanted her to be dependent on him. The truth was that he selfishly wanted her to be grateful, and that her gratitude would bind them together.

Sally went out of her way to be pleasant to Siobhan in an effort to please Michael, offering her tea and cakes. Chattering away to her, Sally let it slip about the lecherous Mr. Gibbs giving her the toffee apple. Siobhan blushed and asked how she knew about it. 'News soon gets around this village. Mrs. Gibbs has a big mouth. I wouldn't get on the wrong side of her if I were you,' Sally advised.

Michael immediately bridled. 'What's this all about? You've never said anything to me about a toffee apple.' Angrily he looked first at Siobhan and then at Sally.

Before Siobhan could answer, Sally butted in. 'Oh, it's nothing, Mr. Gibbs is known for giving sweeties and presents to pretty young girls in exchange for a kiss and a cuddle, that's until Mrs. Gibbs catches him at it.'

Michael jumped up, grabbed Siobhan by the shoulders and shook her. 'Has he touched you?' He did not wait for her to answer. 'I'll kill him,' he said with such viciousness that Siobhan and Sally were frightened, both of them recalling their past experiences.

Siobhan tried to struggle from his grasp. 'You're hurting me, Michael,' she said, tears streaming down her cheeks. Michael saw the tears and immediately let her go, the anger draining from him.

'I'm sorry me darlin'. I'll not be wanting anything to happen to you,' he said, sitting down with his head in his hands.

'Nothing did happen, Michael. He just gave me a toffee apple to eat on the way back to Miss Hazel's,' said Siobhan, rubbing her shoulders.

'And what did Miss Hazel say?' he asked.

'She was very angry and said I should never ever take anything from anyone without paying because they always want something in return. That's why I never told you.'

Sally had been listening intently. 'She's right. They always want something in return, especially men.'

'Ay, both Sally and Miss Hazel are right, so be warned Siobhan,' Michael said, thinking that Miss Hazel seemed a sensible woman.

Eventually, it was time for Siobhan to go and Michael insisted he walked back with her. It wasn't that far, but the lane to the cottage cut through a wood. They walked in silence, each with their own thoughts. Michael's was that the sooner they started their journey to London the better. Siobhan was glad she was going back to Miss Hazel, still shaken by Michael's behaviour. Reminiscent of her father's moods, it made her realize she knew very little about Michael. If what he said was right about men wanting something in return for gifts, hadn't he given her things? What did he want in return, she wondered?

On Michael's return he could not help but notice how quiet Sally was. 'Anything the matter?' he asked. 'You're quiet.'

'Just thinking, that's all,' she answered.

'Thinking what?' he persisted.

'If she wasn't your sister, I'd say you were acting like a jealous lover, the way you lost your temper.'

Taken aback he quickly responded. 'Look, isn't it natural for a brother to look out for his sister?' He would have to be careful. The last thing he wanted was her getting suspicious.

'I wished I had someone to look out for me,' Sally said, feeling miserable.

Michael looked at her for the first time as a person. She looked so miserable and dejected he could not help but feel sorry for her. 'Haven't you any family, Sally?' he asked, taking her hand.

Sally played on his sympathy and told him how her mother, abandoned by her lover, had given birth to her in the workhouse and died a few days after, leaving her all alone in the world. How she had been beaten and forced to work from early morning until late at night. Getting carried away with the story she was elaborating, she told how she was never given enough to eat, fainting sometimes with hunger and how she nearly died with pneumonia. 'I guess Jesus must have been looking after me,' she added, lowering her eyes and forcing a tear to roll down her cheek. She omitted to mention about the Governor or Lord Peter. Michael listened to her story, his soft heart responding impulsively.

'You poor darlin', well it looks as if I'll have to look out for you.'

'Will you really, Michael?' she said, wiping a non-existent tear from her eye. Reaching for the cooking brandy, she poured them both a drink. 'Here's to our friendship,' she added, lifting her glass.   Michael   felt hesitant about his generous offer to look after her, but reluctantly raised his glass. Sally noticed that he shuddered when he tasted the rawness of the drink. 'Bugger this cheap stuff, I'll sneak one of the Reverend's bottles,' she added. Almost a full bottle of the vintage brandy later Michael felt decidedly queasy. He tried to focus, but everything appeared blurred and the room began to spin around. His attempt to get up only landed him back in the chair.

'Oops, I think I'm a wee bit drunk,' he said, holding on to the kitchen table, levering himself up. 'Must go and lie down before I fall down.'

The brandy had little effect on Sally, having drunk it from an early age with the Governor, plus what she helped herself to from Reverend Parker. In fact, she was quite sober. She grabbed his arm and said, laughing, 'Come on, let me help you up.'

She supported him through the door, but the fresh air hit him so hard that it took all his strength to put one foot in front of the other. Michael became helpless with laughter as, with the support of Sally, he zig-zagged towards the barn. 'Quiet,' she whispered, 'we don't want the Parkers to hear.'

Once again, he became hysterical and uttered, 'We don't want the Parkers hearing us now, do we?'

Sally managed to get him into the barn, but it was impossible for him to climb the ladder to the loft where he slept. Michael collapsed on the floor and dragged her down on top of him. Sally took advantage of his semi-conscious state and pressed her lips on his. He attempted to push her off, but in his present state he was too weak. Suddenly he didn't want to push her from him. It had been so long since he felt the sweetness of a girl's lips. Subconsciously, he reached out and pulled her warm body to his. Fired by Sally's passion, he had no control over his manly instincts. Sally used all her sexual experience to arouse him again and again until, exhausted, they both fell asleep.

Michael awoke with a blinding headache and a vile taste in his mouth. Looking around, he wondered why he was on the floor of the barn and not in his bed in the loft. Suddenly, a recollection of the previous night came back to him. 'Jesus, what have I done?' he asked himself. What in heaven's name had made him get drunk? So drunk he couldn't control his emotions! Had he shouted Siobhan's name in his passion? If he had, he was done for! Sally would see he was sent away from here, or worse still he'd be accused of sleeping with his sister. 'Holy Mother, if you make this alright, I'll never touch another drink ever again,' he said to himself as he smoothed down his dishevelled clothing. He washed himself at the yard pump, throwing the freezing cold water over his face to clear his head. He dreaded meeting Sally, but eventually got enough courage to go into the kitchen. In anticipation of coming face to face with her he had rehearsed what he was going to say. His best bet was to pretend he couldn't remember anything about the night's happenings. He was surprised, therefore, to find only Mrs. Bunce in the kitchen. She looked hard at him.

'My, you look rough,' she remarked. 'You aren't sickening for anything are you?' The smell of the bacon cooking started his stomach churning. Mrs. Bunce's offer of a full breakfast was the final straw. He ran from the room and was violently sick. 'Well I never, he must be sickening for something, never known him to refuse food,' she remarked to Sally who had just entered the kitchen. Sally poured a mug of hot sweet tea.

'I'll take this out to him and see what's up,' she said.

Michael doused himself with cold water again and again, supporting himself by clinging to the cast iron pump. He jumped at the sound of

Sally's voice. 'Feeling sick, are we? You poor thing, get this hot sweet tea down you, it'll settle your stomach.' She handed him the mug. 'You certainly had a skin full last night, amongst other things!'

Michael pretended he didn't know what she was talking about. 'What other things?' he asked

'Oh, come on, don't pretend you don't remember, or are you thinking it was a wet dream you were having?' Michael shook his head between gulps of tea.

'Now what would you be talking about?' he answered. Sally stamped her foot in exasperation.

'Oh, you - you know damn well what I'm talking about. Why, you couldn't get enough of me last night - not that I'm complaining.' Michael saw she was getting angry and knew he must keep on the right side of her if he wanted to keep this job.

'Oh, me darlin, so it wasn't a dream then?' he smiled. Sally started to walk away with a smiling face. She suddenly turned and looked at him seductively.

'If it was a dream, all I can say is that you had better have the same dream tonight, because I can't wait to dream with you.' She flounced away, swinging her hips and singing her own adaptation of 'Where have you been all the day, Billy Boy.'

Michael just stood there and groaned. 'Oh no, what have I let myself in for?'

He had indeed let himself in for a load of trouble with Sally. It was the first time in her life she had been in love, and in love she was! All day she could think of nothing else but being in his arms. The thought of him making love to her sent a shiver through her body. Never before had she experienced tenderness with passion when making love. 'He may have pretended he couldn't remember last night,' she thought with a warm glow, 'but I'll make sure he remembers tonight.'

She even made excuses that she had to go out shopping when Mrs. Parker developed one of her headaches. Although it meant her losing her payment she also avoided the Reverend, just in case he wanted to punish her. The whole thing with the Parkers now repulsed her.

Michael had recovered from his hangover and went into the kitchen. His stomach was empty and, as much as he would have liked to have missed dinner, he was starving hungry. Mrs. Bunce remained seated as she served the evening meal. Normally they would have had what was left over from the Parker's meal, but tonight Sally, Michael and cook had stew.

The stew was kept on the boil all the week and each day's leftovers were thrown in. Occasionally, greasy dumplings were added. Sally sat opposite Michael, not saying much, but she kept giving him sly looks and caressing his leg with her foot. 'How the devil am I going to get out of her clutches tonight,' Michael thought, not daring to meet her eyes.

'You're quiet,' said Mrs. Bunce to Sally. 'You ain't catched nothing off Michael have you?' She gave a knowing wink as she said it, but there was no reply. 'Anyway, I'll be off now,' she continued, then hesitated at the door. 'I think I'll take a basin of that stew for my hubby,' said Mrs. Bunce, ladling some into a large bowl. 'He'll enjoy that.' She was not paid very much, so had no conscience about taking food home for her family.

Michael saw an opportunity to get away from Sally. 'I'll help you home with that, Mrs. Bunce, you've enough to carry,' he said as she covered the bowl with a cloth.

'It's too far,' shouted Sally, not wanting him to leave her.

'All the more reason,' said Michael getting up. 'I'll bet it's not too far at all for a strapping chap like myself. Anyway, after all that stew I feel like a walk.'

Sally tidied up the now empty kitchen. 'He won't get away that easy,' she muttered to herself.

At the door of Mrs. Bunce's cottage she asked him in for a cup of tea. He gladly accepted, hoping if he stayed out long enough Sally would have gone to bed. When he entered the cottage he was struck by the sense of warmth and happiness. Mr. Bunce sat by a glowing fire, a contented black cat lay asleep on the ragged hearth rug. Only her youngest daughter still lived at home, her other four children having married and gone their separate ways. The daughter, a pleasant-faced rosy cheeked country girl, got up to pour her mother a cup of tea. 'Don't forget Michael. This is the Michael I've told you about,' said Mrs. Bunce. As if to further enhance her daughter's blushes she added, 'Handsome, ain't he?'

'Not another one,' thought Michael. He didn't want Mrs. Bunce getting any ideas about him being a husband for her daughter. Sometimes he wished he was ugly, then he wouldn't have women falling for him, he thought, gulping down the hot tea. He now needed to extricate himself from this new situation as quickly as possible if he didn't want to upset Mrs. Bunce or the girl. Mrs. Bunce asked him to stay for something to eat, but Michael said that he was still fit to burst from the stew he had eaten earlier. He said something feeble about needing to continue walking to digest it. He could not, however, avoid noticing the look of disappointment on the girl's face. 'Must be careful here,' he thought, especially as Mr. Bunce had said he would be welcome to visit at any time. He walked out into the night air. 'Women! Trouble, all of them, even Siobhan!' he thought, kicking at imaginary obstacles. If he hadn't fallen in love with her he would have been in London by now.

He was standing outside Miss Hazel's cottage before he realized it. It was dark now and the cottage was lit by oil lamps. He could see Siobhan and Miss Hazel sitting at the table studying some book. 'Oh, Siobhan! How I long to hold you in my arms,' he thought, almost shouting out her name. He didn't know how long he stood there, but suddenly the lamps went out and the cottage was in darkness. The cold autumn night made him shiver as he made his way back to the Vicarage. That, too, was in darkness. Hopefully they were all in bed, especially Sally, he thought as he eased the barn door open as quietly as possible. He climbed the ladder to the loft, and, afraid of lighting the lamp, peered down into the darkness for any sign of Sally, but there was none.

'Eh, fancy a grown man like me being frightened of a woman,' he sniggered to himself. 'The sooner I am away from here the better.' With this thought he undressed and pulled the horse blanket over him. Unaware of what had disturbed him, and still half asleep, he moved instinctively towards a warmer patch of straw. Edging forwards he felt something soft. It took only a moment to realize he was touching Sally's naked body.

'What the devil are you doing here?' he shouted, trying to push her away, but Sally's strong arms went tight around him and her thighs held him in a vice-like grip. Try as he might he couldn't shake himself free. He could have used physical violence, but he had never hit a woman and hopefully never would. He tried coaxing her away, saying if the vicar should find them they would both lose their jobs.

'You might, but not me,' she said, trying to kiss him. 'Oh, come on, Michael, what harm will it do? You know how you enjoyed it last time. No one will know, if that's what you are frightened of.' She carried on taunting him. 'Are you a fop or a real man? Or is it your so called sister you would rather be with?' That last comment made Michael do something he had never done before. He slapped her hard across the face, calling her a filthy mouthed whore. The shock of it almost made her loosen her hold, but it also brought out the instinct of survival. She fought with him with all the viciousness of a wild animal. They rolled and wrestled in the hay, Sally punching and clawing, and Michael trying to hold her off. Blood spurted from the scratch marks on his face and body. In the frenzy of sweat and energy, an excitement built up between them, Michael experiencing primitive urges. The odour of body sweat and the defeat of his enemy sent a wave of exultation through his body which, in turn, was followed by a sexual excitement. He took her, ravaging her body, again and again he pounded into her, stamping his male dominance. 'He was King,' went the phrase through his mind each time he climaxed. Exalted, and for some uncontrollable reason, he started to laugh, then Sally started to laugh. All the anger gone from him he lay there content by the side of Sally. Strangely enough, he didn't feel any guilt at all.

Next morning when he awoke, Sally was gone. Still smiling about the previous night's events Michael made his way to the yard pump to ease his bruised and sore body. He stripped to the waist and welcomed the shock of the cold water. Mrs. Bunce was watching from the kitchen window. 'Michael looks as if he's been wrestling with a tiger. Why, his back is covered in scratch marks,' she remarked to Sally. Sally didn't comment, but smiled as she ate her breakfast. She felt more than a little tender herself, and in the next few days she would have difficulty covering up the tell-tale blue black marks of significant bruising. She laughed to herself, thinking of how she had enjoyed the fight. 'What are you laughing at, Sally? It's not like you to be so happy in a morning,' said Mrs. Bunce, puzzled. She wondered if those scratch marks on Michael were the reason for Sally's good humour. Michael's arrival in the kitchen was greeted with a less than subtle addressing from Mrs. Bunce. 'Couldn't help noticing the scratch marks on your body, she asked. 'How did you get those?' Michael stuttered, not knowing what to say, but Sally's monkey cunning concocted a reply.

'I expect you got drunk last night on the way home from the village and fell into a ditch.' Arching her eyebrows to signal him to agree, she went on, 'Now, was that the way of it?'

'You've guessed it Sally! Right tangled up in the brambles, I was, almost ripped the shirt off my back. Teach me to get drunk, hey?' Mrs. Bunce pondered on this. Hadn't he said he was walking off his indigestion when he left her house. Oh, well! It was none of her business and she got on with the cooking.

After that night, Michael changed. It was as if Sally had brought out his darker side. Night after night she would creep into his bed and they would make love, not as ferocious as before, but certainly very passionate.

The hot summer gave way suddenly to the coolness of autumn. There was a nip in the air in the mornings and going really cold at night. 'I'm bloody cold in this loft,' Michael commented to Sally one night after an all too regular tryst.

'Well then,' she replied, 'I will have to see if I can get you moved into the house.' She shuddered at her next thought. 'I don't fancy being naked in here with you all winter,' she said, 'and you won't be able to perform properly if you are cold.'

Michael sat up and looked at her. 'Look, Sally, it is very kind of you, and I'm not ungrateful for all you have done for me, but I never intended to stay, you know. My aim is to take myself and Siobhan to London to make me fortune.' All happiness went from Sally's face and she frowned heavily. Didn't she mean anything to him? Then a recollection came to her. Hadn't he said he would never make love to her? She would think of a way to either go with him or keep him here. With this thought she went happily to her own warm bed.

She had avoided the Reverend's punishment since she had made love with Michael, but knew she couldn't put it off much longer, not if she wanted to get Michael assigned to the attic room in the house. Engrossed in cleaning the study, Sally didn't hear the Reverend Parker enter the room. She gave a squeal of fright when she felt his hands turn her around. 'Now my girl, I have noticed that you have been neglecting your duties. Where have you been getting to?' Casually the Reverend added, 'Mrs. Parker thought she saw you coming from the barn in the early hours.'

'She probably did, Sir,' said Sally. 'I thought I heard a scream and I went to see what it was, but it was only a fox,' she continued, thinking it best not to lie by saying she wasn't there.

'Quite so, quite so, but you have been neglectful and you know the punishment,' he said, reaching for his whipping cane. He pointed to the desk. 'Bend over, girl.' Sally knew the procedure. Dutifully she lifted her skirt and dropped her drawers. The sight of two white buttocks thrust up at him took him near the limit of his self-containment. He punctuated the caning with banal remarks. 'You are a naughty, naughty girl! You know you deserve this caning, don't you?'

'Yes, Sir,' she answered. 'Ouch!' she shouted as the cane came down for the last time. It didn't hurt, but the sound of her acting as if she was in pain thrilled the Reverend. Sally waited a few seconds, giving the Reverend time to compose himself before standing up and adjusting his clothes. The Reverend returned to sit at his desk as if nothing had happened and handed Sally a shilling from the tin cash box.

'You are a good girl most of the time Sally, but if you neglect your duties you know you must be punished,' said Parker in a scholarly tone. 'Now go to Mrs. Parker, she has one of her heads.' Sally unlocked the door and went up to Mrs. Parker's room.

'Another shilling!' she thought. 'If I'm lucky I might use my savings to go to London with Michael.' Michael! Yes, she must ask Mrs. Parker about the room in the attic for him.

Sally gave an exaggerated shiver as she entered Mrs. Parker's room. 'My, it's cold in here, it's a wonder you're not frozen. I bet that's what brought your headache on,' she said as she gently brushed Mrs. Parker's hair. She gradually introduced the subject of the Irishman in the barn, and how he must feel the cold. Mrs. Parker did not take the bait.

'Yes, now you mention it, I am feeling a bit chilled,' she answered instead. Sally proceeded to do her duty and got rid of Mrs. Parker's headache. Before Mrs. Parker dozed off to sleep Sally made another attempt to raise the subject that troubled her.

'With winter coming, I must start lighting you a fire in here. I can't help thinking of that lad in the barn, frozen he'll be when the frost comes. If I may be allowed to use the small bedroom, do you think it would be a good idea to let him sleep in the attic? At least then he won't be too frozen to work?' Mrs. Parker, half asleep, just grunted and Sally chose to take this as a yes. Michael received the news with mixed feelings. One thing was sure, he'd be glad to sleep in a proper bed.

Sally had made up the bed in the attic and warned Michael to be as quiet as possible until she'd had chance to speak to the Reverend. She felt that his conformation was needed for him to be there. Sally lay on the bed and patted the eiderdown. 'There now, nice and comfortable for you, Michael. Want to try it?'

–ooOoo–

The weeks at Miss Hazel's had gone by without incident and Siobhan was surprised how quickly the Sundays came round. Winter brought cold and rain, and the walk through the wood was not very pleasant. The big raindrops fell from the trees, her old umbrella doing little to prevent them from soaking her clothes. She tried to avoid the muddy puddles in the lane, but her feet soon became wet and cold. Siobhan arrived at the Vicarage in a forlorn state. She had to knock hard at the kitchen door before anyone came. Eventually, Sally opened the door. 'Oh! Siobhan! I forgot you were coming,' she said. Then, looking at her bedraggled figure, she motioned her in. 'Come on, dry yourself by the fire! Michael is repairing a leak in the roof, I'll call him.'

Michael came in, all apologetic. 'Oh, me darlin'! Look how cold and wet you are! Pour her a cup of tea, Sally.' Sally was about to say she wasn't her servant, but thought better of it.

'Look luv, if the weather's nasty on another Sunday I wouldn't bother coming,' she said, pouring the drink. At that, Michael reared up.

'If the weather's wet, I'll come to you,' he said. 'Miss Hazel wouldn't mind would she?' This was not what Sally intended, and she now wished she hadn't opened her mouth.

When it was time to leave, Michael walked back with her, but this time Siobhan did not feel happy. The miserable weather did not help, but it was an afternoon that had been such a waste of time. The conversation seemed forced and Michael had resented anything she had to say about her learning. She had foreshortened her stay with the excuse that Miss Hazel wanted her back early. Siobhan could not wait to get back to Miss Hazel's home. Once there Siobhan asked Michael in out of politeness, but he declined, saying he had to get back to finish repairing the leaky roof. Siobhan had to admit she was relieved. Facing Siobhan, and looking into her eyes, guilt swept over Michael about his relationship with Sally. He suddenly pulled her close to him. 'Now, me darlin', if the weather's nasty in future, I'll come to you. We can't have you catching pneumonia - not before we go to London.' Impulsively, he gently kissed her on her forehead. 'You know you are very special to me, me darlin'?' Siobhan wasn't sure, but she thought she saw tears in his eyes!

The weeks continued to pass quickly. On wet Sundays Michael came to visit her, but he sensed she was uncomfortable with him being there. Usually he was never stuck for something to say, but his small talk now seemed boring. It was obvious Miss Hazel was having a great effect on Siobhan's personality. Her strong Irish brogue had softened into a pleasant lilt and she was able to hold an intelligent conversation. Michael realized that if he didn't get her away from here soon she would think herself too good for him.

CHAPTER 7
Parting

Winter started early with a heavy snowfall blocking most of the country lanes. Michael and Siobhan had not met for weeks, both of them making the excuse that it was because of the weather. Siobhan had never been happier. Miss Hazel's nature had softened and she looked on her as the daughter she never had. Their days were full of learning with Siobhan absorbing knowledge like a starving bird with food. In contrast, Michael had become lazy and slovenly, his good looks becoming blotchy and bloated. The sparkle he once displayed had vanished with his now comfortable life. Sally pampered his every whim, prepared to do anything to keep him from leaving. The approach of Christmas saw a slight rise in temperature making the country roads passable.

'Are you going to see your brother this Sunday, Siobhan?' Miss Hazel asked.

'I don't think so,' Siobhan answered. 'Christmas will be here in three weeks, I'll go then.' She rarely thought of Michael now. There was so much to do and learn with Miss Hazel that she hardly ever dwelled on her life before she came to live with this kind woman. It all seemed a lifetime away since she had lived at home with her family, and was terrified of her father and the 'bogey thing'. Suddenly she shuddered, thinking of the night Little Betty had died. At least she had Michael to thank for bringing her away from all that horror. 'I don't know what to give Michael for Christmas' she said to Miss Hazel.

'Why not knit him a warm scarf?' Miss Hazel said. 'I'll teach you how. Go and look in the linen box. I've some balls of wool in there - we can start straight away.'

On Christmas afternoon Siobhan walked to the Vicarage and was surprisingly excited at seeing Michael again. With considerable help she had altered one of Miss Hazel's old dresses to make a green on red tweed cloak. Siobhan's hair had grown past her waist, and with regular washing it was thick and shiny. Regular meals had filled out her figure turning her into a very beautiful young lady. Miss Hazel would look at her and, at times, feel afraid that her beauty would get her into trouble one day. She did her best to keep her in the cottage, but there were times when she had to go to the village for the shopping, always questioning her whether any man or boy had spoken to her. Siobhan mechanically answered 'No', and said that Mrs. Gibbs was always present, but she suspected that Siobhan only said this to stop her from worrying. Miss Hazel knew she couldn't protect her for ever, but while there was breath in her body she would do her best.

As Siobhan reached the Vicarage she saw a decorated Christmas tree in the window. She was just about to knock on the kitchen door when it opened and Michael stood there transfixed and speechless. At first he didn't recognize her.

At last he found his voice. 'Siobhan, me darlin' Siobhan. You look beautiful. I can't get over how you have changed. Why, you are all grown up!' Siobhan, too, was speechless, shocked by his slovenly appearance. His beautiful black hair hung limp and greasy, his defined features had vanished into creases. This wasn't the Michael she knew! How could he have changed so much in so short a time?

A voice came from inside the kitchen. 'Who is it?' said Sally, coming to the door. 'Oh! It's you,' she said, none too pleased. 'What do you want?' Sally's appearance, although not as bad as Michael's, certainly left a lot to be desired.

'I've come to wish Michael a Merry Christmas,' she said, handing the parcel to him. He took the parcel and ushered Siobhan inside.

'Come on in, me darlin'.' Michael opened the parcel and looked at the navy scarf. 'What's this then?'

'I knitted it myself, I thought it would keep you warm.' Blushing, her voice trailed to a whisper, feeling silly now that she had spent so many hours knitting the scarf.

'Why, it's just what I needed,' he said gratefully, then wrapped it around his neck.

'Pity you've nothing for her,' said Sally sarcastically.

'Who said I haven't?' he said, reaching for a bottle of port and handing it to Siobhan. 'I haven't had time to wrap it.' Reluctantly, Siobhan took it from him knowing that he had just taken it from the shelf as an after thought. After a few seconds she handed it back to him.

'Thank you, Michael, but you know Miss Hazel and I do not drink.'

'Do not drink,' Sally mimicked, then added under her breath, 'Miss Hauty Tauty.'

Confused, Michael ignored the remark, but it was not lost on Siobhan. He pulled out a chair from under the kitchen table and put it near the range. 'Come on, sit down. You must be frozen,' he said. He looked at her boots. 'Here, let me have those and I'll dry them. Sally, make some tea for our guest, and cut her a slice of cake.'

Not for the first time Sally considered refusing, but thought better of it. Michael unlaced Siobhan's boots and noticed her shapely ankles - not at all like Sally's thick ones. A thrill shot through his body as his fingers instinctively caressed her small foot. Siobhan also felt a strange sensation come over her, and quickly pulled her foot from his hands.

Siobhan didn't want to stay any longer than necessary with Sally giving her snide looks and Michael acting the way he did. It was too embarrassing and she felt uncomfortable. 'I must go,' she said, making her way to the door. 'I promised I would be back before it gets dark. Miss Hazel worries so much.'

'Look, don't go yet,' said Michael pulling her back. 'You have walked all this way. At least sit down and have a drink and some cake. No wonder Miss Hazel is worried, looking as beautiful as you do.'

'Arrr, it won't be long before a fellow takes a fancy to you and rips those fine clothes off yer back,' smirked Sally.

Quick as a flash, Michael slapped her across the face. 'Don't talk to Siobhan like that.'

'Siobhan, Siobhan. If she wasn't your sister I'd say you were jealous,' she said, rubbing her cheek and leaving the room. Siobhan was horrified at Michael slapping Sally. Without uttering another word she fled from the kitchen.

'Wait!' shouted Michael as he went after her. Grabbing her arm he pulled her close.

'Leave me alone, Michael.' She looked at him in disgust with tears coming to her eyes. 'What has become of you?' she said. Her words hit him hard, and now his eyes filled with tears.

'I'm sorry, I've let you down, but I swear I'll make it up to you,' he pleaded. 'I said I'd always look after you, and I will. I will, me darlin'.' He turned away, tears falling down his cheeks, and with head bowed in shame he walked back into the kitchen. In anger he smashed the bottle of port against the wall. Holy Mother, what had he become? A plaything for a serving wench! He, Michael Rafferty, who had come to England to make his fortune, he that was going to take care of Siobhan and one day marry her. He was going to lose her that was for sure. She was more beautiful than ever and quite an educated lady, good enough for one of the gentry to marry. He'd have to get away as soon as possible before it was too late. Sally, hearing the smash and still rubbing her cheek, came back into the kitchen. Sensing a more subdued mood than a few minutes earlier she slid up to him, stroking his thigh'

'Come on now, darling. Don't let the likes of her upset you,' she said. 'Come upstairs and I'll make you forget all about her.' Michael pushed her away with such force she almost lost her footing. Her face turned red with rejection and anger. 'Upset you, has she, with her fine voice and dainty ways?' she spat out, pushing her face close to his. 'Well, she don't need you now, Miss Hazel has seen to that. Quite grown up isn't she? Some lad will soon have his way with her!' Sally had obviously not learned her lesson from earlier, and continued to taunt him until he could stand it no longer. He gave her another slap, harder than the first, this time sending her sprawling on the hard floor. More angry than he had ever been in his life he held up his hand to strike again. Sally raised her forearms to shield herself from the next blow. Her action brought Michael back to his senses.

'Holy Mother, what has become of me, hitting a woman,' he thought. Then in a calm voice he said, 'I'm sorry, Sally, but I won't stand for anyone talking about Siobhan in that way.'

That night he slept in the barn. There was only one solution - he and Siobhan must leave for London straight away. He hadn't saved that much money, but it would have to be enough. If he left it much longer he would definitely lose her, and with that thought firmly in his mind, he fell into a deep sleep.

Sally crept into the attic hoping to make up with him, but he wasn't there.

Michael awoke early next morning and started to pack his few belongings, but was depressed when he looked through the window and saw that heavy snow had fallen in the night. In desperation he tried to clear a path from the Vicarage, but snow started to fall again. It was no use, he would just have to wait for the thaw.

Sally had watched Michael frantically shovelling the snow from the path. He eventually conceded defeat. 'Given up, have we?' said Sally, who had been watching from the kitchen window.

'Just for now, just for now,' Michael said, but suddenly felt ashamed of the way he had treated her. After all, her only fault was she loved and wanted him. 'Look Sally, I am really fond of you and I'm grateful for all you have done for Siobhan and myself, but it's time for me to leave. You know I never intended to stay, and now I must go to London like I planned.' Sally had been expecting that one day this would happen, but he wouldn't get rid of her that easy.

'Take me with you,' she pleaded, tears filling her eyes. 'I've some money saved. I'd be no trouble.'

'Sally, you are trouble and I cannot have that,' Michael said, 'especially when I'm with Siobhan.'

'Oh! Siobhan, bloody Miss Perfect! Does she know she's going with you to London? Have you asked her if she wants to go?' Sally saw the look on his face. 'No, you bloody well haven't, have you?' A glimmer of hope showed on her face. She went out of the kitchen with tears of laughter streaming down her cheeks.

'Oh! Bugger off and mind your own business,' he shouted after her. However, Sally's comments started him thinking. What if Siobhan didn't want to go with him? No, he was being stupid. Siobhan knew that was his plan all along. That's why he had come to England. His plan, yes, it had been HIS plan – but, Siobhan knew it included her. He would have to be patient and wait for the warmer weather. One thing was certain, he would never have sex with Sally again.

Angry at Michael's continual rejection, Sally vowed to get even with him and his so called 'sister'. Lately she had neglected the Reverend and his wife, tomorrow she would see she got her just punishment.

In the unlit room Reverend Parker was sitting in the big grandfather chair sipping a brandy when the door opened and Sally entered. Hidden by the darkness he observed that she had put on weight, but it suited him, all the more flesh to spank. During the last few weeks with them all confined to the house because of the snow he had not had the opportunity to be alone with her. Watching her, unobserved, brought back all the old longings. Sally knew he was there, in fact she had waited until Mrs. Parker was having a nap, the cook busy in the kitchen and Michael working hopelessly trying to clear the snow. Calculating when he might be slightly tipsy from his third brandy she entered on the pretext of cleaning. She moved her body provocatively, deliberately bending down, thrusting her buttocks in the air. He felt his penis swell and could control himself no longer.

'Sally!' he shouted.

'Oh, Reverend, how you startled me,' she shouted in pretence. 'I didn't know anyone was in here!'

'That was quite obvious from the way you have been attempting to dust,' said the Reverend, getting up unsteadily from his chair. 'My girl, you have sadly neglected your duties. What have you got to say for yourself? Answer me girl.' He was in full command now, just as if he was in the pulpit.

'Nothing to say, Sir, I have nothing to say. I have neglected my duties and you have caught me out,' she said in mock remorse.

'Well! It's punishment time, Sally, isn't it?' he said, hardly able to get the words out in his excitement.

'Yes, Sir! If you say so, Sir,' said Sally, turning the key in the door. Bending over the writing desk she lifted up her skirt. Having left off her drawers, her bare buttocks invited punishment. After only a couple of smacks, the Reverend, filled with excitement, climaxed. Still unfulfilled after Michael's rejection, Sally wanted more. 'I don't think that was punishment enough,' she said to Parker's surprise.

The Reverend, flustered and trying to compose himself, did not understand her. 'What do you mean girl? You want more punishment?' he asked.

'Yes, Sir, I deserve it. I heard it said that squeezing a girl's breasts and biting her nipples is a terrible punishment.' Sally undid her bodice and exposed her breasts. She cradled them in her hands and pushed her chest forward, inviting him to suck her nipples. The Reverend felt the blood rush to his cheeks, he had never seen a woman's naked breast before. Mrs. Parker had always undressed in the dark. His hand went gingerly to touch. Oh! It felt like nothing he had ever touched before, soft and yet firm! She guided his fingers to her nipples which hardened to his touch. Sally pulled down his head. Automatically his thick slobbering lips sucked as a baby would on her breasts. Immediately he felt himself getting hard. Hitching her skirt up she sat on the desk and lifted up his gown. Her legs encircled his fat body and she managed to push herself on to his throbbing penis. She could hardly feel a thing, not after Michael's manhood, but excited by the thoughts of their passionate lovemaking and holding the Reverend tight inside her, she herself managed to climax.

When she loosened her hold on the Reverend he slipped to the floor in a faint. Pulling down her skirt and tying the Reverend's gown she unlocked the door and slipped out to her own room. She poured water from the pitcher into the china bowl and tried to wipe the strong stale smell of the Reverend's body odour from her. The water was cold, but she welcomed it. What had she become, pleasuring herself with that odious pig. 'Michael, what have you driven me to?' she said aloud as tears ran down her face.

--ooOoo–

The weather suddenly turned mild and, instead of snow, the rainfall began to thaw the ice. It had seemed like an age to Michael. Everyday he had become more sullen and short tempered. He avoided Sally where possible, and when they did meet he hardly spoke. Because of the guilty feelings he felt with regard to his treatment of her he could not meet her gaze.

As soon as he saw that the roads were passable Michael could hardly contain his happiness - NOW he could leave!

He told the Reverend Parker he was very grateful for what he had done for him and his sister, but now it was time for him to leave and put his plan of going to London into action. The Reverend stood facing him, his hands holding on to his waistcoat sides in the classic way that always made him feel important and in charge. 'Well my boy. If that is what you want, it's alright by me,' he said, puffing out his chest. 'Best of luck to you and your sister.' His assumption that Siobhan was going with him gave comfort to the Reverend. Thank goodness he would be getting rid of those two, for there had been times when the boy had been in the way, especially when Sally had to be chastised. With him gone he could punish Sally whenever he felt she needed it and when Mrs. Parker had one of her headaches Sally could sooth her. God worked in mysterious ways.

Relieved that the Reverend had not tried to persuade him to stay, Michael went to his room and started to gather his few belongings together. He would have preferred to walk away from the Vicarage without a backward glance, but his conscience would not let him. He had to say goodbye to Sally - after all, she had been good to him. He found her alone in the kitchen. Her back was to him so she did not see him enter. Sensing someone behind her she turned around, her eyes meeting his. 'Well!' she said, frostily. 'Had your eyefull?' His face softened, knowing her anger was just an act she was putting on to hide the hurt she felt.

'I've come to say goodbye, Sally,' he started. 'It's time for me to leave. I've stayed longer than I ever intended. My plan was to go to London to seek my fortune and you've always known that. I'm off to Miss Hazel's to pick up Siobhan, then I'll be gone.'

Sally's face became crestfallen and tears filled her eyes, spilling over and running down her cheeks. He couldn't help but feel sorry for her – after all, she couldn't help falling in love. He lifted his hand to her cheeks and brushed away the tears. 'Now, now, don't cry. You knew one day I would be leaving, I never intended to stay. I never promised you I would.' Sally silently turned her back to him so as he wouldn't see the hurt in her face. Feeling guilty, he put his hand on her shoulder. 'You're a good girl Sally. Had things been different….' He stopped. After all, what else was there to say - he had used her, he knew it and felt bad about it. He turned her around, kissing her tear-streaked cheek. 'You'll soon find someone else, a pretty girl like you.'

Sally held her feelings in check until he was going through the door, then her anger got the better of her. 'Your so-called sister knows she's going, does she?' she screamed.

He turned, the shock showing on his face. Holy Mother, what if Siobhan didn't want to go with him, it had been a long time since he had mentioned it. Shaking himself, he answered himself sharply. 'Of course she knows, that's always been me plan.'

'Your plan may be, but is it hers? Especially now she is settled at Miss Hazel's.' said Sally with a shrill laugh. 'That's made you think, hasn't it, Mr. Michael Almighty Rafferty?'

He slammed the kitchen door shut. 'Of course she would want to come!' he kept muttering to himself on the way to Miss Hazel's.

Still angry, Sally gazed for a long time at the shut door. She'd show him. He wasn't going to get rid of her that easily. She had quite a bit of money saved and when she had saved a bit more she would follow him to London, and with this thought in her mind she felt a lot happier.

The country lanes looked fresh and clean now that the rain had washed the snow away. The odd bird sang out, snowdrops nodded their heads as if saying 'spring is coming'. New life was about to be born. Michael felt his spirits soaring once more as the sun began to appear. 'It's a wonderful morning, so it is, and I'm off to begin a big adventure, me and me darlin'

Siobhan,' he said to himself as Miss Hazel's cottage came into view. He knocked the door loudly, sending echoes through the cottage.

Siobhan opened the door and saw Michael, her eyes opening wide in surprise. 'Why, Michael, what on earth is the matter? Why are you here?' she said, forgetting her manners and keeping him on the doorstep. The words rushed from his mouth.

'Me darlin', nothing's the matter, the snow has gone and I've enough money saved, so get your things, we're off to London as I have always planned,' he finished breathlessly. Siobhan stood there speechless, trying to take in what he had just said. What was he talking about, her going to London?

'Who is it, Siobhan?' said Miss Hazel's voice coming from inside the cottage.

'It's Michael, Miss Hazel,' replied Siobhan, shaking herself back to reality.

'Invite him in, girl, don't let him stand on the doorstep. You are letting in the cold.' Michael followed Siobhan into the kitchen where a fire danced in the black lead grate, reflecting its bright orange and yellow flames. A homely smell of baking bread filled the air.

'What do you mean, get my things ready, we are going to London?' Siobhan asked him with puzzlement in her eyes.

'Off to the big city where the streets are paved with gold. London, like we have always planned.' His voice trailed off as Sally's words rang in his ears '*does your sister know she is going to London?*' It never dawned on him that she wouldn't want to go with him, or that she would have any opinion on the matter, she had always been led by him.

Her answer shocked him. 'Oh! Michael, I could never leave Miss Hazel, she needs me, totally relies on me!' In a firm, but quiet voice she added, 'I cannot go, you surely can see that. Who else would look after her?'

'She could find someone else. We could wait a day or two until she does. I'll bet Sally would know someone.' The words came tumbling from his mouth in a desperate hope to convince her.

She shook her head vehemently. 'No, Michael. No! No-one else will do, I know her ways, I couldn't leave her after how good she has been to me.'

'And I suppose I haven't been kind to you, me who rescued you from the potato field, from your abusive father,' Michael said, raising his voice, full of anger. 'Who do you think you are, saying you are not coming, Miss High and Mighty?'

'London, what's all this talk about London, who's going to London?' Miss Hazel questioned from the bedroom.

'Michael has come to say goodbye, he is off to London,' answered Siobhan.

Michael couldn't believe his ears. 'Off to London! Goodbye!'

'Doesn't your brother want you to go with him,' said Miss Hazel, hobbling from the bedroom.

'No, oh no, he has just come to say goodbye,' said Siobhan, putting her hand on his arm and gently pushing him towards the door. He was outside the cottage before he had a chance to protest. 'I'm really sorry, Michael,' Siobhan said with no conviction in her voice.

Michael was no fool, he could see she wasn't sorry, he had taken too much for granted - he had left it too late, and now he had lost her. 'Don't be feeling sorry,' he said. 'I was only doing it for you, the money will stretch twice as far with only meself to look after.' He smiled, but there was no twinkle in his eyes. 'I'll be off now, but I'll be back when I am rich and famous. Then you'll really be sorry,' he said with bitterness. Her eyes, full of sadness, looked into his. Hesitating, he suddenly grabbed her to him and kissed her full on the mouth. 'I love you, I always have and I always will. Please wait for me, Siobhan, me only darlin'.' Then he was gone.

Siobhan, never having been kissed before, touched her bruised lips. The sensation it sent through her body startled her. She stood in the doorway watching Michael swagger away as if he hadn't a care in the world.

Her thoughts were broken by Miss Hazel shouting her name. 'Siobhan, put the kettle on and start the breakfast, I'm feeling quite hungry.' In silence, Siobhan only picked at her food. 'You are very quiet, my dear. Michael's going has upset you, hasn't it?' said Miss Hazel. Siobhan nodded. 'Oh! He will be back in no time at all when he has made his fortune.'

Miss Hazel did not like to see Siobhan upset - little did she know they would all be upset before Siobhan saw Michael Rafferty again.

CHAPTER 8
The Meeting

With the coming of spring a sprinkling of pale green appeared on the trees, hedges and dark brown earth. Odd snowdrops and primroses added an unexpected colour to the excitement and a new beginning was in the air. New life was being born. Siobhan looked up at a cloudless blue sky, and a surge of happiness filled her body. Michael and the sorrow of his departure were as forgotten as her old life.

Miss Hazel became more agile with the warm weather, and, with the help of a walking stick, she was able to get around unaided. Walking into the back garden, she watched Siobhan planting the spring seeds. The sun was shining on her thick hair which was as black as a raven's wing. Miss Hazel thought how the girl had blossomed and grown. She noted how Siobhan's figure was developing, especially her breasts which were straining against the bodice of her dress, each button looking as if it was about to pop off. She tried to suppress the thought that Siobhan looked positively indecent, the way that dress was pulling across her chest. 'You are growing faster than the plants, young lady,' Miss Hazel shouted. 'We had better get you some new clothes. We will go into the village store and choose some dress material for you.' As an afterthought, she added, 'Better still, go to the Vicarage and ask Reverend Parker to arrange for a carriage to take us into town. I could do with an outing, and a ride out will do us good.'

Siobhan wrapped her shawl around her shoulders and started to walk to the Vicarage. She had not been there since Christmas, and had not liked the way Sally had been hanging around Michael. Sally had looked at her as if she knew she wasn't really Michael's sister, and with Michael gone she felt nervous of seeing her alone.

On the journey from Miss Hazel's cottage to the Vicarage Siobhan continued to think about Sally and Michael. He could have taken Sally away to London with him, but he had said he loved her and he would be back for her - it was all very confusing. As she reached the winding lane, the lovely morning prompted her to sing. Her song was halted abruptly when a horse came galloping around the bend, knocking her into the ditch. The horse reared up, his front hooves grabbing at the air, but, expertly, the rider managed to get it under control. He was about to ride off when he spotted the frightened figure of Siobhan trying to clamber out of the ditch. 'What the devil do you think you are doing, walking in the middle of the path?' he snarled, taking no thought that Siobhan could also have been hurt. 'You could have killed me or crippled my horse.' Poised to gallop off, the rays of the sun suddenly illuminated Siobhan's face as she struggled to her feet. 'What have we here? A beauty if ever I saw one,' he exclaimed with an intake of breath. He alighted from the horse and extended his hand to help her. Taking the outstretched hand she scrambled up the bank, still dazed from the fall.

'Thank you, Sir,' she said. Embarrassed, she attempted to brush the dead leaves and twigs from her clothes. Her shawl had slipped from her shoulders, exposing her tight fitting dress. The rider gazed at her slim girlish figure and her immature breasts straining against the material of her bodice.

'Ready to ripen into womanhood,' he thought, as his green eyes penetrated hers, making her feel shy and uncomfortable. After a pause he spoke aloud. 'I have not seen you before. Where are you from girl?' he said, tapping her on the shoulder with his riding crop.

'From Ireland, Sir,' she stammered, frightened and confused. He laughed out loud at her answer, showing a perfect set of white teeth. The smile lit up the whole of his face. The sun's rays suddenly shone through his blonde hair, creating a golden halo. Siobhan could not take her eyes off his face, thinking she had never seen any man so handsome, like a Greek god in Miss Hazel's books.

'You have walked all the way from Ireland?' he mused with twinkling eyes. Unfortunately, Siobhan did not realize he was joking.

'Oh no, Sir, I was born in Ireland, but now I live with Miss Hazel,' she answered seriously, then added, her voice trailing away, 'I look after her.'

'Miss Hazel! And where does this Miss Hazel live?' he asked.

'At Lilac Cottage, about a mile along the lane,' she said politely.

'A mile down the lane,' he repeated with an air of sarcasm. Siobhan blushed. Had she said something stupid? Why was he repeating what she had said? He noticed the blush and was delighted. 'Shy and unspoilt,' he thought to himself, 'That's a rarity in this village.' He then addressed Siobhan directly. 'And where are you going to now, young lady?' he asked.

With an air of childish innocence, she told him that she was going to ask the Reverend Parker if he would kindly lend Miss Hazel his carriage and driver to take them into Little Chester.

'And why would Miss Hazel want to go into Little Chester?' he said with further sarcasm. Not being used to speaking to men, least of all a gentleman, she spoke trustingly, as a child would speak. She told him that Miss Hazel was going to buy her some material for new dresses, as she had grown out of the ones she presently had. Siobhan's un-sophistication paralleled her beauty, which fascinated him further. He couldn't let this one go - no by God, here was a girl that was worth pursuing, and pursue her he would. 'No need to go to the Vicarage, girl. I will send my carriage to pick up you and Miss Hazel tomorrow morning - can you remember that?' The girl did not seem like an idiot, but you never could tell with these country types. He raised the reins to ride away, but then he stopped and lifted her chin up with his riding crop.

'What is your name girl?' he asked.

'Siobhan,' she answered quietly.

'Well, I'm Bromley – Lord Peter Bromley.' Siobhan stood and watched long after the horse had vanished into the distance. She was reflecting on the events that had just taken place when her thoughts were suddenly broken by a voice.

'What you doing here?' It was Sally. Siobhan told her what had just taken place. At the sound of his name Sally gave a shudder. She had not seen him since that terrible night. 'Well, well. Lord Bromley!' said Sally, eyeing Siobhan up and down. She had forgotten how beautiful the blossoming girl was. In contrast, Siobhan saw something different in the way Sally looked. Her figure and face were bloated and her eyes were red and sore, reminiscent of having been crying. Sally could not help seeing the way Siobhan was looking at her. 'Well! What you looking at?'

'Nothing,' answered Siobhan, pulling herself together. 'It was just a shock seeing you after all this time!'

'Shock! It will be you that's in for a shock if you have anything to do with that Lord Bromley,' said Sally. 'Heard anything from that brother of yours?' she added. She had heard in the village that Siobhan had not gone with Michael to London, news that gave her some satisfaction. 'I told him so,' she thought, 'I knew she wouldn't leave Miss Hazel to go with him'.

'No, I haven't heard from him,' answered Siobhan. 'I expect he is too busy looking for work'

'Very likely, always busy that one, too bloody busy,' Sally said, stemming the flow of tears from her eyes.

Siobhan watched her go, wondering what she meant. She reflected on Lord Bromley, wondering what Sally meant by the remark she had made about him. The happiness she previously felt had suddenly gone as she walked back to the cottage, deep in thought. She repeated to Miss Hazel what Lord Bromley had said about sending his carriage for them, but wasn't prepared for such a hostile reaction. Never had she seen Miss Hazel in such an animated temper, even with her arthritic condition. Miss Hazel stamped her feet and started to wave her stick. 'You stupid girl,' she shouted. 'Haven't I told you time and time again never to speak to strangers, especially men? And now, despite all I have said, trying to protect you, you speak with the most vile creature of them all, Lord Bromley. Heaven help us, that's all I can say.' In shock and close to tears Siobhan managed to stutter a response.

'We need not go, Miss Hazel, we do not have to go, we can send the carriage away saying we have changed our mind.'

'Need not go,' Miss Hazel shouted. 'No one defies the Lord Almighty!'

'He seemed very nice,' said Siobhan, wiping away tears with the back of her hand. Miss Hazel calmed down on seeing how upset the girl was and handed Siobhan her handkerchief.

'I'm sorry for shouting. You weren't to know what a terrible man he is,' she said.

'He didn't seem bad to me,' she said, still wiping her eyes. 'He was very polite.'

'Do not be fooled girl, that's his way,' said Miss Hazel, sitting down exhausted. 'But believe me when I say he is evil, he is the devil himself, but what's done cannot be undone.'

'But what about the carriage he is sending?' said Siobhan, then added with embarrassment, 'We had better not go.'

'We cannot refuse girl, the only thing we can do is to be on our guard,' said Miss Hazel. 'Did he say he would be present in the carriage?'

'No, he just said be sure to tell you he would be sending the carriage to take us to Little Chester.'

'That's something! At least he won't be accompanying us,' said Miss Hazel, with a sigh of relief.

Sally walked back to the Vicarage, deep in thought. She saw how Siobhan had looked at her, and soon everyone would be noticing she was pregnant. What was she going to do? Pregnant, bloody pregnant. It was Michael's, that was one fact of which she was certain. She had some money saved, but not enough to go to London. When she had first missed her period she knew what it meant, having always been so regular. Immediately she visited the old gypsy in the wood who was known for her herbal potions to bring on a miscarriage. But this time nothing had worked - potions, the Reverend's gin, scalding hot baths and more. Sharp branches from the elm tree pushed inside her had caused internal bleeding, and throwing herself down the stairs, not one of her better ideas, resulted in a badly bruised body. 'This one is here to stay my girl,' said the gypsy, shaking her head. 'Other than cutting your belly open and scooping it out, there is nothing else to be done.'

So the little bastard was still inside her, growing bigger every week. Eventually the Reverend would find out, and he would turn her out for sure! Well, when he did she would make sure she got as much money as she could out of him! Then she would go to London and find Michael. He would surely marry her when he knew she was carrying his baby. With this thought in mind her spirits lifted.

CHAPTER 9
The Outing

The following morning the coach arrived as promised, and to their amazement Lord Bromley stepped from the carriage. 'Good morning, ladies,' he said, smiling. He tipped his hat and bowed in an exaggerated fashion. 'On such a beautiful morning I have decided to accompany you. I have business in town, so I thought, why not mix business with pleasure.' Seeing the scowl on Hazel's face he added, 'I trust you have no objections, Miss Hazel.'

'It is your coach, Lord Bromley,' Miss Hazel said quietly. 'It would be very ungracious of me to object.'

Lord Bromley was charming and amusing as they jogged along. Siobhan laughed more than she had ever done before at the stories he was telling. Even Miss Hazel's determination to be curt weakened to a state of mild amusement. 'Why, Lord Bromley, you are making all this up,' Miss Hazel said, now barely concealing her laughter.

'Some of it, perhaps, but most of it is true.' The Lord's eyes were sparkling in the special way he could command when he wanted to impress. 'How beautiful Siobhan was when she laughed,' he thought. She gave him the feeling he was the first one to make her laugh. Siobhan was captivated by Lord Bromley. She had never known anyone like him, so handsome, so gay, you couldn't help but be happy in his company.

Time went very quickly and soon they reached the town of Little Chester. Siobhan's eyes were everywhere - she didn't know where to look first. People were bustling, market sellers were shouting their wares, buskers were dancing and singing. Most of all there was colour, bright colour, everywhere - in the shop windows, on peoples' clothes, and even the colour of the buildings. Lord Bromley made no attempt to leave them. He took Miss Hazel's arm, helping her along the uneven grey cobbled streets. 'You ought to be about your business, My Lord, not wasting your time with us,' Miss Hazel said, wanting to get rid of him. For all his charm she did not trust him since she had heard stories about his madness. Most were exaggerated by re-telling, but she knew that many a fire had started from a single spark.

'Now, Miss Hazel,' he responded. 'What would you do without my arm to support you? You don't want to hold Siobhan back, do you? Look how she is enjoying herself, running from shop to shop.' He looked down at her as if waiting for a response that did not come, then added, 'I can do my business later.'

Miss Hazel looked at Siobhan and felt ashamed. The girl looked like a street urchin. Her clothes were a disgrace, threadbare and far too small. It had not mattered in the cottage, but here, compared with other girls, she realised that this trip was long overdue. As if reading her thoughts, Lord Bromley said, 'You must let me buy the girl a dress. It would give me a great deal of pleasure.' More to himself than to Miss Hazel he added, 'A jewel like that should have a pretty setting.' Miss Hazel reared.

'I can buy the things Siobhan needs,' she shouted. She tried to pull her arm free, but Lord Bromley held it tight, causing her pain.

'Won't hear of it. Won't hear of it. She is an orphan, and, as Lord of the Manor, it's my duty to look after my villagers. You do agree, don't you?' he argued. 'You don't want the village council putting her in the workhouse, thinking you can't look after her properly.' Miss Hazel knew this was more than a veiled threat. Beneath all his smiling charms lurked a viper that would stop at nothing to get what he wanted. She said nothing. After all, what could she say? She would not want to live if Siobhan went out of her life. She would have to box clever and bide her time.

Lord Bromley saw Miss Hazel was angry. He did not want to get on the wrong side of her - it would not fit his plans. His frown disappeared and his charm flowed again. 'I'll tell you what, Miss Hazel. Let me buy a Sunday dress and cloak for Siobhan and you can buy the material for the day clothes she needs.'

Miss Hazel thought for a moment, then agreed. 'Alright, but I don't like it,' she said. 'It isn't right.'

The staff in the salon knew Lord Bromley. Though habitually bringing all his fancy women there to dress, this one was different from the rest. Apart from her beauty, she looked like an innocent child. 'This girl's no floozy,' went the whispers behind the scenes. 'Nevertheless, she would end up like all the rest.' Of course, it was none of their business. Their job was to take as much money as possible from him.

Dress after dress was brought out for Siobhan to try on. Every colour and fabric suited her, from deep blue velvet to crimson chiffon. Both Miss Hazel and Lord Bromley caught their breath at the transformation. He had an appreciation for things of beauty, filling the manor with rare paintings and fine porcelain. Today, his eyes had feasted on a beauty to surpass any object he possessed. 'It's hard to choose,' he said after what seemed like hours of trying on. 'Which one do you like?' he asked Siobhan.

'Oh! They are all so lovely, but not suitable for me to wear in the cottage. Have you anything more plain?' she said to the sales assistant. Shocked, she wondered what ever made her say that. Never had she been so bold, but today was like a drunken reverie. Never in her wildest dreams did she think anything like this would happen to her.

Miss Hazel was taken aback, but Lord Bromley laughed. 'Bring some serviceable dresses for the lady to try on. Leave the velvet dress and cloak. Oh! And the red chiffon with it's matching swansdown wrap! She must have those, and shoes to match.'

There was no protest from Miss Hazel who had fallen into a half sleepy state. They chose two cotton dresses, the most serviceable styles the salon sold. The red dress had to be altered to fit Siobhan's tiny figure. The Lord said he would return in two hours, and that the dress had better be ready. Siobhan thanked him warmly, but said she didn't know when she would get to wear them. 'You never know, my dear. You never know,' he answered softly, winking his eye. 'In fact, put the blue velvet dress and cloak on now and we will go to lunch.' To appease Miss Hazel he let her buy the serge material and practical undergarments.

The tavern was full when they entered, but predictably a table for three was found for their valued client. Many of Lord Bromley's friends were dining. Heads turned as he walked in with a beautiful girl on his arm. Whispers filtered round the tavern, doubtless discussing this new young escort. Oblivious, Siobhan ate her meal in a dream. Lifting an eye she caught the reflection of an elegant, dark haired girl. Was it really her? Miss Hazel, despite deepening tiredness, couldn't help feeling proud of the way Siobhan looked.

Miss Hazel watched the parcels being loaded onto the coach. 'Why, Lord Bromley, you have not attended to your business,' she said, returning to the mild air of sarcasm.

'Forgotten all about it! I can do that any time,' he said dismissively. 'You know I have trouble remembering things when I am enjoying myself so much. I feel positively happy.' For a brief moment Miss Hazel saw the little boy he had once been.

Sleep overcame Siobhan as soon as the coach started off, her head falling against the Lord Bromley's shoulder. He had insisted she wore a corset under the low cut velvet dress, causing her well shaped breasts to be pushed upwards. The jogging of the coach oscillated the exposed flesh in a provocative way. Thoughts of touching them were crossing his mind when he caught Miss Hazel's eye. 'The old witch!' he thought. It was as if she could read his mind. 'Never mind. If I wait, my time will come when Miss Hazel would not be about.'

CHAPTER 10
The Funeral

A few weeks later, events happened that were to change the lives of both Siobhan and Sally forever. Sally and Mrs. Bunce were busy in the kitchen at the Vicarage when the silence was broken by a tremendous crash from the hall. 'What the devil?' exclaimed Mrs. Bunce. They ran towards the source of the sound, only to see Mrs. Parker lying at the bottom of the stairs where she had fallen.

Sally felt for a heartbeat. 'She ain't dead,' she said, trying to lift her up.

'Don't touch her Sally,' said Mrs. Bunce. 'Something may be broken. Go and find the Reverend.' Reverend Parker, mentally distraught at the sight of his wife lying there, started wailing and praying. Mrs. Bunce looked at him in disgust and turned to Sally. 'You go and fetch the Doctor, it's no good sending him,' she said, pointing to the Reverend, who was now on his knees rubbing Mrs. Parker's hands and crying like a baby.

The doctor diagnosed that Mrs. Parker had broken her leg and damaged her back. With great care they carried her upstairs to bed. He left instructions that she was to be kept warm, stressing that if she caught a cold there was a possibility that it could develop into pneumonia. He left laudanum for the pain and a lotion to bring out the bruising.

Mrs. Parker was not a good patient and constantly moaned that Sally was rough with her. She had her running up and down stairs for every trivial thing. Sally wasn't too well herself, feeling constantly sick and exhausted. On one of the days when Mrs. Parker was in a particularly bad mood, no matter how Sally tried to please her, nothing was right. She would no sooner go downstairs, when the bell would ring for her to go up again. If she tried to ignore it, the sound would just go on and on. 'You might as well go up and see what she wants before the sound of that bell drives us mad,' said Mrs. Bunce with a sympathetic sigh.

'I'll stop the old crow,' thought Sally, mixing a cup of hot chocolate and adding a good measure of laudanum. 'That should keep her quiet for a while,' she added, nodding to herself with satisfaction. The extra laudanum did send Mrs. Parker into a drugged sleep, which was appreciated both by Sally and Mrs. Bunce. From then on the hot chocolate concoction became a nightly ritual. Even the Reverend Parker remarked how peaceful his wife had become.

'She must be on the mend, Sally,' he said. 'We'll soon have her up and about.'

The Reverend was wrong - Mrs. Parker was not on the mend. The drugs caused her not to eat, and her weakened state led to the development of pneumonia. Wracked with guilt, Sally was full of compassion and started to care for Mrs. Parker as if she was the mother she never knew. Night after night she sat in the big armchair at the side of the bed, half sleeping, half dozing, to be on hand if Mrs. Parker threw off her bed clothes. One evening, Reverend Parker entered the bedroom, stroking his wife's head, tears running down his cheeks. Remorsefully, he turned to Sally. 'I've been a bad husband, Sally,' he said. 'When Mrs. Parker gets better I'll pay her more attention and try to be more devoted. You have been a good girl, Sally, but I think it will be better if you find another situation. I will give you good references. You should have no problem finding another job.' Sally was too shocked to speak. After he had left the room she pulled the bedclothes off Mrs. Parker in a temper and opened wide the windows. The onrush of the cold evening air caused Mrs. Parker to subconsciously try to grab at the clothes for warmth, but in her weakened state she soon gave up exhausted.

Next day the Doctor called and could not understand the deterioration in his patient. Her fever was much worse. He stressed once more that she was to be kept warm and to try and get her to drink. Naturally Sally assured him that she would do so. 'You look exhausted, Sally. Are you sure this is not too much for you?' said the doctor before leaving.

'I am a bit tired, but Mrs. Bunce gives me a hand in the day. Don't worry about me. Getting Mrs. Parker well is the main thing,' she answered.

With no pang of conscience Sally built up the fire until the bedroom was like an oven. Mrs. Parker started to burn up, the beads of perspiration pouring down her flushed face. Once more Sally opened the windows and pulled back the bedclothes. This time Mrs. Parker made no attempt to pull them back. She stared at Sally with a question in her eyes. 'Why?' they was asking.

A week later, the Reverend suggested that perhaps Mrs. Parker should be sent to the infirmary, but the doctor pointed out that his wife would not survive the journey. He sent for a professional nurse to be in attendance to see if she could bring Mrs. Parker's fever down. Sally became frightened as she foresaw the end of her carefully made plans. Her fears were short lived, however, as Mrs. Parker died on the nurse's second day.

Sally tried not to show the happiness she was feeling. If everything went to plan the Reverend would now marry her and father her child. The Reverend himself was inconsolable, praying the Lord to forgive him for not appreciating his wife. Sally, cunning as usual, sympathised with him and eased his conscience by reminding him what a good husband he had been in allowing her to ease Mrs. Parker's headaches. She knew he was aware of the method she had used. Fear showed in his eyes as he recalled the cure.

'That was in the past, like the punishment I bestowed on you. I trust that you will not mention it again to me or anyone else. If you are a good girl, a just reward will be given to you for looking after my wife.'

'Nothing less than a bribe,' she thought! 'It will take more than a few coins to keep me quiet.' After the funeral she would tell him about the baby.

As the first shock of his wife's death passed, the Reverend realised he may be able to use the funeral to his advantage. He would invite Lord Bromley to attend and, with a bit of luck, there should be a substantial gathering of other influential gentry.

The day of the funeral was cold, but sunny. Many villagers attended, not out of respect for Mrs. Parker, but they had heard Lord Bromley would be there. Initially, he had no intention of attending, but the thought crossed his mind that Siobhan would probably be there. Reverend Parker conducted the service himself, singing his wife's praises. On and on he droned until he sensed the congregation was becoming restless. Lord Bromley's yawn was the final signal that it was time to finish.

The congregation trooped outside, each shaking hands with the Reverend. The gentry were asked back to the Vicarage, but when Lord Bromley declined, much to the disappointment of the Reverend, the others followed suit. Miss Hazel and Siobhan were just about to walk away when a voice calling their names stopped them.

'My dear, dear, Miss Hazel,' said Lord Bromley, 'How very nice to see you. It has been such a long time. I have been meaning to look you up, but I have been away on business,' he said in an exaggerated fashion. Miss Hazel did not want to speak to him and would have ignored him, if it hadn't been for the curious onlookers. She had not seen or heard anything of him since the trip into town. Her fears had subsided as time went by, thinking it was just another whim of the gentry. Even now, looking at him, it seemed as if it had never happened. But to Siobhan it was still very real, as she remembered every minute of that day, and the telling off Miss Hazel had given her. She had warned her of men like Lord Bromley, how they used foolish young girls like herself. Siobhan had listened, and, though not fully disagreeing, in her heart she could not believe that Lord Bromley was like her father. Looking at him now with his striking good looks and perfect manners, she knew she was right. This man could never be cruel. 'I feel I owe you an explanation as to why I have not been in touch since our outing,' Bromley said, walking beside them. 'I have been up north visiting my uncle, but now I am back, so you can be assured I will be looking after the welfare of you both. Now let me start by giving you a lift home. Forster, my coachman, is by the gates with my carriage.' He grabbed at Miss Hazel's arm before she could refuse, and guided her towards his carriage. Miss Hazel wanted to tell him what to do with his lift, but she could not - not without causing a scene. Her reason to be cautious was reinforced by his next comment. 'You see, Miss Hazel, you are not as young as you used to be.' She knew there was a hidden threat behind those words.

The coach stopped and Forster helped them alight, but Bromley just sat there, deep in thought. The words 'Thank you, Lord Bromley,' from Siobhan brought him back to reality.

'What? Oh! Yes, yes. Siobhan, have you still got the red chiffon dress I bought for you?'

'Oh! Yes, Sir,' she replied. 'It's still in its box. I haven't even dare look at it again. Miss Hazel has put it away.'

'I am having a ball at the manor on Saturday,' said Lord Bromley. 'You are invited. You will wear the red dress and the swansdown wrap. Miss Hazel, did you hear what I was saying to Siobhan? The ball on Saturday, she will be coming. See that she is suitably attired in the chiffon dress. Forster will pick her up at 7:30 prompt. By the way, I will send one of the maids over to help you, especially with her hair. See that something is done with it, on top, curls.' He looked at Siobhan, imagining her as she would be on Saturday. 'Roses in her hair,' he rehearsed, 'red ones dotted here and there.' He touched Siobhan's black hair, indicating where they should be put. Miss Hazel went to protest, but his hand gripped Miss Hazel's boney shoulder, pressing hard to emphasise his point. 'Understand?' She winced in pain.

'Yes, Sir,' she whispered. Siobhan was frightened, but excited. Whatever Miss Hazel had said, and she had repeated it many times, she didn't believe Lord Bromley to be evil. He couldn't want her as a plaything to be discarded when he became bored - he was so charming and kind.

Miss Hazel was frightened for Siobhan. Time after time she had warned her, but she wouldn't listen. The girl was in a daze, but Miss Hazel had seen the darker side of Lord Bromley. Her bruised shoulder held testimony to part of it. She had seen the glazed far away look in his eyes. The villagers said he had inherited a madness from his late father who had eventually succumbed to the ravages of syphilis. They thought that, very likely, the son would end up the same way. Miss Hazel could say that Siobhan was sick and could not attend, but he would certainly come after her. Her only option was to ask Forster to keep an eye on her.

At the Vicarage the mourners had all gone, except for Mrs. Parker's distant cousin, Margery, who had travelled down from Scotland. She said she would stay for a week or so to help Reverend Parker sort out his wife's affairs. Sally and cook had put on a grand spread. There had been mulled wine, pork pies, ham and fresh baked bread. Sally felt tired and sat down as the consequences of her pregnancy were beginning to tell. Even Mrs. Bunce noticed a change in her countenance. 'Sally, you don't seem the same girl as you did a few months ago,' she began. 'When you first came to the Vicarage you were always laughing and singing. You were always ready for a joke - a rare treat to see you, it was.' She peered at Sally over her spectacles. 'Anything wrong, girl?' she said, hoping Sally would confide in her.

'I can't go round laughing and singing with the mistress dead now, can I?' she answered.

'Didn't know you were that fond of her,' said the cook sarcastically.

'I didn't dislike her. She was very kind to me,' said Sally. After a pause she added, 'I wonder what's going to happen now. I don't like the attitude of Mrs. Parker's cousin. Treats me like dirt. After all, I've kept this place running for years.'

Unlike Mrs. Parker, her cousin, a widow of five years, was a woman of strong character. She soon exerted her authority over the Vicarage. To her, Sally was just a servant girl, and a sluttish one at that. In the next few days after the funeral Sally was run off her feet with fetching and carrying. The thoroughness by which Sally was required to clear out Mrs. Parker's clothes created the impression that Margery wanted to erase all traces of her relation.   Sally knew she would soon have to act. She would wait until she got the chance to get the Reverend Parker alone, which was proving very difficult, as Margery never seemed to leave his side. Sally got the distinct feeling that Margery saw Reverend Parker as her future husband. She could not let that happen. She had not killed Mrs. Parker for nothing. Sally stopped in her tracks - this was the first time she had admitted to herself that she had committed a murder.

It was the following Saturday morning before Sally found the opportunity to speak to the Reverend Parker. Margery had gone into the village to monitor the ordering of food supplies, feeling there was far too much waste in the kitchen. Sally knocked on the study door. 'Come.' The Reverend Parker was sat in his big leather chair, writing at his desk. He looked up. 'Oh! Sally. I'm glad it's you.' Sally felt her hopes rising. Perhaps he had missed making love to her. She certainly did not anticipate what was to follow. 'I have been meaning to have a word with you. I have been very lax with you recently. Mrs. Parker's cousin has pointed out certain disagreeable aspects in the running of this house. We must start pulling ourselves together. The place is filthy, girl, filthy.' With these words he dragged his finger along the desk. She read the seriousness of his tone, and there was no way that this was part of some new foreplay routine. Sally's fury gave her courage, the words coming spontaneously from her.

'The reason things have become lax, Reverend Parker, is because I am pregnant,' she said forcefully. 'Pregnant, do you hear? And by you.' Her face was flushed with anger. 'Now what do you think about that?' The Reverend fell back in his chair, beads of perspiration forming on his forehead. 'What's Mrs. Parker's cousin going to say about that?'

'Very little!' Margery's voice from the doorway repeated the remark. 'Very little! You don't think I, or anyone else, will believe a little slut like you? Reverend Parker is a pillar of society. No one is going to believe he would take up with a girl like you.' She came closer to Sally until her face was just inches away. 'I'll give you until this evening to get your things together and get out of this house,' she screamed. 'If you are still here tomorrow I will send for the bobbies.'

Sally knew she was beaten. The cousin was right. No one would believe her word against his. She had killed Mrs. Parker, and now only Margery would benefit. As Sally left the room the cousin shouted after her. 'And if I hear the story repeated there will be real trouble for you, Sally Walters. Do I make myself clear?' Margery did not care whether the story was true or not. She only knew that she intended to stay right where she was. She had been a widow long enough. What luck! She now had the opportunity to blackmail Arthur Parker into marrying her, should matters not take her predicted course.

CHAPTER 11
The Ball

By mid afternoon a coach had arrived carrying Lillie Greaves, one of the late Lady Bromley's maids. The tin bath was placed in front of the fire and filled with hot water. Lord Bromley had thought of everything, right down to the rare bath oils and soaps. Greaves had been carefully instructed in every detail of what Lord Bromley expected in preparing Siobhan for the ball. The fragrant smell of perfume filled the cottage as the maid bathed Siobhan. Whilst this was happening, Siobhan's mind went back to when she scrubbed herself at the pump in Michael's yard. To her, it seemed a lifetime ago. The maid did not dare express the thoughts she secretly held: 'Poor child. Did she not know what she was being groomed for?' She could not understand Miss Hazel letting it happen, for it was clear the old lady loved the girl.

Siobhan was instructed to rest whilst her hair dried, and before it was time to get dressed. The big box was opened containing the red chiffon dress and matching satin shoes. The dress was hung up near the dampness of the bath to encourage the creases to drop out. It was far too delicate to think about applying a smoothing iron. Siobhan was so excited she thought she would never be able to rest, but soon fell into a dreamy sleep. She dreamed of herself in the arms of Lord Bromley, the red chiffon dress floating around them as they danced.

Miss Hazel and the maid sat down drinking tea. Now a mature woman, Lillie had worked for the Bromley household most of her life. From early beginnings as a scullery maid she had risen to become Lady Bromley's personal attendant. She had not been a pretty girl, but, in truth, bordering on being ugly had been her salvation. Neither the late Lord

Bromley nor young Peter had been tempted to make advances towards her. She knew how to keep her mouth shut and to turn a blind eye to things she had witnessed. She now shuddered at their recollection. The late Lady Bromley was the reason she had stayed so long at the manor, then after her death she was too old to move on. 'Why are you shuddering,' Miss Hazel asked. 'You are not cold, are you?'

'Oh! No,' said Lillie. 'I think the devil must have walked over my grave.'

Miss Hazel could contain herself no longer. She had kept herself in check all day, but now she let out all her frustration. 'If, by the devil, you mean Lord Bromley, then you may well shudder. What does it feel like dressing a chicken for the roasting?' Anger rose in the maid's stomach.

'How dare you say that to me? You, a retired school mistress, letting it all happen. It's my job to do as I am told. What's your excuse?' Tears that had previously been held in check suddenly filled Miss Hazel's eyes. They brimmed over and ran down her withered cheeks.

'Don't you think that I would prevent this if I could? He's threatened to have Siobhan taken away to the workhouse if I do anything to annoy him.'

'Couldn't you send her away for a while, at least until he has forgotten about her?' said the maid, regretting her earlier outburst.

'If I knew the address of her brother in London I would soon pack her off on the coach. Could you look after her, or at least look out for her at the ball?' pleaded Miss Hazel. 'See no harm comes to her.'

'I will look out for her the best I can,' the maid said, 'but it is Forster who will have the opportunity to see she leaves as soon as Lord Bromley gets drunk. It is usually quite early in the evening that he passes out and doesn't remember a thing. Forster can then bring her home. After that, if I were you, I'd send her away, because once he fancies a girl he's like a dog after a bitch on heat, and won't stop until he's had his way with her. I've seen it too many times.' Suddenly she stopped, realising she was saying too much.   Miss Hazel felt Lillie could be encouraged to reveal more. She loosened the stopper on a bottle of sloe gin that was kept for medicinal purposes. 'Here, my dear, have a drink. It will calm you down.' Miss Hazel poured her a large cup of the home made gin. The maid took a deep gulp. They sat in silence whilst she gradually drank the whole cupful. Patiently, Miss Hazel poured her another, and waited. With the warmth of the fire as a catalyst the gin started to have the effect Miss Hazel wanted. Just a little longer and her tongue would loosen.

'I've seen it all before,' the maid started in a perceivably slurred speech. 'Ever since he was a boy he's been the same. The turns would come and go. One minute he was like an angel, charming happy and gay. The next minute his face would distort and we all knew he was going to have a turn.'

'A turn, you said?' Miss Hazel prompted, as she re-charged her glass.

'Evil! Evil! He'd ride a horse until it dropped down dead! Then when he realised what he had done he'd cry like a baby and be remorseful for a week. Why, I have seen his father beat him until he was bleeding and unconscious. He tried to beat it out of the lad, but he couldn't. You see, he had inherited his father's madness.'

'They do say you can beat the Devil in,' Miss Hazel commented.

'I've said more than I should. I'll have a word with Forster. He'll know what to do. Time to get the girl ready now.'

The maid put the finishing touches to Siobhan's hair, placing the red roses amongst the shining curls that crowned the top of her head. Lillie stepped back, admiring her work. 'You are a beauty and no mistake,' she said. 'You would surely pass for a Lady.' The colour red gave a glow to her porcelain white skin and added fire to her black hair. Siobhan's eyes sparkled like sapphires with excitement. 'Ain't you got a mirror, Miss Hazel? Let the girl see how she looks.' For the moment, the reason for the dressing up was forgotten. Siobhan could only see to her waist in the small piece of mirror in the wardrobe door, but it was enough. She could not believe that this dream-like person was herself. What would Michael think of her now?

'Now, why should I be thinking of Michael,' she thought.

Forster arrived on time. He, too, held his breath when he saw Siobhan. 'My God! You really are a beautiful girl,' he exclaimed.

'I want a word with you, Forster,' said Miss Hazel, calling him into the kitchen. 'Lillie and I have been talking. You know as well as I do why His Lordship wants the girl up at the manor. I can't do anything about it now, didn't have the time, but in the future I will. I will. What I want you to do is keep an eye on her, see that she comes to no harm. Get her away as soon as you can. Will you do that for me, Forster? Will you?' Tears fell once more from Miss Hazel's eyes.

'Aye, Miss, I'll do as you say. I'll do my best to bring her home safe,' he said as he pressed Miss Hazel's hand in reassurance.

The manor house was alight with silver lanterns. Footmen, dressed in silver and black uniforms, helped extravagantly dressed ladies and gentlemen alight from their carriages. Music floated through the open French doors of the ballroom on this most perfect of late spring evenings. Mothers made final adjustments to their daughter's expensive gowns. Bromley was one of the few wealthy, eligible bachelors around. Even with his reputation he would be considered a good catch for any girl.

Lord Bromley felt high with excitement. It was all he could do to stop himself from going to collect Siobhan personally. If it were not for Forster respectfully reminding him that his duty was to be present at the Manor he would surely have gone. He stood proudly in the anteroom of the big hall to meet his guests. Smiling, he held out his hand in greeting, but their names were not registering. His eyes continually wandered towards the drive searching for a sight of his own coach. After a seemingly interminable wait Forster brought the carriage to a halt. Lord Bromley rushed out to greet it, opening the door before Forster had chance to alight.

'Siobhan,' he called softly as he held the red gloved hand and helped her down. Nervously, she alighted from the coach. He stood, as if transfixed, staring into her eyes. As tears filled his own eyes he managed to whisper, 'You look magnificent.' He wanted to kiss her there and then, to hold her to him, but he knew this was neither the time nor the place. With patience, that would come later. He put his hand in his pocket and produced a neatly folded handkerchief. Letting the corners fall away from his open hand he exposed the contents - a necklace of rubies and a pair of matching earrings. 'A finishing touch,' he said, as he gently put the necklace in place. He smoothed away the ringlets of hair to allow him to attach the droplet earrings. She wasn't sure, but it felt as if a butterfly wing had brushed her skin. Lord Bromley's fingers were so gentle against her swan-like neck.

All eyes were on them as they entered the ballroom. Whispers began to fill the room. 'Who was she?' 'Where had she come from?' 'Why had not anyone heard of her?'

Siobhan, oblivious to her surroundings, went through the evening in a trance. She had never been taught to dance, but managed to float around the room, guided by the firm arms of the host. He never left her side. On one occasion, when one of the guests attempted to ask her for a dance, Bromley gave him such a frown that the words stuck in his throat.

As the evening wore on the ballroom became very hot. Although Siobhan had hardly spoken, only to say 'yes' and 'no', she felt she would die of thirst if she did not have a drink. Sensing all was not as it should be, Bromley asked her if there was anything wrong. 'I'm so thirsty, My Lord. Do you think I could have a glass of water?'

'Forgive me, Siobhan, for being so thoughtless. I have been so intoxicated with your beauty I have neglected your needs.'

Champagne and a plate of tit-bits arrived. Thinking it was no more than expensive lemonade she drank it down, and then another. The heat and the champagne combined to make Siobhan very tired, hardly able to keep her eyes open. Lord Bromley noticed, and asked if she would like to rest in the drawing room. Siobhan told him she'd promised Miss Hazel that she would get Forster to take her home early. 'Quite right, too,' agreed Bromley. 'In fact, you go into the drawing room and I'll send for Forster to take you home.' She sat down on the blue brocade chaise-longue, her gaze taking in the magnificence of the room. Large portraits of Lord Bromley's ancestors looked down on her from the high walls. A wood fire blazed in the marble grate, sending a dancing light across the ornate ceiling. It seemed very quiet after the noise of the ballroom. Peacefulness flowed over her, the flickering fire mesmerising what was left of her consciousness.

Lord Bromley entered the drawing room and found her fast asleep. He had to use his self control not to take her there and then, but he knew he must be patient and wait until his guests had gone. Eventually the last ones departed. Bromley went out to the stable and told Forster that the Hadens had taken Siobhan home, and that he would not be called on again tonight. Forster could not argue, but had an uneasy feeling about the explanation. He had not noticed Siobhan leaving. It was not inconceivable that she could have left with the Hadens, but he thought he would stay around for a little longer, just in case.

With all the guests gone, Lord Bromley quietly returned to the drawing room. He gazed at Siobhan and poured himself a brandy, absorbing every detail of her beautiful form, and watching her breasts move up and down to the rhythm of her breathing. The vision he saw was so perfect. The flickering fire played on the red dress and gave the illusion that it was on fire. Never before had he seen anything so lovely. He poured himself another drink. 'No need to hurry', he thought to himself.

Bromley sat there until he could resist her no longer. He went over and gently stroked her face with the back of his hand, and traced the outline of her lips with his finger. She awoke with a start to find his face over hers. At first, her recollection was vague. Then, as he was about to put his lips on hers, her last conscious moments came flooding back to her. She remembered where she was and what was happening. She recognised in his eyes the same look her father had when he was drunk. She started to struggle and tried to protest, but his mouth was already pressed hard against hers. He pushed his tongue deep into her mouth until she started to gag. Feeling as though she was going to be sick she sank her teeth into his tongue. In reflex, he pulled away, his face becoming distorted with anger. 'Why, you little vixen. You don't think I bought you these clothes for nothing, nor given you these rubies.' Savagely, he ripped he jewels from her neck and ears. 'Why do you think you were invited here? Not for your company, that's for sure,' he screamed, then gave out an insane laugh. He started to kiss her more violently. Siobhan could taste the blood from his bitten tongue. She tried to free herself, but the weight of his body held her down. He kissed her neck whilst his hand ripped away the top of her dress. He kissed her shoulders, then moved down to kiss her exposed breast. His teeth bit into her small nipple causing her extreme pain. The more she struggled, the harder he bit. Her terror excited him. He was used to girls being more submissive. This was a new experience, and he was loving every minute of it. His hand slid up under the hem of her dress and tugged down her drawers.

'No! No!' she screamed. He slapped her hard across the face, sending her head back and blurring her vision. She was brought back to reality by the feeling of his fingers probing inside her. He moved his body on top, his weight restricting her breathing. His knees forced her legs apart as he entered her. It felt as if a red hot poker was tearing her body apart. The ordeal seemed as if it would never end. Was this the way her sisters had suffered?

'Little Betty,' she thought, 'Poor Little Betty.'

As it had started quickly, so, mercifully, it stopped when Lord Bromley passed out. The pain was unbearable, but she knew she must get away. Cautiously, she gently wriggled out from underneath the dead weight that held her. Crawling across the room to the door her hands closed around the handle just as two arms grasped her from the back, pulling her to the ground. 'Thought you'd take your leave, did you, my beauty?' Bromley shouted. 'I'm nowhere near finished with you yet.' Siobhan tried to crawl away, but he was too strong for her, tearing at what was left of the tattered dress. He grabbed her buttocks and with a huge thrust penetrated her anus. She let out a scream so loud it alerted Forster who had fallen asleep against the house wall. He rushed inside and located the source of the sound. There he saw a sight he would never forget, Bromley rutting like a pig on Siobhan, who had mercifully fainted. Forster rushed to the fireplace and grabbed a poker. He hit Lord Bromley across the back of the head and dragged him off her. There was blood everywhere.

'Is she dead?' Forster muttered to himself as he went to pick her up. 'No, just fainted', he thought. He looked around for something to wrap the child in. 'God, she's cold,' he continued muttering. He ripped down one of the velvet drapes and wrapped it around her bruised body. Forster carried Siobhan out of the drawing room and through to the French windows. In anticipation of trouble he had not put the horses to rest for the night. He got Siobhan to the waiting coach and managed to lay her on the floor of the carriage. Pushing the horses as fast as he could, he left the driveway of the manor, then slowed to a more careful driving mode so as not to cause the girl any more pain. Although semi-conscious every so often she let out a cry like that of an injured animal. 'The bastard, the bastard,' said Forster to himself. 'Well, he's gone too far this time. It would have to be reported, the doctor would surely do that. What if the girl dies? He would personally see that Bromley hangs for it.' With a shock, a sudden thought entered his head. What if it was Lord Bromley who died - he would have killed him? Bromley had deserved it, but it would be he that would be swinging from the gallows.

He banged on Miss Hazel's door. She had not gone to bed, choosing instead to wait for Siobhan to come home. She had dozed off, but awoke with a start. Why hadn't Siobhan come in, she knew the door was not locked. Miss Hazel instinctively knew something was wrong. She only needed to see Forster holding Siobhan in his arms to know the thing she feared most had happened. Forster walked straight into the bedroom and laid Siobhan gently on the bed. 'Put the kettle and pans on the fire, we must have plenty hot water and salt, plenty of salt. That's good for wounds,' he said breathlessly. With inner strength, Miss Hazel did as she was told. She did not need any explanation - her worst nightmare had come true! Miss Hazel saw all the blood and covered her mouth with her hand in horror.

'My God, has he stabbed her?' she gasped.

'It would have been better that he had done,' answered Forster.

'You don't mean...?' Miss Hazel was too horrified to utter the words, and she didn't finish the sentence. Forster did not mince words when he answered.

'He's an animal - No! He's not good enough to be called an animal. No animal would behave to another as he has done.' Tears fell down Forster's face as he gently unwrapped the blood encrusted cape from Siobhan's battered body. Horrified at the bite and scratch marks, tears continued to fall down Miss Hazel's face. Putting all feeling of horror and embarrassment aside, Miss Hazel and Forster bathed and dressed her wounds the best they could. Siobhan continued to moan and occasionally scream out in pain. Miss Hazel sent Forster into the kitchen as she gently wiped the blood from Siobhan's intimate parts.

'Oh, my God,' she repeated over and over again as she saw the torn flesh. 'Would the girl ever be normal again? Even if her body healed, what about her mind?' she asked herself. Suddenly Siobhan let out a scream and started to thrash her arms and legs about as she had done with her attacker. Forster came running in.

'She's becoming conscious,' he said. 'God knows what she will be like when she realises what has happened?' Miss Hazel gently put her arms about her.

'Hush now, hush, you are safe now,' she said soothingly, holding her as you would a baby. She gently wiped away more blood from her face. Purple bruises had begun to appear where Bromley's teeth had sunk into her flesh. The side of her face where he had slapped her was blue and swollen. Claw marks were all over her body, dried blood encrusting the broken skin. Slowly Siobhan came round, but in her confused state she couldn't remember what had happened to her. She only knew that she was in a great deal of pain. What had Miss Hazel been doing to her and why was Forster there? Suddenly aware of her nakedness she tried to cover herself. Her eyes widened when she saw the bruises and bite marks. Then her memory began to return.

'Lord Bromley,' she uttered with a cry.

'We know dear, we can guess what has happened,' said Miss Hazel, covering her body with a towel. 'But don't you worry now, you are home safe with me.'

'The towel's no good,' said Forster. 'We must keep her warm. Where can I find some blankets?' Miss Hazel pointed to the attic. 'I know this is going to hurt, but I'll be as gentle as I can,' he said as he covered her up. 'Have you any brandy?' he asked Miss Hazel. She gave a nod.

'Only for medicinal purposes, you understand.'

'Well it's needed now,' he said, like it was not the first time he had called on the remedy. 'Give her a good measure with honey in hot water, perhaps it'll send her to sleep, or at least numb the pain.' Miss Hazel did as she was told. Forster waited until Siobhan had reluctantly drunk the brandy before taking his leave. 'I must be off now,' he said. 'God knows what I have done to His Lordship - I may have killed him! If I have, you won't see me again. I'll disappear to beat the hangman!' Half out of the door he turned. 'I'll call at the doctor's, she needs a doctor. I won't tell him what's happened, it will be up to you what you tell him.'

'No! Not the doctor, I don't want the doctor,' cried Siobhan.

'Listen Siobhan, you are hurt more seriously than you realise. If infection gets into those wounds you will surely die.'

'I wish I was dead,' she said. 'Why didn't I die like Little Betty?'

'Well, you did not die, and you are not going to die, not if I can help it,' said Miss Hazel in a voice she would have used to her pupils. 'What's happened has happened! What's done is done and cannot be undone. Forster has risked his life for you! Now, no more talk of dying.'

While she waited for the doctor to arrive, Miss Hazel soothed Siobhan the best way she could and wondered who Little Betty was.

As urgent as going for the doctor was, Forster thought he had better call at the manor first to see what was going on. If he had killed Lord Bromley he'd better get his story right, about the reason he wasn't around. Perhaps they would assume it was a burglar or someone Bromley had crossed who was out for revenge.

Forster arrived back at the manor to find it in darkness. He quietly entered through one of the many doors and made his way to the drawing room. It, too, was in darkness except for the dawn light coming though the window where the drape had been torn down. There was no sign of Lord Bromley. The room had been cleaned. Except for wet patches on the furniture and carpet, you wouldn't have known anything unusual had happened. He didn't want to take the coach out again. If anyone had asked where he was last night he could always say he had taken home a guest who was worse for drink. Saddling a horse, he rode to where the doctor lived.

Forster was surprised to see the doctor answer the door fully clothed. Forster hadn't managed to speak before the doctor started shouting in an angry voice. 'Well, what is it now? Don't say Bromley has taken a turn for the worse? I've told the housekeeper I've done all I can by stitching the wound on his head. I couldn't say whether he has a fractured skull. The best place for him is in hospital, but his Lordship would have none of it. He seems to have lost his memory. As to what happened – the story seems to be that he got drunk, fell and hit his head, knocking himself out. Not that I believe a word of it! Anyway, while all this was going on, where the hell were you?' he asked Forster. So, that was it. Between them, Bromley, the housekeeper and probably the valet had concocted a story, and so long as his Lordship couldn't remember, he was in the clear. Ignoring the doctor's question of where he was, Forster spoke up.

'No! No! I'm not here about Lord Bromley. It's Siobhan, Miss Hazel's ward. She's been hurt, really bad. It's urgent, doctor, or I wouldn't be here.' The doctor looked at Forster and thought the man appeared ill. From the look on his face something was terribly wrong.

'Alright I'll come. Luckily I have not unhitched the horse from the carriage. You go on ahead and I'll follow.'

Forster was waiting by the door of the cottage when the doctor arrived. Without a word he ushered him into the bedroom. The worried face of Miss Hazel nodded towards the bed where Siobhan lay. The brandy had relaxed her and she had managed to doze off. The doctor was shocked to see her battered and bruised face. 'Has the girl been in an accident?' he asked. Miss Hazel didn't answer, but gently touched Siobhan's shoulder. As gently as the touch was, it made her flinch with pain. 'What is it?' she cried out.

'Nothing to be frightened of dear, the doctor has come to examine you,' said Miss Hazel trying to reassure her.

'No! No! I don't want to be touched,' cried Siobhan.

'I'm here to help, Siobhan. You know I wouldn't hurt you,' said the doctor. 'Come on now, be a good girl, let me have a look at you, I promise I'll be as gentle as possible,' he said, as he pulled back the bed clothes. Forster and Miss Hazel had not been able to put a nightgown on her for fear of causing Siobhan more pain. The doctor stepped back in horror as he saw her naked body covered in deep wounds and what looked like claw marks and bite marks.

'Has she been attacked by an animal?' he asked.

'You could say that,' Miss Hazel cried in distress. The doctor examined the marks.

'Why, these are human teeth marks. You don't mean she's been…?' He hadn't completed the sentence when Miss Hazel finished it for him.

'Raped, and worse!' she cried. The doctor looked with pity at Siobhan.

'Look, my dear,' he said. 'This is not going to be pleasant, but if I am to make you well again I will have to examine you, so be a good girl and do as I say, it won't take long.' Siobhan knew that the doctor only wanted to help, but all she wished was to go to sleep and never wake up. He examined her in silence, except for the occasional intake of breath. He ordered Forster to bring a bowl of hot water. Taking a brown glass bottle from his medicine bag he poured some antiseptic into the water. 'This will sting a little, but it will stop any of your wounds getting infected,' he said.

'We did our best with salt water,' said Miss Hazel, feeling a little put out.

'You've both done a grand job, but this will make absolutely sure the wounds heal,' he said. Covering her lower part the best he could so as not to embarrass the girl, he continued his examination. 'Oh! My God, the poor, poor girl. Why she's torn to pieces. She'll need stitches, a lot of them.' The words were out before he could stop them, filling Siobhan's eyes with terror. Instantly the doctor regretted giving vent to his feelings, though never in all his years practicing had he seen anything like it. 'My dear, I am going to give you something to numb the pain, it will send you to sleep for a little while, but when you wake up the worst of the pain will be over, and you will feel more comfortable.' Siobhan was too weak to protest. The laudanum was administered and she felt no more pain. As the doctor worked in silence, Forster and Miss Hazel went into the kitchen where Forster made a pot of tea.

'You had better have some of your medicinal brandy in it,' he said to Miss Hazel as he handed her a cup. 'You look as if you were about to pass out! I hate to leave you, Miss Hazel, but I ought to be getting back - the dawn's breaking. If them at the Manor find me missing they might start putting two and two together!'

'Yes, Forster, you go. You have been more than kind,' said Miss Hazel waving her hand towards the door. Forster popped his head around the bedroom door. 'I have to go now doctor, before they miss me. I'd appreciate it if you didn't say I called you,' he said.

'Yes, by all means, I've nearly finished. A bad thing this, Forster, it ought to be reported. If I did take action, he knows too many people in high places. But mark my words, one day he'll do this to the wrong person. I've had to clean up after too many of his victims, but never as bad as this.' He did not disguise the fact he knew it was the doing of his Lordship.

Miss Hazel insisted on hobbling down the path with the doctor. 'I'll call in tomorrow.' Then looking at the sun rising, he said, 'Well, it's tomorrow now. It's been a very long night. You get some rest - we can't have you ill as well.' As he got onto his carriage, he added, 'You know it would be better if she could go where he won't find her, because if I know that one, he won't leave her alone.' Although he didn't use a name, they both knew he was referring to Lord Peter Bromley.

CHAPTER 12
Escape

After Margery had told Sally to go, she had stormed upstairs to gather up her belongings. 'I'll show them they can't treat me this way,' she muttered to herself, the tears streaming down her face. However, she realised Margery could do exactly as she had said, after all, who would believe a servant girl's word against that of the Reverend. Worse still, if they start inquiring into Mrs. Parker's demise and putting two and two together they might realise she had contributed to her sudden death. Sally became really frightened, she could see herself with the rope around her neck, hanging from the gallows. Her baby would be brought up, like herself, in the workhouse.

Quietly she crept out of the Vicarage, not wanting to be heard or seen. Passing the barn she slipped inside, intent on spending the night in there. Maybe by tomorrow she'd think of what she was going to do. She thought of Michael as she lay on the straw. This was the spot where they had laid together, holding each other and making love. 'Oh! Michael, Michael,' she said, stroking the straw, imagining he was by her side. Eventually she fell into a restless sleep.

Awakened by the cock crowing, and with some difficulty, she stood up. She felt terribly stiff from lying on the straw. Tiny trickles of blood had dried on her arms and legs where the sharp ends of straw had pierced her skin. Making sure no-one was around, she picked up her things and crept from the barn, walking as briskly as she could.

The Vicarage out of sight, she slowed down, thinking of the consequences of her actions. Nothing had worked out as she had planned. Where was she supposed to go now? What on earth was going to happen to her? Feeling sorry for herself, tears filled her eyes. 'Oh! Why was it everything went right for some girls and everything went wrong for her?'

Her thoughts were interrupted by the sight of Miss Hazel's cottage coming into view. There was Miss Hazel walking with the doctor down the garden path. They seemed to be deep in conversation. The doctor was shaking his finger as if stressing the point he was making. He had probably come to see Miss Hazel about her arthritis, but why so early in the morning, when it was just becoming light. Her steps quickened, hoping to reach the cottage before the doctor went. She wanted to hear what was being said, but before she reached the cottage the doctor got onto his carriage and drove away.

Miss Hazel hobbled up the path back to the cottage. Her mind was so full of worry she was not paying attention to the path when suddenly her stick slipped and she fell to the floor. Try as she would she had not the strength to get up. Sally raced to help her. 'Don't worry, Miss Hazel, I've got you,' she said as she helped her to her feet. 'Siobhan, Siobhan,' Sally shouted to alert the obvious source of help. 'Where are you, girl.'

'Get me into the house,' said Miss Hazel crossly. 'Never mind shouting for Siobhan.' Sally was the last person she wanted to know their business. 'You can go now, I can manage,' she said, pushing Sally from her. She tried to walk, but started to fall again. Sally quickly grabbed her before she hit the ground.

'You stubborn woman! Of course you can't manage, you might have broken your ankle. Pity the doctor's gone. Anyway, where's that Siobhan?' she said, almost carrying Miss Hazel into the cottage. Sat on her chair Sally examined Miss Hazel's ankle, twisting this way and that, making the old woman scream with pain. 'No break, just sprained,' said Sally with no feeling of pity for the woman. Miss Hazel's scream awoke Siobhan.

'What's the matter, what is happening?' she shouted from the bedroom. She was attempting to get out of bed when Sally appeared at the bedroom door.

'Not still in bed are…?' her voice trailed off as she saw the state of Siobhan's battered face and shoulders. 'What the hell has been going on?' she asked, her eyes wide open with shock.

'Oh no, not you!' said Siobhan, the same thoughts as Miss Hazel going through her mind. Sally Walters was the last person she wanted to know their business.

'Yes me, and a bloody good job I happened to be passing, or Miss Hazel would still be lying on the path,' said Sally, going close up to Siobhan. 'If you want my help, and you do because there's no-one else, you had better tell me what this is all about,' pointing to Siobhan's bruises. As much as she disliked Sally, Siobhan knew she was right - there was no-one else. She related what she could remember of that fateful night. Sally listened in silence - it brought back memories of how she had suffered at the hands of Lord Peter Bromley. When Siobhan had finished, if she had been expecting sympathy from Sally, she was mistaken. 'Well, girl, didn't I warn you when you first met him, or did you think you were something different, that he would treat you like a lady? Well, now you know, even with your hoity-toity ways, you are just the same as the rest of us. You wouldn't have gone to the ball if your brother Michael had been here. But he's just like all men, uses a girl, then does what the hell he likes.' Having given vent to her feelings, Sally calmed down and saw how she could turn this situation to her advantage. Now all sweetness, she turned on the charm. 'Well it's a good job I'm here, you and Miss Hazel will need looking after,' she said as she straightened the bed clothes.

'But what about your job at the Vicarage?' asked Siobhan.

'Oh! That. I was going to leave anyway. Now Mrs. Parker's gone, I wouldn't feel comfortable up there alone with the Reverend,' she answered. 'I'll make a pot of tea, I dare say we could all do with one.'

Miss Hazel had been listening to what had been said, and she had to agree with Sally, hadn't she also warned Siobhan. She felt she was the one to blame. No matter what Lord Bromley had threatened, she should not have let her go to the ball. She agreed also that it was lucky Sally had come by. Yes, God worked in mysterious ways.

Sally busied herself, stoking up the fire, making tea and cooking breakfast. Siobhan hardly touched hers, but Miss Hazel discovered how hungry she was. On finishing her meal she said, 'Look Sally, I'm very grateful for your help. If you can stay until I'm on my feet again I can afford to pay you a small wage and your food. For the time being you can sleep in Siobhan's bed in the loft, she won't be able to move for a while.'

'But where will you sleep?' Siobhan shouted from the bedroom.

'I'll manage in the Grandfather chair - I doze off in it most of the time anyway,' answered Miss Hazel. Sally agreed, letting them think she was doing them a favour. After all, it had solved her immediate predicament for the time being. During her stay, there may be a letter from Michael, then she would be off to London to find him.

The doctor called the following day and was surprised when Sally let him in. Seeing the look on his face, Sally explained about Miss Hazel falling. 'Good thing you just happened to be passing,' said the doctor with some scepticism. He still had his suspicions about Sally Walters' part in the death of Mrs. Parker, but without proof, there was nothing he could do about it. 'I had better examine Miss Hazel first,' he said, going over to the couch where she was lying. He diagnosed that the ankle was not broken, but badly sprained. Administering liniment then binding it up tightly, he warned her to keep off it for two weeks.

'How can I rest for two weeks? Why, there is Siobhan to look after!' she answered indignantly.

'Don't worry Miss Hazel, I'm here now. I'll look after you both,' Sally quickly butted in.

'What about your job at the Vicarage?' asked the doctor.

'Oh! The Reverend don't need me now, now Mrs. Parker's cousin is there,' she said, busying herself so as they did not see how red her face had gone.

'That's alright then,' said the doctor, going into the bedroom to examine Siobhan. He was pleased with the way her torn flesh was healing, assuring her that she would soon be up and about. He almost said she would be her old self, but he knew that, although her visible scars may heal, the ones left on her mind never would.

At the Manor the housekeeper and the valet were sticking to the story that Lord Bromley had been drunk and had fallen, hitting his head. Lord Bromley, for his part, could not remember what had happened. The only vision that kept coming into his mind was that of Siobhan looking beautiful in the red chiffon dress.

Sally took over the running of Miss Hazel's household - shopping, cooking and, up to a point, cleaning. The cleaning was not up to Miss Hazel's standard, but felt tolerance was a small price to pay for Sally being there. She began to think she had misjudged the girl.

Seven days later the doctor took out Siobhan's stitches. Still very sore, she began to help Sally with the household chores. Miss Hazel's ankle was also healing and Sally began to think that soon she would be no longer needed. Then what would she do?

Lord Peter was also recovering, but he still could not remember what had happened on the night of the Ball. In his sleep he would scream and shout out obscenities until, one night, he remembered attacking Siobhan. Sending for Forster, he asked him, as he had done so many times before, what had happened on that night. 'I've been dreaming that I attacked Siobhan, did I kill her Forster? You must tell me?' He grabbed the coachman by the lapels of his jacket, pulling his face to his. Forster could see the madness creeping into his eyes and he was afraid.

'I have told you, you got drunk, fell down and hit your head. As for Miss Siobhan, I drove her home myself. Why would you think that you had attacked the young lady, what reason would you have?' Lord Peter didn't answer him, he couldn't be sure that Forster was telling the truth. He had the feeling he wasn't, but he would find out when he was well enough. He would go and see Siobhan.

The following night Lord Peter had another attack, more violent than before. 'Where is the bitch I will bloody kill her,' he kept shouting.

The doctor was sent for and he was sedated. Forster, worried about the whole episode, asked the doctor what should be done? He was answered with no uncertainty, 'If it gets out what really happened the authorities will have no option but to prosecute. I couldn't care less about him, it's the girl I'm concerned about. The best solution is that he be sent away to a hospital up north. There are new methods that might cure him of these fits of madness.'

'Not an asylum, then?' asked Forster.

'No, definitely not. I promised the late Lady Bromley that I would look after him after she died. The behaviour of her husband and son killed her you know?' He had been very fond of the late Lady Anne - if it hadn't been for her he would have had her son committed long ago.

'He will never agree to go,' said Forster.

'At the moment, the state his mind is in, he won't know where he is or what is happening to him. I will contact his cousin, he will see to the running of the estate while his Lordship is away. If he does not get better his cousin will inherit anyway.'

In one of his lucid moments and after much arguing, Lord Peter agreed. He did not fancy a life in an asylum. 'After all, a hospital does not have bars, I will be able to leave when I choose,' he thought. His parting words to the doctor and Forster were, 'Tell the little Miss, one day I'll be back for her.' With those words, he gave a laugh that sent shivers down their spines.

On the next visit to Miss Hazel, the doctor asked if he could have a word alone. He repeated what Lord Bromley had said. 'Siobhan must be sent away where he cannot find her.'

'The man is mad,' commented Miss Hazel.

'I know that, that is why, for her own safety, she must leave. What about that brother of hers, in London isn't he, can't she go to him?' asked the doctor.

Thoughtfully, Miss Hazel said, 'I suppose she could.'

'Waste no time then. Get her away as soon as possible,' said the doctor as he left.

Listening to the conversation, Siobhan said, 'Miss Hazel, we don't know Michael's address.'

'And London is a big place, so I have heard,' piped up Sally. Hobbling to the tin box where Miss Hazel kept her important papers she got the key and unlocked it. With a trembling hand she handed Siobhan a letter. 'This is addressed to you. I am ashamed to say I kept it from you, thinking you may leave me and go to London. It was wrong of me, but I did not want to lose you.' Siobhan tore open the letter, dated a month ago. It said Michael had found a job in the dockland, also lodgings with a nice woman called Nellie Bell. He had written an address and asked her to write to him. Siobhan made no comment as she handed the letter back to Miss Hazel who returned it back to the tin box. 'I'm sorry, Siobhan, but I thought it was for the best,' said Miss Hazel.

'Well, at least you know where he is living and the sooner you go to him the better,' Sally commented.

The matter was discussed, and, reluctantly, Siobhan agreed to go. The thought of Lord Peter coming after her terrified her. Why! Oh why had this terrible thing happened just when things were settled for her. She loved Miss Hazel so much, she did not want to leave, but she knew she must. The address was never spoken aloud, and Miss Hazel thought it best that Sally did not know it. She did not trust the girl not to tell if Lord Bromley questioned her, especially if he bribed her with money.

When Sally learned Siobhan was going to Michael she thought of following her to confront him with her pregnancy, but reason prevailed. He could say it wasn't his! What would she do in London if he sent her away? At least for the time being, while Miss Hazel was still infirm, she had a comfortable home here and after Siobhan had gone, maybe Miss Hazel would keep her on.

Miss Hazel instructed Sally what to pack in the carpet bag for Siobhan's journey. 'We can't make it too heavy or else the girl won't be able to carry it. Put a couple of serviceable dresses in, a change of underwear and two warm nightdresses. She can travel in the blue velvet dress and matching cloak,' said Miss Hazel. Siobhan protested on hearing she was to wear the dress and cloak Lord Peter had bought her - she didn't want anything associated with him. 'You have no choice, if you are dressed like a Lady you will be treated as one. You can always get rid of them when you find Michael, until then we must put our feelings behind us and do what is best'.

Packed and ready to leave, tearful goodbyes were said. 'Must I go?' pleaded Siobhan, her arm tight around Miss Hazel. Sally butted in, no-way at this stage did she want Siobhan staying and spoiling her plans.

'Of course you have to go, do you want the same thing to happen to you again?'

Pushing Siobhan from her, Miss Hazel said, 'Now you know it's for the best, and maybe, if circumstances change, you can come back again?'

Forster helped her into the carriage, promising Miss Hazel he would look after her. Waving tearfully, Siobhan began her journey to London.

CHAPTER 13
Nellie Bell

The ride in the carriage was uncomfortable enough, but the journey in the coach was worse, sitting for hours in a cramped position, squashed in with the other passengers. When the coach finally stopped half way to London Siobhan could hardly walk. She had to be helped from the coach and into the tavern. The driver, Forster's cousin, had already been told that the girl was not fully recovered from an operation. As a favour to Forster, would he keep an eye on her. In her weakened state, she was carried upstairs to her room. Although she did not feel like eating, she managed a little of the supper that was brought up to her. Without undressing she lay on the bed and fell into a fretful sleep: a nightmare of Lord Peter running after her, trying to catch her.

Next morning she felt much better and the discomfort from the remainder of the journey was bearable. Listening to, but not participating in, the conversation of the other passengers took her mind off her predicament. Although still in pain, her mind was distracted from it by a sense of excitement. She was going to London, a city where the streets were paved with gold. Much to her surprise, she was looking forward to seeing Michael again.

She did not know what to expect, but one thing was certain, the streets were certainly not paved with gold! On the outskirts of the city, two of the passengers alighted, giving her the opportunity to look from the window. She saw beautiful big mansions that took her breath away. Driving further into the city, fashionable dress shops lined the pavements. Other shops had their windows full of things she had only seen in Lord Peter's manor house.

When the coach finally stopped and the remaining passengers got off, Siobhan thought what a wonderful place it was for Michael to live. It somehow didn't seem to fit the docklands address on Michael's letter. The coach driver saw her troubled face and went over to her. 'Where are you heading for, Lady?' he said, as he took the letter from her. He saw the address he shook his head. 'You can't walk there, Lady, it's too far and too dangerous!' He had given his promise to Forster to look after her, so he hailed a hackney carriage. Most of the drivers knew one another and were friendly. A cheerful faced man got down from the driver's seat.

'What you want, mate?' he asked.

'I've been told to look after this young lady, but I can't take her any further. I've got to plan for the return journey. Can you take her to this address?'

The driver read the address and whistled. 'Cost a fair amount, I'd be riskin' life and limb down by them docks!'

'I can pay,' said Siobhan with too much haste. A glint of greed came into the driver's eye, but Forster's cousin grabbed him by his arm.

'Now listen, mate, this is my cousin's ward, she ain't no rich fancy lady for you to take advantage of - treat her fair or you'll have me to answer to.'

'OK, mate,' he said, stressing the word 'mate' and holding out his hand. 'Keep your shirt on! Seeing she is a relative it'll be a couple of bob.

'You still ain't doing her any favour,' said Forster's cousin.

'Take it or leave it. You want to get another cabby to take her?' he said. The price was agreed, for he knew what the driver said was true. Forster hadn't told him the whole story. Why, for example, the child, for that was all she was, was coming to London. Did her relatives know what they were sending her to? The docklands was no place for this child.

The hackney, with its open front, allowed Siobhan to have a clear view of the streets. Gone were the fancy houses and shops. The dark cloud hanging over the city made Siobhan think they were driving into a storm, but getting closer she saw it was smoke from the sea of chimneys stretched out on the horizon. The smell, at first uncomfortable, soon became unbearable. She had to hold her handkerchief over her mouth and nose to stop herself from vomiting. The cobbled streets were so narrow that at times there was hardly enough room for the hackney to pass along. Several times the driver had to lash out at the ragged children who tried to hitch a ride. The dirty, filthy children dressed in rags reminded her of her own siblings and the hovel in which they lived. At least in their hovel they could run out into the fresh air and play in the fields. These children could hardly see the sky because of the evil vapours that blotted out the sun. The third storeys of the taller houses seemed to gravitate towards each other. Cords that passed from attic windows to the ones opposite were strewn with grey clothes and rags hung out to dry. Through half open windows, she could see dreary rooms with three or more pale-faced women sewing. Many of the rooms were below the level of the street - she dreaded to think what they smelled like. She had to sit right back into the seat to avoid the slops that were thrown from upper windows, and worse, the contents of chamber pots.

Siobhan thought there must be some mistake - Michael could not possibly live in a place like this. She was just about to advise the driver of her concerns when a different smell filled the air. Rounding the corner of a long street she reeled at a sight that took her breath away. Hundreds of vessels looked as though they were on land, their masts in line, their slender rigging making a spider's web. 'The River Thames,' the cabby shouted, as he pointed to the inextricable forest of masts and miles of rope. Men looked like ants, as they weaved in and out, loading, unloading - with the clanking of cables, the clattering of cargo, it was a wonder they heard the orders being shouted. Women and children were salvaging what they could from the piles of rotting fruit and vegetables. There were so many different smells, it was hard to distinguish one from another. The carriage followed the river until the docks gave way to rows of bright painted three and four storey houses, plus many taverns. Siobhan marvelled at the different nationalities of men who were drinking outside these places. Most of them were stripped to the waist, their muscled bodies covered in tattoos and sweat. It was the first time she had ever seen a black skinned man, other than in Miss Hazel's books. This one seemed bigger than the rest of the men, she marvelled at his black tight curly hair. As they passed, he caught her eye and grinned, his perfect teeth gleaming white in contrast to his thick pinkish lips. Shy that he had caught her staring, she shrunk back into the seat. What place was this? Men from all nationalities in all types of costumes hurried about. What would Miss Hazel have said if she could have seen this spectacle?

The coach came to a stop outside one of the more presentable houses. 'Here we are, my dear, 110 Dockside. Not a bad looking place,' said the cabby, feeling easier in his mind that this was where the girl had been making for. She paid the fare and took possession of the coloured carpet bag which held her belongings. Not stopping to see her safely up the steep stone steps to the house, the cabby drove away, intent on depleting his two shillings in one of the taverns.

Siobhan stood looking up at the house, hesitating whether to climb the steps and knock the door, or go away and wait until she saw Michael appear. Doubts began to fill her mind. What if he did not want her with him? After all, he did not know she was coming. There had been no time to send him a letter, and, as she was not really his sister, there was no need for him to feel responsible for her. Then his last words to her came into her mind. Had he not said, 'I love you'?

Plucking up courage she dragged herself and her bag up the steps. She reached up and gave the anchor-shaped knocker a good bang, its sound echoing through the hall. The lack of immediate answer ebbed her courage. She turned to walk away, but then with determination she knocked again. This time the sound of hurrying footsteps partly masked a shouting voice. 'O'right! O'right! I'm coming. I ain't deaf!' A heavy key turned in the lock, allowing the door to open a few degrees. Two heavily mascara'd eyes peered around the edge and viewed the diminutive figure before them - a mere girl and not some undesirable docker. The door was fully opened. The vision that met Siobhan's eyes took her breath away. Unable to speak, she stared at the gigantic woman who stood before her. She seemed all bosom and red hair, which was piled high on her head in curls, making her look even taller than her five-foot eleven. Nellie Bell portrayed a theatrical figure, not only in the way she was heavily made up, but in her flamboyant attire. Her emerald green satin dress clung to her amply shaped figure, helped by a whale-bone corset. Even in the day time, she adorned herself with sparkling jewellery. Equally, Nellie Bell was just as amazed to see a young girl on her doorstep. Crossing her fat dimpled arms she bellowed, 'Well?' Frightened and confused Siobhan didn't answer. 'Come on girl, what do you want? I ain't got all day to stand here!' said Nellie, losing her patience.

'Michael,' Siobhan muttered. 'Michael, I'm his sister. Is he in?'

Nellie heaved up her bosom until they almost escaped their cleavage. 'He don't say nothing to me about a sister?' Her eyes narrowed as she looked Siobhan up and down. 'Sure you ain't one of his fancy bits?'

Siobhan did not understand what she meant by 'fancy bits', so she repeated, 'I'm his sister, Siobhan.'

'And come from Ireland I suppose?' said Nellie, noting the remnants of her Irish brogue. A glance down confirmed that her clothes were of good quality. 'Must be some money somewhere?' she thought.

'We came from Ireland together, but I have been staying …' The sentence remained unfinished as Siobhan collapsed to the floor. The journey and the pain she had endured had eventually taken its toll.

'Ginny! Ginny! Come here at once. Give us a hand,' screamed Nellie, struggling to bring Siobhan to a sitting position. A thin, grey haired woman came running down the hall.

'What's going on?' she asked.

'Never mind what's goin' on, help me get her into the parlour.' Between them, they carried Siobhan in and laid her gently down on the sofa. 'Go 'n fetch her bag, Ginny, before it's nicked,' said Nellie, as she wiped the perspiration from Siobhan's brow. 'Get me the smellin' salts, then brew a pot of tea.' Nellie held the camphor under Siobhan's nose. Coughing and spluttering, she came round, tears streaming from her eyes.

Almost immediately, Ginny came in carrying a tray set out with teapot, sugar bowl, milk jug and three cups. No way was Ginny going to be left out of what was going on! The drink was poured and Ginny offered Siobhan a cup of strong sweet tea. She took it and sipped it slowly in silence. Ginny drank her tea and returned the cup to its saucer with a clatter as confirmation that she had finished. 'Well! What's going on then?'

'Oh, for goodness sake, Ginny, let the girl finish her tea,' said Nellie, trying to replace her cup with less theatricals, but equally eager to know about this girl and her relationship with Michael. With Nellie and Ginny staring at her, Siobhan felt obliged to explain, even if it was a going to be a pack of lies. To kick-start the conversation, Nellie repeated, 'So you are Michael's sister, and where have you been hiding, may I ask?'

'Oh! I haven't been hiding, I have been working for Miss Hazel, a lady crippled with arthritis. When Michael left to come to London, I couldn't leave her - she had been so good to me, and she really needed me.'

'And now? What's changed now? Has she gone 'n died?' Ginny blurted out.

'Oh no, another girl, Sally, who really needed a job, is looking after her, so I was free to come here.' Although it wasn't in her nature to tell lies, she would never tell them or Michael the real reason she had left.

'Funny Michael never let me know you were comin',' said Nellie. 'I didn't see a letter arrive!' then turning to Ginny, she said, 'Did you, Ginny?'

'No Ma'am, no letter at all,' answered Ginny, shaking her head. Thoughts raced around Ginny's mind. 'So that's his sister, is it? That'll put the cat amongst the pigeons! No wonder her majesty is being so nice to the girl. Since that Michael arrived everything had changed. Nothing's too good for him, he's got the best room, eats the best food! She's acting like a love sick schoolgirl over him. Well this girl will upset the apple cart and no mistake.'

'What are you mumbling about Ginny,' said Nellie, accustomed to her inability to think in silence.

'Nothing, just thinking,' answered Ginny, her thin arms hugging herself with anticipation of the events that would surely follow.

Siobhan thought quickly. 'What, Michael didn't get my letter? Well I sent it some time ago!' Lies upon lies, she thought.

'If he's not expecting you, he's going to get quite a shock when he finds you here,' said Ginny gleefully, priming herself for some domestic excitement. On hearing these words, Siobhan's fears were increased. Before Nellie could question her further, there was the sound of the back door opening.

'Anybody in?' shouted a voice that Siobhan recognised immediately.

'In here,' shouted Nellie. Siobhan's heart started to pound and she felt as if she was going to faint again. Michael popped his head around the door, ready to pull a funny face or make a witty remark, as was his usual practice. The expression on his face froze as he saw Siobhan sitting there. He blinked his eyes in total disbelief of what he was seeing.

'Surprise, surprise! Your sister's here,' said Ginny somewhat theatrically, unable to await his reaction. Michael stared in disbelief. One word penetrated his mind. Had Ginny really said 'sister'? Holy Mother, thank God she had kept to the lie. He had a good thing going here and wished to keep it that way. He knew Nellie Bell had taken a fancy to him and was very happy with the situation.

He looked Siobhan up and down, taking in every detail. She was even more beautiful than he remembered. She seemed all grown up, a real little lady, and her clothes, they must have cost a pretty penny. He couldn't fail to notice how pale she was, the dark circles under her eyes giving her a haunted look! Something was wrong alright and he was determined to find out what it was. He pulled himself together. 'Siobhan! Holy Mother, what are you doin' here? How on earth did you get here? Is there anything wrong?' He could not get the questions out fast enough.

'Give the girl a chance to answer. Why, you're firing questions at her as if they were bullets?' laughed Nellie, always happy to see Michael.

'It's just that I am surprised, so I am. Why on earth didn't you write? I could have rented a room for you.'

'I did write, but the letter must have got lost,' answered Siobhan, blushing with guilt. Michael knew Siobhan well enough to know she was lying. Why the rush? He knew something was wrong - it was written all over her face. And the fine clothes she was wearing, where did they come from? Things were far from right.

'No need to worry about a room, she can stay here,' said a smiling Nellie, looking at Michael and sensing something was going on. Her years of experience had taught her that it wasn't what people said, but the way they looked when they said it. 'That reminds me, Ginny, I thought I told you to air the bed in the small room for Siobhan. Go on now!' Waving her hand impatiently, Ginny knew Nellie hadn't given her the order, but she knew her mistress had an ulterior motive.

'Cup of tea, Michael?' said Nellie.

'What's that?' answered Michael, not listening.

'Tea, a cup of tea?' said Nellie. Not waiting for an answer she poured one for him and another for Siobhan. Deep in thought they all sat in silence, drinking the tea they didn't want. It was quite obvious that nothing was going to be said whilst Nellie was in the room, so, making her excuse that she was going to help Ginny, she left. Nellie knew better than to stand outside the door listening. The old days had taught her a lot. Every room in the house had a peep hole where she could spy and listen to what was going on in an adjacent room - you couldn't be too careful when you took in lodgers. She hurried to the room above, rolled back the carpet and peered through a small hole in the floorboards. She could choose to see or hear, but not both. On this occasion listening would have to suffice.

Michael was the first to speak. 'Well, me darling, let's be having the truth. What's gone on? And where did you get those fine clothes?'

'The truth?' stuttered Siobhan.

'Yes, b' Jesus, the truth. I know you well enough to know when things aren't right. What made you come here and who in hell is looking after Miss Hazel?' Siobhan shut her eyes, unable to look at him. The blood drained from her face as she wondered how on earth could she tell him what had happened? She started to shake her head in despair. Michael, shocked that she had arrived with no explanation, started to get angry. 'Well, come on. Let's be having it?' he said, grabbing her by the shoulders and shaking them. Siobhan cried out in pain at his touch. Surprised at the cry, Michael shrunk back. 'Mother of God, Siobhan, what's the matter? I didn't mean to hurt you.' He had hardly touched her, but it had obviously caused her great pain. Tears started to fall down Siobhan's cheeks. 'I'm sorry, me darlin', I didn't mean to hurt you,' he repeated. 'I wouldn't hurt you for the world,' he said, wiping away her tears.

'It was not your fault.' All these lies and pretence was too much for her to bear. She blurted out the name of Lord Bromley!

'Lord Bromley! Lord Bromley! What on earth are you talking about? What the hell has Lord Bromley got to do with anything?' asked Michael as Siobhan sobbed hysterically.

Nellie didn't know what to do - it was clear the girl was in some sort of trouble. She wanted to wait and hear more, but with the sound of Ginny's footsteps rushing downstairs to see what all the crying was about, she decided it would be better if she, too, went down. Nellie followed Ginny into the parlour. Ginny rushed and put her arms around the distraught Siobhan. 'What on earth is the matter, girl? He hasn't been upsetting you, has he?' she said, giving Michael an accusing look.

'Mother of Jesus! I haven't touched her,' Michael snapped in self-defence.

'Come on now, girl, it's all been too much for you,' said Ginny, putting her arm around Siobhan's shoulders, unintentionally causing her to wince once more. 'You come and have a nice lie down,' she said, leading Siobhan out of the room. Nellie and Michael stood in silence, watching. Every step Siobhan took on the stairs caused her pain, but she managed to get to the bedroom without collapsing. Ginny shouted to Michael to bring up Siobhan's bag. At the bedroom door Ginny grabbed the bag and pushed him back into the corridor, saying, 'Off with you, this is women's work.'

Walking downstairs, Michael couldn't imagine what it was all about. Lord Bromley? Sally had hinted she had been very friendly with him at one time, but he thought she had only said that to impress him. He went into the kitchen where Nellie sat pouring a tumbler of brandy. She handed it to him, then poured one for herself. 'What a carry on, hey, Michael! Here, drink it up and I'll pour you another - you look as if you could do with one!' He took it gratefully, downing it in one gulp. Nellie observed him with slanting eyes. 'You never mentioned your sister before, Michael.'

'What?'

'I said, you've never mentioned your sister before,' repeated Nellie in a tone that required a response.

Michael, pulling himself together, said dismissively, 'Didn't I? I don't know why I didn't. Yes, she's me sister alright. Our Mammy and Pappy are dead, we've no brothers or sisters, so it was my duty to look after her. We came over to England to make our fortunes.' He tried to make the story sound convincing, although his mind was in turmoil.

Nellie sat in silence for a while sipping her brandy. 'What do you make of it then?' She was about ask about Lord Bromley, but remembered in time that she wasn't supposed to know his name.

'What do I make of it, Nellie? Holy Mother, I've no idea,' he said, shaking his head. 'And that's the truth of it.'

'When Ginny comes down, maybe she'll be able to tell us more,' said Nellie, staring at the rich brown liquid in her glass.

CHAPTER 14
Ginny

Ginny led Siobhan across the bedroom and sat her on the white wicker chair. 'Sit there my dear, while I remove the warming pan from the bed,' she said. Siobhan did as she was told, too exhausted to think for herself. Ginny looked at Siobhan and was filled with pity for her. She looked very fragile. 'Now girl, stop your crying, nothing is so bad it can't be put right.' Going over to her she gently eased her out of the chair. 'Let's get you undressed and into bed.' Ginny picked up Siobhan's bag. 'Now, let's see if you have a nightdress in here.' She noticed with surprise that none of her clothes were of the same quality as the blue velvet gown and cloak she was wearing. The limited contents were made of cotton and serge material. Ginny took out a cream flannelette nightdress, holding it up to shake out the creases. Trying to make light of the situation, she commented on the embroidery that decorated the garment's collar and cuffs. 'You do this girl?' Siobhan nodded. 'It's very pretty, you have a fine hand,' said Ginny, easing off Siobhan's cloak.

She went to undo the dress, but Siobhan suddenly cried out, 'No, it's alright, I can undress myself.' She couldn't let this woman see her bruised body.

Ginny saw she was agitated. 'Alright dear, no need to get upset. You get undressed and get into bed while I fetch you a glass of warm milk.'

In the kitchen Nellie and Michael looked at her questioningly. 'Well!' said Nellie 'What have you learned?'

'Only that the girl wouldn't let me undress her,' said Ginny. 'Nearly went hysterical when I tried to help. I managed to remove her cloak, but

I could see it caused her pain.' She sighed as she poured milk into the saucepan. 'That girl's been badly beaten if you ask me.'

'Holy Mother! Siobhan beaten?' said Michael with indignation. 'Who would have done such a thing? Why, she is so small and gentle, she wouldn't give anyone cause to beat her.'

Nellie puffed out her chest, straining not to reveal the only name she knew. 'Can't you think of anyone that would harm her?' Once again, she bit back the name of Lord Bromley. 'And another thing, she ain't so little. In case you haven't noticed, she's almost a woman. That dress and cloak she was wearing must have cost a fortune. Have you asked yourself where that money came from?'

Ginny chipped in, 'Well the rest of her clothes don't match the quality of the blue velvet, very home-made they are. I'll take her up this cup of milk.' She hesitated, turning towards Michael, 'unless you want to do it.'

'Yes, I'll take it up,' he said, reaching for the cup.

Nellie poured out a glass of brandy. 'Take her this as well, it will help her sleep.'

Michael knocked on the bedroom door. 'I've brought you up a cup of hot milk.'

'Come in, Michael,' said Siobhan, pulling the sheet up under her chin. She had managed to undress herself despite the level of pain.

Handing her the glass of brandy, he said, 'Here, me darlin', get this down you with the warm milk, it will help you to sleep.' She was well aware the brandy would make her sleep. If she hadn't had a drink at the ball she probably wouldn't be in the situation she was in now!

'No thank you Michael,' she said, pushing the glass away, 'but I will have the milk.' As she reached for the cup the sheet fell away, revealing her neck and chest. She quickly went to retrieve the sheet, but it was too late - Michael had seen the damage Lord Bromley had caused.

'What are those marks on your throat, Siobhan?' asked Michael going closer for a better look. Siobhan grabbed the sheet, but Michael had already seen enough.

'Why! Those are love bites!' he uttered in disbelief - he should know, he had given enough of them in his time. Anger welled up in his stomach, making his chest feel that it was about to explode. The blood rushed to his head as he shouted, 'Holy Mother of Jesus! What the hell's been goin' on?'

The shouting reached Nellie and Ginny in the kitchen. Ginny was about to run upstairs, but Nellie grabbed hold of her. 'Let them get on with it, it's their business, not ours.'

Ginny reluctantly slumped back in her chair, audibly muttering, 'Ar! And you'll make it yours when the time suits you.' Both women sat in silence, straining their ears trying to hear what was being said.

Siobhan sobbing, pleaded, 'Don't shout, Michael, please don't shout. It wasn't my fault.' Her body was quaking with fear. Michael shook his head in disbelief. He wiped the beads of perspiration from his brow, then covered his eyes with his hands, trying to blot out what he had just seen. Her sobs brought him back to reality. As he looked at her tear-stained face pity overtook the anger he was feeling. Calmer now, sat down beside her, stroking her hair.

'I'm sorry, dearest, for upsetting you,' he began, 'but I've got to know what has happened? After all, I'm the one who brought you to England and I swore to look after you. Me darlin', come now, tell me what happened? I'll find out sooner or later, even if it means me travelling back to Little Chester.' Siobhan's tear-filled eyes looked into his and she could see he meant what he said. The last thing she wanted was for him to go back to Little Chester - Lord Bromley would surely find out where she was and come looking for her.

Wiping her eyes, she slowly began to tell him about the first encounter she had had with Lord Bromley, the way he had almost ridden her down, knocking her into the ditch, the meeting with Sally and her warning. 'If only I had listened to her,' she said.

Michael did not interrupt the telling of her story, although it was all he could do to keep himself from screaming out. She omitted some of the sordid details, there was no need. From the moment she told him Lord Bromley had attacked her he could imagine what had happened, but never in his wildest imagination would he have guessed the full extent of the assault. When she had finished, Michael was stunned into silence. Thoughts raced around his mind - scenes of his beautiful, innocent Siobhan being raped by that animal was too much for him to bear. He let out a cry that echoed through the house.

The sound that reached Nellie and Ginny was so full of pain that it made their hair stand on end. 'My God, what was that?' Nellie said as she made for the stairs with Ginny in close pursuit. They went into the bedroom to find Michael pacing up and down, tearing at his hair.

'I'll kill the swine!' Michael was yelling over and over.

'Kill who?' asked Ginny.

'That dirty swine, Lord fucking Bromley. That's who.'

'But why?' asked Ginny innocently.

'Why? You ask why? I'll show you why!' In his deranged state, he tore at Siobhan's nightdress, exposing her naked, battered and bruised body.

Unspeaking, the women stood paralysed with horror. Crusted-over claw and bite marks covered most of her body. The bruises were coming out on her breasts, colouring them blue and purple, still raw from Bromley's teeth marks.

Ginny was the first one to break the awkward silence. 'My God, girl, no wonder you didn't want me to undress you!'

Nellie Bell hadn't seen anything as bad as this, even in the old days when one of her prostitutes had been with a rough customer. 'God knows what her lower half was like,' she thought. Coming to her senses, the Nellie of old took charge. 'Cover her up, for God's sake. We don't want her catching pneumonia on top of everything else!' Turning to a stunned Michael, she pushed him towards the door. 'You stop that blartin'. What's done is done and there's no changing it! Go and fetch Doctor Round from 11 Chorley Street, and hurry.'

'No doctor! No doctor!' screamed Siobhan.

'My girl, you are having a doctor whether you like it or not,' said Nellie. 'If an infection sets in you'll be a gonna and no mistake. If you die in this house questions will be asked and the Peelers will be here.'

'What if the doctor won't come on a Saturday?' asked Michael, coming back into the room.

'He'll come alright. Just say Nellie Bell wants him, he'll come running,' said Nellie with conviction.

She was right. Leaving his meal on hearing the name Nellie Bell, Doctor Round did as he was bid. Nellie knew far too much about him from the old days, things he would like to forget now he was a respected doctor in the community.

While the doctor examined Siobhan, in the kitchen Michael went over in his mind what Siobhan had told him. She had given him a brief outline, but what had she left out? A hell of a lot, going by the state of her body. Holy Mother of Jesus! What was Miss Hazel thinking of, letting Siobhan go to the ball at the manor? So many questions went unanswered in his mind. The whole thing was a nightmare. His Siobhan, pure and innocent, was now defiled. He had rescued her from the abuse of her father, only to be raped by that bastard. He would make him pay. Holy Mother, he would make him pay, then he would kill him. This thought gave him some comfort.

The doctor managed to examine Siobhan, despite her protests, aided by the sedative effects of laudanum. He was a kind man, and was as gentle as possible so as not to cause her more pain than necessary. Ginny supplied the requested hot water and towels, whilst Nellie looked on, not believing what she was witnessing. The poor child had almost been torn apart.

Doctor Round finished his examination. 'She's already been seen by a doctor and he's done a good job, nice and clean. She is healing nicely. I'll leave you some ointment - see it's applied on her wounds once a day. With what that child has gone through, it's a wonder she is alive! I wish I'd got the brute here!' Nellie saw the doctor to the door. On the top step he suddenly turned to her, saying, 'I won't ask you what happened, I know better than to pry - I learnt my lessons in the past. I'll just ask you one thing, did you have anything to do with this? Not procuring again are you, Nellie?' It was no use feigning indignation, Nellie knew he was remembering the old days, when neither of them were too particular where the pennies had come from.

'On my oath, Ted Round. I gave up that way of life years ago.' Then looking him straight in the eyes she added as a bit of devilment, 'It's about the time you did, too.' His eyes dropped from her gaze - he knew she was telling him the truth. She shut the door behind him and, her hand still on the knob, stood reminiscing about the old days - not the bad times, but the happy ones. She could have married Ted Round - he had asked her enough times. At sixty he was still an attractive man, but, regretfully, now married. Her thoughts were broken by Michael's appearance from the kitchen.

'How is she?' he asked.

'She will be fine, Michael,' said Nellie, putting her arm through his as they walked back to the kitchen. Michael would have gone up to see Siobhan, but Nellie told him that the doctor had given her a sleeping draught and she was best left to get some rest.

'The bloody bastard, I'll do for him, I'll make him suffer as he's made Siobhan suffer,' he said, banging his fist on the table.

'Sit down, Michael, I want to have a talk to you,' said Nellie in a serious voice. 'The best thing you can do is to treat her as if she has got an illness. Don't ever mention what has happened. I know it's going to be hard for you to hide your feelings, but believe me, it's best for Siobhan. She can stay here and I'll see she is looked after, but Michael, this isn't a charitable institution. Her keep will have to be paid for, and the doctor's bills. I don't think that's being too hard on you, is it?' Besides, it will give Michael a reason to go to work, she thought.

'Holy Mary, Nellie! You have been more than kind takin' Siobhan in. Of course I'll pay for her keep. And I'm sorry we have brought all this trouble to you.' His thoughts returned to Siobhan. He started to cry again, but this time all the anger he had felt had been replaced by pity.

Nellie cradled his head to her bosom. 'Now, now, Nellie will take care of everything,' she said as she kissed the thick black curls on top of his head. She had been tempted to kiss his lips, but thought better of it - that time would come in the future.

Siobhan awoke from a deep sleep, imagining for a moment she was in her own bed at Miss Hazels. The realisation of where she was cascaded the terrible nightmare onto her. She blushed, remembering the doctor examining her private places. Private places? She had no private places now. Michael, Nellie and Ginny had all seen her battered body. Her attempt to get out of bed coincided with Ginny's entrance into the room. 'Now, now, my girl, stay where you are. You're looking better, that sleep has done you good. I'll go to the kitchen and get you something to eat,' she said, returning to the door.

'Wait Ginny, I must use the potty!'

'Of course my dear, I never gave it a thought. Come on, I'll help you onto the commode.' Modesty gone, Siobhan let her help. It was all she could do to contain her cries as the warm urine scalded her wounds. Glancing at the sunlight shining through the slit in the curtains, she asked the time. 'Three thirty,' answered Ginny.

'The house is so quiet. Where is Michael?' she asked.

'At work, my love. Michael's at the docks 'til 5 o'clock as usual, and Nellie's collecting her rents. She owns lots of properties you know!' Reflected pride sounded in her voice - she was very proud of what her mistress had achieved.

'They work Sundays?' Siobhan asked.

'Sunday, it ain't Sunday girl, it's Monday. You've slept a whole day away,' laughed Ginny. 'I bet you're hungry? I'll nip down to the kitchen and get you something to eat. Now what do you fancy?'

'I do feel hungry,' said Siobhan, 'but don't go to too much trouble, tea and toast will do, I don't want you running after me Ginny, I have caused you enough disruption.'

'You'll do no such thing. The doctor said you're to stay in bed restin' 'til the next time he calls, and that, my girl, is what you will do!' said

Ginny with authority. In no time at all she appeared with a tray laden with scrambled egg on toast, a glass of fruit juice and a pot of tea. Two cups on the tray ensured Ginny would have an unarguable reason to stay in the room. 'I'm sitting here until you've eaten every mouthful,' she said.

Ginny sat there watching Siobhan. This girl could have been her own daughter, had things been different.

The eggs and toast tasted good. Siobhan was more hungry than she thought, and managed to finish off the last mouthful before her eyes began to close. Shaking her head trying to arouse herself, she said, 'I've had enough sleep, I can't be tired, but I can't keep my eyes open, Ginny.'

'It's the sleeping draught the doctor gave you. The more relaxed you are the quicker you will heal. Don't try to fight it, just close your eyes and I'll be up later,' said Ginny as she removed the tray and went down to the kitchen.

Monday was washing day, come rain or shine. Nellie kept to a strict routine in running the boarding house. 'It's the only way to keep on top of things,' she said on a regular basis. In the last few years the boarders had been few - only those Nellie had taken a fancy to were allowed to stay. 'It's not like the old days when I needed the money,' she had explained to Ginny. Nevertheless the household routine had remained: Monday washing, Tuesday ironing, Wednesday shopping, Thursday baking, Friday cleaning. Saturday and Sunday were the days when they took things easy.

This Monday, Ginny was breaking the routine. It was a sunny day, the washing had dried, so today she would iron. No matter how long the whites were boiled they never lost their grey appearance due to the polluted air from the docks - the constant smell of burning oil and rotting cargo rarely left the air. With the inhabitants' lifelong exposure they were never conscious of the smell, and were oblivious to the topping up it got with each new crate that became damaged, spilling its contents onto the quay. No-one bothered to clear it away. Beggars, children and those on hard times scavenged amongst the mess, grabbing at anything that may be of use. Sometimes a kind docker would deliberately damage a crate, especially one containing vegetables, to help feed the starving families.

Lifting the flat iron from the black lead grate, Ginny spat on the base to test its temperature. 'Well, the house routine is broken for this week, and it will be for many weeks to come if I'm any judge of it!' she thought as she gently ironed away. In the quietness, her mind began to wander back to the time when she had first met Nellie Bell, all those years ago.

She had been a girl of thirteen when, tired of her father's drunken beatings and abuse, she had run away from home. Begging and stealing, she kept herself alive, sleeping at night in whatever shelter she could find. On one occasion she was caught trying to lift the purse from a gentleman's pocket. He had grabbed her by the arm and was about to call the Peelers when she begged for mercy. 'I'm sorry Sir, truly I am, don't send for the Bobbies!'

He looked her up and down. 'She is a pretty little thing, and young,' he thought to himself. 'Her breasts are just starting to form. I bet she is a virgin!' Still holding her wrist in a tight grip he said in an authoritative voice, 'Are you truly sorry?'

'Yes Sir, Oh yes Sir,' she said, tears of fright running down her dirty cheeks.

'Then come with me,' he said, pulling her along the street.

'You ain't turning me in?' she appealed, hanging back.

'No, I am not turning you in, but I want to see how sorry you really are?' he answered. They passed along a few streets and entered a lodging house. Flinging his captive inside, he barked an order to the old woman who came out to greet him. 'Wash the girl and put her in something clean, then bring her up to my room. You know my needs.' Ginny did not know what to make of it all. She tried to escape, but a burly man blocked the front door. What were they going to do to her? She was soon to find out.

She was dragged screaming into the man's room. The door slammed shut and was locked from the outside, preventing any escape. He threw her on the bed and raped her, all the time repeating, 'Tell me again how sorry you are.' After a while she stopped struggling, after all it was of no use as he was much stronger than her. How long he violated her she didn't know. After the first burning pain it was all a haze. Eventually he rolled off her exhausted. 'Now you can consider yourself punished!' he gasped. As a final gesture he threw a half sovereign at her, saying, 'You won't do it again, will you?' He burst out in hysterical laughter.

She banged on the still locked door until the old woman let her out. 'Waren't so bad, was it?' she said with a toothless grin. 'Think yourself lucky he's a gentleman and always pays for his pleasures. Better than beggin'. Hey! Why don't you come and work for me, you ain't a bad looker and you'm young. They likes um young, the gentry,' she said, handing back her ragged clothes. She put on her dress and ran from the house as fast as she could. She felt sore inside, but as the woman had said, it wasn't too bad and she did have the half sovereign. The money soon spent, she began

126

to reflect on what the old woman had said. On one particular rainy night, feeling cold and hungry, she went back to the house where the man had taken her. So began her life as a prostitute.

She had been given a few rough clients, but the burly man soon dealt with them. She made enough money for food, decent clothes and a warm place to sleep, much preferable to winter months on the streets. Her periods had never been regular, so when she missed a few months she didn't really notice. It wasn't until she started to feel sick and put on weight that it dawned on her she must be pregnant. It didn't unduly worry her as many of her fellow prostitutes had got pregnant. An old woman known as Granny Price got rid of the unwanted pregnancies and the girls were soon back at work. Ginny shuddered as she remembered the filthy room. She had attempted to get off the blood stained table, but Granny Price had already put a chloroformed cloth over her face to dull the pain. Pain, Oh, the pain, she grimaced. Now thinking of it, she heard Granny's voice saying, 'You've gone further than I thought, nearly five months. Wouldn't have started it if I'd known, but it's too late to stop now.' She had heard someone screaming and realised it was herself. After what had seemed an eternity of coming round, Granny's voice started to register. 'It's all over now, the little blighter's out, she had put up a right fight, had a devil of a job to prise her from you.' The meaning of her words didn't register until some time later. A little girl, she would have had a baby girl.

Tears rolled down Ginny's face as she recalled the horror. She hadn't thought about it in years, but young Siobhan had triggered her worst memories. She tried making herself a cup of tea to take her mind off the past, but memories kept creeping back.

Weak from the loss of blood and hardly able to walk, Granny Price had showed no mercy as she turned her out into the street. 'You'll be as right as rain in a week's time' Granny assured her. 'I've packed your insides to stop the bleeding.' She had wanted her away as soon as possible - the girl might die. It weren't her fault, the stupid cow should have come to her sooner. Stumbling along the cobbled stone streets, she held onto the house walls to steady herself. She had no idea where she was going, the rain was beating down, soaking her to her skin. Too weak to proceed she lost consciousness and slid down the wall and onto the floor. Blood running down her legs mixed with the rain, causing a scarlet stream in the gutter.

Nellie was seeing one of her clients off her premises and noticed the trail of blood. Out of curiosity she followed the gutter upstream to the figure slumped on the ground. Her instinctive reaction was to assume the woman had been knifed. Gently easing the body over she exclaimed, 'Why, it's a young girl!'

Ginny's eyes fluttered open, staring straight into Nellie's. 'Help me!' she uttered. Normally Nellie would not have got involved - it paid in these parts to mind your own business, but hearing that plea for help, her heart melted. Ginny was carried back to Nellie's brothel, attended by Doctor Ted Roberts. He didn't give much hope for her survival, but he did what he could for her. By a miracle, after a month she had improved, but it was not a full recovery. The doctor had told her that her womb had been damaged and that she would never be able to have children. He hadn't told her what he had told Nellie, that her insides had been butchered.

From the day Nellie took her in she had been her devoted slave. Not that Nellie had asked anything from her, but had remarked in her blunt manner, 'You ain't pretty enough or got the figure to work in my brothel, but, if you want, you can be the general dog's body. Can't pay much, but you will have a roof over your head and food in your belly.'

Finishing her tea she stood up and started ironing. 'Ar, that must have been thirty years ago,' she mumbled to herself. She had seen Nellie through the good times and the bad times. Ginny laughed to herself, remembering the scrapes she had helped Nellie get out of. And here she was again, helping with this Michael and his sister's troubles. She knew Nellie had fallen for the lad - there were times when Nellie let her heart rule her head and there were always tears to follow.

The ironing finally finished, Ginny took it upstairs to the linen cupboard. Passing Siobhan's room she opened the door quietly and went in. Looking at her lying there she thought how beautiful she was. Her black curly hair covered the pillow, tears still wetting her thick eyelashes and her rosebud mouth still quivering with emotion. She's a beauty and no mistake, no wonder that Lord Bromley lusted after her. I shouldn't wonder if he don't come looking for her. What would happen if he found her? That brother of hers, for all his brave talk, couldn't be relied on. Far too weak. Another thing, there's something queer there. He don't act like her brother. Maybe she was wrong, but her gut feelings rarely let her down. Still muttering to herself, she continued as if talking to an invisible person. She'd help as much as she could, but Nellie Bell's word was law and this girl wouldn't fit in with her plans for Michael. Her mistress lusted after the lad and, knowing Nellie, by hook and crook, she would have him.

A banging on the front door broke the silence. Siobhan awoke with a start. 'It's alright child, it's only Nellie,' said Ginny, leaving the room to attend to her mistress.

'Ginny! Ginny! Where the bloody hell are you?' bellowed Nellie, heading for the kitchen.

'Keep your hair on. I'm here, and it's a cup of tea you'll be wanting, no doubt?' said Ginny, putting the cast-iron kettle on the black lead range.

'You've guess it Ginny, but while it's brewing I'll have a large brandy,' she said, sitting on a chair and kicking off her shoes. Rubbing her feet she continued, 'You'd swear I was robbing them the way they reluctantly hand the rent over. My feet are killing me, Ginny, I'm getting too old for this rent collecting!'

'I've told you before, I'll do it for you,' Ginny answered, pouring out the drink.

'You! You collect the rents? You're too soft hearted. Any sob story and you'd end up giving them money.'

'Hire a collector, then,' Ginny said as she brewed the tea.

'Couldn't trust them. No, it looks as if I'll be collecting 'til the day I drop,' she added, finishing off her brandy.

'You could sell the properties,' said Ginny, testing her.

'I'll have to if it really gets too much for me. That's unless I get a young husband to help.' She gave Ginny a crafty look. Ginny didn't comment or audibly mumble, this time she kept her thoughts to herself. So that's her plan, is it. I wonder if Michael will have a say in the matter.

Next morning Michael reluctantly went to work. He had wanted to stay at Nellie's to look after Siobhan, but as Nellie had pointed out, what good would he be hanging around the house, and he could loose his job if he took time off. He needed that job more than ever now that Siobhan was here - he couldn't expect Nellie to pay for the doctor's bills. Anger welled up inside him again as he thought of what Lord Bromley had inflicted on his darling, innocent Siobhan. He had let her down. Hadn't he always promised to take care of her? He would regret to his dying day that he hadn't insisted she came with him to London. By all the saints, he would have his revenge on his Lordship.

As he got to the Quay, it never ceased to amaze him how insignificant the men were against the big cargo vessels. The whole place was a hive of activity and noise. 'Come on, Rafferty! Get to it, unless you want to be laid off. Plenty more to fill your place,' shouted a big burly foreman. Michael hurried to get in line with the other men that were unloading. He was kept busy all day and didn't get any time to dwell on Siobhan's predicament.

CHAPTER 15
Seduction

Michael took the long way home from his hard day's work. He wanted time to think - he couldn't believe it had only been a few days since Siobhan had arrived and turned his world upside down. Usually on a Saturday night he'd be down at the local tavern, 'The Pipers', drinking with the other dockers where they would be spending most of their hard earned wages. Docker's wives were lucky if their man came home first to clean up - at least then they would get a chance to wheedle some money out of him for the housekeeping.

Dockers hailed from every nationality, they were rough and tough, but most had a heart of gold. Saturday was the only night they let off steam, usually ending up in a free-for-all fight, but with no ill feeling the next day. Michael spent very little, saving every penny so he could go back to Little Chester a rich man. One docker had called him 'tight-fisted'. After a fight that lasted over an hour, they both collapsed in blood and sweat with no-one the clear winner. This was the first and last challenge Michael faced. After that he had been treated with respect and was now fully accepted as one of them.

When he had first arrived in London he was in high spirits, expecting the pavements to be paved with gold, as his friend Patrick had said. He soon realised the pavements were filthy dirty, the gutters running with household slops. After a while he had got used to the stagnant smell that hung over the city, a far contrast to the sweet air of the Irish countryside.

After being turned away from several jobs, he was about to give up hope when he met Nellie Bell. He had found temporary lodgings in one of the back street boarding houses where the caretaker had agreed a few days temporary rent for a room until he met the owner for her approval. 'Mrs. Bell likes to vet every client, she's had trouble in the past and she don't want any more,' said the caretaker, taking a chance with Michael, who seemed a decent enough chap. He would be damned by Nellie if a tenant was undesirable, but she would go mad if she knew he'd turned down business. From the moment Nellie Bell set eyes on Michael she had taken a shine to him. Young, virile and handsome, he reminded her of one of her old lovers.

It felt as though she was buying a horse, the way she had looked him over, walking around him muttering, 'fine shoulders, good strong legs, he'll do very nicely.' At last the inspection was over. 'Well, Michael, you can have one of my rooms, but not here,' she said. 'I need someone to protect me at night. A rich woman like myself is in constant danger from burglars. You can have a room there if you want.' Nellie puffed up her chest and narrowed her eyes, a trait he would come to realise meant, 'Defy me if you dare!' He initially declined the offer, explaining he was happy with the room he was in (recalling the trouble with Sally living in, and he didn't want a repeat with this woman). The caretaker cringed as he listened to Michael - no-one defied Nellie Bell. If she wanted something she got it, moving heaven and hell until she did. Uncharacteristically, Nellie had suddenly gone all coy saying, 'Would you have an old woman go unprotected?' There would be little rent to pay, and all his food would be found. She knew a foreman at the docks who would find him a permanent daytime job. Hearing that, he would be a fool not to take up Nellie's offer. He moved into Nellie's house and she was as good as her word - the foreman at 'Prestons' owed her a favour and found him a job. It soon became apparent that there were lots of people who owed favours to Nellie.

He knew the day of reckoning would come when he would have to re-pay his favour. She wanted his body, but he had kept her at bay until now with the odd embrace. She had often remarked that there was more to life than a kiss and cuddle. She was free and he wasn't married - or was he?

If Siobhan hadn't turned up when she had, he would have succumbed. There were plenty of prostitutes hanging around the docks and 'The Pipers', but he had never paid for sex in his life, and he had no intention now. He didn't fancy Nellie, but he had his needs. As he passed a woman selling flowers his thoughts turned to Nellie. She had come up trumps again - what would have happened to Siobhan if Nellie had turned her away? Impulsively he bought three bunches of flowers, saying to himself with an air of optimism, 'Holy Mother of Jesus! I've a feeling everything is going to be alright.' He ran the rest of the way to Nellie's home. Nellie was overcome with emotion when Michael gave her the flowers, her eyes becoming moist. 'Thank you, dear, but you shouldn't have spent your money on an old woman like me.' She looked at him coyly waiting for him to contradict her - she wasn't disappointed.

'Jesus, you old? Never. Why, you're in your prime. Many a young girl wished they looked like you!' Michael said, laughing.

Siobhan came down for supper. The tension seemed to have lifted, with Michael telling them amusing stories - some true, some that he had made up. With tears running down her cheeks, Ginny said, 'That's never the truth?'

'I swear it is, by the Holy Mother,' said Michael, his eyes looking up to heaven.

'Why, Michael Rafferty, you blasphemer!' said Nellie, playfully clouting him.

Ginny noticed Siobhan yawning. Still very weak she suddenly felt tired. 'Come, girl, off to bed with you, we don't want you overdoing it,' said Ginny, helping her up.

'You go to bed as well Ginny, leave the washing up 'til in the morning, it's been a long day for all of us,' said Nellie, wanting to be alone with Michael. 'Come on Michael, you and me will finish off this bottle of brandy in the front parlour. And bring a shovel full of fire to put in the grate, it's gone quite chilly.'

They sat comfortably in the warmth of the fire, and in the glow of the oil lamp. Maybe it was the atmosphere or the brandy that made Michael look at Nellie, but in the soft light she looked beautiful. 'You know Nellie, you're a fine looking woman and no mistake,' said Michael twiddling her ringlets with his fingers. 'You've got pretty hair, I bet it's passed your waist?' Saying that he took out the combs that were holding it, letting the thick hair cascade over Nellie's shoulders like a red cloak, the colour having been enhanced by a henna rinse. She looked at him coyly, the years disappearing from her face as she recalled the young girl she had once been. Michael kissed her passionately on the lips, then her neck. Gently he entered her and came almost immediately. He attempted to withdraw, but Nellie held him fast. With all her expertise she coaxed his body until, at last, they noisily climaxed together.

The sound woke Ginny. 'She's got him at last. No good will come of it!' she muttered, then went back to sleep.

Michael lay back and immediately fell asleep. Nellie looked down at him, thinking how wonderful it had been to feel young again. She thought she would never experience this feeling again, but also knew he would regret the whole episode in the morning and pretend it had never happened. Nellie looked on, philosophising over her life with all its ups and downs. It hadn't been a bad one, she had had more than most. If this thing with Michael only lasted a few weeks it would be a bonus - if not, she must look on this as her swan song and, My God, what a duet they had sung! Gently kissing him on the forehead she covered him with a shawl and went to bed.

Next morning they were all late arising, the breakfast being prepared nearer to dinnertime. 'It looks as if Sunday Dinner will be served tonight,' Ginny said, clearing away the breakfast things.

'It's alright by me, I was planning to go for a drink at The Pipers,' said Michael. Then remembering Siobhan he stopped, looking guilty. Nellie had been right, Michael was pretending nothing had happened last night.

'Don't worry about Siobhan,' said Nellie. 'I'm taking her to Old Isaacs, the pawnbroker, to sell that blue velvet cloak and dress.'

'Right' said Michael, he didn't say anymore, but thought 'that's one thing less to remind her of the past'.

CHAPTER 16
Old Isaac

Every day Siobhan got a little stronger. Feeling guilty about imposing on Nellie, she asked Ginny if there was any sewing she could do. 'Ah, lass, there's plenty of mending to be done, especially on Nellie's clothes,' answered Ginny with a laugh. 'She insists she isn't putting on weight, but the splits in her clothes says summat else! I sometimes let the seams out before they split, just to avoid embarrassment.' Examining her needlework, Ginny marvelled at how neat the repairs were. 'You're a good little seamstress and no mistake!'

'Miss Hazel taught me,' said Siobhan with pride. 'I made the dress I'm wearing, and my nightdresses and underwear.'

'Not the blue velvet though?' said Nellie entering the room.

Siobhan lowered her eyes and answered quietly. 'No, not the blue velvet.' The mere thought of it made her feel sick. She never wanted to see it again. 'Mrs. Bell, do you know where I could sell it? It's far too fancy for me to wear,' said Siobhan, not looking up.

'I do know someone who will buy it from you,' said Nellie with a glint in her eyes. 'Old Isaac, the Pawnbroker, in Rifle Square. You won't get much for it, but anything is better than nothing. I'll take it round for you, if you like.' Nellie had had dealings with Old Isaac over the years, and he had always been fair. The blue velvet was good quality and should fetch a good price. Ginny looked at Nellie and screwed up her eyes. She knew what she was up to - she would take a nice cut out of the deal. Many a prostitute who had fallen on hard times had given her things to sell, and Nellie had never failed to make a good profit. Nellie was a business woman first and last. 'There's no sentiment in business,' she had been heard to say on more than one occasion, but to Ginny this time was different.

She felt sorry for the girl and piped up, 'Why don't you take it yourself, Siobhan? I'll go with you.'

Had Ginny gone soft in the head? She knew the arrangement Nellie had with Old Isaac. 'You can't be spared,' Nellie said. 'You've enough to do here. If Siobhan wants to go herself then I'll go with her. With me, she will get a better deal!' Then under her breath, and staring at Ginny, she added 'Satisfied!' Siobhan, oblivious to the tension between the two women, and to the sarcastic remark, answered that she would like to go with Mrs. Bell as she had been cooped up in the house long enough. Thus it was agreed - the following day they would go to Old Isaac. Siobhan knew she was doing the right thing in selling the blue velvet outfit. Every time she looked at it, it reminded her of that terrible monster, Lord Bromley. When he had bought her the outfit he had been charming - she could not believe his transformation. What had made him change? Perhaps he really was mad, as Sally had said.

In spite of these awful memories, she could not help but feel a sense of excitement at the prospect of going to Isaac's with Nellie. She had not been out of the house since she had arrived and the only bit of London she had seen was through the carriage windows. She put on one of the serviceable grey serge dresses and the bright paisley shawl Miss Hazel had given her. Nellie, as usual, was dressed flamboyantly in a gold satin dress and a dark brown fur cape. Her red hair was piled high on her head, on top of which was perched a small black ostrich-feathered hat. Diamante earrings swung from her ears, almost reaching the matching necklace that adorned her throat and terminated somewhere in her cleavage. What a pair they made, Nellie, a towering, colourful, six feet tall in her high heels and the soberly dressed, beautiful, petite Siobhan. It was all Ginny could do to stop herself from laughing out loud.

To Siobhan's disappointment they travelled to the Pawnbrokers by carriage. 'Is it too far to walk?' asked Siobhan.

'You're damn right it is, especially in these flippin' shoes!' replied Nellie. Siobhan didn't respond, but wondered, if Nellie's shoes were so uncomfortable, why was she wearing them?

The carriage arrived, taking them through grey, winding, cobbled streets. As with her last journey through the docks, the streets were so narrow there was barely enough room for the carriage, and, as before, the journey was hampered by ragged urchins climbing on board until discouraged by the driver's whip.

The carriage came to a sudden halt on the outskirts of a square. It was market day and the whole area was covered in stalls, some bright, some dull, but all attended by traders shouting their wares. A delicious smell of baked potatoes and hot chestnuts filled the air and, although Siobhan wasn't hungry, the smell made her mouth water. 'Can't take you any further, there ain't enough room for me carriage,' shouted the driver, alighting from his seat. 'You ain't got far to walk, you can see Old Isaac's balls hanging down from here!' the driver said, laughing out loud.

'There's no need to be crude!' said Nellie, suppressing her laughter. The course comment left Siobhan wondering what they were laughing at.

Eventually they reached a small dingy shop. Hanging from the sign there were three brass balls, the centre one hanging lower than the other two, and above, the word 'Pawnbroker'. Siobhan had experienced a range of shops selling specific items, but what sort of shop was this? The two windows were crammed full with everything you could think of, from jewellery to stuffed animals. Nellie had difficulty pushing open the door to the shop because of the iron security bars that stretched from top to bottom. The smell of dust and must hanging in the air caused Siobhan to start coughing. She had never been in such a place. Floor to ceiling was piled high with clothes. On the shelves that filled one wall stood china, glass, brass, everything you could imagine. At the end of the shop was a counter – metal netting protecting the expensive items that were displayed under the glass top.

With the ringing of the door bell, a sound of shuffling feet was heard from behind a beaded curtain that separated the shop from the back room. A withered hand pulled the curtain aside, followed by one of the oldest faces Siobhan had ever seen. Typically Jewish, Mr. Isaac had a large hooked nose, on which were perched a pair of gold spectacles. He was dressed in a shabby black pin-striped suit and on his head was a black velvet scull cap. His straggly white hair mingled with his long grey beard. Coming forward, he screwed up his eyes, then recognised who it was. 'Ah, Nellie, my dear, dear Nellie,' he said in broken English. They embraced each other with the familiarity of old friends. 'Now what can I do for you, my dear Nellie?'

'A favour.' She saw his eyes narrow – in his line of work he didn't like doing favours.

'This child has an outfit she no longer needs.' He started to shake his head, but Nellie, taking no notice, continued. 'Listen, before you dismiss it, have a look. It is of the finest quality. Come, Siobhan, show Mr. Isaac what you have!' Siobhan came forward with her parcel. As she came into the light Old Isaac let out a gasp and clutched Nellie for support. 'Caw Isaac! You ain't gonna pass out?' said the startled Nellie. Beckoning to Siobhan she said, 'Help me get him sat down!' They half carried, half dragged him into the back room, where they lowered him into a chair. Frightened, Nellie said, 'Come on Isaac, you ain't dying on me are you?' Turning to Siobhan, she indicated where a decanter was kept. 'Fetch the brandy!' Trembling, Siobhan went to the decanter and, without being told, poured two glasses. She knew Nellie would need a drink after this shock. Was the old man dying? 'Good girl,' said Nellie, taking one of the glasses and putting it to Old Isaac's purple lips. 'Come on you old bugger, take a sip. I ain't goin' to let you die before we've done business.' The brandy caused Isaac to splutter and, opening his eyes, he looked at Siobhan and the fear in her eyes.

'Don't be frightened, child, Old Isaac is not ready to meet his maker yet!' he said, smiling and showing his few remaining discoloured teeth.

'I should bloody well hope not,' said Nellie 'You gave me the fright of my life. What on earth was the matter with you, you looked as if you had seen a ghost?'

'Thought I had, Nellie!' he answered. 'This girl, Siobhan, is so much like my late wife.' He could see now that, although the girl was very much like his beloved Maria, there were differences. The girl had large blue eyes in contrast to his Maria's brown ones.

Not one to miss an opportunity, Nellie said, 'In that case you'll give her a good price for her gown and cloak.' At this they both laughed.

'Let me have a look what you have, child?' Isaac said, attempting to get up. Isaac fingered the blue velvet and he realised it was made of the finest fabric. Now how did this girl come by it? And what was she doing with the likes of Nellie Bell?

As if reading his thoughts, Nellie said, 'This is Siobhan Rafferty, my lodger's sister. They are staying with me until they can find a place of their own.' Holding the dress and cloak up to the light, he saw they had hardly ever been worn. Once again the thought went through his mind, how had this girl come by it?

'I'll give you five guineas for them,' Old Isaac said, bracing himself for Nellie's onslaught.

'Five guineas? Five guineas? Twenty-five is more like it!' said Nellie. The haggling went on with Siobhan not understanding any of it. At Mr.

Gibbs' shop you paid what he asked, or not at all – to her it was as if they were playing some sort of game. And to both of them that is what it was - there would be no fun in it if it wasn't done this way. It was agreed that the price paid would be fifteen guineas, including a cut of three for Nellie. It was more money than Siobhan had ever dreamed of.

'Thank you Mr. Isaac,' she said with gratitude.

'I'll take care of your money for you,' said Nellie. 'After all, it's got to last you 'til you get a job. You can't live in London for nothing, and you can't expect Michael to work his guts out to keep you,' she added.

'No, I don't expect Michael to keep me,' answered Siobhan. 'You are right Mrs. Bell, I must get a job!'

Old Isaac looked at her, thinking she was such a pretty little thing, just like a young Maria. It would be a joy to have her around. 'If it's a job you're after, why not here? I could do with some help, especially with the bookkeeping.' He held out his hands, twisted and bent with arthritis. 'My hands aren't so good these days.' Siobhan was silent, thinking how his hands reminded her of her mothers.

'Didn't you hear Mr. Isaac's offer?' said Nellie, prodding Siobhan in her side. 'A job, you can have a job here if you want?'

A smile lit up her sad face. 'Of course I would love to work here, but I don't know anything about bookkeeping or shop work.'

'You can read and write can't you girl?' asked Old Isaac.

'Oh! Yes, and I can add up. Miss Hazel was a good teacher.'

'That's settled then,' said Isaac beaming. 'You can start tomorrow, 7 o'clock sharp. I'll give you a week's trial to see if you suit me and I suit you.'

On the way home Nellie chattered away, but Siobhan wasn't really listening. All she could think about was how pleased Michael would be when she told him.

Unfortunately his reaction was not as she expected. The fact was, he didn't want her to be away from the house in case anything else happened to her. Nellie sensed this and understood his feelings, but he couldn't keep the girl wrapped in cotton wool. She voiced her opinion. 'Look, Michael, Isaac is a good man, miserly, but on the whole he is a gentleman. He wouldn't do anything to harm Siobhan.' He shook his head.

'How will she get there? It's quite a distance, she'll probably get lost?'

'I'll walk with her and meet her afterwards,' piped up Ginny.

'And who'll do your work, I'd like to know?' said Nellie, giving her a scorching look.

'I'll fit my work in, don't you worry about that,' said Ginny with anger in her voice. 'Miserable bugger, slave driver!' thought Ginny in her usual style.

'Don't think I can't hear your mutterings. I have to be a bloody slave driver, or no work would ever get done around here,' said Nellie, feeling put out.

So it was settled. Siobhan was to start work the next morning. Although still feeling weak, she managed to be ready for 6 o'clock, thinking it would take an hour to walk the distance. Michael had already gone to work, and Nellie rarely arose before 9 o'clock. Siobhan couldn't understand why Ginny was loitering at the breakfast table.

'Shouldn't we be off, Ginny, if I'm to be there for 7 o'clock?' She knew she was being forward in hurrying Ginny, but she didn't want to be late.

'Don't you trouble yourself, Siobhan. I'll get you there in time. We ain't bloody walking, we'll take a cab to Isaacs.'

Siobhan stared at her in amazement. 'Won't that cost too much?'

'Let me worry about that,' said Ginny. 'I've got to go to market, so I'll use that as an excuse.'

The shop was already open when Siobhan arrived - it had been since 6 o'clock. Many a customer, desperate for money, had been known to knock on Isaac's door no matter what the hour. Isaac patiently took her through the rudiments of the pawn business. 'A customer brings articles in - it could be anything from clothes to a stuffed animal.' With this statement he extended an open palm to a deer's head mounted on the wall. 'I offer them an amount of money for it, and, if they agree, I give them the money and a ticket bearing a future date, plus the amount they would have to pay to get it back - that's if they want it back. Most of these articles people don't come back for. The money they pay to get an item back is more than I gave them - that's how I make a profit.' The open palm now panned the items that cluttered the shop. 'Most of this stuff will never be re-claimed by the due date, then I have to sell it.' He sighed, adding, 'Ah, it's a hard life!' To Siobhan, it didn't make sense. Why pawn something, then pay more to get it back again? She voiced this to Isaac. 'You see, my dear, Mondays they need their working clothes, so they pawn their weekend clothes. Then come the weekend, when they have been paid, they redeem the best clothes, and so on. Then some, like yourself, have no further use for the article. Of course, the better quality items I sell on to a high class shop in the city.'

'Oh!' said Siobhan, then looking around, asked, 'Is that where the blue velvet will go?'

'Yes my dear, some nice young lady will soon be wearing that.' Siobhan hoped it would bring her better luck it did her.

The day went very quickly. Siobhan made herself busy by dusting and tidying. In no time at all a worn out Ginny arrived to collect her. 'Come, come Ginny,' said Isaac. He motioned her into the back room and poured her a cup of tea.

'Something stronger wouldn't come amiss," she said, relaxing in a comfy chair. 'I'm getting too old for all this walkin'. As much as I would like to walk with you, Siobhan, I'm afraid it's too much for me, what with doing the cookin' and cleaning for Nellie. The spirit's willing, but the flesh is weak, as they say.'

'I don't mind walkin' now I'm stronger,' said Siobhan feeling guilty, although she, herself, felt worn out.

Isaac had schooled himself to be hard hearted, but this time he felt sorry for the girl. From bits of the conversation he had heard from Nellie, he gathered that she had been ill. The girl looked frail, but she had worked hard today and she looked so much like his Maria. Rubbing his hands together, a trait of his race, he said, 'I'll pay for you to have a cab to get here in the mornings.' His generosity fell short of offering one for the return journey.

Amazed, Ginny said, 'Are you sure?'

'I'm sure, and for today only,' he said with a smile, but stressing the "only", 'I'll pay for one to take you home as well.'

At dinner, Siobhan answered all the questions Michael fired at her. Did she like it? What was Mr. Isaac like? Had he treated her well? 'Oh for goodness sake!' said Nellie. 'Leave the girl alone, can't you see she is tired. Siobhan, eat your meal and then go to bed - don't forget it's another early day tomorrow.' She continued, tired of hearing Michael's questions. She felt irritated with him. Since they had made love he seemed to be avoiding her, but tonight she would make sure he didn't. Michael was about to follow Siobhan and Ginny upstairs when Nellie grabbed hold of his arm. 'Stay and have a drink with me, Michael, I'm feeling a bit melancholy tonight.' Half of him wanted to go, the other half wanted to stay. Not having much will power where women were concerned, he followed her into the parlour, half anticipating what would happen. It wasn't very long before the relaxing effect of the brandy succumbed to the temptation of Nellie's voluptuous breasts. He was once again engulfed in her body.

Each morning for the first week, the carriage came to collect Siobhan to take her to Isaacs. The time spent working in the pawnshop went very quickly, seeming to Siobhan that no sooner had she arrived at the shop, than it was time to make her way home. Isaac had taught her how to enter the transactions into a ledger, a skill that she soon mastered. The shop had been transformed. Siobhan had tidied up, putting the items in some sort of order. All the bed linen was stacked in neat piles, clothes were put on hangers and hung up on rails. Isaac had been reluctant to spend the money buying the rails, but at Siobhan's suggestion he managed to get some second-hand ones from the market. The china and glassware had been washed, and gleamed on the shelves. 'Next week I will polish these, if it's alright with you, Mr. Isaac,' Siobhan said, looking at the discoloured brassware. She had taken for granted that her services were being retained.

'Anything is alright with me, girl. You have made a real difference to the appearance of the shop,' said Isaac, confirming Siobhan's thoughts. 'Maybe next week you can have a go at the shop windows?' There was a long pause before he added, 'You realise, Siobhan, the carriage won't be picking you up next week. I can't let all my profits be swallowed up when you have a perfectly good pair of strong legs, and by now you should know the way. The summer's coming, the mornings will be getting warmer and lighter, so will the evenings!' Siobhan didn't argue. She thought Mr. Isaac had been more than generous sending the carriage in the first place. He had formed the habit of closing the shop at the end of the day (an act hitherto unknown) and walking with her a short distance towards home. He enjoyed their chats as they walked together, though in truth, it was he that did most of the talking. It had been so long since he had had someone to converse with. Although he had only known Siobhan a few days, he felt close to her, as if she was the daughter he could have had, if the Lord hadn't needed Maria. Reminiscing, he told Siobhan how he and his wife had come over to England from Germany to get a better life. 'You see Siobhan, the Jewish race is despised all over the world. In England people are more tolerant, but you notice, even here, we are treated with suspicion. That's why most of us live in our own little community.'

'But why, Mr. Isaac? Why don't people like you?' Siobhan asked perplexed, forgetting completely the shunning she and Michael had experienced in Liverpool.

'Oh! It's not me as an individual. It's just that Jews have a reputation for making money,' he said, 'and then being mean with it,' he added almost mischievously.

'You haven't been mean to me!' responded Siobhan.

'No, not you, my dear, you are different. You are so like my darling wife, Maria, when she was young. She died giving birth to our daughter, my little girl who only lived a few hours. She was so perfect, like a china doll. I asked myself why the Lord had to take them, but I dare say he had his reasons.' He wiped a tear from his eye. 'Time heals everything, they say, but I still feel the pain at losing my wife and child.' Siobhan felt pity for Old Isaac, but could find no words of comfort to say to him. They walked in silence, and, before they both knew it, they were at Nellie's.

'Why, we are here already,' said Siobhan. 'Why don't you come in and have a cup of tea. I'm sure Nellie wouldn't mind.' She placed her arm in his and led him up the steps to the front door. Feeling very emotional and weary, he didn't protest.

Nellie was surprised and delighted to see the old man. 'Have we enough food for another one for dinner?' shouted Nellie to Ginny in the kitchen. Isaac protested, but Nellie insisted. 'An it ain't pork, either!' she said smiling.

'What was wrong with pork,' thought Siobhan, but chose not to ask.

Isaac, Nellie, Ginny, Siobhan and Michael sat at the large kitchen table eating the appetising meal. Although it was only beef stew it was delicious, especially the big fluffy dumplings. It was the first time Michael had met Isaac, and was relieved that Siobhan should be working for such a man.

The meal over, Isaac called a carriage to take him back to the shop. He had enjoyed the evening, a sharp contrast to eating on his own, but what a waste of money! – the food, the shop had been shut for hours, and the cost of the carriage! He must be going soft in his old age. Then a thought came over him. What was he saving all this money for, anyway? He had plenty, and was getting no younger. From now on he was going to have some of those little luxuries he had always denied himself. He would start by buying himself a new suit - he had felt ashamed tonight sitting at the table showing the threadbare cuffs on his suit and shirt. With that thought he felt happier than he had done for a long time - he even gave the carriage driver a tip. In total disbelief, the man stared down at the coin in his hand.

CHAPTER 17
Big John

Siobhan had regained most of her strength and was much stronger now. She could walk back and forth to the shop without feeling any discomfort and, being familiar with the route to Nellie's and the numerous narrow cobbled streets, they no longer confused her. She was accustomed to the street urchins and beggars that loitered in the dark alleyways and ignored them. The word had circulated that she was under Nellie Bell's protection - they knew that Nellie, the wealthy landlady, had influence with the peelers and left her alone. That is, except for one rainy evening, when a gang of youths sheltering in an entry grabbed her.

'Now here's a nice bit of class, if you like, lads,' said one of them.

'I wouldn't mind wearing that skirt meself,' said one of the girls. 'Mine's all worn out. Her boots are gooduns, bet her drawers are too!'

Different voices shouted different comments. 'Let's see, shall we?" said another, as several hands lifted up her skirt. Siobhan tried to stop them, but there were too many.

'Oh please, God,' she prayed, 'Not again!'

Just as her clothes were about to be removed she heard a roar. A voice bellowed out, 'Leave her alone or I'll break your bloody arms.' Hearing those words, and who was saying them, they all fled in terror. Siobhan looked towards a gigantic man standing in the entry. As he approached she saw it wasn't a man at all, but a very tall fattish youth.

'You alright, Lady?' he said in a surprisingly gentle voice.

'Yes! Yes, thank you,' she answered, not totally sure that her situation had improved - his appearance was so menacing, with his long greasy black hair.

'Come on, I'll walk with you to Mrs. Bell's,' he said, extending one of the largest hands she had ever seen.

'You know Mrs. Bell then?' she said in surprise.

'I donna know Mrs. Bell, only of her,' he answered, not letting on he had followed her going back and forth from Isaacs and watching to see she came to no harm. From the first moment he had seen Siobhan walking with Ginny, he had made it his business to find out all about her. In all his twenty years he had never seen anyone so beautiful. Compared to his size she was like a little doll - and for the first time in his unloved life, he had fallen in love. Siobhan was reluctant to walk with this menacing looking youth, but she was afraid to refuse in case he got violent. He saw the fear in her eyes and felt sad - the last thing he wanted to do was frighten the girl. Too shy to say anything to reassure her, he walked with her towards Mrs. Bell's in silence. Siobhan didn't know what to say either. Every now and again she would take a look at him out of the corner of her eye. The rain was still pouring down and she could see he was getting soaked.

'Would you like to share my umbrella?' she asked out of pity.

He blushed and said, 'No thanks, I'm used to the rain!' He didn't add, 'If I held it over me there would be no shelter for you'.

When they reached Nellie's, Siobhan extended her gloved hand. 'Thank you very much, Mr. …?' then asked, 'What is your name? Mine is Siobhan Rafferty.' The name Rafferty came easily to her now.

'John, me name's John, Big John I'm known by.' Uneasy, he gently took her hand. He had always had to be careful in touching people and objects. As the old lady he lived with was always reminding him, 'You don't know your own strength, John.' On one occasion whilst playfully stroking a kitten, he had accidentally broken its back. He had cried for days over the incident.

Siobhan did not mention the encounter, in case Michael stopped her going to Isaacs. To her surprise, Big John was waiting for her the following day after Isaac had left her. 'Thought I'd see you home, in case those ruffians attack you again,' he said, blushing once more. Siobhan didn't protest, for some unknown reason she trusted him. Every evening he would be there, rain or shine, waiting for her. Gradually, some of John's shyness having waned, he started to talk with Siobhan. She asked how he could spare the time to walk with her. He said he hadn't got a full time job, but just did odd jobs for people. Siobhan started to look forward to his company, and she certainly felt safe from being attacked.

'Have you any family, John?' she asked curiously. He hesitated before answering. No-one had ever cared enough to ask before. He decided to tell her the truth.

'My mother was a prostitute, she gave me to an old lady who had no children of her own.'

'I'm sorry,' said Siobhan, wishing she had never asked.

'Don't be sorry, the old lady has been good to me, and, after all, my mother could have got rid of me. I ain't done so bad,' he said philosophically. Although John told her personal details about his life, Siobhan was very economical with the truth about hers. She told him of Ireland, sticking to the story that she and Michael were orphans. The story was becoming very easy to her now - the fact was, she half believed it herself. She told him about Miss Hazel, and how happy she had been with her.

'If you were so happy, why did you come to London?' he asked.

'Michael wanted me with him. He had promised to look after me,' she said, thinking – if you only knew the truth.

'And has he looked after you?' he asked, wondering where was he when she was attacked?

'Yes, yes, I suppose he has in his own way,' then added, as if reading his thoughts, 'He can't be with me all the time, he works on the docks.'

'If you were me sister, I wouldn't let you walk the London streets alone!' he muttered to himself. Siobhan heard but did not comment.

Working at Isaac's, the weeks seemed to fly by. Siobhan couldn't say she was happy, but she didn't feel unhappy either. Her life had fallen into a routine, with Big John walking her to work and back again from where she left Mr. Isaac. She saw Michael in the evenings when they all sat down to dinner. Sometimes they would play a game of cards, with Nellie almost always winning. Other times she would sit and sew while the others talked and drank beer or brandy. Michael sometimes went to the 'Pipers' tavern, taking Nellie with him, though Nellie did most of the paying as Michael was saving hard for a place of their own. Siobhan earned four shillings a week, three of which she gave to Michael to help to pay for her keep. She still had most of the money Miss Hazel had given her, securely sewn into the lining of her skirt. Miss Hazel had told her about 'keeping money for emergencies'.

It was Saturday night and Michael was feeling guilty that he had paid little attention to Siobhan. Most of his thoughts had been occupied with work and with Nellie. Well, he would remedy that. 'How would you ladies like to come for a drink and a bite to eat with me?' he asked, all smiles.

'Don't say you're paying,' said Nellie immediately.

'Hey, of course I'm paying, Holy Mother I wouldn't be asking if I wasn't! And not the 'Pipers' either! Somewhere a bit special,' he said, getting carried away with the idea. Siobhan said she didn't want to go, but when Ginny said she wouldn't go if Siobhan didn't, she agreed. Nellie was over-dressed as usual and Ginny put on her best outfit – in contrast, Siobhan looked dowdy in her grey serge dress.

Nellie looked her up and down. 'You can't go out looking like a school teacher! You can borrow one of my shawls.' Fetching a brilliant jade-green silk shawl from upstairs, she draped it around Siobhan's shoulders. Immediately it transformed her appearance, the jade colour enhancing her porcelain skin and jet black hair.

They took a carriage into the city and stopped at a posh looking hotel. The four of them trooped in, but soon began to feel very uncomfortable as the rest of the guests and waiters looked at them with distaste. Nellie was about to shout, 'What you starin' at?', but thought better of it. The humiliation of being thrown out would have been too much, so, pre-empting the situation she whispered to Michael, 'Come on, let's get out of here and find an ale house?' Much to the relief of the staff, they departed.

They enjoyed the meal, normal food, but cooked in oils and herbs that made it taste very different. 'I must try cooking steak like this,' said Ginny, savouring every mouthful. Michael appeared to pay for the meal, but Nellie had slipped him some money towards the bill.

On arriving home, Siobhan and Ginny went straight up to bed. Nellie, tired of making love in the parlour and finding it more that a little uncomfortable at her age, picked up the brandy bottle and two glasses, and indicated to Michael to come up to her bedroom. That night Michael's lovemaking was sensitive and tender. When it was over, instead of going to his own room, Michael fell into a deep sleep in Nellie's feather bed. Nellie, on the other hand, lay awake staring at his handsome face, tears running down her cheeks. Tears for her youth - not as it had been, but as it could have been if she had met someone like Michael.

Ginny noticed Michael's bed hadn't been slept in. She didn't comment, but thought 'about time too, that sofa was doing Nellie's back no good at all.'

Siobhan got up feeling sick, but put it down to the rich food she had eaten the night before. The rest of the week she not only felt sick in the mornings, but was physically sick as well. A week later Siobhan thought she could no longer blame it on the food.

Ginny, who didn't miss anything that was going on, asked Siobhan straight out, 'You ain't pregnant, are you girl?'

Siobhan blushed and answered, 'Of course not.' The comment started her thinking back to when she had her last period. Thinking of the ball and Lord Bromley's attack, it suddenly dawned on her pregnancy could be a possibility. She looked at herself in the mirror and saw the same look that her sisters had before their bellies began to swell. Her hand immediately went to her mouth to stifle her cry of anguish. She refused to believe that she could be pregnant by that brute, but as the weeks went by she started to put on weight. Even Michael commented on it.

'Siobhan, me darlin', by the Holy Mother, I swear you are getting bonnier every day,' then whispered, 'but don't get too bonny, you don't want to look like Nellie.'

Ginny, sharp as a needle, overheard. When Michael was out of earshot she confronted Siobhan. 'It's no good denying it Siobhan, you are pregnant and in another month everyone will know.'

Siobhan started to cry. 'Oh! Ginny what on earth am I going to do? I can't have that monster's baby.' Ginny held out her arms and hugged her tight. Thoughts raced around Ginny's mind. Should she help the girl get rid of it? She decided that she would - nothing drastic, she didn't want her to end up the way she had!

'I could mix you a potion - maybe that will bring on your period?' She avoided saying 'get rid of the baby.'

That day Siobhan went to Isaac's as usual, but she didn't feel at all well. 'My dear Siobhan, I've been thinking you haven't looked well for a while. Why don't you stay at home for the rest of the week?' he said, concerned. 'In fact, go home now, I'll call a carriage to take you.' Siobhan protested, but Isaac insisted. In the carriage she looked out for Big John, knowing he would be waiting for her. Over the weeks she had become quite fond of him. Spying him, she told the driver to stop.

'John, John,' she shouted towards him. He realised who was calling and ambled over to her.

'Siobhan, what's the matter? Where are you going?' he asked full of anguish.

'I don't feel very well, so Isaac's sent me home,' she answered.

He opened the door and without being asked he got in beside her. Immediately the carriage tipped to one side with his weight. 'I thought you'd been looking pale, you ain't really ill are you, Siobhan?' he asked. He couldn't bear the thought of her being ill and not being able to see her. Since they had met, she had become the most important part of his life. She told him that Isaac had given her the rest of the week off, so it would be no use waiting for her. This made him very sad, not seeing her for a whole week! What if she was really ill, how would he find out how she was getting on? He voiced his fears to her.

'Just knock on Nellie's door and ask,' she said, not seeing a problem.

'Would they tell me?' he asked, not believing.

'Of course! I will leave instructions that if you come to the door, they should let you in to see me,' she said, noticing the gratitude on his face.

Ginny waited until Michael had gone to work and Nellie had gone out to do her rent collecting before she heated up a mixture of quinine and gin. 'Here, drink this as hot as you can,' she said, handing the cup to Siobhan. It was all she could do to swallow the bitter tasting liquid. Ginny then made her take a hot bath. When nothing happened after the first drink, they tried it twice more. Apart from making Siobhan dizzy it had no affect on the pregnancy. In despair, Siobhan asked Ginny if there was another way, but the alternative made Ginny shudder.

'No my dear, I think the little un is here to stay,' she answered.

'Oh! Ginny, what on earth am I going to do? I can't give birth to that monster's baby?'

'There ain't nothing you can do,' said Ginny. 'One thing is certain, in a few weeks you won't be able to hide your condition from anyone! If I were you, I'd come clean and tell your brother and Nellie. After all it weren't your fault!' said Ginny

'I'll give it a few more weeks, then I will tell them,' she said, hoping against hope that she would have a miscarriage. As it happened, the decision was made for her. One evening, a month later, Michael commented once again after dinner about her appearance.

'You know, little sister, London must really suit you, you will have to either get a new dress or let that one out before the seams burst?'

Nellie suddenly looked up. These last few months she had hardly looked at the girl, her thoughts having been filled with Michael. What Michael had said made her look at Siobhan, then, like a bolt of lightening, it struck her. The girl was expecting! Before she could stop herself, she voiced her thoughts. 'You're pregnant!'

Michael nearly choked on his brandy. 'Holy Mother Mary! Are you?' he said, looking at her in disbelief.

Ginny answered for her. 'Yes, I'm afraid she is, and has been since she arrived - if some people had taken time to notice!' The point wasn't lost on Michael who had the decency to look ashamed, but Nellie only felt annoyance.

'Well, what do you intend to do? And why didn't you tell me about it, Ginny?' Ginny ignored the last question, but answered for Siobhan.

'It's too late to do anything about it, we've tried certain things, but they didn't work, and I wasn't having her go to any backstreet abortionist. Remember what happened to me?' Michael's mind raced with thoughts of what he could do. Although he still loved Siobhan, he didn't want to disrupt the comfortable situation he was in now. The conversation went back and forth, Michael, Ginny and Nellie discussing what should be done as if she wasn't there. Siobhan sat there only half listening. Her thoughts were of Lord Bromley - no way was she giving birth to his bastard, hating the thought of his evilness growing inside her body. If only she could rip it out before it consumed her completely. Where were these backstreet abortionists? She would go to one of them! So preoccupied with their opinions, they didn't notice her slip upstairs. She unpicked the stitching in her shirt and pocketed a sovereign.

Siobhan ran along the quay towards the backstreets, passing several prostitutes. One of them deliberately sidestepped so she bumped into her. She grabbed Siobhan's arm, saying, 'Hey! What's the hurry little un? Who you runnin' from?' She looked into her face then exclaimed, 'Why, ain't you one of Nellie's 'so-called' guests?' In the foray Siobhan's shawl fell from her shoulders, revealing her protruding stomach. 'Oh! Pregnant are we?' she said, her red lips twisting into a sneer. Siobhan began to cry, the emotion she had held back over the weeks flooding out. Suddenly ashamed of making fun of the girl, the prostitute put her arm about her, saying, 'Now, now! Don't upset yourself. I'm surprised Nellie let this happen. I take it you don't want it?'

'No, No, No, I hate it!' cried Siobhan, her hands ripping at her stomach.

'I know someone who could help you,' said the prostitute. 'Have you any money? It can't be done for nothing!'

'Yes, I have a sovereign, would that be enough?' she said, holding the sovereign tight in her hand.

The prostitute's eyes narrowed with greed. She would have stolen the money from the girl if Nellie had not been involved.

'Yes, that'll be enough. Come on, the sooner we get you seen to the better.' The prostitute dragged Siobhan through the back allies until they stopped at a foul smelling place behind some warehouses, the cobbles covered with the slime of rotting fruit and vegetables. Stopping at an end terraced house, the prostitute banged on the door and shouted, 'Edna, Edna, you awake?'

The door opened slightly and a face peered out. 'Is that you, Polly? What ya want?'

'A customer, I've got a customer for ya!' said the prostitute, pushing the door open and pulling Siobhan along behind her. The stench that greeted Siobhan made her retch, it was all she could do to stop being sick. A bent old woman squinted at her and laughed, showing blackened broken teeth.

'Too drunk to do anything tonight!' said Edna tottering on her feet.

'Perhaps a sovereign will sober you up, you old hag!' said the prostitute, grabbing at the gin bottle that Edna was about to up-end. She pushed Siobhan into what was supposed to be a kitchen. Several cats scurried out, leaving behind the strong smell of feline urine.

Siobhan shuddered. She was just about to run away when Polly and Edna came back into the room. Edna had had the decency to put on a pinafore that was once white, but was now grey with blood stains of passed abortions. If that wasn't bad enough, she held in her hand a long, thin bone knitting needle. Polly followed her, carrying a rusty bucket, steam rising from its contents. A filthy towel hung over her arm. Putting them down, Polly pulled an old wooden table into the middle of the room beneath a hanging oil lamp. She quickly removed the stained newspapers and mouse droppings that covered it. 'Don't you ever clean up after you, you dirty cow? Where's some clean paper?'

Edna laughed and pointed the knitting needle towards the corner of the room where two more cats had made it their bed. 'Bloody cats!' shouted Polly as she shifted them away.

In a more soothing voice, Edna approached Siobhan. 'Come on, lie on the table. Polly remove her underclothes!' Polly helped Siobhan onto the table, her hands removing her shoes, stockings, and finally her drawers. 'That's right, let the dog see the rabbit! I'll soon have the little blighter out,' cackled Edna.

Siobhan shut her eyes tight. 'I'm in a nightmare, surely to God, this is a nightmare!' she thought. 'It couldn't be really happening?' No wonder Ginny didn't want her to come to a place like this.

'Don't be frightened, girly,' said Edna, her face coming closer to Siobhan. The gin fumes and body stench of the woman nauseated her, making her retch once again. Opening her eyes she could see Polly about to stuff a filthy rag into her mouth, whilst Edna was pushing open her legs, ready to insert the sharp pointed knitting needle. Siobhan pushed Polly's hand away and screamed and screamed.

The next thing she felt was the cold air on her face. Had she died? Was she being carried high, as if floating to heaven? Siobhan opened her eyes, and in the light from a street lamp, the last thing she saw before passing out was Big John's face staring down at her. He carried her in his arms and ran with her through the alleyways, not stopping until he reached the house where he lived. Breathlessly he kicked at the door. The old lady opened it, saying in a surprised voice, 'What the devil's goin' on?' She noticed the bundle he had in his arms, she asked, 'What the hell have you got there?' John didn't answer, but lay Siobhan down gently on the couch.

'Hurry, mother, get her some brandy!' The old woman was so taken aback, she didn't argue, but did as she was told. John held Siobhan's head up and made her take a sip.

The old lady noticed Siobhan was wearing neither shoes nor stockings and feared the worst. 'My God! John, what have you done?' she cried.

He gave no answer - his mind concentrated solely on the plight of Siobhan. Thank God he had seen her walking with Polly, the prostitute. He had followed them, wondering what on earth Siobhan was doing out at that time of night, and particularly with someone like Polly? When they entered Edna's house, everything fell into place. All these weeks when Siobhan hadn't felt well - her pale drawn face and the dark circles around her eyes. She couldn't be having a baby, he reasoned, she couldn't be. Why, she never went out on her own, and he had been with her on the journeys backwards and forwards to work. Perhaps that was why she came to her brother, because she was in trouble. He must be wrong, but everyone knew what Edna did - she was well known for her abortions. She was nothing but a murderess. Many a young girl had died after going to her, or worse still, had lived, diseased and rotting from the inside. He hadn't known what to do. He could have gone rushing in, demanding to know what was going on, but, after all, it was none of his business! However, at the first scream he kicked the door open to see Edna about to insert the needle into Siobhan.

The brandy had its affect, bringing Siobhan back to her senses. The first thing she asked was, 'Did she do it?' her voice hesitating on every word.

'No, I heard you scream and saved you just in time,' said Big John with as much calm as he could muster. 'Whatever made you think of doing such a thing?' he added in disbelief. 'Why! The woman's a murderess!'

Siobhan put her hands to her face and cried, 'Thank God, Oh, John, thank you.' At that she flung her arms around him. They held each other, their tears mingling. John's adopted mother looked on, not believing her eyes. If ever there was a case of beauty and the beast, this was it!

Ginny was the first to realise Siobhan wasn't at home. She had gone up to her room thinking she had gone to bed, but on seeing it empty she called her name in case she was in one of the other rooms. Dismayed, she had come downstairs. 'Here we are, talking as if the girl wasn't here,' said Ginny, 'discussing what she should or shouldn't do. If she's overheard us, no wonder she's run off,' she said, addressing Nellie and Michael.

Michael looked shame-faced. 'Holy Mother! Where the devil would she go? I'll go and look for her,' he said, putting on his coat.

'Hold on, I'll come with you,' said Ginny, wrapping a shawl around her shoulders.

Ginny walked along the quay and Michael searched the narrow streets and alleyways. Unsuccessful in their efforts they both arrived back at Nellie's feeling very tired.

'No luck then?' said Nellie, pouring them a hot drink.

Ginny sat down, kicked off her shoes and rubbed her feet. 'Can't think where the girl's got to!' she said, shaking her head. 'We'll have another look tomorrow, it will be easier in the daylight.'

Michael wept as he held his head in his hands. 'It's all my fault, I should have taken better care of her!'

'It's no good blaming yourself,' said Nellie, feeling very much her sixty years. 'We're all to blame. Let's go to bed and get some sleep, we'll need to be fresh for tomorrow!'

Siobhan didn't want to go back to Nellie's that night, the shock had left her exhausted, and the last thing she needed was another interrogation.

Next morning Siobhan awoke shaking from head to toe. John wanted to fetch the doctor, but Siobhan declined. The doctor would only tell Nellie and she wasn't ready to face them yet. 'You can go to Isaac's and say I'm not well, so I'll not be in today,' she said, pulling the blanket around her.

John was only too pleased to do what Siobhan wanted. 'I'll go, but before I do, you must get some food down ya, and a hot drink. Mother, get Siobhan something to eat while I am out,' he said, already part-way through the doorway.

His mother looked bewildered. 'He don't tell me nothing. Still, he ain't a little lad no more!' she muttered to herself.

When John reached Isaac's he was out of breath from running most of the way. It was early, the dawn was just breaking and the shop wasn't open. It seemed an age before Isaac opened the door in a sleepy state, squinting at the figure before him. He had never met John before. Seeing this gigantic man with an abundance of black covering his head and face, he attempted to close the door, but John's foot prevented him from doing so. 'The shop's shut! Go away!' said Isaac in a frightened voice.

John stammered, 'I've come with a message from Siobhan.'

Hearing the name, Isaac's manner changed. 'Siobhan, what about Siobhan? What have you got to do with Siobhan?'

'A message, I've come with a message,' repeated John, still a little breathless.

'You had better come in, I'm catching my death out here,' said the old Jew, leading the way into the back parlour. 'Now what is this all about?' John repeated what Siobhan had told him to say. The old Jew was too worldly-wise not to realise there was more to this than was being said. Cunningly, he offered John a cup of tea and made him sit down. As John became more relaxed he asked him how he knew Siobhan, and whether it was through Nellie?

The mention of Nellie's name triggered John to repeat what Siobhan had said to him, but then continued, 'Siobhan doesn't want Nellie or Michael to know.'

'What must we not let Nellie or Michael know?' said Isaac gently, coaxing an answer that would otherwise not be forthcoming.

'About the baby, she doesn't want them to know about the baby, of course,' he said, getting agitated.

'Now calm down. What did you say your name was?'

'I'm John… John,' he said ringing his hands in frustration. He began to realise in his slow mind he shouldn't have mentioned Nellie, and had now said too much. Oh, what was he to do now?

It was dawning on Isaac that this was not a man, as he had first thought, but a big youth who was none too bright. He put his hand on John's shoulder and said in a calm voice, 'Siobhan wouldn't mind me knowing. I am her friend, just like you. She trusts you, doesn't she?' At that John nodded. 'And she trusts me, else why should she send you to me?'

It took a few minutes for this statement to sink into John's mind, but when it did John related all that had happened to Siobhan. If Isaac was shocked, he didn't show it. His race was schooled into hiding their true feelings. Inwardly he was appalled. How could this be? Siobhan pregnant? And how could Nellie and that brother of hers let her run to an abortionist? One thing was certain, from here on he would look after her. He put on his heavy black overcoat and said, 'Come on, John, I'll call a carriage. I'm coming back with you - and I'm taking charge from now on!' Upset and confused, John did as he was told.

CHAPTER 18
The Pawn Shop

John's stepmother dithered about, not really knowing what to do. To her, Siobhan seemed a very grand lady. What on earth was John doing with such a person? Although she loved him dearly, she knew he wasn't the same as other youths, and never had been. She had told him he was adopted, but the truth was he had been left with her to look after by a prostitute who had never come back for him. Always bigger and strong than his peers, he had earned money from an early age doing odd jobs. He'd had no schooling, so couldn't read or write. The one thing he was good at was counting money - on the odd occasion when someone had tried to cheat him, thinking him simple, they soon found out to their cost, with a bloody nose as a reminder.

The door opened and in walked John and, much to Siobhan's surprise, Isaac. He went right to her, putting his arms about her saying, 'My dear child, John has told me all that has happened to you.' Embarrassed, Siobhan blushed and looked down, unable to meet his eyes. 'I don't know how all this came about, but knowing you, I know you wouldn't be the one to blame. What I can't understand is, where was your brother while all this has been going on?' he asked, shaking his head in disbelief.

Isaac casting doubts on Michael caused her to speak up. 'Oh! Michael didn't know, it happened before I came to London. They didn't know where I was going. Last night, while they were talking, I ran out of the house.'

Isaac was alarmed. 'So they don't know where you are?' he exclaimed. 'Why, they must be out of their minds with worry. We will have to get you back as soon as possible.'

'No! No! I can't face them. They were all discussing me as if I wasn't there,' cried Siobhan

John had been listening, and eagerly offered, 'She can stay here!'

Isaac saw his stepmother about to object. 'That is kind of you, John, but it wouldn't be practical, especially when the baby arrives,' he said. After a slight pause he added in a gentle voice, 'Siobhan, would you like to come and stay with me for a while? I have just the bedroom for you.' The question took Siobhan by surprise, and needed a few moments for it to register. When it did she decided that, for the time being, it seemed to be the only answer. It would give time for Michael to get used to the idea of her having a baby. But then again, he really wasn't responsible for her, after all she wasn't really his sister.

So it was decided that Siobhan would be living with Isaac for a while, and he sent John to find a carriage. Isaac said it was only fair that they called at Nellie's to tell them what was happening, and to collect her belongings. Siobhan dreaded facing Michael, but she knew she had to let them know.

Without waiting to be asked, John got into the carriage with them. He was not going home until he saw Siobhan safely at Mr. Isaac's. On the way to Nellie's they met Ginny and Michael who were still out searching for Siobhan. There wasn't room in the carriage for them all, so Michael sat with the driver and John followed on foot. Back at Nellie's house Siobhan was bombarded with questions. 'What was she thinking of going off like that?' 'Where had she been?' 'Didn't she realise how worried they had all been?'

Nellie was really angry. 'You are nothing but a selfish girl,' she shouted at Siobhan. 'Why, your poor brother has been out of his mind with worry. Him and Ginny are fair worn out from tramping the streets looking for you. Michael has lost a day's work - if he gets laid off it's all your fault!' On and on she went until Siobhan burst out crying, saying how sorry she was. Michael didn't go to console her, agreeing with Nellie that Siobhan had been thoughtless.

It was Ginny who went to Siobhan, putting her arms around her. 'Now, now my dear, don't cry. Nellie doesn't mean it, it's because we were all so worried. Where did you go? To Mr. Isaac's?'

Isaac would have answered 'yes' to save a lot of explaining, but John piped up, feeling very important, 'No she didn't, she went to Edna, the murderess!' Then, puffing out his chest in pride, he added, 'and I saved her!'

They all went silent whilst the meaning of his words sank in. Of course, Nellie and Ginny knew all about Edna, but Michael hadn't a clue. 'Holy Mother of Jesus, who's Edna?' he asked with more than a little sarcasm in his voice.

'She's an abortionist!' said Nellie, blunt as usual.

'Holy Mary, you haven't, have you Siobhan? She didn't do it?' questioned Michael.

'No she dain't, I saved her!' piped up John once more, milking his few minutes of glory.

Nellie sat down and indicated to Ginny. 'Get the brandy, I think we all need one.'

Nellie and Michael had brandy whilst Ginny made tea for the others. They all sat in silence, each occupied with their own thoughts. John, however, not used to the subtleties of life's complicated moments, spoke up. 'She's goin' to stay at Isaac's.'

'What?' all three said at once. Isaac quickly explained, and much to Siobhan and Isaac's relief, no-one objected. Secretly, Michael and Nellie were relieved. Ginny was the only one with reservations - she had grown fond of the girl and was going to miss her.

As Michael loaded Siobhan's few possessions onto the coach, he whispered in her ear, 'Me darlin', take care of yourself. I'll come to see you on Sunday.'

The carriage stopped outside the pawnshop, greeted by several people waiting to do business, not believing the shop was really closed. 'It has never been known,' remarked one customer, 'Not even on Christmas day.'

'I cannot do anything now,' Isaac said firmly to them, 'A family crisis!'

'But I need some money to feed my children!' piped up one woman who looked half starved herself.

Isaac put his hand in his pocket, fetched out a handful of coins and distributed them amongst the waiting people. 'Here, these will tide you over until I resume my business. Now be off with you!'

The astonished customers went away, looking incredulously at the money and muttering, 'What's come over the old miser?' said one. 'And what's that Big John doing carrying the girl?' said another.

Isaac led the way upstairs, followed by John carrying Siobhan. She did not know what to expect. If the bedroom was anything like the rest of the house it would be full of clutter, but when they entered one of the bedrooms she could not believe her eyes. It was the prettiest room she had ever seen, decorated in pale pink and white. Fresh flowers filled several vases, their perfume filling the air. A big four-poster bed with lace drapes stood in the middle of the room. On a light mahogany dressing table with a white profiled marble top lay silver backed brushes and picture frames.

Isaac moved about the room with renewed vigour, excitedly giving orders to John. 'Place Siobhan on the chaise-longue, then go and fill the warming pan with hot coals to air the bed.' John was at his best when given worthwhile things to do, so gratefully did as he was bid.

'What a beautiful room. Whose is it?' she asked whilst the two of them were alone. She knew it couldn't be his, because he slept downstairs in a comfortable arm chair.

Isaac looked around the room with nostalgia, then picked up one of the framed photographs. The picture was of a woman not unlike herself. 'It was my Maria's room. I keep it like this in memory of her.'

Siobhan felt awkward and didn't want to impose on this man's grief. Voicing her reluctance, she said, 'I'll stay in another room. I don't want to...' Before she could say another word, Isaac placed an extended index finger against her lips.

'Siobhan, it is as if this room has been waiting for you. Do not be afraid, there are only good spirits here.'

With rest, Siobhan soon recovered, falling into an easy routine of serving in the shop, cooking and cleaning. Isaac did not expect her to do these jobs, but Siobhan insisted that being busy took her mind off her pregnancy. Michael came to visit her every Sunday as he had promised, and Ginny popped in whenever she found time. Once or twice Nellie had come, but only when she had something to pawn for a customer. John proved himself useful doing odd jobs and dealing with customers that became aggressive.

Mr. Isaac did not have many friends, but on the rare occasion he had supper with them he would take Siobhan along. No-one passed a remark as to how much she resembled his late wife.

At Isaac's insistence, Doctor Round called regularly to check that all was going well with Siobhan. Although she wasn't very big, he said she was in perfect health and should give birth to a healthy baby. Siobhan, on one occasion, heard the doctor and Isaac talking. 'How did this young girl get herself pregnant? She seems so innocent?' Siobhan held her breath fearing the doctor would tell Isaac everything, but, respecting his profession, said only, 'Isaac, we are good friends, but I cannot betray patient confidentiality. Perhaps you should ask her directly.'

That evening Siobhan was particularly subdued, pondering on what the doctor had said. She knew Isaac was too much of a gentleman ever to ask her, but felt that his kindness towards her would surely merit his knowing the truth. The opportunity came when Isaac remarked how quiet she was, and asked was she worrying about anything?

'I feel I owe it to you to tell you about myself, and how I became pregnant,' she answered.

'You owe me nothing, my dear. It is true I have wondered how an innocent girl like you came into this situation, but I am prepared to let it rest at that.'

This time Siobhan placed a silencing index finger against her lips, indicating that she would like to begin explaining what had happened to her. She started at the very beginning, about the hovel, her abusive father, Michael bringing her to England, Miss Hazel. Then she hesitated as tears filled her eyes, thinking how she missed the old school teacher.

'Don't tell me any more dear if it is going to cause you pain,' said Isaac, tears filling his own eyes.

Siobhan wiped away her tears and said, 'No, now I have started, I want to tell you everything.'

She went on to tell of Lord Bromley, of the ball and finally the rape. When she had finished, Isaac was too shocked to speak, anger filling his body. If only he were younger he would seek out this Lord Bromley and kill him. What was her brother thinking of, leaving her behind? But, of course, the final shock was that Michael was not really her brother.

At last he found his voice. 'No wonder you wanted to get rid of the baby. But there is an old saying, "out of evil cometh good." When the child is born, instead of feeling hate for it, reminding you of that loathsome creature, I will find you both a good home with a family who will not know your background.'

Siobhan felt as if a big weight had been lifted from her. She had no doubts that Isaac would keep what she had told him to himself, but felt she had to ask. 'You won't repeat what I have told you, will you? Especially about Michael not being my brother!'

'Need you ask? You can trust old Isaac. I'll not breathe a word to anyone,' he said, getting up and putting his thin arms around her in reassurance.

The weeks and months went by. Michael kept his promise and still visited her every Sunday. If he sensed hostility from Isaac he never mentioned it. Although he still loved Siobhan, he had once again fallen into the trap of a woman. With Siobhan no longer around he and Nellie made love regularly, not bothering to hide the fact from Ginny, who, used to Nellie's ways, wasn't shocked. She just hoped her mistress would not get hurt.

Siobhan's labour pains started early one morning. Big John, who seemed always to be around when he was needed, was sent to fetch Dr. Round. It wasn't a comfortable birth because of all the scar tissue from the attack, but eventually the plaintive cries of a baby girl filled the house. Siobhan had prepared herself to have nothing to do with the child, but from the moment the doctor put her daughter in her arms, she fell in love with her. 'Oh! She's beautiful,' she exclaimed, kissing the baby's crown on which golden down was already appearing.

'What shall we call her?' said Siobhan, looking at them both.

'Amy,' said Big John almost instinctively. He didn't know why he had said that name, it just seemed to pop into his head. Only his subconscious knew it was the name of his biological mother.

'Amy, I like that,' repeated Siobhan, then, fully aware of the effect it would have, she added, 'but I like Amy Maria better.'

'Thank you,' said Isaac glancing at the picture of his late wife.

Ginny came bustling around as soon as John bought the news, and announced to Nellie without asking for her permission, 'I'm staying over there until Siobhan can manage on her own!'

You could not mistake who the baby's father was, much to Michael's dismay. She was nothing like Siobhan in looks or colouring. 'You aren't keeping it, are you?' he asked in disgust.

A shocked Siobhan looked at him. 'She is of my flesh too, she cannot help who her father is. And "It" has a name. She is called Amy Maria.'

Michael was too taken aback to say any more, but he vowed if that was her attitude he wouldn't be coming to visit so frequently.

The house had become alive again with the sound of Siobhan and Amy's laughter. Isaac had never felt happier.

CHAPTER 19
Judas

From the day Siobhan left, Sally wanted to stay at the cottage and make herself indispensable to Miss Hazel. The first few weeks had been difficult - Miss Hazel, heartbroken at Siobhan's leaving, hardly spoke to her. After a letter had arrived from London, reassuring Miss Hazel that Siobhan was fit and well, and comfortably settled in with Michael at Nellie Bell's boarding house, Miss Hazel became more sociable. The letter said she had got herself a job in a pawnbroker's shop owned by a Mr. Isaac, who was very kind to her.

Sally was filling out in a way that she couldn't put off much longer. She would soon have to throw herself on the mercy of Miss Hazel and tell her about the baby she was expecting.

The summer had begun and the seeds Siobhan had planted had blossomed into flowers. Miss Hazel took great delight in sitting on the wooden bench in the garden awaiting the afternoon tea Sally would prepare and take out to her. She had even managed to learn basic cooking skills - today it was fruit cake that accompanied the afternoon cup of tea. It had become accepted that Sally would sit taking tea with Miss Hazel. Most afternoons she would chatter away about nothing in particular, but today she said nothing.

'You're very quiet today, Sally?' commented Miss Hazel.

'I've something I have to tell you. You will find out sooner or later anyway, but I am having a baby,' said Sally, coyly lowering her eyes in mock shame.

'I'm not blind, Sally. I had noticed,' said Miss Hazel, taking hold of her hand. 'And if you are worried, I have no intention of turning you out -

have no fear, I'm not that heartless. No, my dear, you and your baby have a home here for as long as you like.'

It was the first time anyone had ever been kind to her without wanting something in return. Tears of gratitude filled her eyes as she went over and threw her arms around the old lady.

Sally's baby was born a month before Amy. It was a boy, a great big bonny boy weighing ten pounds, with thick black curly hair, just like his father. From an early age there was a glint of mischief in his blue eyes. Naming him Michael confirmed Miss Hazel's suspicions of who the father was.

From time to time a letter would arrive from Siobhan, tactfully omitting to say she had a child. With similar reserve, Sally begged Miss Hazel not to let Siobhan know she had given birth when replying to the letters.

Young Michael was a constant joy to both of them. Sally felt she was really loved, and loved just for being herself. Time had flown by. Michael had been a good baby, much to Sally's relief, generally sleeping through the night so Miss Hazel was not disturbed. Michael was now two years old, but he had been walking from the age of one. Miss Hazel would chase him around the garden, hobbling on her stick. Siobhan, occupied with little Amy Maria and helping Isaac, wrote less frequently to Miss Hazel, finding it increasingly difficult not to mention her daughter.

Young Michael had taken the place of Siobhan in Miss Hazel's heart - not that she had forgotten about her, but she had stopped worrying as her thoughts were increasingly taken up with the boy. She felt she must do something about making his future secure, since if she were to die intestate, the cottage and her remaining money would go to his Lordship's estate, and she wasn't having that. She hadn't thought of Bromley in a long time, but, as far as she knew, he was still in the hospital up north.

True to the old adage 'think of the devil he is sure to appear', Miss Hazel had hardly finished thinking about him when the sound of horse's hooves was heard in the lane. Curiously, Sally peered through the lace curtains. 'Oh, my God!' she shouted. 'It's Lord Bromley!' Instinctively she bolted the door. Putting her finger to her lips, she indicated to Miss Hazel to be quiet. Luckily, Michael had fallen asleep. Lord Bromley stopped the horse outside the cottage gate as though to alight, but changed his mind and rode off. Sally, watching from behind the curtain, let out a sigh of relief. 'What do you make of that?' she asked Miss Hazel.

Miss Hazel had gone pale and was shaking. 'I thought it was too good to be true that we had seen the last of him,' she said with a tremble in her voice. 'We can expect trouble. Sally, no matter what pressure he puts on you, you won't tell him where Siobhan is will you?'

'Of course not. As if I would,' said Sally, none too convincingly. But if he threatened to harm her son it would be a different matter.

His Lordship had already made inquiries about Siobhan, first from Forster who had said he had taken her home when the ball had ended. Nothing was mentioned about the rape. He had asked the villagers if they had seen her, but, suspecting what had really gone on, thought it was safer to say nothing.

The next day he rode once again to Miss Hazel's, but this time he banged on the door. At first, both Sally and Miss Hazel made no attempt to open it, but the noise soon had the predictable effect on young Michael. Faced with a screaming child, Sally had no option but to open the door. Lord Bromley pushed Sally to one side and searched the cottage, then went back into the garden. Progressively unable to control himself he shouted, 'Where is she?'

'Where is who?' asked Sally, trying to feign innocence.

Lord Bromley stormed back into the cottage, still shouting. 'You know damn well who! Siobhan! Where is the little cow?' He could feel the blood rushing to his head.

At the words 'little cow', Miss Hazel put aside all fear and lost her temper. 'Siobhan is no little cow. What you did to that innocent child does not bear thinking about. To call you an animal is too good for you. You are a lecherous beast who should be put down.' He went to hit her, but her words curbed him. 'You hit me, or harm Sally or Michael, and I will go to the magistrates in Liverpool and tell them everything. There are witnesses - Sally here, the doctor - and Forster. We are all fed up with you getting away with murder. Think yourself lucky this time you were only sent to hospital. Next time, for all your influence, it will be the gallows.' She picked up her stick and pointed to the door. 'Now be off with you, and if you come here again I'll do as I've threatened.' Bromley was so taken aback at this outburst from the old lady that he did as he was instructed. Sally quickly shut the door and bolted it. She turned to Miss Hazel who, worn out, had collapsed into a chair.

Whilst away having treatment, Lord Peter's fits had become less frequent. He used his cunning to give the appearance of a model patient, wanting a formal discharge as soon as possible. He remembered little of what happened the night of the ball. One thing that did stick in his mind was how beautiful Siobhan had looked in the crimson red dress. He could not get the image of her out of his mind, it was like a torment, the lust he felt for her.

When he returned to the manor from his ride to Miss Hazel's cottage, he summoned Forster. Fearfully Forster entered Lord Bromley's study, anticipating that one day his Lordship would want to know what really happened the night of the ball. Bromley stood in front of the window, his back to Forster, rhythmically tapping his thigh with his riding crop. It made Forster uneasy, and thought he would have to be very careful with what he said. The last thing he wanted was his Lordship having one of his rages. After what seemed an age, Lord Bromley turned around. He was smiling, thinking that the best way to get the truth from this man was to treat him as he would a close friend. He invited Forster to be seated and poured two large brandies. Not asking whether Forster wanted one, he handed him a glass. Lifting and offering his own glass as he would for a toast he began, 'Forster, I want to thank you for helping my cousin run the estate whilst I have been away.' Forster went to protest, saying that the estate manager had done most of the work. 'He may have done the work, Forster, but you have worked for my family longer than any of the other staff. You know how things should be done, know the ropes, so to speak.' Forster didn't answer, knowing this wasn't the reason he had been summoned. Sooner or later his Lordship would get to the real point. Bromley finished his drink and poured himself another, unable to hold back his intended questions any longer. 'Forster, what really happened the night of the ball? I know they said I had been attacked, but it has been going over and over in my mind - I cannot think that is the truth.' Lashing his crop hard on his desk he shouted, 'The truth Forster! I want the truth.'

Forster had had enough of covering up for his Lordship. If the truth resulted in his dismissal then so be it - he had enough money saved to last him the rest of his life. He looked his employer in the eye. 'My Lord, you are not going to like this, but you want the truth, so here it is. You almost killed the girl - if I hadn't come in when I heard her screaming, you sure as hell would have.' Forster suddenly felt an uneasiness inside. Despite the invitation to be open, a lifetime in service made it difficult for him to speak to his master in that tone.

Shocked at his servant's frankness, Bromley tried again to recall that night. 'What was I doing, beating her?'

'I wish to God it had only been that,' Forster said, anger boiling up inside him as he recalled the scene. You raped her and buggered her. There was blood everywhere. You almost tore her in half.'

Lord Bromley stood in silence for a while, digesting what Forster had said. 'So my fractured head was your doing?'

'Yes, My Lord, I had to do something, you were out of your mind,' replied Forster.

'Out of my mind? Out of my mind?' repeated Lord Bromley to himself. He pulled himself upright and regained a posture of authority. 'You may go now, Forster,' he said in a quiet voice, as though they had been discussing some trivial estate matter. Forster was part way through the door when a final question was asked. 'How many people know?'

'Myself, the doctor, Miss Hazel, Sally,' listed Forster, unsure whether he would have preferred there to be more or less. 'I don't know who else. When I returned after taking Siobhan home and fetching the doctor, dawn was breaking. I went into the drawing room and everything had been cleaned up, the blood, everything, you wouldn't have known anything had happened, except for damp patches on the carpet, oh, and the missing drape I'd wrapped Siobhan in. The footman told me you had been attacked. He didn't elaborate about what he knew or thought, and the staff never discussed it - well never in front of me.'

So Miss Hazel was right. If the magistrates in Liverpool got to hear of the episode it would be jail for sure. The judge in Chester had turned a blind eye to his mad outbursts - he had been well paid to do so - but in Liverpool it would be a different matter. He would put all thoughts of Siobhan out of his mind, what was she to him anyway, there were plenty other girls around who would be only too willing to accommodate his needs.

After the episode with Lord Bromley, Miss Hazel seemed to age. Her upset nerves had caused her arthritis to worsen. 'I'll soon not be able to get about, not even on my sticks,' she thought, as though talking it through with another person. 'I must do something about making provision for Sally and young Michael when I die,' she continued, recalling the fate of her estate should she not make a will. 'When I feel a bit better, I'll go up to see a solicitor in Chester.'

Both Sally and Miss Hazel had been surprised when Forster had called. Embarrassed by the hindsight of his former boldness he told them what had gone on between his Lordship and himself. 'I don't think he'll bother you again, he knows he's gone too far this time, after all his mother isn't alive to protect him.' Seeing Forster, it presented the opportunity Miss Hazel had been waiting for. She asked him if he could fix her a carriage to take her and Sally to Chester. She had some business to attend to.

So it was arranged. Miss Hazel, Sally and young Michael went off to Chester. She gave Sally some money and she sent her off shopping while she attended to her business. It was a real treat for Sally who hadn't been out of the village for years. She bought Michael some sweetmeats and he was as good as gold munching away while she looked in the shop windows at things she knew she could never afford. A familiar voice behind her made her go cold. 'Pretty, are they not? Pity you will never be able to afford such things.' Frozen to the spot, she could not speak. Michael looked up at Lord Bromley and offered him a sweetmeat. 'What a good looking little chap,' he said, ignoring the infant's outstretched hand.

'You leave him be!' said Sally, pulling Michael to her.

'Oh for goodness sake, I mean the boy no harm. All I want is for you to tell me where Siobhan has gone.'

'I don't know,' she lied.

'Come on, you must have some idea,' said Lord Bromley, slowly and deliberately taking out his purse.

'Ireland, she's gone back to Ireland,' said Sally, disorientated and frightened for Michael.

'Now I know that's not true,' he said with all the calm he could muster, counting out gold sovereigns from the purse into his hand. 'Would twenty shiny gold sovereigns refresh your memory?' Twenty sovereigns! It was a fortune and would be security for her and Michael's future. He saw her eyes fixed on the money. 'Not enough, hey? Let's see.' He counted out ten more. 'Now do you remember? I will not harm her, I promise you. After all, it's not as if you owe her anything, is it?'

Sally was in turmoil as thoughts raced around her mind. Thirty sovereigns. Through Siobhan she had lost Michael. Lord Bromley was right - she owed her nothing. Anyway Michael was with her and would protect her. She, on the other hand, would never get another chance like this. She held out her hand.

'Oh! Don't you trust me? Very well.' He poured the money back into the purse, and for a moment she thought he had changed his mind. Instead, he raised her hand with his and placed the purse in her palm. 'Can't have the money falling on the floor, can we?' he said as he tightened the grip on her wrist. 'Now where is she?'

'London, she's gone to her brother in London,' she said. Although his grip was hurting, she doggedly held on to the purse.

'Now come on, I've paid you for more information than that,' he said, tightening his hold still further.

'Dockland, Nellie Bell's boarding house in dockland,' she blurted out, tears from the pain now running down her face. The inquisitive Sally had found Miss Hazel's key to the tin chest and read Siobhan's letters.

'Thank you, Sally. Enjoy your thirty pieces - not silver, but it comes to the same thing in the end,' he said, letting go of her hand and laughing as he walked away.

Thirty pieces of silver! She knew what he had meant. She was a Judas, but Siobhan had been no friend of hers. With this money, she and Michael would not have to go to the workhouse when Miss Hazel died.

'You are in a happy mood,' Miss Hazel commented on the way home.

'Well it's been a nice day out for me and Michael. I've bought him some new clothes and myself a dress, second hand, but they've hardly been worn.'

'Well I'm going to tell you something that will make you even happier,' said Miss Hazel. 'I have been to solicitors, Dallow & Dallow, to make my will. You will be pleased to know I intend to leave the cottage and any money I have to you and Siobhan. The cottage cannot be sold without the other's consent. So, my dear, you and Michael have a home for as long as you like.' She beamed at Sally as she finished talking. Sally was shocked. She had never thought about ownership of the cottage, or that Miss Hazel had any money. Then the terrible realisation of what she had done dawned on her. In betraying Siobhan she had betrayed Miss Hazel and now, with what Miss Hazel had just told her, she need not have done it. Seeing Sally's face Miss Hazel said, 'Aren't you happy, dear?'

'Of course I am. It's just that I wasn't expecting it. No-one has ever looked out for me before. I don't deserve it,' she said with regret.

'Of course you do dear. Why, haven't you looked after me like a daughter?' said Miss Hazel, consoling her.

'Yes, I have,' thought Sally, then recollections of Mrs. Parker crossed her mind, hadn't she looked after her like a daughter?

CHAPTER 20
The Search

Lord Bromley had not felt so excited for a long time. He enjoyed a chase, and this was the chase of all chases, the search for Siobhan. He would get Forster to take him to a cousin up north, then stay a while before taking a carriage to London.

He had not been to London for a number of years, but now walking through its busy streets he had forgotten how stimulating the atmosphere was. Well dressed men and women paraded through Hyde Park. He was in no real hurry to find Siobhan – first he would have a little fun. Being the depraved person he was, he soon tired of the eloquent company in his Gentleman's Club, making his way eastwards until he found a reasonably clean tavern and booked a room there. He downgraded his flamboyant dress to a more modest attire, not wanting to draw attention to himself.

Yes! He was certainly going to have a bit of fun. At the manor everything he did was seen and was talked about by the village busybodies. Here he could do anything, be anybody he wanted. The one thing he thought he would never get used to was the stench of the streets, their gutters running with urine, excrement, dead rats, and maggots squirming in rotting carcases. No wonder people were dying from disease. Dockland was just as bad, but here the stench was replaced by rotting fruit, meat and fish. As the days went by the smell seemed a part of life and he ceased to notice it.

On every corner there were prostitutes for the picking, and his Lordship did some picking. After a while he began to tire of the ordinary whores – with his perverse nature he required more unusual amusement. He had become very friendly with a woman called Dolly. Following one of their bedroom encounters he said, 'Look Dolly. All this is very nice, but a fella like me has more exotic tastes.' Not put out by his request, and knowing her limitations, she pretended to give it some thought.

'I know what you want, Guv, a gent like you wants something a bit out of the ordinary,' she said at last.

'Could you help me, Dolly?' he said as he puffed at his opium pipe. The blue smoke drifted in front of his eyes as he languished on the bed. Dolly thought how he looked like an angel with those golden curls and creamy skin, but she had only to look into his eyes to see the devil in there.

'If you've the money, Guv, you can buy any pleasure you want, and Dolly knows where to shop for it.'

'Money's no object Dolly,' he answered, dreamily overcome with the drug. Dolly made enquiries at one of the famous brothels and found the Madam had girls and boys that would satisfy every man or woman's needs.

'Why the hell can't he come here?' the Madam asked with indignation.

'He is a very private Gentleman. He dresses a bit ordinary, but I think he is in disguise - maybe he is royalty, who knows! He's got plenty of money, that's the main thing,' answered Dolly.

Next day she knocked on Lord Bromley's door and on entering started to cough from the opium fumes. 'Caw! You'll have to get rid of this stink and get the room tidied up,' she said, waving her arms about. 'No high class girl could perform in this atmosphere. Cough her guts up she would! Don't the maid clean in here?'

'I do not want maids poking about. Can you clean the room up for me?' He tossed some coins on the bed. 'Then get some girls!'

He selected a white satin shirt, the smooth material against his body giving him a sensuous feeling. His black velvet breeches fitted tight against his well shaped thighs. He pulled on his shiny leather boots, the heel built up to give him extra height. Looking at himself in the mirror, he tied his red cravat and was well pleased with his appearance.

He sat waiting with anticipation. He was tempted to have a smoke, but he wanted to keep his mind clear, to savour every moment. After a while be became impatient. Where the hell was the girl? He reviewed mental pictures of what she may look like, ranging from a diminutive oriental girl to a big, fat bellied buxom wench.

'Enter,' he shouted in reply to a knock on the door. Nothing prepared him for the vision that appeared. A scarlet satin cloak enveloped the Negro girl from her shoulders to the floor. Dark eyes fringed with black curly lashes looked at him from below the tiny black curls that covered her well shaped head. She had high cheek bones and an aquiline nose. Her lips, like those of most Negros, were full, the scarlet rouge making them glisten like ripe plums.

An arm appeared from the cloak, her fingers drooping downwards as an invitation to kiss her the back of her hand, and displaying her nails extending like red painted talons. 'My name is Salome,' she half whispered in a husky voice.

He stepped forward, amazed to see she was equally as tall as he, despite his enhanced heels. 'Let me take your cloak,' he said softly. Politely ignoring him she turned away and undid the fastener, letting the cloak fall to the floor, leaving her completely naked. With an intake of breathe, Lord Bromley stepped back, his eyes taking in her majestic figure. The flames from the fire danced over her back, highlighting her curves. She slowly turned to face him. 'You are magnificent!' he said. She smiled, showing a perfect set of white teeth. 'Would you like a drink?' he asked, pouring them without waiting for her to answer. She accepted, the red talons suggestively curling around the stem. Lord Bromley lifted his glass in a toast, oblivious to her previous introduction. 'Your name?' he asked.

'Salome,' she said again in a voice that was both rich and husky.

'Salome,' Lord Bromley repeated. 'The name suits you.' He drank his wine with one swallow then started to undress. 'I feel positively overdressed,' he said in jest.

Salome stepped forward and started to unbutton his shirt. 'Let me help you. I like undressing a man, to me it is all part of sexual foreplay!'

This was a new experience for him. The women he had used and girls he had raped had all been too frightened to say anything. Her actions were slow and sensual, caressing his body as each garment was discarded. To remove his boots she guided him to the bed and gently pushed him down. Standing in front of him she held the heel with one hand and the toe with the other, then with a quick jerk the boot was off. Even with her long nails she expertly undid his breeches, further tightened by his erection straining at the material. Premature excitement had already made a damp circle on his white silk underpants. Pulling them down over his narrow hips she let her tongue follow her hands, licking at his bare flesh. It was all he could do to hold himself back from exploding. Now naked, he moved further onto the bed, making room for her. To his amazement, instead of taking a position where he could lie on top of her, she straggled across him. 'You have a fine body,' she said, stroking his chest. 'It will be a pleasure to make love with an Adonis like you!'

In her profession she was used to making men happy, be they fat, bloated or deformed. Those with obvious sores she had refused to lie naked with, being very proud of her magnificent body. No way did she want to catch anything that would mark it. Usually with these men they would have to be satisfied with a hand stimulation. But this man was different. His body was as perfect as her own - she was going to enjoy tonight. Even if she wasn't being paid handsomely for her services, she would have gladly made love to him. Before he realised what was happening, he was inside her, it felt hot and silky He couldn't stop himself from bucking like a stallion. Within seconds he had climaxed and flopped back onto the pillows. Embarrassed at his lack of self-control he didn't know what to do or say. He opened his mouth to apologise, but she put her hand over his mouth. 'Shush, don't say anything,' she said, 'We have all night. Rest a while, then we will really make love!'

They enjoyed each other through the whole of the night. The noise could be heard in the room below, but the tavern keeper knew better than to interfere when this particular Gentleman was entertaining. It was his business alone - he didn't care what this guest did, he was paying, and paying more than all the other guests put together.

The night finished with Bromley being made love to like he had never experienced before. Exhausted, they lay in front of the fire, their bodies glistening from sweat.

Lord Bromley awoke in a state of complete disorientation. For a moment, he could not think where he was, and he hurt, hurt all over. Blood had dried from the deep claw marks that covered much of his body. Then he remembered Salome. Where was she? With difficulty he stood up, blue marks starting to appear within the redness of the wounds, no doubt mirroring some of the discomfort his past victims had experienced at his hands. She was gone, only her musky scent remained. The mantle shelf no longer held the sovereigns he had counted out at her insistence when she arrived. He drank a large brandy and crawled into bed.

Exhausted, he slept until mid-morning. His body ached all over, he could hardly move. Dolly had certainly supplied a prostitute who was different from anything he had ever experienced before. The heavy warm musk smell that clung to his body reminded him of the previous night's activity. A feeling of nausea came over him. Immediately he went over to the jug and pitcher, and, although the water was cold, he scrubbed himself all over, trying to rid himself of Salome's odour.

Feeling hungry he walked to one of the many taverns. He never ate where he was staying, self-consciously believing all eyes were upon him. He wondered if he would see Siobhan today, but he didn't feel ready to go to the address Sally had given him. There would be time enough, but first he felt he must cleanse himself of his recent perversions. In his distorted mind he felt than an assignation with a virgin would be the answer. He did not have to go far looking for Dolly, having no idea that most of the time she had been following his movements, keeping just out of sight. Dolly was still curious that he may have been someone important, an idea reinforced by his readiness to part with whatever she said was the going rate for his particular request. The possibility of further money from blackmailing him was never far from her mind.

Dolly suddenly appeared from one of the side alleys. 'Hello Guv,' she said, careful not to address him as 'Sir' or anything more grandiose.

Surprised, he gave a start. 'Oh, Dolly! What are you doing skulking around? I hope you're not following me?' he asked in an annoyed tone.

'Certainly not, Guv,' she said, running along side of him. 'I live around here. Did I do good for you last night?'

'Yes, you did, but it is an encounter I do not wish to repeat. Perhaps next time, something more genteel, a virgin may be!'

'It'll cost you! Virgins are hard to find around here. She'll be young as well - if you don't catch 'em young they'm soon got at!'

'I can pay, you know that, but no tricks - it's a pure virgin I want,' he said, thinking it would remind him of Siobhan.

'Right you are, Guv,' said Dolly. She was about to run off when Bromley shouted after her.

'Not for a couple of days!'

'That Salome too much for you, was she?' Dolly thought to herself. The scratches on his face hadn't escaped her notice. 'She'll kill a client one of these days.'

Dolly had no problem finding a young girl who's mother, for the right money, would be willing to let her daughter spend the night with a gentleman.

'See that she is scrubbed clean. The gent can't stand filth - and dress her in these clothes,' said Dolly, throwing a bundle of clean white garments at the mother.

The girl was only eleven years old - in dockland that was old enough to go with a man. Her mother had told her what was expected of her, that it may hurt a bit at first, but after that it wouldn't be too bad. She was to do whatever the gentleman asked of her and not to make a fuss. If she was a good girl, a whole Guinea would be hers.

Accompanied by Dolly the girl arrived, dressed demurely in a white cotton dress and ankle socks. 'I thought I had better bring her myself as she's never been with a man before. She knows what's what, but you will be gentle with her, Sir, won't you?' said Dolly, as she left the room. She came back immediately. 'I'd better have the money now, like I promised her mother,' she said. Bromley counted the sovereigns into her hand. 'Better safe than sorry,' Dolly thought. 'You never know what state he'll be in when he has had his pleasure with her.'

The girl stood wide eyed with fear. Her mother had explained what was going to happen - after all, it was only what her father did to her mother and she seemed to like it. And she was to have a whole guinea if she was good! With this thought in her mind she smiled nervously at his Lordship. 'That's right my child, smile. There is nothing to be afraid of,' said Bromley as he poured two glasses of Madeira. 'Here drink this, it will relax you!' He led her to a chair near the fire. 'Now you sit there and drink the wine - there are chocolates in that dish, eat as many as you like while I go and get changed.' He went first to the door, locked it and removed the key. 'You never know, the child might run off,' he thought.

He emerged from the room he used for dressing wearing his scarlet satin house coat. He approached the child, but with the drink and the heat from the fire she had fallen asleep. He picked her up gently and laid her on the bed, gently removing her shoes and socks. He tried not to look at her calloused feet and thin bruised legs. The action of having her drawers removed awoke her and she tried to snatch them back up. 'Now, now, you know why you are here,' he said quietly. 'Didn't your mother tell you to do what I wanted you to?' With these words he met with no more resistance. She lay there, naked, her pathetic little body trembling with fear.

Stroking her barely formed breast buds, he murmured in encouragement, 'So firm and so white.' He teased her small pink nipples and they responded to his touch. He kissed her all over, savouring the sweet smell of her youthful flesh. He looked at the lack of pubic hair, and went to part her legs. She instinctively closed them tight, ignoring all the words her mother had said - she wasn't supposed to resist, she was supposed to be submissive. The blood started to rush to Bromley's head, anger filling his mind. He had tolerated enough of resistance with that Salome - she had used him, now he was the user. He tore off his house coat and straggled over the girl. 'Right, you won't open your legs, so perhaps you will open your mouth,' he said in anger. He grabbed her cheeks, forcing her mouth open and pushed himself inside. The child started to heave. 'Don't you dare be sick, you little whore,' he said thrusting in further. Retching, she was violently sick – the chocolates, the Madeira. He let out a disgusted cry and smashed his fist into her face, so hard it broke her neck. Now in one of his mad states, he did not notice she was dead. The animal in him took over and he used her as he had used Siobhan until, exhausted, he collapsed in the blood and vomit.

Bromley awoke, shivering. He reached out his hand and touched a cold body next to him. He recoiled in horror, re-living the night's events. He had killed the child. Now what was he to do? He would wait for Dolly, she would help him – after all, it was as much her fault as his, she shouldn't have brought this child to him. He wrapped up the girl in a sheet, then cleaned and dressed himself. The time seemed to drag. Eventually a knock came at the door. Dolly entered and put her hand to her nose - the smell was worse than the docks.

'What the hell's been goin' on?' she asked, looking at the blooded bundle on the bed.

Bromley sat down, his head in his hands, snivelling. 'It's all your fault. Why did you bring an inexperienced child here?'

'Here, don't you go blaming me,' she said indignantly. 'I only brought what you asked for.'

'What are we going to do, Dolly? The child is dead,' he said, pleading.

'What are WE going to do? Don't you mean YOU?'

'Oh Dolly! You have got to help me. I'll make it worth your while,' said Bromley.

'Worth my while, hey. Okay, but you'll have to help me - I can't do it on my own and we daren't trust anyone else,' she said, thinking of the money.

'You don't mean I'll have to stay here with this dead thing until tonight?'

The words filled Dolly with disgust. 'This dead thing is someone's child. Her mother will have to be paid off or she'll go running to the Peelers.'

'Yes, yes, I'll agree to anything, as long as you get me out of this mess,' he said.

'I'll bring some clean sheets. You clean the room up the best you can. That'll help you pass the time until I come back.' She left without waiting for an answer. Bromley vowed that if he got out of this mess he would go back to Little Chester. This was all Siobhan's fault, and she wasn't worth getting hanged for.

Dolly returned with a large sack in which to put the body - it would be less noticeable than a white sheet. Bromley put the child in the sack, and then made up the bed with the clean linen she had brought with her. 'If I were you, I wouldn't come back here after we have got rid of the body,' she advised.

'I was thinking the same thing myself. I'm leaving London altogether,' he said as he packed his belongings. As an after thought he asked, 'What did the mother say?'

'Haven't told her yet, but she will probably welcome one less mouth to feed. I've no doubt she'll pretend to be sad and say she'll be going to the Peelers, but when I point out she gave the girl to me, knowing what was going to happen, she'll change her tune. Mind you, Guv, she'll want payin!'

'Yes, yes Dolly' he said, tipping a pile of gold sovereigns on the table. 'That's all I have available - I must keep some money to get back home!'

Dolly scooped up the money. It would do alright, more than alright, she thought.

They crept down the back stairs. She made Bromley conceal the body under his cloak while she carried his bags, the noise of the customers in the tavern drowning their footsteps. 'Follow me,' said Dolly once they were outside. They weaved in and out of several alleys until they stopped near a quiet part of the river. 'Here, this will do. Pick up some of those big stones and put them in the sack. We don't want a floater on our hands.' Trembling, he did as he was bid. Dolly produced a piece of rope from her pocket and told Bromley to tie it around the top of the sack. They dragged it to the bank and heaved it into the river. A pattern of bubbles formed as the sack sank out of sight.

Dolly didn't wait to say goodbye. She wrapped her coat around her and ran as fast as she could away from this devil of a man. She had done wrong for sure, but now, with this money, she could make a fresh start.

Relieved it was all over, Bromley instinctively went to find a carriage, but, to his dismay, discovered this was not the sort of area where they plied for hire. He walked along badly lit streets trying to find somewhere he recognised. He felt very tired and decided to take some rest until it was light. He found a derelict shed in which he soon fell into a deep sleep.

The noise of the dockers woke him up. He crept out of the shed and began walking away towards the 'Dockland Inn'. 'Dockland? Wasn't that the place Siobhan had gone to be with her brother Michael?' he thought.

Out of curiosity he walked until he came to a row of Georgian terraced houses, all painted in bright colours. He entered a nearby tavern and ordered a breakfast and a beer. Beer seemed to be drunk with everything. Getting into conversation with one of the bar staff he asked if he knew of a clean lodging house in the area. The man named several, including Nellie Bell's. Bromley suppressed his immediate reaction.

'Which one would that be now?' he asked casually.

'It's the pink one, you can try if you like,' said the barman, 'but since the Irish couple came to stay she don't seem interested in takin' in anyone else.' Reinforcing his wish to be a fund of all local gossip the barman added, 'Now what would you be doin' in these parts?'

Lord Bromley was off before the barman got a reply. Concealed behind a stack of crates he watched the door of the pink house. His patience was rewarded when a handsome young man with black curly hair came out, followed by an elderly, tall, thin woman. He followed them at a safe distance. They hadn't gone far when the woman turned up one of the streets. 'Give my love to Siobhan,' the man shouted.

'What luck! She will lead me straight to Siobhan,' he thought, all intentions of going back to Little Chester forgotten. He walked quite a distance through winding streets and alleyways. Occasionally the woman would stop, gossiping to people she met. At last, she entered a square where traders were setting up their market stalls. Through the crowds he lost sight of her, then spotted her just as she was entering the doorway of a pawnbroker's shop. 'Now what?' he reasoned to himself. 'Is this where Siobhan is? Shall I go in? Better not. I'll wait here awhile to see if she comes out again, after all she may be just going to pawn something.'

After waiting a while, idling the time looking on stalls, there was no sign of her coming out of the shop. He entered a tavern in the square where he ordered a drink and sat watching through the window. He was rewarded when the door opened and out came the woman pushing a perambulator. Then another woman appeared, waving them off. His heart stopped as he caught his breath - it was Siobhan, more beautiful than ever. It was all he could do to stop himself from rushing out to her. No! He had come this far, so he must be patient a little longer. He must plan this properly, he thought, as he sipped his hot mulled wine. A baby! Was Siobhan married? If so, to whom?

After a while the barman began to look at him with interest, obvious that he was watching or waiting for someone. Curious, the barman walked over to him. 'Not turned up, has she?' he commented, with a mild air of sarcasm.

'Seems that way,' said Bromley standing up. He was just about to leave when he saw the woman with the perambulator return and enter the shop. 'On reflection, I'll wait a few more minutes. Another of your splendid beers, if you please, barman.'

The woman did not come out immediately. He knew he dared not risk going in the shop while she was there, but eventually he left the tavern and skulked about waiting. It was getting dark and the market traders were starting to pack up. Bromley was cold and stiff from hanging around. He was just about to leave and come back another day when the door of the pawnshop opened and out came the woman he had followed. Once again, Siobhan waved her off.

He waited a few minutes before entering the dark, musty shop. With slow shuffling steps Mr. Isaac came forward. 'How can I help you, Sir?' he said, wondering what a Gentleman like this was doing in his shop?

'You can help me by taking me to Siobhan,' Lord Bromley said through clenched teeth.

Isaac realised immediately who the man before him was. 'I don't know anyone of that name,' he said, trying to bluff.

'Don't lie to me, you old fool. I've seen her. Now where is she?' Bromley said, forcing his way past. Isaac tried to stop him, but he was too frail. Bromley brushed him to one side with the back of his hand, knocking him to the floor. As he fell, he caught his head on the counter and hit the floor with a bang, knocking him unconscious.

'What's the matter, Mr. Isaac?' asked a voice from upstairs.

Bromley raced up the stairs two at a time. Siobhan thought she was having an hallucination. 'No, it can't be,' she shouted.

'Oh, but it is. Your one and only Lord Peter Bromley,' he said, grabbing her by the arm. 'You didn't really think you could escape me, did you Siobhan?' Screaming, she tried to struggle from his grasp, but he was far too strong for her feeble frame. The commotion awoke little Amy who started to cry. Attracted by the noise Lord Bromley let go of Siobhan and went over to the cot. There he saw the child's golden curls – the very image of himself. For a moment he was taken aback, then picked up the child.

'No! No! Leave her alone,' said Siobhan, trying to grab the child from his arms. As if sensing something was wrong, Amy started to struggle to free herself.

'Oh! A fighter like her mother, hey,' laughed Lord Bromley. Siobhan began to fear for Amy's safety.

'Please put her down. Do what you like to me, but please don't hurt my child,' she pleaded. Gently, he placed Amy back in the cot, then went over to Siobhan.

'So I can do what I like to you, can I?' Stroking her cheek, he said in a quiet voice, 'I don't want to hurt you, Siobhan, I never did want that. You see, you are so beautiful that I cannot help but want you. Don't you understand that I love you. If you loved me in return, you, me and the child could be so happy,' he said, tears filling his eyes.

'I could have loved you once with your handsome looks and charming ways, but then you turned into the vicious animal you are.' she cried, tears falling from her eyes. 'Love you? I hate the very thought of you!'

'So be it!' he said, taken aback. He grabbed at her dress, tearing it down and exposing her naked breasts. Screaming, she tried to run downstairs, but he snatched at her hair, pulling her back into the room. Bromley threw her onto the bed and lifted her skirt. He was struggling to undo his breeches with one hand when he was dragged from the bed onto the floor. Before he could defend himself a big fist hit him in the face again and again. Blood spurted from his nose and mouth as a heavy boot kicked at his ribs. It all happened so quickly he hadn't time to cry out.

'Stop it! Stop it, John. You'll kill him,' said Siobhan, trying to pull Big John off Bromley's battered body. John moved back, only to take one more mighty kick at the body before him. This time it did not move - Lord Bromley was dead.

'Oh! My God! John, what have you done?' said Siobhan in a shocked whisper. They both stood there paralysed to the spot, gazing at the still body. Amy's cry brought them back to reality.

'Isaac, where is Isaac?' said Siobhan. Until now, she had not given him a thought.

'He's on the floor downstairs. I had to step over him to get to you,' said John, still in shock.

'On the floor?' repeated Siobhan as she ran downstairs. Cradling Isaac's head in her arms, she wept. John slowly came downstairs and, seeing Siobhan weeping, he didn't have to be told that Isaac, too, was dead.

'What are we going to do, Siobhan?' said John. The shock had reverted him back to his childish ways. Something had to be done, and done quickly.

'I'll go to meet Michael from work,' said Siobhan. 'You comfort Amy. Lock the door and do not open it to anyone until I come back.' John looked at her stupefied. She held his arms and shook him vigorously, hoping to bring him back to his senses. 'Do you understand, John?' she shouted.

Slowly he nodded. 'We'm in trouble, much trouble,' he said to himself as he locked the door after her.

Siobhan wrapped her shawl over her head and around her body, not wanting anyone to recognise her. With the river mist beginning to thicken it was difficult to pick out Michael. Dockers rushed past her, chatting and joking, until she recognised Michael's laugh. She shouted to him.

'Siobhan, what on earth are you doing here?' he said, going towards her. Putting her arm through his, she led him away from the other workers.

'Oh Michael, a terrible thing has happened. Lord Bromley...' She got no further.

'Lord Bromley, he's here? I'll kill the bastard!' shouted Michael.

'He's already dead. Big John killed him when he attacked me at the shop.'

'Good for him!' said Michael, not thinking of the consequences of this action.

'We'll have to get rid of the body, Michael. You'll help won't you?' she pleaded.

'Of course me darlin', haven't I always told you I'll look after you. Now tell me what happened?' he said. As they walked along, Siobhan related the recent events.

'Isaac's dead?' Michael repeated in shock.

Trembling, Big John let them into the shop. Michael went over to where Isaac lay and felt for a pulse. 'Holy Jesus, he's dead alright! The sooner we get the doctor the better, much longer and rigor-mortis will set in.'

'What about Lord Bromley?' Siobhan said.

'Holy Mary! I'd forgotten about that bastard. Where the devil is he?' questioned Michael. Siobhan nodded towards the stairs.

Michael saw Bromley's body and smiled. 'Couldn't have done better myself,' he said. 'The bastard deserved it!'

'What are we going to do with him?' asked Siobhan. Michael's reactions seemed oblivious to the fact that there was a murdered body on the floor.

'Be Jesus! Let me think.' They were silent while Michael considered his response. To Siobhan it seemed an age before Michael spoke. 'I've got it. First, we get Dr Round to look at Isaac and write out a death certificate - we'll keep his Lordship hidden in the bedroom. While I'm fetching the doc, John, you wrap the body in a sheet and find a sack and put him in. Better remove all his clothes as well. Yes, and shave his hair off - if anyone finds him he will be harder to identify. My God, I'm a genius!' Michael said with satisfaction. John nodded his head in agreement.

'What shall we do with the body afterwards?' said John, wondering if he had missed the main tenet of Michael's solution.

'By all the saints, I never thought of that?' Michael answered.

Then all three said in unison, 'Throw it in the river!'

'Now, John, don't forget what I have told you,' said Michael. He went over to Siobhan and put his arms around her. 'Don't worry, me darlin', Michael will look after you.' He meant it. As all the old loving feelings he had for her filled his heart he knew he meant it.

Siobhan and John worked in silence. Amy had fallen asleep, sucking her comforter. It was a good job that Big John was a strong chap, because Bromley was no lightweight. The rug that he had fallen on held most of the blood. It was taken up and hidden with the body. Siobhan looked for the odd spots of blood and wiped them away.

Siobhan heard a carriage stop and ushered John through the back door, signalling him to stay there. She opened the shop door to admit Dr. Round and Michael, who was trying hard to act as naturally as possible.

'A sad thing, hey, Siobhan. Do you know what happened?' the doctor asked, examining Isaac.

'I think he must have fallen. I was upstairs getting Amy to sleep and when I came down, that's how I found him. Oh! If only I had been downstairs, maybe I could have saved him,' she said with genuine tears falling from her eyes.

'He couldn't have been pushed, could he?' asked the doctor dismissively. 'Has the cash box been tampered with?'

'No, the shop was closed for the night, the door had been bolted,' said Siobhan without hesitation.

'Good girl!' thought Michael as he smiled at her.

'There you are then, he must have fallen and hit his temple. A tender spot the temple.' He wrote out the death certificate as he was speaking. 'Michael, I'll help you carry him to his chair, can't leave the poor chap here!'

'Except for the wound on his head he looks as if he is sleeping,' commented Siobhan.

The doctor, satisfied that nothing untoward had taken place, left the shop. Big John was called back in.

'Mother of Mary! Thank goodness you kept your head when he asked you if there might have been an intruder. Now for his Lordship - when the dockers are out of the taverns and the streets are clear, then we will move him.'

While they waited, Siobhan and Michael discussed what should happen to Big John. At times, when he wasn't quite himself, there was a chance he would let something slip. John stood very pale and still, listening, then he started to shake. 'Why, John, what's the matter?' said Siobhan throwing her arms about him, 'Were you cold out there?'

'I'm scared, scared of being found out and hanged. I must go away. If I stay here I know I'll give myself away. Mother can always tell when I have done something wrong,' he said, starting to cry like a baby.

'Hmm, and if you get caught we'll all get caught,' said Michael, now frightening himself. 'After all, we were all in this together. There is a way out! There is a ship sailing tomorrow for the Americas. I could get you a passage on that,' said Michael, thinking the sooner he's out of the way the better.

'Why, John wouldn't be able to manage on his own?' Siobhan said frowning.

At this, John straightened up. 'Of course I would!' then added, in a monotone voice, 'Anyway, I can't stay around here!'

'That's settled then,' said Michael. 'Tomorrow I'll get you a working passage.'

Between them they carried the body of Lord Bromley through the empty streets to a quiet part of the river. The weighed-down sack was thrown in, neither of them aware that this was in the exact spot Dolly and his Lordship had disposed of the murdered child.

John sailed for America the next day. He asked Siobhan to let his stepmother know, saying that an opportunity had come along, so he had taken it. Siobhan gathered as much money as she could spare, but John insisted that she gave it to his stepmother, because without his odd job money she would find it hard. As Siobhan said her goodbyes, she thanked him for all he had done for her. Pressing a sovereign in his hand, she added, 'Take this for luck, you never know when you will need it?' Giving John the money brought back memories of Miss Hazel and the money she had given her when coming down to London. All that seemed an age away. She hadn't written since she knew she was pregnant, feeling too ashamed and, strangely enough, Miss Hazel's letters had suddenly ceased.

Back in Little Chester Miss Hazel's health had taken a turn for the worse. She was now totally crippled by her arthritis and was confined to bed. Sally had been a godsend, seeing to her every need - even little Michael helped to fetch and carry. Miss Hazel knew she hadn't got long in this world, but she felt she could go to her maker with a contented mind. All her affairs had been put in order - the only thing that troubled her was that she would love to see Siobhan once more. It had upset her when her letters stopped coming, but she guessed she had her reasons. She knew she was alright, because Forster had asked his cousin to look out for her. Forster knew about the baby, but thought it better to say nothing. After all, if Siobhan had wanted Miss Hazel to know, she would have written to tell her.

With a shaky hand, Miss Hazel wrote a letter to Siobhan explaining that she had left the cottage and any residual money jointly between her and Sally. She told her how, when she had come to live with her, it had given her a new lease of life, that she loved her as she would a daughter, but deeply regretted that she had not protected her as she should have done. She hoped to be forgiven. She explained how Sally had been a godsend, and how her son Michael had been a joy. The letter ended with, 'Goodbye my darling Siobhan, Miss Hazel.' She put it in an envelope and addressed it, but did not give it to Sally to post. She still had reservations about Sally's loyalty. She put the envelope in the locked tin box until the doctor or Forster could post it.

That night, feeling she was ready to meet her maker, Miss Hazel shut her eyes and slipped away.

Sally read the letter. With Miss Hazel's money and the cottage, for the first time in her life, Sally felt secure and she did not want Siobhan coming and disrupting things. She never let Siobhan know of Miss Hazel's death.

CHAPTER 21
Changes

Isaac was buried in full Jewish tradition and Siobhan was amazed at how many people attended. The quiet clothes of Ginny contrasted with those of Nellie, over-dressed as usual in an outfit of black chiffon and satin. Her head was adorned with a cartwheel hat trimmed with ostrich feathers, making Doctor Round embarrassed to be seen at a funeral with such a flamboyant figure clinging to his arm.

Isaac had left instructions that, should anything happen to him, Siobhan was to go to his solicitors, where they knew what his requests were. Michael insisted on accompanying her to the solicitor's office. They were both taken aback by the enormous wealth Isaac had accumulated. He had left generous amounts to various people, but the bulk of it was left to Siobhan with a trust fund for little Amy. Siobhan went weak when she heard the amount she would inherit. A glass of brandy, that she would normally have refused, stopped her from fainting. Both Michael and Siobhan walked from the solicitors in a daze. 'Me darlin', you're set up for life now. Never again will your belly rumble for lack of food,' said Michael, thinking that if he hadn't rescued her she would still be living in a hovel. These thoughts, he knew, would be wise kept to himself.

Since the night Isaac had died, Michael had stayed at the pawnshop. He had helped Siobhan to arrange the funeral and sort out Isaac's papers. 'Michael, without your help I never would have managed. It's been so good of you, but isn't it time you went back to work?' said Siobhan, feeling guilty at taking up so much of his time. The statement took Michael by surprise - he had got used to having an easier life, and Siobhan had not been mean with money, paying him the same amount as if he had been working at the docks. He knew he must play his cards very carefully if he was to share in Siobhan's good fortune.

'You're right. I've spent more time helping you than I intended - but just to be on the safe side, I think I ought to still stay here until you have sorted out what you are going to do in the future,' he said feigning concern. 'Holy Mary! I wouldn't sleep easy in my bed at Nellie's knowing you were here all alone!'

A week later he arose early to go to the docks. Siobhan had packed his lunch as she had seen Ginny do. Off he went, whistling, appearing as if he was glad to go.

Siobhan felt very alone when he had gone, the place was so quiet. She had become used to Michael's cheery personality, and also his help in the shop. She felt she owed it to the memory of Isaac to keep open the shop he loved so much. Never before having had money of her own before, she couldn't get used to the fact that she would be working for pleasure, not necessity. However, by lunch time, she felt she could cope no longer with customers coming in and out. Amy seemed to need more attention than usual. Normally Ginny popped in around noon, but today, for some reason, she had not turned up. Siobhan had no idea that Michael had not gone to his job at the docks, but had wandered around wasting away the time.

After two hours, knowing Ginny would be up, Michael called in at Nellie's. Putting on a glum face, he let himself in the front door and walked into the kitchen. Ginny was busy preparing the breakfast. 'My, that smells good!' he said.

Ginny gave a squeal. 'Oh! Michael Rafferty, you'll be the death of me one of these days. What are you doing, creeping up on folk?'

'Sorry Ginny, didn't mean to frighten you. I've come for a bit of comfort, so I have.'

'Well, Nellie's still asleep, if that's the comfort you be lookin' for,' she said, grim faced.

'Holy Mother, Ginny. What sort of fella do you think I am? I've lost me job. I stayed away too long helpin' Siobhan, and they've filled me place!'

'Well you can't blame them,' said Ginny as she poured him a mug of tea. 'There's plenty o' men wanting jobs. I'm going over to visit Siobhan later.'

Michael acted surprised, not wanting Siobhan to know he had called at Nellie's. 'Didn't she tell you she would be out most of the day? She's got to sign some papers at Isaac's solicitors.'

'No, she didn't. I could have traipsed all over there for nothing. That girl has too much to cope with, if you ask me,' said Ginny, handing him a plate of bacon and eggs.

This was just the reaction Michael wanted, and heartily agreed with her. 'You're right there, Ginny. I would offer to help her with running the business, but she might think I was trying to run her life.'

'She could do with someone to help her, and someone she can trust. The time I do spare with her is getting too much for me. I ain't getting' any younger, neither is Nellie. By the way, although I've never agreed with you and her, she has really missed you not livin' here,' said Ginny, looking straight at him, then added, 'Nellie's been good to you.'

'Jesus, don't I know that, but what can I do? She's me sister after all. I can't leave her in the lurch, now, can I?' said Michael, acting concerned.

'If she could find herself a decent husband, that would solve the problem,' said Ginny, watching for Michael's reaction.

He threw down his knife and fork and exclaimed, 'Holy Mother. Ginny, don't you think she has had enough of men, what with that Lord Bromley and everything that's happened?' he said. The thought of Siobhan with a husband made him lose his appetite.

Ginny put down her own knife and fork. 'I suppose you're right, but you never know as time passes,' she said. 'Changing the subject, what's happened to that Big John who used to hang around? I ain't seen him about lately, and he wasn't at the funeral!'

Michael did what he was good at, concocting a story. 'Big John! Well, Ginny, this is between you and me - it's to go no further, Siobhan wouldn't like it.' All ears, Ginny gave the promise she had no intention of keeping.

'When he knew Isaac had died, John asked Siobhan to marry him. When she said she couldn't, he had one of his turns and hit her.'

A shocked look came on Ginny's face as she exclaimed, 'Oh! No!'

'I couldn't believe it meself. I was out at the time. I came back just in time, or I don't know what he would have done. Siobhan ran to me crying, and John ran out of the door - we haven't seen him since. Siobhan, being the girl she is, made me call at his stepmothers' who said he'd got a working passage to the Americas.' Michael smiled internally at the credibility of the story he'd made up.

'Well, would you believe it. I always thought there was something funny, the way he used to hang around.' She couldn't wait to tell Nellie.

'What's all the noise?' said Nellie, appearing from upstairs. 'Why Michael, how are you, my boy? Come and give Nellie a hug,' she said, holding out her arms. She enveloped him and whispered in his ear, 'The bed is still warm!'

Remembering Ginny's words of how good Nellie had been to him, he whispered back, 'Lead the way.'

Michael arrived back at the pawnshop, pleased to see it closed, fitting in with his theory that Siobhan was not coping. He found Amy and her mother fast asleep on the bed. Siobhan never looked more beautiful - if only people did not think of them as brother and sister, he could ask her to marry him. She awoke to find him staring at her. 'Oh, Michael, it isn't that time already, is it? I haven't cooked your supper,' she said, getting off the bed.

'It's only mid-afternoon – they'd given me job to someone else. I have been hunting for work until now and I'm worn out,' said Michael, looking downcast. 'There's just no jobs to be had!'

'Oh Michael! It's all my fault for keeping you here helping me.' Then a thought struck her. 'There is a job here if you want it. Being on my own all day, I realise that I can't manage to run the business and look after Amy.' He seemed to hesitate. 'Unless it's not manly enough for you?' she added.

'Holy Mother, I don't need hard work to prove I'm a man. Hard work only breaks your back. Siobhan, I will be pleased to help you. Didn't I always say, me darlin', I'd look after you.' Saying this, he took her in his arms and swung her around until their laughter woke Amy.

Michael took to working in the shop as if he was born to it. His easy Irish patter charmed not only the ladies, but the men as well. The shop was doing well, and Siobhan thought it only fair that Michael should have some of the profits, as well as a wage. For the first few months Michael still visited Nellie, taking her for a drink at the Pipers, then back to bed. However, she soon felt that Michael's visits came out of a sense of duty, and that their lovemaking had lost its ardour.

Working and seeing Siobhan every day rekindled the old feeling of love he had for her. She would look up and find him watching her. Looking into his blue eyes, she frequently felt a shiver go through her body.

Amy was growing bigger by the day. Michael and Siobhan would often take her to a quiet part of the river on a Sunday. They would laugh when passers by remarked how fair she was compared to her parents. 'Holy

Mother, I wish I was her daddy,' he started in all seriousness. 'Nothing has worked out the way I had planned for us. The only thing that's come good is that we are still together. You know, Siobhan, I fell in love with you the first moment I saw you in the potato fields. What a dirty little scrap you were, but all I saw was beauty under all the grime.' He turned her face to look at him. 'Now look what a fine lady you have become. I still love you, Siobhan, and I always will. You are my little darlin'.' With that, he pulled her to him and kissed her gently on the mouth. For a minute they stood staring into each other's eyes, their tears mingling as he pulled her to him again. To Siobhan, it was the sweetest feeling she had ever experienced, not vicious like Lord Bromley's kisses, but gentle, almost like little Amy's. Then the realisation came to her that she loved him, and always had.

Shyly she whispered, 'I love you, too, Michael.' Hand in hand they walked back to the pawnshop, every now and again giving a little skip of happiness. Although Michael longed to make love to her, he knew he must not rush. When the time was right it would happen. He still visited Nellie, but couldn't bring himself to make love to her. She thought the reason was that she was looking old and he no longer fancied her.

One day Nellie suddenly announced to Ginny, 'I'm selling all my properties. I've had enough of trudging the streets collecting rents. You and me are going to see the world before we are both too old!'

Ginny initially doubted her sincerity. 'And what's brought this on all of a sudden? It's not because Michael's not beddin' you anymore?' Ginny didn't mince her words - she had known Nellie too long to do that. 'There's plenty of others that would gladly take his place,' she added.

'Trust you to call a spade a spade,' said Nellie. 'There may be others, but I really cared for that boy. He was the first man to treat me with tenderness.'

'I hear the French are very tender and romantic,' said Ginny, trying bring cheer to Nellie.

'You could be right. France will be our first stop. You never know, Ginny, you might even find yourself a fella - I hear they like a more mature woman!'

'Ah, get on with you,' replied Ginny, though not averse to the prospect.

The properties were soon sold, all except for Nellie's own house - it would be there if ever they wanted to return. She asked Michael to keep an eye on it for her, and, if he wished, he could live there. Michael said he would be only too willing to look after the house, but Siobhan needed him, so he would stay at the pawnshop.

He was not sorry to see Nellie go. For a long time now he had felt uncomfortable when he visited her. Siobhan was very upset when she heard Ginny was also going. 'Oh! Ginny, I'm really going to miss you, you have been like a mother to me,' she said clinging to her.

'I'm going to miss you and little Amy. You have been the daughter I never had. You never know, we might be back sooner than you think, you know what Nellie's like,' said Ginny, with tears in her eyes.

Michael, Siobhan and Amy waved them off from the quayside. Nellie, in her colourful outfit, stood out from all the other passengers. 'By all the saints, I do believe Nellie's already got one of the stewards by the arm,' he said, laughing, thinking, it wouldn't be long before he's in her bed. Good old Nellie, she's certainly one on her own.

That night Michael sat thinking about Ginny and Nellie. Weren't they now the only two in London who thought him and Siobhan were brother and sister. Only Dr. Round knew the truth, never even hinting to Nellie over the years that they were not related. With Michael and Siobhan working together in the shop, most customers thought they were man and wife. At the weekend, if it was fine, he would suggest they go out for the day and he would propose to her.

The Sunday weather could not have been better. From early morning the sun shone, with not a cloud in the sky. Michael looked through the shop window. 'What a lovely day,' he said, 'Let's go by the river and take a picnic. What do you say, Siobhan? The fresh air will do Amy good.'

Michael was right - Amy would enjoy a day out. They packed a hamper and hired a carriage to take them out of the city and into the countryside, instructing him to return for them in the late afternoon. They ate the delicate meat sandwiches Siobhan had carefully prepared, plus a selection of iced cakes. Fruit tasted all the sweeter out in the sunshine. With a full stomach, Amy soon fell asleep. 'What a grand day,' Siobhan commented. 'I'll be sorry when the carriage comes for us.'

'It won't be for a while yet,' Michael said, producing a bottle of wine. 'We have plenty of time to celebrate.'

'Why, Michael Rafferty, you know I don't drink, and anyway, what would we be celebrating?' she asked, her big blue eyes twinkling.

'You might like a drink to celebrate me asking you to marry me – that's if you accept,' he said, kneeling down in front of her. 'Siobhan, will you be my wife?'

Startled, she exclaimed, 'Oh Michael, I couldn't.' Michael was taken aback. This wasn't the answer he expected.

'Why ever not,' he said in an angry voice. 'You say you love me, and God knows I love you – always have, right from the beginning. Is it that you think you are too good for me, now you have Isaac's money?' The thought had crossed his mind that if they were to marry it would be his money also.

Hearing the anger in his voice, she exclaimed, 'Of course not. I could never think myself too good for you. Where would I have been if you had not rescued me from that hovel?'

'What is it then?' asked Michael, this time tears filling his eyes. It seemed an eternity before she answered.

'After my experience with you-know-who, I feel I could never be a proper wife to you. I could not let you touch me….' She hesitated. '…that way.' Tears now filled her eyes.

'Me darlin', do you think that because I was your husband I would force myself on you? If it makes you feel better we could have separate rooms. Me darlin', when you make love with me it will be because you want to, you can be sure of that, so you can.' Michael finished with a nod of his head, to confirm what he said he meant.

'If you are sure, Michael, that is the way it will be, then I will be only too happy to marry you,' she said smiling.

He grabbed her to him. 'Me darlin', darlin', Siobhan. I swear I will make you the happiest woman alive, or my name isn't Michael Shamus Rafferty.

'I didn't know your middle name was Shamus?' giggled Siobhan, tweaking his nose.

The wedding was a quiet affair. The fewer people that knew about it the better, seeing they had been living together since Isaac's death. Dr Round had given Siobhan away.

'It's a pity Big John isn't here to witness this happy day,' said the doctor, then added thoughtfully, 'Funny how he suddenly decided to go to America.'

'He was always a bit odd,' said Michael, not wanting to be reminded of that episode. The doctor did not say any more, but he felt there was more to it than Michael or Siobhan were saying.

They celebrated the day with a special tea. Siobhan had made a small wedding cake covered with white icing and pink roses, and sporting a statue of a bride and groom in the middle. The doctor had bought a bottle of champagne that initially reminded Siobhan of the last time she had drunk it at the ball. However, not wanting to put a damper on the day, she concealed her true feelings and gently sipped from the glass. 'After all,' she thought. 'This is Michael's and my special day and with Lord Bromley gone, I no longer have anything to fear.'

At the end of the evening Siobhan felt uneasy. Had Michael meant what he had said about separate rooms? With a big yawn Michael stretched his arms and announced, 'Come on me darlin' time for bed!' Siobhan froze. Michael lit two oil lamps and, handing one to her, kissed her on the cheek. 'Off to bed, you must be exhausted after the excitement of the day?' he said, gently pushing her towards the stairs. She was still apprehensive, but at the top of the stairs he entered his own room, saying, 'Goodnight, my dearest love.'

Siobhan undressed, not knowing whether to be glad or sorry, and feeling a slight disappointment. Didn't Michael desire her? Perhaps he still thought of her as his sister? 'I'm being ridiculous,' she thought, as she put on her best nightdress. 'I really don't want him to make love to me.' She lay, pondering, well into the night.

Michael, on the other hand, lay in bed, filled with desire for Siobhan. It had taken all his self-control not to enter her bedroom and make love to her. He wanted her so much, but he knew he must be patient - she would come round in time when she felt she could trust him.

Next morning Siobhan waited for some recriminations from Michael - after all, it wasn't the way a wedding night should be! However, the more normal Michael acted, the more guilty it made Siobhan feel. This went on for a week, each night Michael going to his own room. Siobhan lay awake most nights thinking of him. 'What is the matter with me, aren't I desirable?' she thought, running her hands over her smooth slender body.

Michael was already up cooking the breakfast. 'Oh there you are, I was going to surprise my wife by bringing her breakfast in bed,' he said, laughing.

They sat together eating, Michael acting as if he was on top of the world, joking, making her laugh. Their merriment woke Amy who started to shout. Michael got up to fetch her, but Siobhan stopped him. 'No Michael. I'll get her, you finish eating your breakfast.'

That night, when Michael went into his room, he found Amy there in her cot, fast asleep. Perplexed, he went into Siobhan's room to find her standing dressed in a silk nightdress, looking at herself in the cheval mirror, the light from the oil lamp illuminating her beauty. He went over and turned her around to face him. 'Are you sure this is what you want?' he asked. Without words she guided him to the bed. He knew he must not rush things in case his actions reminded her in anyway of Lord Bromley's attack. He began by laying beside her on the bed, making no attempt to remove her nightdress or his own clothes. His kisses were as gentle as a brush from a butterfly's wing. He stroked her hair, neck and shoulders. When he reached her breasts he felt her small nipples harden to his touch, teasing them until she could stand it no longer. She prompted him to undo the buttons on her nightgown by undoing some of them herself. Michael removed his own clothes then pulled a quilt over them to keep out the cold. They touched each other, Siobhan shy at first, soon lost her inhibitions as she became aroused. Michael made love to her gently until they were both satisfied. Their emotions spent, they lay back, falling asleep in each others arms.

As dawn approached they made love again, this time Michael using all his sexual experience to give Siobhan the ultimate pleasure. She went from one ecstatic height to another, all her inhibitions having disappeared. For Michael this was a new experience - it was making real love because of the love he felt for Siobhan. Previously with other girls it had just been lust.

CHAPTER 22
The Fire

These were happy times. Days drifted into weeks, weeks into months, and months into years. The only thing that marred Michael and Siobhan's lives was that Siobhan had not conceived a child. Siobhan secretly thought that it was through the damage that had been done to her insides by Lord Bromley. Michael said he wasn't disappointed, after all he had Amy. 'And don't I look on Amy as me own daughter. Don't she call me daddy?' he would say if Siobhan brought up the subject. There has been no need to tell Amy that he was not her father. She adored him and he doted on her. At times, Siobhan felt jealous at the bond they seemed to have.

Amy had grown into a beautiful, tall, young girl, with creamy skin and long blonde curly hair. She featured Lord Bromley, even to the way she regally held herself. 'Thank goodness she hadn't inherited his nature,' thought Siobhan, for Amy was kind and caring with a gentle temperament.

Michael and Siobhan had sent her to a private girls' school. At first she felt out of place when one of the bullies had found out that her parents kept a pawn shop, but Amy's sunny nature soon won over the other pupils. As time went on her origins were forgotten.

Michael had settled down. He no longer felt the need to go off drinking or seeking the company of other men and women. He had all he wanted at home. Siobhan even had to insist that on Saturday evenings he went out to the local tavern to socialise with the market traders. When he returned, they all sat down for a special supper. Amy boarded during the week at St. Prides' School for Young Ladies, so when she came home at weekends it was always treated as a special occasion. Amy kept them amused with stories of the other pupils and teachers. She was a great mimic, taking off the voices of some of the upper crust girls. 'Honest, Mom, they speak as if they had a plum in their mouth,' Amy said, after taking off one particular girl.

Laughing until the tears ran down Michael's face, he said, 'Mary, Mother, if you don't take after your father for your story telling.' From the day Michael moved into Isaacs', he had looked on Amy as his daughter, the episode with Lord Bromley put well behind him.

He stood up and went over to the chiffonier to pick up a letter which he handed to Amy. 'We had a letter from Nellie and Ginny. Be Jesus, they don't half get about - they are in Monte Carlo now!'

Suddenly, his expression changed, becoming very serious. 'I've been thinking,' he said. 'Why don't we sell the business and go travelling like they've done, before we are too old to enjoy it?'

All merriment went from Siobhan's face as she repeated, 'Sell the shop?'

'Why not, we have enough money to last us 'til the end of our days. And it would give Amy a chance to speak some of those foreign languages she's been taught?'

'Can I come too?' chipped in Amy, full of excitement.

'Holy Mary! You don't think we'd leave you behind!' Still in shock, Siobhan said nothing. She watched Amy and Michael getting excited at the thought of the countries they would visit. 'Me darlin', what do you think?' asked Michael.

'I don't know, said Siobhan. 'The suggestion has completely taken me by surprise. What will we do when we have finished travelling? The money won't last that long, and I hope we are going to live forever, well, long enough to see our grandchildren at least!'

'Mother!' Amy exclaimed, blushing. 'Give me chance. I haven't even got a beau!'

All the happiness had gone from Michael as he sat there in silence. Uneasy, Amy didn't know what to say. Siobhan felt guilty, as if she had thrown a bucket of water on his plans. Then she started to smile. 'I know, we could rent the shop out for a year. It would always be here if we wanted to come back.' Both Michael and Amy looked at her, their hopes rising. It was eventually agreed that they would find a reliable tenant for the shop and a trustworthy rent collector.

Over recent weeks the shop had been particularly busy. Times were hard and people were pawning everything they didn't need, and sometimes things they did, often demanding more money for their goods. Then when the time came to redeem them, they hadn't the money. Siobhan felt sorry for the families with children, but as Michael had pointed out, their husbands drank most of their wages away. One particular family, the Howards, were always pawning working clothes for Sunday clothes and vice versa. Mr. Howard was a rough, hard-drinking docker. He reminded Siobhan of her father, and his children always seemed to be half starved. Many times, after the weekend, Mrs. Howard sported a black eye. 'I don't like serving her, Michael,' said Siobhan, sorting out some children's clothing. 'I feel so sorry for those children. It's a good job it's summer or the poor wee things would be frozen.'

Michael was watching her. 'I know what you're going to do - give those clothes to the Howards,' he said. 'It's no good Siobhan, they will only try to pawn them back to us. Next time Mrs. Howard comes in, leave her to me, me darlin'. I know you feel sorry for them, but if you do it for one, everyone will expect it!'

Sure enough, on Saturday morning Mrs. Howard walked in with the money to redeem Mr. Howard's weekend clothes. Michael sorted out the dark navy serge suit and white collarless shirt. It was the fashion, instead of clipping on a collar to the shirt, a scarf or muffler was worn around the neck. 'Don't forget the red muffler,' hissed Mrs. Howard through split lips.

Michael counted her money. 'Mrs. Howard, you know you haven't got enough money here to redeem all three items,' he said.

'Oh, Mr. Rafferty, please let me have them. I daren't go back without all three,' she said pleading.

'You need more money, Mrs. Howard. We gave you extra last week because you said you needed it for a sick child's medicine. We can't keep doing it. This isn't a charity?'

'Oh, don't say that, Mr. Rafferty. He'll kill me if I don't take all his clothes!' cried Mrs. Howard. Normally, Michael would have obliged, but it was getting beyond a joke. If every customer was treated leniently, they would soon have no business to sell, he thought.

'I'm sorry, Mrs. Howard. If I do it for you, everyone will expect it. Take the suit, that's all you have the money for!' Mrs. Howard ran from the shop, the suit over her arm. Within minutes, the door flung open and Mr. Howard stomped into the shop.

'Where's the rest of my bloody clobber?' he said, slapping his fists on the counter.

'Look Mr. Howard, I've explained to your wife, no money, no clothes!' said Michael trying to keep his temper.

Mr. Howard went red in the face and started to shout abuse at Michael. 'Why, you Irish pig, who the hell do you think you are, coming over here taking our jobs? Gimme me clothes, or I'll tear your bleeding face off.' Michael stood firm, saying in a calm monotone voice. 'No money, no clothes!'

Howard threw some money at him and grabbed the shirt and muffler. 'I'll see you pay for this, Rafferty. Mark my words, you'll regret this day!' He flung open the door and charged into the street.

Siobhan appeared from the back of the shop and asked Michael, 'What was all that arguing about?'

Michael tried to make light of the matter, saying casually, 'Oh, it was just Howard getting excited about the cost of redeeming his clothes. He paid up in the end though!' He didn't mention the threat Howard had made.

He didn't take the threat seriously. Feeling light-hearted about their forthcoming holiday, he went to the Tavern as usual, not noticing Howard lurking in an alleyway. Howard waited until the market square was deserted. Most people on a Saturday night either went out drinking or had a grand Saturday supper to end a hard week of working. Carefully, Howard poured paraffin through the letterbox of the pawn shop, soaking the wooden door and floor, and then drenched the window sills. He lit a strip of paper and pushed it through the letterbox. Soon, the whole of the front of the shop was ablaze.

Siobhan and Amy were upstairs. They always took particular care of their appearance, making their Saturday night suppers a special occasion. Amy was the first to smell the smoke. Opening her bedroom door onto the landing, to her horror she saw the downstairs engulfed in flames. 'Mother! Mother!' she shouted, crashing open Siobhan's bedroom door. There was no need to say anything more - Siobhan herself could smell the burning.

'Oh my God, Amy, what on earth shall we do? I know, pour water over a blanket. We'll try to battle through the flames to the back door!' They doused a blanket with the water from the jug and pitcher, but it was hopeless. The heat was too intense, the bright orange and red flames licking at everything burnable.

'It's no good Mother, let's shout for help from the windows.' With a great effort, they prized open the sash window. 'Help! Help!' they shouted.

Already people had gathered and had made a human chain, passing buckets of water down the line, hoping to douse the flames. 'Hold on, Mrs., we've sent for the fire engine, it should be here any minute,' said one helper.

Just then the fire engine's bell could be heard ringing. The horse drawn vehicle came tearing into the square, the horses hooves slipping on the wet cobbles. To stop the horses bolting they wore blinkers to prevent them from seeing the fire, and the strength of several men to hold them still. The fire hoses were unwound and water pumped through.

Siobhan and Amy were hanging out of the window gasping for air. 'Shall we jump, mother?' asked Amy in desperation.

'We will have to take the risk of killing ourselves. That way is better than being burnt alive!' answered Siobhan.

From the back room of the market tavern Michael heard the rumpus. 'Holy Mother, what's all the racket? What's goin' on!' he said

'Your bloody shop's on fire, that's what, and your wife and daughter are trapped inside!' said the man, dragging at Michael. When these words sunk in, Michael let out a howl and ran from the tavern as fast as his legs could carry him. From the light in the sky there was no need to question if the man was telling the truth. Pushing his way through the crowd, Michael could see Siobhan and Amy hanging from the upstairs window, calling frantically for help.

'Siobhan,' Michael screamed, waving his hands.

Siobhan looked down to where the voice came from and waved back, shouting 'Michael, Oh! Michael, help us!'

Before anyone could stop him, Michael ran through the burning door of the shop. The water had doused the flames from the stock, but the wooden beams still burned. Rushing to the back kitchen where the fire was still raging, he went to pump water into the sink. He screamed as his fingers touched the hot cast iron handle. Wrapping his scarf over his hand he started to pump furiously, putting in the plug to fill the sink to the top. He wanted to rush up to Siobhan and Amy, but he knew he wouldn't stand a chance if he didn't protect himself from the hungry flames that were licking up the staircase. He soaked his hair and doused his coat in the sink. With the coat over his head he ran up the blazing staircase. He had avoided being burned, but his clothes were beginning to smoulder. 'Siobhan!' he shouted.

She and Amy came running from the bedroom. 'Michael, Michael,' screamed Siobhan as she snatched the coat from Michael and throwing her arms about him.

'Enough of that, me darlin', we must get you out of here before the staircase burns through. Is there any water in the pitcher?' said Michael.

'We have already used it. Here, this blanket is still wet.'

'Cover both your heads with it and follow me,' shouted Michael.

Siobhan looked at the red and orange flames devouring the wooden stairs, some of them already collapsed. 'We'll never get through that wall of flame,' she screamed.

Michael turned to her and said, 'Me darlin' we have no choice. Now follow me and keep that blanket over the both of your. Right, now, come on as quick as you can'. Siobhan could hardly breathe with the heat, and could smell the singeing of human hair. Miraculously they reached the kitchen. 'That's me girls, not far to go now. But be careful of the falling beams!' said Michael, pushing the two of them before him.

The charred debris crunched under their feet as they made their way to what was left of the shop doorway. The fresh air stung Siobhan's nostrils as she stepped from the shop. 'We are safe!' she said. It was then she realised Amy was not behind her. Looking back into the flames she saw Amy had fallen and Michael was helping her up. 'Amy, Michael!' she screamed, turning to rush back.

A fireman grabbed hold of her. 'One of ours will get them,' he said as he waved a man forward. Michael all but threw Amy towards the fireman, and in doing so fell himself. Stumbling to his feet Michael started to follow, but one of the burning beams fell, knocking him to the floor.

'Dad!' screamed Amy. 'My dad, my dad!'

Another firemen rushed in to free him, but it was no use, the beam was too heavy. Another two came to help lift the burning beam. Siobhan and Amy were crying and screaming, 'Get him out! Get him out!'

Eventually Michael was freed, but his body had been crushed and badly burnt. As he lay on a make shift stretcher, Siobhan stroked his blackened face. 'Michael, Oh Michael!'

His eyes opened. His thick lashes had been burnt to stubs, but his blue eyes still managed to shine as he whispered through blistered lips, 'I told you I'd look after you, me darlin', didn't I?' He tried to smile, but he hadn't the strength. Siobhan watched as the sparkle slowly faded from his eyes. Michael Rafferty was no more.

CHAPTER 23
Going Back

Without Michael, Siobhan's life seemed empty - he had been with her since she was fifteen years old. Now, although she had Amy, life seemed to lack purpose. She and Amy, having lost the shop, had moved into Nellie's boarding house. Siobhan could not ask her permission because she had no idea where she and Ginny were. Sending a letter to their last known address, she informed them of Michael's death after saving them both from the fire.

Luckily, the shop's takings had been banked the day before, but all the linen and clothes had been burnt to a cinder. Most of the china had cracked with the heat, and the melted jewellery had been stolen by scavengers. With every day that passed Siobhan seemed to withdraw into herself. Amy realised she must do something before she lost her mother altogether. The idea suddenly came to her. 'Mother, why don't we go on that holiday we were planning before father died? I'm sure he would want us to,' Amy pleaded.

'Oh Amy. It would not be the same without your father,' Siobhan said wistfully. Gradually, Siobhan began to reflect on Amy's suggestion, thinking that she wasn't being fair to her daughter. After all, she was still young. She should be happy, not dragged down by her mother's sorrow. The next day she sprung the surprise. 'You're right Amy, your father would not want us moping around. We will go on a journey by sea - not a long one like Nellie, just for a month.' So it was agreed. Amy had lots of fun choosing the clothes that they would take with them. Siobhan's heart wasn't in it, but for Amy's sake she tried her hardest to be enthusiastic.

On the ship, Siobhan remembered the old rusty wreck that she and Michael had boarded to cross from Ireland to England. This ship was quite different, like a floating hotel. Their cabin was luxurious. The floor was covered in thick red carpet, and the windows had matching velvet drapes. Each mealtime was a banquet, with every type of food you could imagine. Both Siobhan and Amy started to put on weight, unable to resist such wonderful delights – but not the wine, that was one thing they chose to leave alone. 'If we put on any more weight we will not be able to get into our clothes,' said Amy in disgust, trying to button up her bodice.

'Then we will have to buy some more,' answered Siobhan with a laugh, realising that for the first time in ages she was actually enjoying herself.

All the passengers wanted to know who they were. Conversation stopped as they entered the dining room, for they made a stunning pair, Siobhan with her jet black hair and Amy with her blonde curls. No-one could believe they were mother and daughter. Except for a few character lines, Siobhan had not aged at all. The men on board, whether young or old, tried to flirt with them, even the ship's crew. Every evening the Captain insisted they sat at his table, giving the excuse that two women on their own should be looked after. At bedtime they would giggle like two school girls over the day's events.

Many times Siobhan thanked God that Big John had saved her from having an abortion, and for the joy this girl had given her. Siobhan was afraid that all the attention Amy was getting would go to her head, but she need not have worried - Amy was far too sensible to be fooled into thinking they meant it.

'Aren't you attracted to any of the young men, Amy?' Siobhan asked.

'Mother, they are all very pleasant and I am flattered, but when I fall in love it will be with someone like my father,' Amy answered wistfully. If only she knew who her real father was, she wouldn't think that way, reflected Siobhan with a level of guilt. She must never find out his true identity - Michael, Nellie, Ginny and herself had agreed that years ago.

The time was drawing near for the end of the holiday. Siobhan's enjoyment had taken away some of the sadness of losing Michael, but now she must think of what they were going to do in the future. The money that had been saved would not last forever. They had lost a lucrative business in the fire, and this excursion, however enjoyable, had cost a fortune. Amy must have read her thoughts, because she asked, 'Mother, what are we going to do when we get back? Stay at Nellies?'

'I've just been thinking about that very thing! We can't keep staying at Nellies, it isn't ours. In any case, there's a chance she will tire of travelling and want to come home. Amy, although we're not short of money, it is a limited amount and will soon dwindle, especially in London. How would you like to go back to where your father lived when we came to England – Chester?' She didn't mention Little Chester. 'I could buy or rent a cottage and perhaps we could both find work. Who knows, I might even open a pawn shop there,' said Siobhan, the idea growing stronger in her mind.

'I'll find work mother, you have worked hard enough all your life, it's time for me to put to use the schooling you have given me,' said Amy with conviction.

The journey back to Chester brought back painful memories for Siobhan. Seventeen years previously she had travelled from Little Chester to London, racked with pain from the rape ordeal at the hands of Lord Bromley. How she had survived without going out of her mind she didn't know, but she must not think of those depressing times, after all there had been plenty of happy ones. She regretted not keeping in touch with Miss Hazel. She had tried, but was too ashamed to tell her about Amy. When she didn't hear from her she had let the correspondence lapse altogether. She supposed that by now Miss Hazel must have passed away, although she was never sure of her age. Her thoughts were interrupted by the shouting voice of the coach driver. 'We're at Chester, all off.'

How quiet everything seemed in comparison with the hubbub of London. Amy remarked on it immediately, but Siobhan replied, 'This is positively noisy, compared to some of the little villages.' They had brought only a small amount of luggage with them, the rest would follow when they had found somewhere to live. They booked into a hotel, feeling tired after their journey, and it was decided to wait until the next day before looking around.

Siobhan's first call was to Dallow and Dallow, the firm of solicitors that Miss Hazel had used. Of course, they would not recognise her because Miss Hazel had always insisted on visiting their office alone, but Siobhan felt she could trust them, as Miss Hazel had done. For some unknown reason she felt quite nervous sitting in the reception, waiting to see one of the partners. Sensing her mother's feelings, Amy clasped her hand, saying, 'Everything's going to be alright mother, we have quite a bit of money, enough to secure us a small house or cottage.'

When they entered the office of young Mr. Dallow he hardly bothered to look up from his books, indicating with his quill for them to be seated on two stand chairs by the wall. He was sick and tired of the Irish pleading poverty. The name 'Mrs. Rafferty' said it all - probably being sued for bad debts.

'Well, Mrs. Rafferty,' he started, emphasising the Irish surname. He was just about to ask what their problem was, when he looked up and saw two of the most beautiful women he had ever seen in his life. Words stuck in his throat and it took a full minute for him to recover his composure. Immediately he was around the other side of his desk arranging two leather-bound seats. 'Do come and sit here, my dear ladies. Smith, bring in a pot of tea for Mrs. Rafferty and ...' He hesitated.

'Miss Amy Rafferty, my daughter,' said Siobhan, answering his unspoken question.

'Would tea be alright, or perhaps a light sherry?' he asked, bending over backwards to accommodate them.

'Tea will be fine, Mr....?' It was Siobhan's turn to cause mild embarrassment, as the young man had not had the manners to introduce himself.

'Oh! Mr. Ronald Dallow at your service,' he said nervously, realising his mistake in assuming his new clients would be a pair of Irish tinkers. He now observed that their clothes were of the finest quality, and could see breeding in the daughter's face. She reminded him of someone, but for the moment he couldn't think who.

Siobhan explained her situation, that, although not without means, she could not afford to waste the money they did have. Although young Mr. Ronald listened to what Siobhan said, he couldn't take his eyes off Amy - the delicate way she held her tea cup, so gracefully. He had immediately fallen in love with her. Pulling himself together, he attended to the primary matter of Mrs. Rafferty, that of finding a house or cottage at a reasonable price. As for her running a pawn shop in Chester, it was unthinkable, not without a man at her side. He surmised that, in all probability, she had married beneath her, with her husband running the business. He shuddered at the thought of this delightful creature mixing with the ruffians that frequented such places. He had great difficulty in keeping these thoughts to himself. 'First things first, Mrs. Rafferty, we must find you somewhere to live. I will arrange for your money to be transferred to a bank in Chester. As for employment, I come in contact with lots of influential people, I'm sure we can find a position for Miss Amy. Teaching the piano, tutoring children of the upper classes - I take it someone as genteel as yourself is qualified to take on such tutoring?' he said. He probably didn't mean to sound condescending, but his manner grated on Amy.

Not having spoken before, Amy put on an exaggerated haughty voice. 'Of course, Mr. Dallow, I was educated in London at the Prides' School for Young Ladies.' Siobhan hid her amusement, knowing Amy was putting on the clipped voice for Mr. Ronald's benefit. But Ronald Dallow was far from being put out - he was highly delighted, much to his father's dismay that his son was a snob. He said he should have some news for them in two days time, and, if permitted, he would collect them from their hotel and discuss it over dinner. Siobhan would have liked to decline his offer, realising the pompous sole he was, but if he could find Amy or herself employment it would be sensible to accept his invitation.

Over the next two days Ronald Dallow, spurred on in feverous anticipation that a relationship might develop with Miss Amy Rafferty, did his utmost to find a dwelling and employment for them. He was successful in two out of three of his tasks. Burning with excitement, he picked them up from the hotel. At the sight of Amy, he felt himself overcome with emotion. He had never seen anyone look so beautiful - the word beautiful seeming inadequate to describe the picture she made. She was dressed in a pale green silk dress, trimmed with a darker green velvet, bringing out the colour of her eyes. She wore a cloak of the same material as the velvet trim, and this was lined with the same pale green silk of her dress. The bodice had a sweetheart neckline that showed the swelling of her ripe young breasts. Minute buttons went from the neckline to her small waist, which was exaggerated by pin tucks. Her golden hair fell loose in waves and curls that reached way down her back. It glinted in the light from the hotel fire.

If the sight of Amy wasn't enough, Siobhan looked equally breathtaking - dressed in pale cream trimmed with dark blue. The cream taffeta contrasted with Siobhan's hair, which after her thirty-six years was still blue black and as abundant as Amy's. Being older, Siobhan wore her hair in a chignon at the nape of her neck, and covered in a net decorated with seed pearls. Ronald Dallow had never felt so proud in his life, or for that matter never would again, as he escorted one on each arm into one of Chester's finest restaurants. He hoped that some of his acquaintances would see him. He had few friends - from an early age his life had revolved around work.

As they entered, all eyes were upon the contrasting pair, one so dark and the other so fair. The manager stopped what he was doing and rushed to greet them. Ronald Dallow had never received such attention. The restaurant was lavishly furnished with expensive furniture and drapes, huge ornate guilt mirrors adorning the walls. Siobhan, catching sight of their reflection, could not help but feel proud, and thought how far she had come from her early days in the potato field. She did not dwell on these thoughts - tonight she and Amy were going to enjoy themselves at the expense of the pompous Ronald Dallow. 'I hope you have some good news for us, Mr. Dallow,' asked Amy.

'Ronald, please, you must call me Ronald. I have only had your acquaintance for a few days, but I feel we have become friends. The answer to your question is yes. I have what I consider good news for you, very good news indeed,' he said in an excited high pitched voice that almost became a squeak. Wanting to hold their attention for as long as he could, he said he would tell them his news over coffee. Siobhan and Amy got through the meal with little effort, not having to contribute to the conversation. Ronald Dallow was in full flow, and all they had to do was agree with him. Amy, out of devilment, kept nudging her mother's foot at certain ridiculous statements that the stupid man was saying. Eventually, when he had exhausted the topic of himself, he announced, 'Now the good news. I have found Miss Amy a post as governess to the children of Lord Ernest Bromley at the Manor.' He didn't see Siobhan's face turn deathly white. 'They are aged just four and five, so they will only need the basic teaching, for which I am sure you have the qualifications, Miss Amy?'

'Yes, yes, of course Mr. Dallow.' She couldn't bring herself to address him as Ronald. 'At the school in London we were tutored not only to be ladies, but to earn our own living, if the need arose.'

'And now the next bit of good news, there is a cottage at a reasonable rent not far from the Manor in the village of Little Chester.' He beamed as he sat back in his chair, thumbs in the armholes of his fancy waistcoat.

Siobhan could not speak. Amy, on the other hand, was delighted, but noticed her mother's silence. 'Aren't you pleased, mother?' she asked. Siobhan could give no reason for her objection without telling of her contact with the Bromleys. After all, perhaps this was her destiny, that she should always be connected with Little Chester and the manor.

Breaking away from her thoughts, she answered. 'Of course I'm pleased dear, I was just taken by surprise that Mr. Dallow could solve two of our problems so quickly.'

Once again Ronald Dallow beamed with satisfaction. 'Unfortunately, I have not found a situation suitable for you, Mrs. Rafferty.

'Mother has no need to work if I am earning,' said Amy, reaching for her mother to reassure her. 'I trust the salary will be adequate?'

CHAPTER 24
The Manor

Ronald Dallow had arranged an interview for Amy at the Manor the following week. At the same time they could also view the cottage. He said he would escort them, making every excuse to be in Amy's company. 'That man is so boring, I cannot wait until we are settled and there will be no need to endure his company,' Amy said, pulling a face. Siobhan, pre-occupied with her own fears at going back to Little Chester, didn't answer. She had asked Mr. Dallow if there were any other positions for Amy, and if there were other cottages vacant other than in Little Chester. He had answered, in no uncertain terms, that the position at the Manor and the convenience of the cottage being so near were the best that he could find. Amy had thought it perfect, providing Lord Bromley found her suitable, and if the cottage wasn't in good condition they could soon get it put right.

So there was no arguing, unless she was prepared to tell Amy the truth about her experience at the Manor and her connection with Little Chester. Maybe one day she would, but not for a long, long time.

Siobhan had to stop herself from shaking as they approached Little Chester. It seemed to her that it was only yesterday that she went to the village shop on errands for Miss Hazel. She wondered if Mr. & Mrs. Gibbs still kept it.

The carriage travelled along the road that ran alongside the high Manor wall, then it turned off down a narrow lane. After a short distance it stopped.

'We are here, ladies,' announced Ronald.

Both Siobhan and Amy looked in wonder at the fairy-tale cottage upon which the sun was shining. It was built from grey stone with a dark grey slate roof. As they walked up the paved path the scent of rose bushes filled the air. Three steps lead the way to an elevated wooden floor porch surrounded by a white balustrade. An old rocking chair broke the silence as it gently rocked back and forth in the slight breeze.

Mr. Dallow unlocked the black painted wooden door to reveal a large kitchen-dining area, very much like Miss Hazel's cottage. Instead of one bedroom, there were two fairly large ones, each opening from the kitchen. A veranda at the back housed a water pump and a brown stone sink. In the back garden was an overgrown lawn that led to a small fruit orchard. The garden front and back needed tidying up, but one could see that it had once been loved. Siobhan, even with her reservations about living in Little Chester, was won over by this idyllic cottage. 'Do you think it will suit you?' asked Dallow.

'More than suit, Mr. Dallow, it is perfect!' said Amy, not waiting for her mother to answer.

'That's settled then. Tomorrow you have an interview at the Manor,' he said addressing Amy.

Siobhan declined to go with her, making the excuse that, as all their furniture had been burnt in the fire, she would be shopping for essential items like beds, linen, pots etc. Ronald Dallow quickly offered Amy his services. Much as she would have loved to decline, she felt too nervous to go on her own.

Next day she dressed in a simple gown of grey linen trimmed with white lace. Even in the plain dress and her glorious hair scraped back, she still looked as beautiful as ever. Ronald Dallow was proud to be escorting Amy to the Manor.

Amy was shown upstairs to the nursery by the housekeeper. To greet her was Lady Bromley and her two children. Feigning shyness, they hid behind their mother's skirt. Gently pulling them forward, Lady Bromley said, 'Come children, do not pretend you are shy, we all know what little devils you can be.'

Lady Laura Bromley was small with dark hair and an olive complexion, large brown eyes dominating her pretty face. Amy thought she had a foreign look about her. Lady Bromley immediately put Amy at her ease by sending for a tray of tea. She also ordered that Mr. Dallow be offered tea in the library, where he occupied his time sifting through books, hoping to find something that would be of use to him.

The children were introduced to Amy - Thomas, the elder, and his sister, Elizabeth. Amy could see that although she was the younger, Elizabeth was the boss. Both had dark hair and olive skin, but although the girl resembled her mother, the boy's features were more angular with high cheek bones. One could see that, when he grew to be a man, he would be a very handsome fellow.

Lady Bromley questioned Amy about what qualifications she had to tutor her children. Amy omitted to tell her that her parents had owned a pawn shop, not that she was ashamed of it, but she felt Lady Bromley would not approve. Instead, she said her parents were in drapery, which was not a complete lie.

The children, knowing the reason she was there, tested her out by asking her childish questions. When it became obvious that they had taken to her, Lady Bromley made the decision that she would give Amy a month's trial and she would start the following Monday.

Ronald Dallow, nosey by nature, managed to open the large roll top desk that stood in the corner of the library. Looking through the drawers he found some old letters regarding the disappearance of Lord Peter Bromley. It had been assumed he was dead, and after seven years was declared so. His next in line, cousin Ernest Bromley, inherited the title, the Manor and its land. Ronald remembered there had been much speculation when Lord Peter Bromley had disappeared. It was rumoured that he had gone completely insane and was locked in an asylum far away. Finding nothing else of importance he closed the desk. He was getting bored - it seemed an age since Amy had gone up to the nursery. Opening the door he went into the entrance hall, hoping he could hear some sound to indicate the interview was at an end. His eyes were drawn up the wide staircase to a large portrait on the wall of the first landing. He mounted the stairs to get a closer look - it could have been a portrait of Amy, the likeness was uncanny.

'Unbelievable!' he said to himself. Just then Amy and Lady Bromley appeared from the floor above. Being too late for him to return to the library, he had no alternative but to stay where he was. 'You will have to excuse me, Lady Bromley, but my attention was arrested by this portrait of the late Lady Bromley. So like Amy, don't you think?' he said, hoping to take the attention off his wandering around.

Annoyed at the impudence of the fellow – she had already taken an instant dislike to him – she did however look at the portrait, and then at Amy. 'Yes, I can see there is a slight resemblance, mainly the colour of the hair,' she said in agreement. She turned away to address Amy. 'I will not be here when you arrive on Monday, but Nanny will show you around.'

On the way back, and feeling very pleased with himself, Dallow said, 'So you got the position then?' He hoped Amy would be grateful to him. Pre-occupied with thinking of her likeness to the portrait, she did not answer.

Excited, Amy enthused to her mother about the children and Lady Laura Bromley and how pleased she was at getting a month's trial, but Siobhan felt very uneasy about the situation.

While Amy was at work, Siobhan was busy decorating and furnishing the cottage. Not wanting to spend their savings unnecessarily, she visited the second-hand shops for pieces of furniture that could, with a little care, be made to look like new again. There was an auction at a farm within walking distance, so she went along.

The day was sunny and the auction had attracted quite a crowd. Bric-a-brac was amongst the first of the lots to be auctioned. Siobhan managed to buy some quality pieces of china, having learned the quality and value from her time with Isaac. An oil painting of potato pickers in an Irish field came up for auction, reminding Siobhan of her humble beginning and feeling she must buy it, no matter what it cost. The artist was well known for his Irish landscapes, with quite a few dealers making initial offers, but as the bidding got higher, one by one they dropped out until there was only Siobhan and another gentleman left. The other bidder was behind Siobhan, so she couldn't see who it was - she knew he was a gentleman by the sound of his voice. The man looked at the petite figure in front of him, curious to see the face of this person whose black hair hung in curls past her waist. The gentleman graciously dropped out of the bidding, letting Siobhan purchase the painting. The auctioneer closed the bid. 'Sold to Mrs. Siobhan Rafferty.'

At the end of the auction she collected her goods. Outside, several carts and carriages plied for hire, hoping to take buyers and their purchases home. Siobhan stood with packages at her feet and the precious painting, which she had paid much more than she intended to do, in her arms. A gentleman appeared beside her. 'You have a fine painting there,' he commented. 'Does it have a special meaning for you, seeing as your name is Rafferty? Is Ireland your home country?' Siobhan looked up to see, although elderly, a tall handsome gentleman. She did not like this stranger questioning her, and felt anger rising inside. As if reading her thoughts he apologised. 'I'm sorry, I didn't mean to be intrusive, but I had dealings with a Miss Hazel many years ago and your name was mentioned. I am a solicitor you see, Miss Hazel's solicitor. The late Miss Hazel, I should have said.'

Siobhan started in astonishment, hoping to have severed her link with the past. 'You were Miss Hazel's solicitor, she is dead then?' The gentleman nodded in confirmation. 'I thought she may be, after all, it has been nearly twenty years since I lived in Little Chester.'

'Let me introduce myself, I am Mr. Benjamin Dallow, of Dallow and Dallow, Solicitors. I only go into the office one day a week now, my brother and his son run the Chester branch,' he said extending his hand.

'So Ronald Dallow is your nephew?' said Siobhan, as she took his hand.

'You know Ronald?' he asked frowning.

'Yes, he found myself and my daughter our cottage and also found Amy a position as the children's tutor at the Manor. We are very grateful to Mr. Ronald.'

Looking at her standing with her purchases around her, he said 'Look, Mrs. Rafferty, let me give you a lift home. We can talk on the way. I have a few legal matters I wish to discuss with you.' Seeing a startled look come into her eyes, he added, 'There is nothing to be alarmed about, you will find it is all to your advantage.'

On the way to the cottage the solicitor explained about Miss Hazel's will and that Siobhan was a beneficiary. Miss Hazel had left her a sum of money, which had been gathering interest, and half the cottage in which Miss Hazel had lived.

Although in her mind she knew, she had to ask. 'And who has been left the other half of the cottage?'

'To Mrs. Sally Rafferty. She must be in some way related to you, having the same name,' he said, frowning, and wondering in what way they were related. This Mrs. Rafferty was an exquisite lady, in a completely different class from Sally Rafferty! 'After Miss Hazel's demise, we tried to contact you, but no-one knew where you were, not even the other Sally Rafferty.' Taken by surprise, Siobhan could not think quickly enough to make up a lie. As much as she dreaded meeting Sally again, and to satisfy her curiosity she knew she must, first she would go to the solicitor and find out more.

A meeting was arranged for her to visit the office of Dallow and Dallow the following day to discuss Miss Hazel's will. Until she knew more, she would not mention it to Amy. It was a surprise when Siobhan expressed her wish that she wanted to see him without the junior Mr. Dallow being around. The last thing she wanted was that snob interfering in more of her business. 'Not that I am ungrateful to Mr. Ronald, but...'

She got no further with the sentence when Mr. Benjamin raised his hand to interrupt. 'I quite understand. Master Ronald is a bit over-enthusiastic at times, and not everyone's cup of tea.'

'To say the least!' replied Siobhan, under her breath.

Sitting in the office of Mr. Benjamin Dallow, Siobhan was surprised at the amount of money with interest that Miss Hazel had left her. The money would more than ease her conscience about over-spending on the oil painting. 'Now, what about the cottage? By rights, you are entitled to half of its value,' said Mr. Benjamin, flicking through the papers. 'Mrs. Sally Rafferty could be forced to sell it if she hasn't the money to buy your half?' He could see she was puzzled and asked, 'Is there anything you want to ask me?'

'You say her name is Mrs. Rafferty, has she a husband?' The name Sally was using puzzled Siobhan.

'A husband was never mentioned, but she has a son. Miss Hazel also left him a small sum of money. From what I can remember he was a handsome little chap with black curly hair, very much like your own. Are you sure they are no relation? Your husband's brother's wife perhaps?' Siobhan was deep in thought. A handsome little chap with dark curly hair - the boy must be Michael's, the coincidence was too great.

'How old would you say the boy is now?' asked Siobhan, ignoring his question.

'How old? Let me see, it's been ten years since Miss Hazel died, the boy must have been about eleven then, so that would make him twenty-one years old now.'

'Twenty-one years old,' repeated Siobhan, the same age as Amy. Sally must have been pregnant when she came to look after Miss Hazel. Was the boy really Michael's son? She had to go to see for herself.

In the distance she could hear the voice of Mr. Dallow. 'Are you alright, Mrs. Rafferty? You seem to have gone into a world of your own?'

'I am fine, Mr. Dallow, it's such a lot to take in, the cottage, the money and maybe a sister-in-law I did not know I had. Please forgive me, but before I make up my mind about the cottage I would like to visit Mrs. Rafferty. I would hate to turn someone out of their home,' she said, getting up to leave.

'I understand, Mrs. Rafferty. In the mean while I will have the money transferred into your bank account, if that will suit you? And when you have made up your mind about the cottage, let me know. If you wish, address the letter to me personally to make sure no-one else gets involved.' He did not mention a name, but they both knew who he meant. He started to write down the address of the cottage when Siobhan stopped him.

'There is no need to give me the address of Miss Hazel's cottage. You see, I lived with her myself when I was young.'

As she went from the office, Mr. Benjamin Dallow was tempted to ask her how she came to be living with Miss Hazel, but reflected that it was none of his business. Nevertheless, he would enquire, for the whole situation intrigued him. What could a genteel lady like Siobhan Rafferty have in common with the coarse Sally Rafferty?

Siobhan was shaken when she heard Sally was now known as Mrs. Rafferty. Michael could not have married her, but from the description of the boy, it could be his child. Was this the reason, many years ago, he suddenly decided to go to London? No, she could not believe Michael would desert a child of his. She would not rest until she found out the truth. Tomorrow she would visit the cottage and see for herself.

That night, Amy remarked about how quiet her mother was. Siobhan gave the excuse that she felt exhausted after a hard day cleaning the cottage. She had not told Amy about her visit to Dallow and Dallow - she would, but not until she discovered the truth about Sally and the boy. Likewise, Amy had not mentioned her likeness to Lady Bromley's portrait. The fact was that her day had been taken up entirely with teaching the children, and it had gone completely from her mind.

Trembling, Siobhan walked up the familiar lane to Miss Hazel's cottage. Nothing had changed, it could have been only yesterday when she had walked the same route. Mr. Gibb's village shop was still there, but under a different name now.

As the cottage came into sight, Siobhan felt the urge to turn back. What did it matter if it was Michael's son or not? But it did matter, she must summon enough courage to go on. The cottage seemed much smaller than she remembered, but the garden was still full of hollyhocks and other colourful flowers. The fence was in good repair and had been newly painted. At least Sally is looking after the place, thought Siobhan.

She opened the garden gate and was about to walk up to the cottage door when it opened and out walked a young man - it could have been Michael when Siobhan had first known him. She felt her knees go weak, and the next thing she knew she was lying on the old familiar chaise in the parlour. A glass of water was being handed to her by a woman. She was older and plumper, but unmistakably, it was Sally.

'Here, get this down ya!' Sally said, thrusting the glass at her. 'I'll need something stronger myself. Thought I was seeing a ghost, I did!' She took a gulp from the glass of brandy, then said, 'Now, what the devil do you want?'

The boy was standing in the doorway watching, his mind confused. He could tell by her clothes she was a lady, but what was she doing here? And his mother, why was she so hostile towards her?

Sally, suddenly aware that he was still there, turned around and said in a soft voice, 'You get off to work son, you don't want to get the sack for being late do you?'

'But mother!' he was about to protest when Sally interrupted him.

'Don't worry son, this lady and I are old friends. We have a lot to talk about, in private. Go on now, see you tonight,' she said as she gently pushed him out of the door. Sally stood, her hand on her hips, her eyes glinting ready for what she thought was about to come. 'Well, what brings you here after all these years? If you think you are going to claim half of this cottage you can think again.'

Sitting up, Siobhan shook her head in denial. 'No Sally, I have no intention of claiming half the cottage Miss Hazel left to me. I came because I learned that you are known as Mrs. Rafferty and wondered who you had married?'

Sally's attitude softened when she heard Siobhan was not there to claim her half of the cottage, but hardened again when Siobhan asked about her marriage. 'There ain't been a marriage,' she suddenly answered with venom. 'Your brother scarpered before I could tell him I was pregnant. I was going to follow him to London, but with all the goings on, with you being attacked.......' Siobhan winced at the mention of that episode of her life. '... and Miss Hazel's fall, I had my hands full. I got used to livin' with the old woman and she, God rest her soul, got used to me. She loved my son, Michael, as if he were her own grandchild, taught him to read and write, and me, taught me an all. No, Michael Rafferty, although still in my heart, took second place. My son has been my life!' Unable to control herself, tears begin streaming from her eyes.

Moved by the sight of hard-faced Sally in tears, Siobhan got up and put her arm about her. 'Here don't cry, come on sit down. I'll put the kettle on and make us both a cup of tea.' Siobhan instinctively reached for the tea and teapot - it was where it had always been. Pouring the water from the kettle, which was always boiling on the black lead grate, was so familiar that it seemed she had never been away. Sally accepted the drink gratefully, her hand shaking with emotion. Siobhan sat by her, sipping her tea, her mind was racing with the thought – should she tell Sally that Michael wasn't her brother? She decided that it was time the truth came out, after all what did it matter, now Michael was dead.

So she began. 'I've something to tell you Sally, and I do not want you to interrupt until I have finished.' Sally looked at her in surprise, her own sorrow forgotten with her curiosity in what Siobhan was going to say. 'First of all, Michael was not my brother.' Sally went to interrupt, but Siobhan's raised hand stopped her. 'Please do not say anything until I have finished my story - if you do I will not go on!'

'Alright then, but I always thought you two were too close for brother and sister,' Sally said, then seeing Siobhan's face, added 'Alright then, I'll shut me gob.'

Siobhan started her story right from the time when Michael rescued her from her abusive father. She omitted to mention that Amy was Lord Bromley's child, or about his murder. When it came to the part where Michael had died saving her and her daughter from the fire, Sally let out a cry. 'Michael dead, Michael dead!' Fresh tears fell from her eyes. 'I really loved him you know Siobhan,' she said, looking into Siobhan's eyes, that were also full of tears. 'He'd like that, Michael Rafferty having two women crying over him,' Sally smiled through her tears. 'So you have a daughter, what's her name?'

'Amy, I called her Amy,' then she corrected herself. 'We decided on Amy.'

'Is she dark like you and Michael?' asked Sally.

'No, strangely enough, she is fair,' said Siobhan, then changed the subject. The less said about Amy the better. 'Well, I must be going now, I have a lot to do. Don't worry, I will inform Dallow's that I relinquish all my right to the cottage,' Siobhan said.

Sally got up and reached for Siobhan's hand. 'Thank you, not that I don't deserve it. We have been through a lot you and me. Let's hope we live with our children in peace from now on.'

CHAPTER 25
Young Michael

Amy was having trouble controlling her charges, they were so excited at the prospect of seeing the new pony that had been bought so that Elizabeth could learn to ride. Master Thomas had been having riding lessons since he was five, and now Miss Elizabeth was of an age when she too must learn, as all the gentry's children did. The morning was bright and sunny - the children's excitement was catching and Amy could not help feeling a surge of expectancy. She had not been down to the stables before, but the children showed her the way, running on in front of her. They shouted with joy when they spotted the sweetest small white pony in the paddock. The sound of their voices brought the groom rushing from one of the stables.

'Hey, what's all the noise? Frighten the little thing to death you will!' he shouted playfully.

'Oh Michael! She is adorable, it is a girl is it not?' Elizabeth asked, already running towards the paddock.

'Not a girl, a filly, if you don't mind Miss Elizabeth, let's get the names right from the start,' said the groom, laughing. Amy stood, unable to move, for the groom looked like a young version of her father and, stranger still, had the same name.

Michael, suddenly concious of the governess staring at him, began to feel uncomfortable. Aware he was none too clean, as he had been cleaning out the stable block, he began to apologise. 'I'm sorry Miss, I haven't had time to tidy myself up, you are earlier than I thought.' His country brogue, instead of her father's Irish lilt, broke the spell.

'Do not apologise. It is I who should be doing that for staring, but you bear a striking resemblance to my late father. His name was Michael, the same as yours,' she said suddenly blushing. This time it was Michael who stood transfixed - he had never seen anyone so beautiful. Even from where he was standing he could see the pale green of her eyes sparkling under the shade of thick black eye lashes, unusual on a person with hair as gold as sunlight. Although she wore a bonnet, he could see strands of golden curls that had escaped. Her perfectly shaped mouth was captivating, showing her white pearly even teeth.

When he realised she was speaking to him he pulled himself together. 'Your father, you say?' At least that much had sunk in.

'Yes my late father, you look like a younger version of him.' She once more repeated that his name was also Michael. Perhaps the youth is a bit deaf or backward and he didn't understand what she was saying. Michael was thinking the same – she must think him an idiot! The children's squealing saved them both embarrassment.

'I want to ride her now!' shouted Elizabeth. 'Oh please Michael, let me,' she pleaded.

Michael walked towards Elizabeth and knelt down in front of her, so that his eyes would be on the same level as hers. 'Now you know that is not possible, we have to have the right size saddle made before you can ride her, and you must have the correct riding clothes.' When she started to stamp her foot, demanding to be lifted onto the pony's back, Michael said in a quiet voice, 'Why don't you think of a name for her, you can't keep calling her 'she', now, can you?'

Elizabeth thought for a moment, then said, 'You are right Michael, while Thomas has his lesson I'll sit here with Miss Rafferty and think of a name for my beautiful pony.'

Realising the name Elizabeth had used to address the governess, an astonished Michael said, 'Miss Rafferty? Your name is Rafferty?'

'Yes, it's Amy Rafferty,' she answered, wondering what had it got to do with him?

'My name is also Rafferty,' he announced in disbelief.

'Michael Rafferty. Your name is Michael Rafferty?' In shock, Amy supported herself on the wooden fence that surrounded the paddock. Not only did he look like her father, he had the same name. Regaining her composure, she asked, 'Do you live with your father?' If so, out of curiosity, she must meet this man.

214

'No, he was drowned, died before I was born, and I was named after him. My mother always says I'm the spitting image of him. Do you live with your parents?' He knew he shouldn't be asking personal questions of the governess, as she was far above his station, and obviously a lady.

'My father is dead also, he died in a fire saving my mother and myself, that is why we moved from London – to forget. Strange isn't it that your father and mine had the same name,' she said, deep in thought. She must question her mother when she got home.

Michael was thinking he would ask his mother if they could be in any way related.

Amy felt her skirt being pulled. 'Miss Rafferty, you are not listening. I am going to call my pony Princess, because she is beautiful, like a princess.' With the children claiming their attention, they had no more time to discuss the coincidence of their names.

Both Amy and Michael could think of nothing else all day but about their fathers bearing the same name, and both were eager to question their mothers.

Rushing into the cottage, Michael blurted out, 'Ma, you'll never guess, the new governess at the Manor has the same surname as us, and what's more her father was called Michael, the same as mine. Could we be related?' Sally stood rooted to the spot, the colour draining from her face. This was the moment she had always dreaded, that her son should find out he was a bastard. Her mind raced. Should she tell him the truth or continue the lie?

Composing herself, she asked, 'How did you find out?'

'She brought Master Thomas and Miss Elizabeth down to the stables to see the new pony, and when I heard Miss Elizabeth call her Miss Rafferty... well it went from there.'

Sally decided to bluff it out until she found out what Siobhan had told her daughter.

'Hey, that is strange, but Rafferty is a common Irish name and I suppose Michael is too. I don't recall your father ever saying he had relatives in these parts,' she said, not daring to look him in the face.

'Oh, they don't come from around here, they have come up from London after the death of Mr. Rafferty,' he said, washing himself at the sink.

Every time Sally saw her son's well shaped body, she remembered Michael's with longing.

'London! Well, there must be thousands of Rafferty's there,' she said, passing the incident over. 'Now put your clean shirt on and get your dinner before it gets cold.'

They ate in silence, each deep in thought, then Michael blurted out, 'She is very pretty!'

'Who's pretty?' said Sally, dismissively.

'Miss Rafferty, she's just not pretty, she is beautiful.' Then with a dreamy look coming into his eyes, he added, 'The most beautiful girl I have ever seen.'

'You had better not let your girlfriend hear you say that,' said Sally, smiling and thinking how he shared his father's roving eye.

'Mary's not my girlfriend. I just take her out sometimes,' said Michael, wholly denying his mother's remark.

Siobhan had been going through the same questions with Amy. The thought briefly went through her mind – should she tell her the truth, that Michael Rafferty was not her real father? But if she did, the whole story of the rape would come out. How could Amy live with the knowledge that her real father was a mad rapist. She managed to brush it off as coincidence, the same as Sally had. Amy seemed to accept this explanation and no more was said on the matter.

Although Amy did not mention Michael to her mother again, he was on her mind. She found she could not wait until each riding lesson took place. The more she talked with Michael the more she realised her first impression of him was entirely wrong. Far from a simple mind, he was intelligent and quite well educated. When she asked where he had gone to school, he explained that the old lady they lived with, a Miss Hazel, who was a retired school teacher, had taught him from an early age to read and write, this gave him a thirst for knowledge and to try to improve himself by watching how the gentry behaved.

This impressed Amy, and although they did not have much time to talk, that which they did have was spent in lively discussion. Watching the children riding, Amy said, 'I wish I could ride!'

'I'll teach you,' offered Michael.

'His Lordship wouldn't let you use your time in his employment teaching me to ride, and her Ladyship couldn't spare me either. I'm only here to teach the children,' answered Amy.

'I could teach you on Sundays. I have most Sunday afternoons off, except when his Lordship has guests,' he said, full of enthusiasm.

'I haven't a horse or saddle,' Amy laughed. Her laughter was like the tinkling of a mountain stream to his ears.

'His Lordship lets me borrow his horses, not the thoroughbreds, but they are decent enough. I could borrow a saddle and I'm sure you could find something suitable to wear.

So Amy's lessons began. She kept her meetings from her mother, feeling she would not approve of her seeing a groom. When asked where she was going, Amy said her Ladyship had asked her to do extra duties. It was the first lie she had ever told her mother. They met most Sunday afternoons, except for the ones when his Lordship needed Michael.

Amy had adapted one of her serge skirts into one suitable for riding. Michael kept it hidden in one of the lockers at the stables.

It was a glorious summer for both of them. Amy had never been so happy. She lived from one Sunday to the next, and was so disappointed when they could not meet. Michael felt the same way. He would go about his work singing, always on the look-out for nya sight of Amy. 'I reckon you'm in love,' one of the old hands remarked. 'It ain't natural for a chap to be so happy as yo am.'

The man was right, he was in love, in love with Amy Rafferty. When he looked at her riding by his side, her golden hair blowing in the wind, her cheeks flushed – a lump would come into his throat. She was indeed the most beautiful girl he had ever seen, but it was not just her beauty that captivated him - it was her pleasant nature and their lively discussions. He started to buy a newspaper to read about what was going on in the country, so that he would be knowledgeable on current topics.

'What you suddenly took to reading a newspaper for?' Sally asked one night as he sat engrossed.

'Got to keep up with the news, Ma. I can't let the gentry think I'm an ignorant person, now can I? If it wasn't for Miss Hazel I would be as ignorant as the rest of the people around here,' he added.

'I hope you don't include me in that, and I hope you're not getting ideas above your station,' she said, but felt proud that her son wanted to better himself.

'Ah, go on! You're me Ma, the wisest woman in the world,' he said teasing her.

The situation between Amy and Michael could have gone on forever, if nature hadn't intervened. One glorious afternoon when they were out riding and full of high spirits, Amy started to canter away from Michael. Laughing, she urged her horse to go faster and faster.

'Stop, you silly girl, you're not experienced enough to handle the horse at that speed!' shouted Michael. The moment he said it, the horse attempted a jump, unbalancing Amy and throwing her to the ground. 'Amy, Amy!' cried Michael, as he bent over her, cradling her face in his hands. 'Are you alright, darling?' He said darling without thinking. She opened her eyes, wondering if she had heard correctly.

'You called me darling,' she said, staring into his blue eyes, which, as usual, had a twinkle in them.

'I'm sorry. I shouldn't have taken such liberties,' he said, stifling the urge to kiss her.

'Oh Michael! I want to be your darling,' she sighed. They couldn't contain their feelings any longer, the passion that had been building up over the months broke forth and their lips met. Michael pressed his lips tight to hers. A sensation arose in Amy that she had never experienced before, she wanted – she didn't know what – only that Michael and she should be one. Michael was having great difficulty in keeping his passion in check. He turned away from her embrace. 'Michael, what is the matter?' asked Amy, feeling rejected.

'My darling Amy. If I don't pull away from you now, I don't think I can stop myself.'

Amy, who was not ignorant in the ways of men and women, and equally full of passion, said 'I want you to, Michael. I love you.'

'I love you too, but I am not making love to you in a field like some common village wench, you mean more to me than that. When we make love it will be after we are married,' he said, lifting her from the ground and holding her close.

'Is that a proposal, Michael Rafferty?' she said teasing.

'I'm not proposing now. When I do it will be properly, with a ring. I mean to marry you Amy, if you'll have me? I fell in love with you the moment I saw you,' he said clasping her hands.

'I must have fallen in love with you at the same time, and I will marry you Michael, with or without a ring,' she said, not thinking of what her mother would say.

'Now, don't take this the wrong way Amy, but for the time being I think it best if we keep our relationship to ourselves,' he said, dreading telling his mother.

So they agreed to keep their secret, but as with most plans, they rarely turn out the way they are intended. Sally was being served in the village store. Mr. Gibbs, the previous proprietor, had long since died. The present owner, trying to be friendly, enquired, 'How's your Michael doing, Mrs. Rafferty?'

A voice behind her piped up. 'He's doing fine, according to my husband. Romping in the field with some lassie.'

Sally turned to face the woman and uttered a good natured laugh. 'Ain't that what young men are supposed to do? He's been seeing Mary Evans for a while now.'

'Oh, it weren't Mary. My husband says she was a beauty, long hair, all curls, colour of ripened corn, he said,' the woman replied maliciously.

The storekeeper, taking an interest, piped up, 'I don't know who that could be then, no girl like that in this village.'

Sally, upset that Michael had never mentioned another girl, shouted, 'It's a pity your husband has nothing better to do than be a Peeping Tom!' then stormed out of the shop.

'Well!' exclaimed the woman, 'What's got into her?'

Sally could hardly wait for Michael to come home to interrogate him. The last thing she wanted for her boy was that he should get some girl pregnant. Michael came in, cheerful as usual, to find his mother sitting stone faced in the chair. 'What's the matter Ma, you look upset?'

'I am upset, bloody upset, what with you being the talk of the village. Who's the fair haired girl you have been lying in the grass with?' she asked, her face blood red with temper.

Michael went to her and placed his arm around her. 'Now Ma, don't upset yourself, I was going to tell you, but not until I was ready to get engaged to her.'

'Her, who's her?' Sally asked.

'Amy Rafferty, the governess at the Manor,' explained Michael. His voice went soft as he said, 'We love each other, Ma.'

It took a few seconds for the words Michael had uttered to sink in. Amy Rafferty, Siobhan and Michael's daughter, young Michael's half sister. Sally grabbed him by the shoulders and screamed, 'Have you had your way with her? Have you?'

Taken aback, Michael stepped back from her. 'Ma, what's got into you, you're getting hysterical?'

'Oh, my God, Michael! Answer me, have you had your way with her?' she asked in a calmer voice.

'Not that it's any business of yours, but no, I haven't. I respect her too much. We can wait until we're married,' he said, answering her question as calmly as he could.

'Married! Married! You can never marry that girl!' shouted Sally.

'And why not? You probably think she's above my station, but ...'

Before he got any further, Sally blurted out, 'You can never marry because her father and your father are the same man. She is your half sister Michael, do you hear me, your half sister!' she screamed into his face.

Michael collapsed onto the sofa, the words sinking in. 'My half sister! I don't believe you. You're only saying that to keep me with you,' he said shaking his head in disbelief.

'I've done some wicked things in my time Michael, but I would never be so wicked as to tell you a lie like this. My son, it is the truth. I wish it wasn't, but it is. Do you think it really was a coincidence that her father was named Michael Rafferty?'

Pulling his head into his hands, he started to sob, knowing what his mother was saying was the truth. 'How, Ma? How did this happen?'

'I never wanted you to find out,' she began.

Michael interrupted, 'You were never married to my father, were you?'

'No, Michael, by the time I found I was pregnant your father had already left for London, but knowing him, he would surely have stood by me.' She proceeded to tell him the whole story. When he went to interrupt she silenced him, as Siobhan had silenced her. 'No, let me finish, now I have started.' When she concluded, they both sat in silence, then Sally said, 'I guess I should have told you a long time ago, but I didn't want you to know that ...'

He finished the sentence for her '...that I was a bastard! Oh Ma! I would have preferred to know about my father, rather than let me fall in love with my half sister. No wonder there was a bond between us from the start. You say her mother came to see you, what was she like – fair like Amy?'

Sally had never thought it through before - the girl's hair colour was described as ripened corn – how could it be? Both Siobhan and Michael had jet black hair.

'Ma, was she beautiful like Amy?' he asked again.

'Oh, yes! She was beautiful and innocent. No wonder Lord Peter Bromley lusted after her,' she answered dreamily.

'Lusted after her. What do you mean, mother?' Michael asked.

Sally hesitated, then said, 'Well, now I have started I might as well tell you all I know. Lord Bromley became obsessed with Siobhan from the moment her set eyes on her. He liked them young and innocent. Dressed her up in fine clothes and invited her to a ball at the Manor. That's where it happened,' said Sally, shaking her head.

'That's where what happened?' asked Michael.

'The attack, Bromley attacked and raped her,' replied Sally. 'Miss Hazel was worried beforehand that something like that may happen.'

'Then why didn't Miss Hazel stop her from going?' asked Michael, perplexed.

'She did object, but it was no good. Lord Bromley threatened to have Siobhan taken away from her, saying she was too old and crippled to look after a child. The old lady had no choice but to let her go. She asked the coachman to watch out for her. He did so as far as he was able, but it was no use. I don't know exactly what happened. All I know is that it was him who brought her home all bruised and blooded. Bromley had attacked her – a terrible sight, so I believe. It was then I happened to be passing Miss Hazel's cottage, and I was called in to help. We got Siobhan away to London to be with Michael in the hope that Lord Bromley would never find her.' She omitted the part where she had sold her London address to Bromley . 'I never thought I would ever see her again. How I wish she had never come back. If she hadn't we wouldn't be in this mess now.' Sally held out her hand, saying, 'Pour me a drink, luv, all this talk has worn me out.'

Michael poured a drink for his mother and himself. He sipped his drink, trying to take in all that he had been told. He said thoughtfully, 'I suppose after promising to look after her, my father married her out of pity. Do you think Amy knows what happened?'

'I don't know, son, I shouldn't think so, neither Siobhan nor Michael would want her to know,' Sally said, thinking perhaps that was the reason Michael did marry Siobhan, to look after her. After all, he had saved her from her abusive father and brought her to England. Somehow, she felt better about Michael Rafferty now.

'What happened to Lord Bromley? Wasn't he punished?' asked Michael.

'No, them sort are above punishment. They say he was locked away in some asylum up North. Anyway, no-one has ever seen or heard from him since.' Again, she blotted from her mind the money for betraying where Siobhan had gone.

'What am I to do now, Ma? I still feel love for Amy. I guess I will have to tell her that she is my sister and that we can never be together,' he said sadly, tears filling his eyes.

'I can't see that there is any other way son. I wonder if it would come better from her mother. Yes, I think that would be the kindest thing to do. I'll go and see Siobhan, then it will be up to her what she tells her daughter.'

'Siobhan won't want Amy to know about Lord Bromley, especially with her working at the Manor,' said Michael, wiping away his tears. 'What a mess Ma!' he said, grasping his mother to him. 'Thank you for bringing me up on your own, and for trying to protect me, even though it was all a lie.' Although it broke Michael's heart to do so, it was agreed that he should act normally with Amy until Sally had the chance to speak to Siobhan. 'Find out where they live? I don't want to ask Dallow and Dallow - the less they know the better,' Sally asked.

Amy could sense the change in Michael until, at last, she couldn't hold back her feelings any longer. 'Michael, have I done anything wrong?' she asked while the children were having their riding lessons.

'I don't know what you mean, Amy. Of course you haven't done anything wrong. Is this because I can't see you on Sunday? I told you that his Lordship wants me here. He has a buyer coming to see one of the horses.' It was a lie, but he had promised his mother that there would be no more Sunday outings.

'I'm going to miss you, Michael,' she answered, a look of sadness on her beautiful face. His heart wept to see her so unhappy, longing to hold her in his arms.

'I'm going to miss you, Amy. If you tell me where you live, I'll meet you somewhere near, if I can get away,' he said cunningly. It was a way of getting her address. It was like the sun coming out from behind the clouds when she heard his words.

She gave him the address, then added, 'You must not come to the house. I'll keep a look out for you if you give me some idea of the time. Then I'll come out to meet you.' At the thought that she might see Michael on Sunday, she spent the rest of the children's riding lessons in a happy mood.

Michael felt really bad for tricking her into disclosing her address and fuelling her hope that he might meet her. Why, oh why did they have to be related? He wished he had never met her, for the heartache he felt was too much to bear. He couldn't go on working at the Manor where he could bump into her at any time. One of them would have to leave, and he guessed it would be him.

Sally made plans to visit Siobhan. If she went early in the morning there was a chance she would catch her before she went out. The cottage was quite a distance away, but Sally, ignoring the cost, hired a coach. She asked the driver to drop her off some distance away, saying she would walk the remainder of the journey. The early morning mist had lifted and the sun was rising in the blue sky. Already the leaves had started to change colour, a sign that autumn was approaching. Near the cottage she saw a girl come from its front door, saying a polite 'good morning' as she passed Sally, thinking it was early for one of Siobhan's customers to call. Siobhan had started to earn money by sewing and dressmaking for people, as she had always been good with a needle. Sally noticed the sun shining on the girl's golden curls bulging from under her bonnet. After only a glance she could see the girl was a beauty, and must be Siobhan's daughter Amy. It was no wonder Michael had fallen in love with her. But there was something that troubled her about the girls looks, something other than her fair hair. She waited until Amy was out of sight, then went up the path and knocked on Siobhan's door. It took Siobhan a few moments to register who was standing there. The last person she had expected to see was Sally.

'Well ain't you gonna ask me in?' said Sally, pushing her way past.

Siobhan recovered her composure. 'There wasn't much point in asking,' said Siobhan, sarcastically. 'What can I do for you? I have told you I lay no claim to the cottage, but I'm afraid I need the money Miss Hazel left me. After the fire I had very little money left.'

'You've got it wrong. I've come on a much more serious matter – Michael and Amy,' she said. Without waiting to be asked she sat down.

'About your Michael and my Amy. What about them? I wasn't aware they knew each other,' she said indignantly.

'Oh, they know each other alright, know each other too well,' answered Sally with a sneer. 'You had better put the kettle on. We'll both need a cup of tea when you hear what I've got to say!'

Puzzled, Siobhan did as she was bid. The tea poured, Siobhan lifted her cup and said, 'Now, please tell me what this is all about?' For a while, Sally irritably sipped her tea. Impatient to hear what Sally had got to say, Siobhan snatched the cup from her. 'Oh, for goodness sake, tell me what you have come here for!' Sally began to tell Siobhan the whole story of how Michael was the groom at Bromley Manor, how they had met and fallen in love, and how they had been seen romping in a field by a villager.

'Oh no!' Siobhan exclaimed. 'They haven't made , you know....!' she cried out loud.

'No, thank goodness. Michael said they hadn't, they were waiting until they get married.'

'Get married!' Siobhan repeated.

'So you see, Siobhan, I had to tell Michael the truth about who fathered him and that he and Amy were half-brother and sister.'

There was a long silence before Siobhan spoke. 'You told him everything, about Lord Bromley attacking me?'

'I had no choice. I guessed you hadn't told Amy, so I swore Michael to secrecy.'

'Thank goodness for that at least,' said Siobhan with a sigh.

'Why I am here, apart from telling you about the feelings they have for one another, is for you to tell Amy why they can never marry. It's not going to be easy, but a damned sight easier than I had it, telling my son he is a bastard!'

'So many lies,' Siobhan said thoughtfully.

'And more to come I have no doubt. Well now, I've had my say, I'll be getting along.'

As Sally got up to go, Siobhan held out her hand to her. 'Thank you, Sally for letting me know.'

After Sally went, Siobhan's thoughts were all jumbled up. What could she say? Tell Amy the truth that she wasn't Michael's child? No, she must never find out who her real father was, even if it broke her heart believing she could not marry Michael Rafferty.

When Amy came home she did not have to broach the subject - Amy pre-empted the conversation. 'Was that one of your customers I passed in the lane this morning?'

Siobhan took a deep breath. 'No dear, it was Michael Rafferty's mother.'

Amy gave a start, 'Michael's mother! Michael who?' she asked, feigning innocence.

'Don't pretend you don't know who Michael Rafferty is. You have been seen kissing him in a field,' said Siobhan, angry now that her daughter was going to lie to her.

'Mother, I wanted to tell you, but we decided to wait until we were ready to get engaged.' Proudly she added, 'We are in love and he has asked me to marry him.'

Feeling sorrow for her daughter and the lie she was going to tell her, Siobhan hugged her close. 'My darling daughter, sit down, I have something to tell you.' She told her the lie that she and Michael had the same father. At first, like Michael, she did not believe it, but then it suddenly made sense. That was the reason Michael resembled her father and the coincidence of their surname. Amy buried her face in her hands and wept until there were no more tears left. Without another word she ran up to her room, locking the door. Later, as Siobhan knocked on the door offering her supper, she was abruptly told to go away.

Siobhan retired to her bed, but the sound of Amy's sobs kept her awake. Over and over in her mind she wondered, would it be better to tell her the truth? No, she decided anything was better than that - the girl would get over Michael in time.

A thought went through Amy's mind - How long had Michael known? Was that the reason for his strange behaviour and the reason he couldn't see her on Sunday - why hadn't he said? She couldn't leave it like this and must speak to him.

Next morning, not wanting her mother to hear, she crept out of the house before dawn had broken. She went straight to the stables and hid, waiting for Michael to arrive. She must have nodded off to sleep, for when she awoke the sun was already in the sky. Shaking herself and smoothing down her clothes, she looked around. Michael was nowhere to be seen. Impatient, she saw old Jake and asked where he was.

'He ain't come in today, Miss, unusual for him,' he answered.

'You don't happen to know where he lives do you Jake?' she asked.

'Not exactly Miss, somewhere outside the village, I think. Not sure though,' he said, curious to know why the governess should be asking such a question.

Amy hired a carriage to take her to the village. It's a tiny place, someone must know where Michael lives she thought. She entered the village shop.

'Can I help you Miss?' the owner asked, surprised at seeing a well dressed stranger in his shop.

'I wonder if you know where the Rafferty's live?' she asked, oblivious to the stares the other customers gave her.

The shopkeeper gave her directions, then cheekily added, 'May I ask what you be wanting them for?' Amy ignored his question and went from the shop in the direction he had given her. The shopkeeper turned to one of his customers.

'What you make of that then?' he said.

'She fits the description of the girl my Harry saw Michael Rafferty romping with in the field,' said one of the women.

'Her's probably found her's got a bun in the oven!' said another, laughing alone, before being joined by the others.

Sally opened the door at the sound of the loud knocking. 'Alright, no need to knock the door down!' Her mouth dropped open as she saw who was standing there.

Before Sally could say anything, Amy blurted out, 'Is Michael in? I must speak with him.'

'You had better come in. How did you know where we lived, anyway?' she asked.

'The shopkeeper told me,' answered Amy.

'The village shop?' asked Sally. Amy nodded. 'That's put the cat amongst the bloody pigeons. The whole village will know now.'

'I'm sorry, but there was no other way I could find out,' apologised Amy.

'Anyway, now you are here, what do you want?'

'I want to speak to Michael,' said Amy, agitated.

'He ain't here, he's gone away to see about another job. After what has gone on between you and him, he felt he could no longer work at the Manor,' said Sally, feeling no sympathy for the girl. How dare she come here demanding to speak to him.

'Where has he gone?' Amy asked, oblivious to Sally's attitude.

'I don't know, and it's best if you don't either. The only thing to do, feeling the way you do about each other and knowing nothing can come of it, is to keep apart.'

'Even if I did not love him, he is my half brother, after all,' Amy replied.

'I don't care if he is your whole brother. It's best you keep away from him. A pretty girl like you will soon fall in love with someone else. I was always falling in and out of love at your age,' Sally lied. She had only ever loved one man, and that was Michael Rafferty.

Dejected, Amy went from the cottage. The thought kept going around in her head – she must see Michael. He had to come home some time, she would hide in the ditch and wait for him.

Sitting in the ditch at the end of the lane, she felt quite comfortable. The warm sun blazed down on her, and the buzzing of the honey bees lulled her into a deep sleep, dreaming of herself in Michael's arms. A sudden downpour awoke her, and at first she didn't know where she was. She must have been out of her mind, hiding in a ditch like a common tramp. Her mother would be worried to death, wondering where she was, and Lady Bromley would not be too pleased that she had not turned up for work. She must get home as soon as possible. All these thoughts went through her mind as she attempted to climb out of the ditch, but, with the rain, its banks had become slippery. Try as she might to get out, she just kept slipping back. With the aid of a tree root she managed to get half way up, but suddenly it gave way, throwing her backwards, where she hit her head on a boulder, knocking her unconscious. The rain beat down on her, soaking her through.

Eventually the rain stopped and the harvest moon began to appear from behind the clouds. Michael trudged up the lane feeling very weary, having been unsuccessful in finding a job. One like he had now at the Manor would be hard to find, he thought. His eye was drawn in the moonlight to something in the ditch. He went over, and to his astonishment saw the moon casting its light on a woman's hair. He knew that hair, no-one in these parts had hair that colour. 'Amy!' he shouted, trying to drag her out of the muddy ditch. 'Oh my God! She is dead?' he said to himself when she did not move. Taking her in his arms she started to moan. 'Oh thank God, she is alive. Amy, Amy,' he shouted, shaking her by her shoulders. He noticed the blood streaked in her hair. Picking her up as if she were a feather, he ran to the cottage, he kicked at the door. Alarmed, Sally picked up the poker ready to defend herself from whoever it was.

When she saw Michael and the girl in his arms, she screamed 'What's happened?'

'No time to talk now, Ma, get these wet clothes off her and put her into bed while I fetch the doctor,' he said, laying her on the sofa.

By the time the doctor arrived, Amy was tucked up in bed in one of Sally's flannelette nightdresses. No matter how many blankets Sally covered her with she could not stop her from shivering. Even the stone hot water bottle had no effect.

The doctor examined the cut on her head, which looked worse than it was. 'She has caught a severe chill,' he said. Michael had told him where he had found her. 'She will be lucky if it doesn't turn into pneumonia. Keep her warm and try to get her to drink plenty of hot liquid. What the devil she was doing in the ditch I don't know. She wasn't robbed was she?' he asked Sally.

'No, no, her purse is here. There's nothing been taken from it as I can see,' said Sally.

'We will soon find out when she comes round,' said Michael. He had a feeling his Ma knew more about this than she was saying in front of the doctor.

CHAPTER 26
The Truth

Despite constant care, Amy's chill did develop into pneumonia. Siobhan had been told, and came to look after her daughter, sleeping on the sofa at night and refusing to leave Amy for a second.

Michael resumed work at the Manor, taking a note from Siobhan explaining that Amy was very ill and if her job as governess was still available when she was well then she would be glad to return. Siobhan did not know whether Amy would want to return, but she wrote it anyway. The question was whether Amy would ever recover.

Siobhan blamed herself for not confessing that she was not Michael's sister. Sally blamed herself for not being sympathetic to the girl's feelings and sending her away. And Michael blamed himself for leaving without a word of explanation to Amy.

A fire was kept burning in the small cast-iron grate in the bedroom - the doctor had stressed that she must be kept warm. For Sally, the situation brought back memories of Mrs. Parker's pneumonia, and how she had killed her. 'I've been a wicked person, but please, God don't let me be the cause of this beautiful girl dying,' she prayed. 'If she lives I promise never to do an evil deed again.'

The only name uttered from Amy was that of Michael. Delirious, she would mutter 'I don't want to live if I can't have Michael.' Over and over she would repeat it.

'I cannot understand it,' the doctor commented. 'She seems to have lost the will to get better. The pneumonia has gone, but she does not seem to be improving.'

Michael was at work, and Sally and Siobhan were taking a rest with a cup of tea. Siobhan had been pondering over what the doctor had said. It may give her back the will to live if she was told the truth about her father, but the shock may cause a relapse. As if reading Siobhan's thoughts, Sally suddenly spoke. 'If only they weren't related, none of this would have happened, but then again, if you had not come back from London......'

'And I could say if Michael had not been killed in the fire,' Siobhan interrupted. 'So many ifs,' she said, 'but there is one 'if' I can put right.'

'What's that then?' said Sally, eagerly.

'Michael was not Amy's real father,' Siobhan said in so quiet a voice that Sally could hardly hear what she was saying.

'What! What's that you said? Michael was not Amy's father. I thought there was something bloody strange, her hair being so fair.' Then the full realisation hit Sally. 'I knew she reminded me of someone, it was Lord Peter Bromley. After he raped you, you found out you were carrying his child.'

'Not until I had arrived in London,' explained Siobhan.

'Well, I'll be blowed, said Sally in a daze. 'Did Michael know?'

'Yes, Michael knew,' Siobhan answered

'And he married you anyway?' exclaimed Sally.

'Yes, we brought her up as Michael's child, and she's never believed any different.'

'And you were going to let her go on believing it, knowing it would be breaking both their hearts?' Sally said in disbelief.

'What would have been worse, Amy knowing her father was a murderous madman and she was born from rape?' said Siobhan, weeping at the thought of it.

Sally was quiet, letting the knowledge sink in, then a thought struck her. 'You could say that you had fallen for a sailor, he got you pregnant, but was drowned before he could marry you. And Michael, who swore to always look after you when he brought you to England, and because he had always loved you, married you and looked on Amy as his own.' Getting carried away with her story, Sally added, 'and in time you fell in love with him.'

Siobhan thought for a while, then said, 'It does sound feasible, but your Michael knows I was raped. He's not a stupid lad, won't he put two and two together?'

'Michael doesn't know you were carrying Lord Bromley's child - I didn't myself know until you just told me. No, Siobhan, he will be so happy that they are not related and he would not want to do anything to prevent them getting married. You had best go and tell her, even if she doesn't appear to be listening. I'm sure if you tell her often enough it will sink in,' finished Sally, who was smiling for the first time in many weeks.

It was decided to tell Michael first, that no way were Amy and he related. Siobhan dreaded telling him after the heartache he had suffered from not knowing the truth, but Michael simply overflowed with happiness. If he suspected anything different he never said. He did ask that he could be the one to try telling Amy the good news.

The first time he tried there was no response. After the third attempt Amy's eyes began to flutter open. 'Michael, what did you say?' she asked. Once more he repeated it. The sudden realisation of what he was saying was as if someone had waved a magic wand making her want to live again.

'How did you find out?' she asked.

'Your mother will explain,' said Michael, calling Siobhan into the bedroom.

After Siobhan had told Amy the made up story that Sally had concocted, Amy, too delighted to be angry with her mother for deceiving her for all those years, did not reproach her.'

'No-one could have loved you better if you had been his real daughter,' Siobhan added.

'I know, Mother, to me he will always be my real father,' she said, the sparkle returning to her eyes.

From that day on she started to recover. Lady Bromley was only too delighted to give her back the job as governess, having hired a temporary governess while Amy was ill. Both Master Thomas and Miss Elizabeth shouted, 'We are glad to have you back, Miss Rafferty, we hated Miss Grimshaw!'

Everything seemed to be going to plan for Amy and Michael's wedding on a date set for the following Easter. 'Oh mother, I do not know whether I can wait that long. Easter seems such a long time away,' Amy said impatiently.

'Amy, it will come around quickly enough. Get Christmas over and it will soon be here. After all, it will take me that long to make your dress. I want it to be the best of its kind,' said Siobhan.

'Mother, with you making it, it will be, because I know every stitch will be sewn with love.'

Tears came into Siobhan's eyes. 'Oh, you darling, darling girl,' she said as she thanked God everything was turning out well.

Siobhan had been right. No sooner had Christmas come, which the two families celebrated together, than Easter was upon them. Lord Bromley had let one of the estate cottages to Michael, and, as a wedding present, said they could live rent free for a whole year.

'It's more than generous of him Ma,' Michael said as he told her.

'And by rights the whole estate should be Amy's,' Sally thought, but kept it to herself.

The authorities had long since given up searching for Lord Peter Bromley, assuming he had died after escaping from the asylum in Scotland. The estate had then passed to his cousin, Ernest Bromley.

Master Thomas and Miss Elizabeth, excited at the coming wedding, begged to attend. 'I want to be bridesmaid,' cried Elizabeth. 'I have never been a bridesmaid!'

'And I want to be the ring boy,' joined in Thomas, feeling that was an important role. The children continued nagging until, in the end, and for the sake of peace, Lord and Lady Bromley agreed. The villagers were heard remarking that it had never been known for the gentry to attend an employees' wedding. Most of them intended to be there to watch, even if it meant standing outside the small family church on the Bromley estate.

George Dallow, who had become a family friend since he had met Siobhan at the auction, was honoured when he was asked to give Amy away. Although he was much older than Siobhan, they enjoyed the same things. He often took her to auctions that he thought she would be interested in, and, as a special treat, to the theatre.

Over the past months Siobhan had worked until the small hours of the morning making sure all their outfits were finished on time. Amy's dress was made from the finest white brocade, the tight-fitting bodice embroidered with gold thread and hundreds of seed pearls. It had a V-neckline and tiny pearl buttons fastened down the back from the neck to below the waistline. The headdress was also made of pearls, making the shape of large flowers, from which a veil of delicate lace reached the ground and met the long train of the dress.

Amy cried with delight when she tried on the finished dress. 'Mother, it's the most beautiful dress I have ever seen. None of her Ladyship's dresses can compare with this one!'

'That's because every stitch I've sewn with love, my darling daughter,' Siobhan answered proudly.

Sally's outfit was a different matter. Because of her dowdy colouring it was hard to choose a colour that would flatter her. At last, an emerald green velvet, trimmed with a pale green satin, was chosen. To get it to fit was awkward, as Sally had really let herself go, and was very much overweight. On a promise that she would lose weight, Siobhan said she would leave her outfit until last. Her own dress was made of a heavy pale blue satin, trimmed with dark blue velvet. Both outfits had a short cloak to match, a precaution against the appearance of a late frost.

Michael's suit was hired. As he said, 'I'll never need a wedding suit again, Ma, it's a waste of money to buy one.' It was pale grey with gold brocade waistcoat and cravat. Master Thomas had a suit in the same style, and Miss Elizabeth's dress was of gold to match the cravats.

'You'd think the queen was getting married,' remarked Sally. 'All this fuss and palaver, I don't know when I will ever wear my outfit again, I'm sure! If you ask me, it's a waste of money – the whole thing is a waste of money!' She still had her spiteful streak.

'Well, we're not asking you, Ma, and as you're not paying for it. If I were you, I would keep my opinions to myself. As for your gown, who knows, when I've gone, you may find yourself a husband,' said Michael, laughing. Sally huffed, but said nothing, then smiled to herself - who knows, with less weight, she may even do that!

Siobhan, opening Amy's bedroom curtains, exclaimed, 'Oh Amy, it's a beautiful morning, not a cloud in the sky. It's going to be a perfect day.' And so it was, the spring sun shining to take the chill from the air.

The small estate church and its grounds were full. Villagers from miles around had come to see what was special about the wedding that the Lord and Lady felt they should attend. Not only that, but their children were taking part.

Michael and the congregation waited impatiently for Amy to arrive. Before the music started the sound of 'Ah' could be heard from outside the church, and Michael knew his bride-to-be was about to appear.

Amy stood in the church doorway, the sun streaming in from behind her, lighting the embroidery on her dress and her golden hair. The vision made the congregation catch its breath. They had never seen any bride look so radiant and so beautiful.

The wedding service went to plan. Even Thomas, who took his duty very seriously, behaved perfectly. He handed the ring to Michael on a cushion. Elizabeth's eyes did not leave Amy's train, ready to smooth it when it was crumpled. The sight of their children brought tears to the eyes of the Lord and Lady.

Michael's throat went dry at the sight of his bride and wondered what Amy saw in an ordinary fellow like him. He was so very lucky and he would do his utmost to make her happy. Ronald Dallow, who had not been invited, came along out of curiosity and was thinking the same thing. Why had she picked this country-yokel instead of someone refined like himself?

Both Siobhan and Sally cried openly on seeing the happy couple walk from the church in a shower of rose petals and cheers from the crowd.

'Don't they make a handsome couple' said one of the villagers. 'I can't get over how much she resembles his Lordship. Funny that!'

'You don't think she's a blow-by, do you?' said someone.

'You never know, she certainly has an air about her, and what with his Lordship being here,' replied the former person.

Another whispered, 'We'll see. As they say, blood will out.'

And how right that turned out to be.

Lightning Source UK Ltd.
Milton Keynes UK
03 March 2011

168569UK00002B/2/P

Seaside Gardening

F. W. SHEPHERD

Cassell

The Royal Horticultural Society

THE ROYAL HORTICULTURAL SOCIETY

Cassell Educational Limited
Villiers House, 41/47 Strand
London WC2N 5JE
for the Royal Horticultural Society

First published 1990

British Library Cataloguing in Publication Data
Shepherd, F. W. (Frederick William),
  Seaside gardening.
  1. Great Britain. Coastal regions. Gardening
  I. Title   II. Series
  635.90941

  ISBN 0-304-31967-8

Photographs by Michael Warren, Harry Smith Collection and Andrew Lawson

The map on p. 9 is Crown Copyright and is reproduced, with minor adaptations, by permission
of the Controller of Her Majesty's Stationery Office

Phototypesetting by Chapterhouse Ltd, Formby
Printed in Hong Kong by Wing King Tong Co. Ltd

Cover: Headland, a clifftop garden in Cornwall
Frontispiece: rock roses like Helianthemum 'Cerise Queen'
flourish in a sunny spot regardless of wind
Back cover: 'Mrs Popple' and other fuchsias are a familiar
sight in seaside areas of the mild southwest (photographs
by Michael Warren)

Contents

Introduction

To those who have visited the seaside – and who has not? – gardening by the sea may bring to mind bright displays of spring bulbs or summer bedding. Others will remember windswept trees and shrubs, with sometimes unfamiliar plants crouching in their lee. But those who have the good fortune to live and garden near the sea will know that the brilliant bedding displays are rarely possible for them, because time and money are not always available and because such displays must be well sheltered from the winds.

The many who think of retiring to a seaside town or village or buying a holiday home on the coast, and who wish to start or continue gardening as a hobby, must appreciate that they will enter a new phase in their gardening experience. In addition to the new problems, mainly caused by the stronger winds, they will still face all the old ones. Weeds, sometimes of a different kind, will continue to grow – frequently, in the milder districts, later in the autumn and earlier in the spring. Diseases and pests still appear. Mowing, quite often right through the winter, and pruning still need attention. Other hobbies, such as sailing and fishing, may also compete.

However, against the problems and distractions of seaside gardening there are advantages that new seaside gardeners should not forget. They can take heart that many plants, probably new to them, thrive in very windy situations, and that other plants, rare in inland Britain except in greenhouses, can be grown in the milder coastal gardens. There are, therefore, two distinct types of garden that can be planned by the seaside gardener. The first, amply sheltered, would include many tender or half-hardy plants, providing new variety of shape, colour and scent; the second would consist entirely of wind-hardy plants needing little attention.

This book sets out to tell of the differences between seaside and inland gardening, to explain the difficulties and to assist in overcoming them. We will limit our scope to those situations that are within reach of onshore winds carrying salt and, in some cases, sand from the shore. We will first consider the two significant climatic factors that affect the seaside garden – immoderate winds and moderate temperatures.

Formal bedding on the seafront at Bridlington, Yorkshire

Wind and Shelter

DAMAGE FROM WIND

The most important feature of the seaside climate is undoubtedly the wind. It is stronger when coming in over the uninterrupted surface of the sea and it picks up salt spume from the waves and, in some places, fine sand from the shore to add to its damaging abilities. Wind may bend, break, scorch, tear and uproot plants and some of this damage is increased when salt and sand are included in the assault. Many good garden plants of inland gardens are not accustomed to such attacks and suffer accordingly, but from the coasts of numerous countries have come plants that survive and even thrive in the presence of wind, salt and blown sand. We will discuss them later, as it is to them that we must turn both for protection and to supply the chief inhabitants of exposed gardens.

In general, wind reduces temperatures. In winter, however, light onshore winds from over the water, which is at a higher temperature than the earth, maintain slightly higher temperatures. Thus, where the sea has an effect, average temperatures are often lower in summer and higher in winter. The provision of shelter reduces wind speeds and the consequent lowering of temperatures, but fortunately does not counteract the warming effect of onshore winter winds (see figure 1, p. 9).

Damage by wind allows fungus diseases to enter and spread more readily in many plants. The spores of some fungi causing plant diseases can only enter the plant through damaged tissue and this is often found on leaves, branches, flowers and fruit that have been exposed to strong winds. At the same time, the moister atmosphere by the sea improves the conditions in which diseases thrive.

Wind-shaped thorns and other trees on the coast suggest long periods of strong gales from off the sea, but the shaping is not usually caused by persistent winds. It is nearly always the result of pruning by the wind, perhaps only once a year, when really strong salt-laden gales kill or shorten all new growth directly exposed to it. After such wind-pruning, the unexposed twigs and branches will

Plumes of the pink pampas grass look particularly fine in the wind and are relatively unharmed by it continue to grow more or less horizontally to leeward and the well known leaning tree will develop.

It must not be thought that winds only flow onshore or from one direction. Even with the so-called prevailing winds, it is rare for more than 40% of the wind to come from one of the four quarters of the compass, or more than 25% from the southwest, which is usually the source of the strongest and most frequent winds. Strong winds can and do come from all quarters. Overland winds may bring less damage than the salt-laden sea winds but, in winter when from the north and east, they may carry snow and frost that are equally damaging.

On the east coast, where the onshore winds are, in winter, the cold winds, protection from their combined effects is even more important. The farther south and west one goes, the less important will be the freezing effects of onshore winds, although salt damage will occur. However, protection will still be needed against winds from other quarters, unless the garden is naturally sheltered by hills or woodlands on the landward side.

THE EFFECT OF BARRIERS

Before looking at the means of providing shelter, let us consider the effect of barriers on windspeed and direction. Wind is, of course, air moving from an area of high pressure to one of lower pressure. It moves more or less directly and at more or less even speeds over water or flat land, but swerves and eddies when obstacles of any kind are interposed. Wind cannot be stopped, but it can be deflected or filtered.

A solid barrier deflects wind and, when this happens, the speed increases over the top and at the ends of the barrier. This can often be noticed at street corners or between two solid hedges, where the wind is diverted and the air whistles round or through at greater speeds. Immediately behind a solid barrier, there will be an area of comparative calm; further away, the wind will drive downwards from the high pressure area in front of and above the obstacle to a relatively low pressure space from which the air has been kept by the barrier. Thus, in the lee of a solid windbreak some shelter can be found, but a little beyond it there will be an area of turbulence and wind eddying where more damage will be caused to plants and other vulnerable objects.

A permeable barrier, on the other hand, allows some wind to pass through at reduced speeds, while sending some of it over the top or around the ends in the same way as a solid wall. It will be obvious

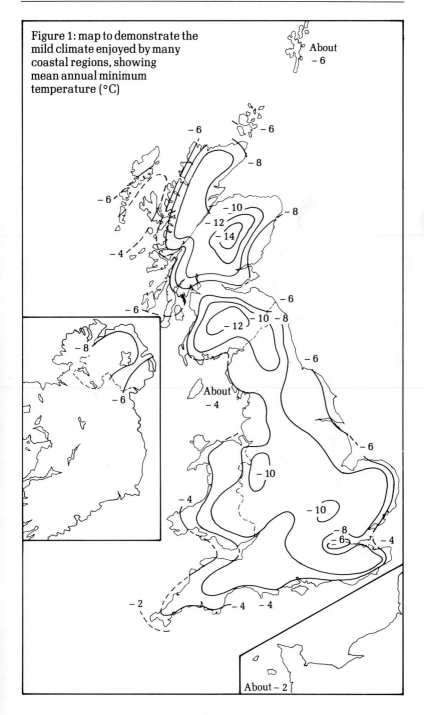

Figure 1: map to demonstrate the mild climate enjoyed by many coastal regions, showing mean annual minimum temperature (°C)

Direction of wind

95%   85% ▌hedge   35%   75%   95%
5 H   2H   5H   10H   20H

    a Cross-section, to scale, of a hedge at right angles to the direction of wind, showing percentages of original wind speeds (measured at ground level) at various distances (in heights of hedge) to windward and leeward of the hedge

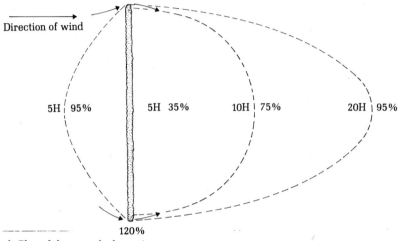

Direction of wind

5H ¦ 95%   5H 35%   10H ¦ 75%   20H ¦ 95%

120%

    b Plan of the same hedge as in *a*

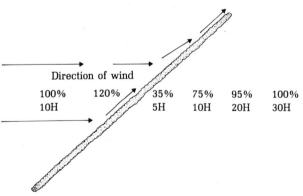

Direction of wind

100%   120%   35%   75%   95%   100%
10H   5H   10H   20H   30H

    c Plan of a hedge at an angle of 45° to the wind, showing percentages of original wind speeds in relation to the hedge (measured along line of original direction of the wind and not at right angles to the hedge)

Figure 2: the effect of a permeable barrier on wind speeds

that wire netting or similar very permeable screening will allow much of the wind to pass through at almost the original wind speed, whereas a thickish hedge will allow far less to pass through and at considerably reduced speeds, although it may cause some eddying to leeward.

Much research has been conducted into the behaviour of wind and it is known that the optimum permeability for a shelter is about 60% solid to 40% aperture. This significantly reduces wind speeds but causes little turbulence. The lath fences once widely used to protect flower crops in the West Country, and still available in a few places, are near this optimum degree of permeability. The wooden laths, 1 in. (2.5 cm) wide and spaced 1 in. apart, plus the cross-timbers on which they are mounted and the broad bracing diagonals, produce a ratio of about 60:40.

The diagrams in figure 2 illustrate patterns of the wind when blowing against a permeable barrier such as a hedge, trellis or screen. It must be remembered that they are somewhat simplified. Each situation will be different and may produce areas of exposure or shelter that need to be studied on the ground and taken into account before planning any additional protection.

As well as its permeability, the height of a barrier (expressed as H) has a direct relation to wind speed. Quite simply, a solid barrier will give good shelter up to a distance of 2H (i.e. twice the height of the barrier) and there will then be an area of turbulence up to 7H away. A barrier of 60:40 permeability (as shown in the diagrams) will produce little turbulence and will reduce wind speed at ground level up to a distance of about 20H, but with the maximum protection only within about 5H.

PROVIDING SHELTER

Armed with this knowledge of the effect of shelter on wind, and bearing in mind the necessity of good shelter for almost all seaside gardens, how do we set about providing it? As always, each situation will need special attention, depending on its size, slope, shape, aspect and the surrounding shelter and on the wishes of the gardener. Larger gardens, of more than say 50 yd (45 m) across, will probably require tall shelter belts of suitable trees, while in smaller gardens, living hedges or artificial fences will be necessary.

Most gardeners will wish to preserve any existing attractive views from the house or garden. The competition between the pleasure of the scenery and protection from the wind has to be faced in almost all seaside gardens, with the additional problem of reduced sunshine and increased shade caused by shelter, particularly on the east and west where the shadows are long. Short of having a well sheltered garden with little or no view or, alternatively, ample views but little wind protection, the only solution is to provide several low screens at intervals across the garden over which the eye can roam to any distant horizons.

Shelter belts

A shelter belt may be defined as two or more rows of trees unpruned and growing to their full height and spread. Three rows are often recommended and even wider belts have been planted in exposed country, usually for the protection of farmsteads or livestock and the ultimate production of timber. Two rows will suffice for most garden purposes and, taking a long term view, will enable a third row to be planted some years later when the first two are beginning to become thin at the bottom.

× *Cupressocyparis leylandii* 'Castlewellan' makes a good tall hedge or shelter belt, but is less vigorous than the Leyland cypress itself

Young, suitably spaced trees will soon provide some shelter and, when mature, they will give permeable shelter and good protection for the garden and the plants established in their lee. The area protected obviously increases as the trees grow. Thus, when they are 50 ft (15 m) high, land up 250 ft (76 m) away in the lee of the belt can be well protected and there will be some protection at up to 1000 ft (305 m) away. Trees take time to grow and we cannot all afford the time allowed by Osgood Mackenzie, at Inverewe in the north of Scotland, who planted *Pinus radiata* and then left it for some 25 years before planting his garden! Useful shelter will usually be produced within ten years and meanwhile temporary artificial shelter or quick-growing hedges can be used and, if necessary, removed as the shelter belt becomes effective.

Trees for a shelter belt or for any other purpose in windy situations are best planted as young seedlings or even younger plants from cuttings. Older, large trees have too much top in relation to the amount of root, making them likely to be blown over by strong winds, and staking is expensive and often useless in exposed positions. The seedlings may be described as 1 + 1 plants in catalogues, which means that they have spent one year in the seed bed and one year lined out before being lifted for planting in their permanent positions. Very few trees are raised from cuttings, the most noteworthy exception being the hybrid Leyland cypress (see p. 14). Young plants should have the opportunity of making good new root systems before the tops become too large and top-heavy. They will benefit from protection in the early years when establishing themselves (see p.17) and also need to be kept clean and free from weeds.

Thorough cultivation of the ground and the elimination of perennial weeds in a strip of land 12 ft (3.6 m) wide are good preparation for a two-row shelter belt. The young trees, in their two, or at most, three rows, should be planted as 'staggered' rows and not opposite each other. For most species, 6 ft (1.8 m) each way is a suitable distance. Towards the end of winter is probably the best time for planting and firming in. Earlier planting may lead to loosening during a long wet winter and later planting may be followed by a dry spell that makes establishment difficult. After planting, application of a residual herbicide such as simazine, between the trees but not on them, will help them to make a good start without competition from weeds. There should be no further cultivation of the ground because this could damage the roots and loosen the soil around them, which might result in the young trees being blown over before they were properly established.

After the first year of clean ground and following the application of simazine or a similar weedkiller, grass may be sown between the rows. This will curb weeds and hold the roots of the trees firmly in place, but it should not be sown right up to their stems. In a few years, no further restriction of weeds will be necessary. The grass may need cutting for another year or two, or until the overgrowth of tree branches keeps it in check, and weeds around the base may require attention if they are growing so tall as to shade and damage the lowest branches of the young trees. Thereafter, ordinary garden weeds will do little harm to the trees. The worst weeds in a shelter belt are such competing plants as brambles, ivy, elder, thorn, ash and sycamore, which should be dealt with as soon as they appear.

The choice of trees to form a shelter belt by the sea is limited. As with so many decisions in gardening, a careful study of neighbouring plantings and a word or two with those who garden in the locality will be helpful. The most effective trees are evergreens, which will give protection all the year round. In the south and west of Britain, the quick-growing, massive Monterey pine, *Pinus radiata*, from a very limited district on the west coast of North America, is as good as any. Singed by salt spray but quickly recovering and remaining upright and firm at the roots, it grows 2 ft (60 cm) or more each year after becoming established. The beach pine, *P. contorta*, comes from a much wider area of the west of the United States and Canada, with consequent variations in growth and usefulness. The variety *latifolia*, known as the lodgepole pine, is the one usually planted for shelter purposes in this country. It probably survives colder conditions and is therefore more widely used in the colder parts of the country.

When closely clipped, as it so often is, the Monterey cypress, *Cupressus macrocarpa*, is a great disappointment, but when allowed to grow untrimmed as a shelter-belt tree, it is one of the toughest of all trees for the seaside in the mildest regions. The Leyland cypress, × *Cupressocyparis leylandii*, has been widely planted in recent years and somewhat maligned for its instability. Like all the others, only very young trees must be planted. Being a hybrid and raised from cuttings, there is no tap root and the two or three main roots tend to grow horizontally. Newly rooted cuttings (never transplants or plants raised overlong in containers) should be permanently planted as soon as the site is clean and deeply

Pinus contorta var. *latifolia*, a reliable shelter-belt tree for coastal sites

cultivated. Only then will the roots spread quickly and a little downwards to support the rapidly growing tops. Shallow soils over chalk or rock are not suitable for this tree, as the roots do not seem able to penetrate into the lower crevices as do those of some of the pines.

The European evergreen oak, or holm oak, *Quercus ilex*, is slower-growing than any of the others already mentioned, but is just as stable when properly planted and longer-lived. It is distinctive in form and growth. Probably the main cause for complaint in tidy gardens is that it sheds its considerable load of leaves in the spring and early summer when all thoughts of leaf-collecting have long since passed.

Among deciduous trees, ash, *Fraxinus excelsior*, and sycamore, *Acer pseudoplatanus*, will provide some protection on exposed sites, although they will always be wind-shaped near the coast and therefore less effective than the evergreens. The loss of leaves in the winter reduces their efficiency as shelter, but this may be useful if the plants or garden only require shelter in the summer. There may be some advantage also in that the leafless trees allow a little more light into the sheltered area.

Shelter-belt trees are just as much living, growing and, later, decaying features as any other plants. They need regular if not frequent attention – the removal of weeds in the shape of competing trees and of broken branches and dead trees if they occur. All shelter belts are best thinned as they grow. This will enable the remaining plants to grow into massive trees that will stand firm and provide shelter for a long time to come. The gardener arriving in an established garden is more likely to face these problems of maintenance than one who has recently planted a shelter belt.

At some stage, almost every shelter belt will become thin at the bottom, leading to wind damage through the gaps. This can often be overcome, if there is space, by planting an additional row of trees of the same or similar species. They are planted just beyond the spreading branches of the original trees, within the span of the roots, and individual preparation of the place for each tree will be necessary. Where there is a choice, the lighter side of the shelter belt is preferable, enabling the young trees to make reasonable growth and gradually merge into the existing line.

The alternative is to plant one of the rather few shrubs that will grow well under all but the heaviest shade. Thick pines are unlikely to permit such plantings to succeed, but an existing open shelter belt may well benefit from infilling. There is one attractive evergreen shrub, *Griselinia littoralis*, that will grow beneath moderate shade in the mildest parts and fill in gaps between trees (see p. 22).

16

Sea buckthorn, *Hippophae rhamnoides*, is useful by the sea as an outer screen or wind-hardy shrub

Although not frost-hardy, it will also make a very useful hedge in the open in warmer coastal districts. Other shrubs that can be used for infilling are native holly, *Ilex aquifolium*, and some of the evergreen oleasters, including *Elaeagnus* × *ebbingei*, *E. pungens* and several of its variegated forms, and *E.* × *reflexa*. The latter, in particular, tends to produce climbing branches that may eventually smother the main trees if these are not growing very vigorously. If the site of the shelter belt is very exposed, any underplanting of shrubs or additional rows of trees will almost certainly need some artificial shelter in their first few years.

Outer screens
The importance of protecting young trees in a shelter belt while they become established has already been mentioned. In the teeth of the wind, near the shore or cliff edge, any rough vegetation will be welcome protection for a newly planted shelter belt or more formal hedges. Native gorse, elder, sycamore, sea buckthorn, ash, blackthorn and quickthorn, with the inevitable brambles, may be left 3–6 ft (0.9–1.8 m) wide where there is space on the windward side of the plants. They will be singed and tattered and, although

17

never reaching any great height, will provide some protection in the first years. They will later prove the point that there is some shelter on the windward side of windbreaks, and will be seen to grow taller than normal as the shelter belt too makes growth.

If it can be established, the New Zealand flax, *Phormium tenax*, will stand boldly in exposed situations (see p. 33). So also will some bamboos, particularly *Pseudosasa (Arundinaria) japonica*. They will look bedraggled after every storm, but will send up new growth each spring that will provide some shelter at the lower levels. Bamboos are particularly good in moist rich soil (see p. 56).

Hedges

A single row of trees or shrubs, trimmed to a predetermined height and breadth, can make a formal hedge. A single row of shrubs, or of a mixture of shrubs, left untrimmed, becomes an informal hedge. Almost any shrub can be used for an informal hedge, although the number that will survive in seaside conditions is much smaller. Shrubs that can be clipped to formal hedges are less plentiful and, of these, very few indeed can be planted by the sea.

As with a shelter belt, good soil preparation and the removal of perennial weeds, and using young plants and keeping them weed-free all contribute to the early and successful establishment of a hedge. When possible, planting a hedge against small-mesh wire netting or similar screening encourages more rapid and upright growth. Weeds must be controlled as they compete for food and water, so reducing the rate of growth and, what is worse, may smother the lower branches and leave them permanently bare. A single row of hedge plants is easier to keep weed-free and is less costly than a double row, which has no real advantage.

Most of the suitable hedge shrubs may be planted 1–3 ft (30–90 cm) apart and, except for those intended to form a single stem, such as certain conifers, they are best hard-pruned after the first year of growth. This involves the removal of at least half the length of the leading shoots and trimming the more or less horizontal shoots to leave them 6–8 in. (15–20 cm) long. The initial pruning will encourage a good thick bottom to the young hedge and, as the seasons pass, trimming should be designed to produce a broad base and narrow top. This shape not only tends to preserve the lower branches, because they receive more light than when the sides are vertical or undercut (as so many hedges are), but also reduces the risk of the tops being broken out by heavy snow. With the bottom forming a solid barrier and the top a permeable one, a hedge of this kind makes an almost ideal shelter, with good protection at ground level and a filtering top that reduces wind turbulence.

The range of seaside shrubs that can be considered for use as hedges is greater than that of trees for shelter belts, but they are still few in comparison with the number available for planting inland. The genus *Escallonia*, from the shores of South America, contains some of the best seaside hedges, especially *E. rubra* var. *macrantha* and the two cultivars raised in Cornwall, 'Crimson Spire' and 'Red Hedger'. These are wind- and salt-tolerant and fairly frost-hardy. Many of the others are too flimsy or more tender and, although they make attractive semi-formal hedges, are not really suitable for providing shelter. The cheapest method of forming an escallonia hedge is to plant cuttings in a single row from late October onwards, having prepared the strip of ground for the hedge early in the autumn. The cuttings, of current year's growth up to 12 in. (30 cm) long, are inserted with at least two thirds of their length in the soil and about 1 ft (30 cm) apart. They should not be pushed in as this is likely to damage the base and impede rooting. In

Some escallonias provide excellent seaside hedges

most circumstances, the cuttings will have rooted by the spring and some growth will have appeared by the autumn. They may then be lightly pruned and, if kept free from weeds, are quite able to reach 6 ft (1.8 m) in height within three years of planting. Plants raised elsewhere from cuttings and planted in their permanent site in the spring may suffer some setback, but soon become established to attain a similar height if conditions are good.

Escallonias may be clipped twice or more each year, when they have made good growth in the early summer and again in the early autumn, and will then form a solid evergreen hedge rivalling close-clipped yew or privet in appearance. Clipped only once a year, in July, they produce short growth before the winter and carry a striking display of red flowers in late spring and early summer. They may be 'burnt' by strong gales and lose many of their leaves in the coldest winters, but will recover the following spring.

In addition to the oleasters for use in partially shaded conditions (p. 17), some others including the deciduous *Elaeagnus angustifolia* and *E. umbellata* may be trimmed into quite useful hedges, resisting much of the wind that may be experienced by the sea. Trimming once a year during the late summer will keep them moderately formal, while left untouched they form a strong but spreading barrier. They are not quite so quick-growing in the early stages as escallonias, but when established many make rapid growth.

Some of the numerous New Zealand olearias are useful hedges in

Tamarix ramosissima 'Rosea' thrives in exposed coastal places

the milder districts, although they are generally better when untrimmed as informal barriers. They are evergreen, with small daisy-like flowers, and mostly very wind-hardy. *Olearia × haastii* is the hardiest and thrives inland in the north of England, but it is not very tall or quick-growing. It can be made into a neat formal hedge, of up to about 5 ft (1.5 m) high, almost anywhere. With grey holly-like leaves and broad panicles of small white flowers in June and July, *O. macrodonta* is more satisfactory as an informal hedge up to 15 ft (4.5 m) high than when close-trimmed (see p. 29). If killed to the ground in very cold winters, it usually grows again from the base. *Olearia virgata* behaves in the same way, growing even more rapidly after being cut back by a very sharp frost. It has the advantage that, although not looking very ornamental, the dead branches will remain in place to provide some shelter while the new growth is appearing. This shrub has somewhat rosemary-like leaves and an upright habit and is best left untrimmed to withstand the severest gales. Even faster-growing but even less frost-hardy is *O. traversii*, which is quite often killed except in the mildest districts. It is so quick-growing that its roots rarely keep it erect unless it is strongly staked or hard-pruned in the early years to reduce the imbalance between root and top growth. Nevertheless, planted young against good artificial shelter and with half its annual growth removed in the first three years, it makes a most attractive and useful hedge in warmer areas.

Several others daisy bushes, such as *Olearia albida*, *O. avicennii-folia*, *O. paniculata*, with wavy-edged leaves rather like *Pittosporum tenuifolium*, and *O. solandri*, looking like a tall golden-leaved heather, may be used as mostly quite narrow, informal hedges in suitable climates. From the related genus *Senecio*, *S. reinoldii* has some of the toughest wind-resistant leaves of any New Zealand shrub, but is better when allowed to form a rounded shrub than when trimmed in an effort to make a formal hedge. It has been known to succumb in sharp frosts. Other lower-growing and somewhat spreading senecios are also wind-hardy and some are more frost-hardy. *Senecio greyi*, *S. monroi*, and the hybrid *S.* 'Sunshine', evergreens with grey foliage and yellow flowers, would make informal lines of low-growing protection where taller hedges are not wanted.

Euonymus japonicus is usually undamaged by the worst gales and is frost-hardy in most parts of the country. Strange as it may seem, the exception is in the milder areas, where the plant goes on growing long into the autumn and, when this growth is hit by a sharp frost in the new year, is killed back to the older wood. It is, however, a most useful evergreen hedge plant – if not a very attractive one – for almost all seaside gardens. There are also variegated cultivars.

The tamarisks are well known seaside shrubs, deciduous, wind-hardy, frost-resistant and providing good permeable shelter. They have been trimmed to make semi-formal hedges, but do not survive long in that condition. There are several species – *Tamarix gallica*, being regarded as a denizen of this country, and *T. parviflora*, *T. ramosissima* (*T. pentandra*; see p. 20) and *T. tetrandra* from southern Europe and western Africa – all of which will serve well as informal screens or even thrive in the outer defences with the commoner natives (see p. 17).

Of other shrubs that can be used as more or less formal hedges in the milder districts, *Griselinia littoralis* (p. 16) has a very compact root system, which makes it easy to transplant as quite a large

Griselinia littoralis, a versatile seaside shrub that can be used as a hedge, filler or in its own right

shrub. *Fuchsia magellanica* var. *gracilis* and *F.* 'Riccartonii' are attractive flowering hedges in seaside areas of the southwest. The latter is the stronger and will reach 6 ft (1.8 m) in two or three years when the winters are relatively frost-free. They usually grow again from below ground after hard frosts have struck and, in the warmer parts, will reach even double that height. *Pittosporum tenuifolium* stands a certain amount of wind in milder regions, but needs complete protection when it is being grown for its evergreen foliage. Stronger-growing and altogether more wind-resistant are *P. crassifolium* and *P. ralphii*, but they are quite tender and really only suitable as hedges, for which they are used in the Isles of Scilly. *Muehlenbeckia complexa*, sometimes known as the wire netting plant, has very thin wiry stems that will scramble upwards and over any plant or fence and quickly makes an almost impenetrable mass of twining shoots in milder areas. Some of the dwarfer and close-growing hebes, such as the *Hebe × franciscana* hybrids, are sufficiently wind-hardy to make useful low hedges near the coast.

Artificial shelter

Walls and stone-faced banks make permanent boundaries and provide solid shelter that can be useful in protecting trees and shrubs while they are becoming established. Wooden fences of various kinds, including the standard lath fences (p. 11), wire and plastic netting and various other plastic fences all make good temporary screens against which hedge shrubs can grow more readily to serviceable heights (see p. 24).

Where a fence forms the boundary between two plots, it is always as well to talk to the neighbour before making any planting on or adjacent to the boundary. If complete agreement is reached, the new hedge may be planted as close to the boundary as possible and will grow through the fence to be trimmed by each on their own side. After all, most people want a good hedge and a single line of one kind is far better than two, which often make the hedge so wide that trimming of the top becomes almost impossible. The temporary and sometimes not very sightly fences can then be absorbed in the hedge, improving the appearance of the garden and retaining its original purpose of defining the boundary and keeping out unwanted cats and dogs. However, if the neighbour insists on a different hedge or wishes to see only the fence, it may be necessary to plant the hedge or shelter belt some distance from the boundary, to allow enough room to prune the plants on your own side and to prevent the trees or shrubs from growing over the neighbour's land.

Whatever is chosen as a temporary artificial fence, it is of the

greatest importance that the stakes and other supports are adequate. A fence that stands and provides shelter for almost the whole year and then blows over in an exceptional gale is worse than useless. This is because many plants, when protected from wind, expand and grow more openly than they would without shelter and if, after a year of good growth, the protection is suddenly removed, the damage is greater than ever. So stout supporting posts should be deeply set in the ground, with struts or wires all strongly held together by screws or nails, and should enable the fence to withstand the occasional hurricane. Remember, too, that gales often bring rain and that the additional weight of the water makes fences even heavier and more difficult to support.

ACHIEVING AND MAINTAINING ADEQUATE SHELTER

It is not always possible to ensure that shelter is of the optimum 60% permeability, particularly with shelter belts and hedges, which vary with the seasons and conditions and as the plants grow. Measuring their permeability is also very difficult.

Viewed from right angles, a shelter belt or hedge may appear quite solid and, from a more acute angle, very solid, but when the leaves and branches move in the wind, it may actually be too open or permeable. However, observation of the effect of the wind on plants in the lee side will provide a clue as to whether the shelter is sufficient. As a general rule, it may be said that, if moving figures can be seen but not identified through a hedge or shelter belt, the amount of shelter is about right and no changes need be attempted.

If a hedge is too solid, it may be thinned by trimming more closely to remove the mesh of small twigs that thicken it; if it is too open, one or both sides may be trimmed less closely for a year or more. It is less easy to improve a shelter belt, which is not trimmed, although the main fault – gaps at the bottom – can usually be overcome by additional planting (see p. 16).

Rigid artificial shelter in the form of lath or similar wood fences can be measured to assess the degree of permeability. Unlike a living screen, it will not alter. Flexible shelter, such as plastic fencing, may be less effective than it appears because it gives way under pressure, allowing more wind to blow through and at greater speeds to cause increased damage on the lee side. Additional layers of material should then be provided for reinforcement.

Above: plastic netting creates a serviceable windbreak
Below: a fine bedding display at Torquay, Devon

Types of Seaside Garden

Having considered the main problem of seaside gardening – the wind and how to reduce its effect – let us consider the gardening alternatives that can be practised by the sea. The various forms of gardening to be found in Britain are so numerous as to be almost endless, depending as they do on the wishes of the owner and on the size and conditions of the plot. Where there is room, a framework of trees and many shrubs among lawns can provide a reasonably work-free garden. Add herbaceous flower and bulbs and the work required will increase, while even more labour is necessary with biennials and annuals, whether sown or bedded. Almost all these types of ornamental gardening will need good protection in windy conditions. Alpine or rock gardening perhaps needs less shelter, as many alpines come from fairly exposed situations, but the plants demand quite a lot of attention to keep them in order and weed-free.

Enthusiasts for individual plants or groups of plants are widespread. One has seen gardens of roses, of irises and even of pelargoniums, and many gardeners devote their energies to chrysanthemums, dahlias, sweet peas or daffodils. If, as is often the case, the purpose of the specialism is exhibition, the need for shelter is paramount. The same applies to growing hardy fruit, for one's own use, and vegetables, if the show bench is in mind, when wind damage can be very limiting.

We will return briefly to the special needs of these various gardens in seaside conditions, but there are really two possibilities by the sea that should be considered – a garden of wind-hardy plants; or a garden consisting of plants only on the verge of hardiness, which have, in the past, tempted so many gardeners in the mildest districts.

THE WINDSWEPT GARDEN

Before shelter is established or even without any intention of providing it, the gardener may rely entirely on wind-hardy plants for the framework or the whole of the garden. Such an unsheltered garden can be economical of time and energy, requiring little

The Brazilian *Tibouchina urvilleana*, a tempting shrub for gardeners in warm districts by the sea

27

pruning, clipping, staking or tying and generally smothering most weeds, thus reducing the amount of weeding and hoeing. It does however, lack many of the well loved features of other gardens. It is quite unsuitable for most of the usual herbaceous plants, annuals or bedding plants, and fruit and vegetable gardening is more or less impossible. It can be open and sunny on the few calm bright days, but is not tempting to work in or for relaxation on the many days when wind is blowing.

Lawns

If the garden is large enough, there may be space, on a suitably maintained lawn, for garden sports. Bowls and croquet do not need the formality of a rectangular plot and can be played on an irregular lawn among beds and borders of shrubs. A single rink for bowls should be 42 × 7 yd (38 × 6 m), although a full green must be 42 × 42 yd (38 × 38 m) with adequate surrounds. Croquet requires 32 × 28 yd (29 × 25 m), but enjoyable games can be had on other sizes and shapes. About 40 × 22 yd (36 × 20 m) overall is necessary for lawn tennis, with enough surrounding netting if the game is not to become too exhausting from chasing errant balls to all parts of the garden. Golf putting can be accommodated on quite a small lawn and does not need the careful levelling of some other games, but the grass must be finely cut and any competitive matches take up an extensive area.

Shrubs

There is a range of wind-hardy and attractive plants which can fill the windswept garden and which, as time passes, will provide sheltered pockets where even greater variety can be introduced. Where there is room, any of the trees and shrubs already mentioned as suitable for giving shelter and many of their relatives may be planted in borders, groups or as individual specimens around and in ample lawns, to form a pleasant, easily run garden. Less space obviously makes it impossible to use trees or larger shrubs, but there are others to enhance even a small garden.

Of the considerable number of species and cultivars of escallonia, most are evergreens and make rounded shrubs, some with arching branches. The colour range is from the intense white against shining foliage of 'Iveyi' – one of the tallest – through many pinks, including the well named 'Apple Blossom' and 'Peach Blossom', to the deep reds of the glossy-leaved *Escallonia rubra* var. *macrantha* and its hybrids, including *E*. 'C. F. Ball'. Most escallonias are generous with their small flowers and are covered with colour for several weeks, from late May, when *E.* 'Pride of Donard' commences, to October when *E.* 'C. F. Ball' and others finish.

The oleasters also make strong, solid, rounded shrubs with handsome foliage but inconspicuous flowers. *Elaeagnus × ebbingei* has striking shining leaves which are silvery beneath and the somewhat similar *E. pungens* has a number of variegated cultivars that add all-the-year interest to the garden. There are several others that are sufficiently different to provide variety in a windswept garden (see also pp. 17 and 20). All produce small white flowers in the late summer and well into the autumn, giving a pleasant perfume at that time of the year.

Few of the olearias (p. 21) are sufficiently frost-hardy to be included in the unsheltered windswept garden, except in the mildest climates, but where they can be relied upon, they will contribute their attractive, daisy-like, slightly scented flowers to the scene.

Two of the large-leaved senecios, *Senecio reinoldii* and *S. elaeagnifolius*, are well able to withstand the strongest of winds, but have been killed to the ground in colder winters. Another large shrub,

Olearia macrodonta withstands wind, but may be cut back by severe cold

Cotton lavender flowers throughout the summer, given a position in full sun

almost a tree as it ages, *Griselinia littoralis* (p. 16) has pale bold foliage and is a good plant for the exposed garden.

The more compact lavenders and the cotton lavender, *Santolina chamaecyparissus*, remain unharmed in windy situations. Other grey foliage shrubs that grow well in salt-laden winds include the rock roses, *Helianthemum* and *Halimium*, with similar single rose-like flowers. Several of the small-leaved cotoneasters are low wind-resisters, with white flowers in spring and coloured leaves and berries in autumn. *Cotoneaster horizontalis* really needs a wall or bank against which to spread itself, but *C. microphyllus*, *C. dammeri*, *C. adpressus* and *C. conspicuus* are all admirable for the front of the border. Many of the heathers – *Erica* and *Calluna* species and cultivars – are sufficiently wind-resistant, provided the soil is not

The striking *Yucca gloriosa* 'Variegata' is frost-hardy

alkaline. As can be seen in a number of well known gardens, including the RHS Garden, Wisley, heathers can be a most attractive feature in the right surroundings. Their wide range of flowering periods and extensive spectrum of foliage colours enable a garden of great variety to be planned (see also the Wisley handbook, *Heaths and heathers*).

The native sea buckthorn, *Hippophae rhamnoides*, grows best on sandy shores, but is useful anywhere by the sea and provides a more open form than many of the shrubs already described, with decorative orange fruits during the winter. Several of the yuccas, with their sharp leaves and striking spikes of white flowers, are valuable for contrasting with the solid shapes of wind-hardy shrubs. In the same way, bamboos will break the line of shrubby

31

borders (see p. 56). They will look rather tatty after the fiercest gales, but produce a new crop of shoots each year. The rounded outline of a single plant of the pampas grass, *Cortaderia selloana*, is relieved in early autumn by its spectacular plumes, the clear white of 'Sunningdale Silver' being among the most striking. These may be battered rather earlier in the winter than in more sheltered gardens, but will have served a useful purpose for a while (see p. 6).

Bulbs
Within the framework of hardy shrubs, much colour and interest can be added from the start by planting bulbs which, together, can provide flowers for some nine months of the year. Crocuses can be chosen to flower from autumn to spring in varying colours, starting with the many forms of *Crocus speciosus* and its relations in October and ending with the popular yellow *C. flavus* and its garden hybrids in March. The so-called autumn crocus, *Colchicum autumnale*, and its many relations produce the first crocus-type flowers from September onwards, but they have large, rather intrusive leaves the following spring. Two other crocus-like bulbs are the bright yellow *Sternbergia lutea*, flowering in the autumn, and the reddish purple *Bulbocodium vernum* in early spring. The numerous forms of snowdrop, *Galanthus*, can be had from January through to March and there is also an autumn snowdrop, *G. reginae-olgae*.

In the mildest gardens, daffodils can be in flower from late autumn through to May. *Narcissus* 'Scilly White', found against many south-facing walls, and the Dutch yellow trumpet daffodil, *N.* 'Rijnveld's Early Sensation', flower in early January. Others continue through to the time when *N.* 'Double White' finishes the season as the earliest tulips appear. In all but large gardens, the smaller daffodils are best. The species *N. minimus*, *N. cyclamineus*, *N. bulbocodium*, *N. jonquilla*, *N. triandrus* and the native *N. pseudonarcissus*, with all their numerous cultivars, may be damaged by the strongest winds, but will provide some colour every year in the shelter of developing shrubs. Most of them are best in short grass which is not cut until the leaves are dying in July (see also the Wisley handbook, *Daffodils*).

Many tulips are not so happy in their ability either to stand the wind or to persist unlifted for many years. However, some of the dwarf, so called botanical tulips are worth including for flowering

New Zealand flax, *Phormium*, makes good wind-resistant clumps

in the late spring before the larger ones. *Tulipa batalinii*, *T. clusiana*, *T. fosteriana*, *T. greigii*, *T. kaufmanniana* and others, with their smaller hybrids, bring a range of colour when grown in sun with some shelter. The specialist bulb catalogues will suggest many more less common bulbs that can give interest and colour throughout the summer until the montbretias (now grouped under *Tritonia* and *Crocosmia*) come into flower in late summer and autumn. The mildest gardens will also allow the planting and flowering of two different plants sometimes known as naked ladies – *Amaryllis belladonna* and the nerines. Both flower in warm places from late August through to late October (see also the Wisley handbook, *Growing dwarf bulbs*.)

Thus, for the gardener who will accept the limitations of the effect of the wind, there are many hardy trees and shrubs that can create the framework of a not too labour-intensive garden, which will consolidate into an attractive maturity making even less demands on time and energy. If greater variety and colour are required in the early years, numerous bulbs can provide them.

THE HALF-HARDY GARDEN

Turning now from the really windswept to the more sheltered garden, let us consider the possibilities, particularly in the milder southern and western districts. As we have noted, the shelter may be provided by natural features of hills and woods, or it may have been introduced in the forms already described. Apart from the wind, the other main factor that may limit plant growth will be soil. As in any garden, chalk, limestone, or, near the sea, most blown sand with its particles of broken seashells, will usually restrict ornamental gardening to plants that will grow in alkaline conditions. This eliminates camellias, rhododendrons and most other ericaceous plants and applies to much but not all of the coast. Badly drained soils are inhibiting too, but this condition can generally be overcome. Soils of whatever type may also be shallow over solid rock or too much broken stone. This is difficult for gardening of any kind and adds to the problems of establishing and maintaining good shelter belts where they are needed. However, thorough preparation of the sites for planting and no further disturbance of the surface will do much to overcome the handicap.

Where there is shelter and the climate is less harsh than normal, there is a great temptation to try to grow the many attractive plants that thrive in warmer countries or are to be found under glass

The lovely *Magnolia liliiflora* grows to about 10 ft (3 m) high and across

elsewhere. Such plants often survive and even flourish for several years and then succumb in the severe winters that occur periodically – as in 1946/47, 1962/63, 1981/82 and, in south and west Cornwall and Scilly, in the early weeks of 1987. Gardens can be devastated when short sharp conditions assail tender plants, but not all is lost because some are merely killed above ground level and others are damaged only on the last year's growth that has gone on developing long into the mild autumns. It is a risk that many gardeners in the warmer regions are prepared to take.

Trees, shrubs and wall shrubs

Among the trees and shrubs that prefer sheltered mild conditions are some that are reasonably hardy but benefit from the milder springs in which to flower without the risk of damage from late frosts. They also enjoy the higher rainfall that usually occurs in these parts of the country. Magnolias, particularly those that grow into tall trees, such as *Magnolia campbellii* and var. *mollicomata*, *M. delavayi*, and *M. × veitchii*, are really at their best in open woodland by the sea. Similarly, the medium-sized species such as *M. liliiflora*, *M. sinensis*, *M. × watsonii* and *M. wilsonii* are more likely to flower successfully in the milder areas.

The earliest rhododendrons require protection from wind and also have a greater chance of displaying their flowers to perfection in mild gardens where late frosts are less common. This large genus provides great variety of size, colour and time of flowering, shape and size of leaf, but almost all need an acid soil. They range from the towering *Rhododendron arboreum* and some relatives, reaching 40 ft (12 m) in height, to *R. radicans* and *R. forrestii*, clinging no more than a few inches above the ground. There are red flowers of every hue, through pinks to pure white, with orange and similar colours and some nearly blue among the purples and mauves. They first appear before Christmas and some go on well into the summer. The leaves vary from those almost 20 by 8 in. (50 by 20 cm) of *R. grande* and others in the same group to the tiny leaves of some azaleas, with a variety of greens on the surface and bronzes and darker colours beneath. Several species from southeast Asia are too tender for any outside garden in Britain, but a few that are borderline will survive for many years. *Rhododendron nuttallii*, *R. veitchianum*, *R. virgatum*, *R.* 'Countess of Haddington' and *R.* 'Fragrantissimum' are among those that provide scent and colour where shelter from wind and frost can be given (see also the Wisley handbook, *Rhododendrons*).

Camellias, once grown as greenhouse or conservatory shrubs, have long been found quite hardy in most parts of the country, but they need protection from strong winds and are usually at their best where mild springs will not damage their flowers. Their shining foliage is attractive all the time and the white, pink or red flowers of the numerous cultivars may, in the milder districts, last from November to May (see also the Wisley handbook, *Camellias*).

Many of the wattles or acacias will grow and flower well for a few years, only to be killed in the occasional cold spell. Even then, they may only be cut back to the ground, leaving a number of new growths to appear near, and sometimes at a distance from, the base. Some are useful wall shrubs, although the mimosa, *Acacia dealbata*, which is probably the hardiest, makes quite a thick trunk and is really too strong to grow beside the average wall. *Acacia armata*, *A. longifolia*, *A. rhetinodes* and *A. verticillata* are other wattles that may be planted in the mildest gardens, either against a wall or in a sheltered corner.

There are several most attractive abutilons which thrive in warm districts. *Abutilon vitifolium*, with large, open, lavender-coloured

The fast-growing mimosa, *Acacia dealbata*, flowers in early spring

flowers and deeper purple and white forms, is so fast-growing and floriferous that it should be tried wherever some mild winters can be expected. It grows to at least 10 ft (3 m) in a very few years, to make a striking display in early summer, but, even without frost-damage, its natural life seems to be short, since a plant will die suddenly after a very free-flowering season. Replacements can be raised easily from cuttings – of the cultivars and hybrids – or by seed, and these quickly fill any gaps. *Abutilon megapotamicum* is another rather straggling, tender shrub, with somewhat fuchsia-like flowers of yellow and red. It does best against a south-facing wall and then survives most winters. It can be in flower for some eighteen months given a mild winter.

Ceanothus in many forms can be found for the open ground or to help clothe sunny walls. Some of the hardiest are the deciduous hybrids, such as *Ceanothus* 'Gloire de Versailles', raised in France many years ago. Others, less hardy and evergreen, range from *C. arboreus* 'Trewithen Blue', growing to 12 ft (3.6 m) and more, with bold leaves and blue flowers over a long period, to *C. divergens*, *C. prostratus* and *C. thyrsiflorus*, which are almost ground-clinging

Ceanothus arboreus 'Trewithen Blue' is a vigorous spreading shrub

and suitable for contrasting with the dwarf cotoneasters. 'Trewithen Blue' is often seen as a wall shrub, but it will stand alone in mild districts and, anyway, needs ample wall space. *Ceanothus dentatus*, *C. rigidus*, *C.* 'Autumnal Blue', *C.* 'Southmead' and several others are more compact and suitable for smaller walls.

The south and southerly walls of the house and other buildings are always valuable places on which to grow some of the most tender wall shrubs and climbers. Even there, they may be lost in the rare, usually brief, winter frost, although if there is due warning and action is prompt, temporary protection with netting, hessian, straw or bracken can save many of them. Among others, two cassias, with yellow pea-like flowers, have come through many recent winters with no more than severe cutting back. *Cassia corymbosa* is hardier than *C. obtusa*, but both provide good splashes of yellow in late summer and autumn where they succeed (see p. 58). The New Zealand lobster claw, *Clianthus puniceus*, a straggling shrub with huge pea-like red flowers, needs a warm wall for protection and support. Its white form is less striking unless against a red brick wall. In the angle of a southwest wall, it may be

Clianthus puniceus bears its unusual flowers in spring and early summer

Feijoa sellowiana has the bonus of attractive evergreen leaves with white undersides

worth trying the almost tender *Tibouchina urvilleana* for its large purple flowers that continue through summer (see p. 26). It requires protection in all but the mildest winters. *Itea ilicifolia*, with evergreen holly-like leaves and very long catkins in summer and autumn, will fill quite a large wall and is hardier than some of those mentioned here. Very well drained soil against a warm wall will suit *Feijoa (Acca) sellowiana*, a South American shrub with striking dark red and white flowers and, after the warmest summers, edible egg-shaped fruits.

Some of the relatives of the wind-hardy shrubs already mentioned are not very hardy and do better in the shelter of the mild seaside garden. They include *Olearia* × *scilloniensis*, which smothers itself every spring with the purest white flowers, and the *O. phlogopappa* 'Splendens' group, producing similar masses of pink, mauve and blue michaelmas daisy-like flowers in the summer. *Olearia semidentata* will be cut to the ground in the colder winters, but often survives for several years and is well worth planting for its larger than usual mauve flowers during early summer. Although some of the hebes, particularly *Hebe dieffenbachii* and *H.* × *franciscana* 'Blue Gem' and other cultivars, are very wind-hardy, many of the more colourful need the protection of other shrubs or hedges in coastal gardens. Many are hybrids with larger leaves and flower

The flame creeper, *Tropaeolum speciosum*, will climb up to 10 ft (3 m)

spikes: 'Alicia Amherst', 'Miss E. Fittall', 'Purple Queen' and 'Simon Delaux', together with the 'Wand' series in a wide range of colours, all produce valuable flowers over a long period.

Climbers
There are many beautiful climbers and scramblers that add greatly to gardening by the sea, planted among wall shrubs or on suitable bare walls. *Lapageria rosea*, the national flower of Chile, climbs along erect wires or through open shrubs to produce large, delicate, red, pink and white flowers in late summer and autumn. It prefers some shade and ample moisture and, if growing from beneath good ground cover, withstands most winter frosts; in many years the whole plant survives to maintain plentiful aerial growth. Three of the herbaceous tropaeolums will scramble through wall shrubs and others growing in the autumn. *Tropaeolum speciosum*, with scarlet flowers, seems to thrive best in the west of Scotland and is very fickle in approval of its surroundings. Good plants should be planted from pots in late spring and are happiest in the shade of established shrubs in peaty soils. Similarly, *T. tricolorum* and *T. tuberosum* need shade at their roots, the former flowering quite early in the spring and the whole plant dying back before midsummer.

Several of the passion flowers, particularly *Passiflora caerulea*, the hardiest, provide interesting shape and colour on almost any wall. *Berberidopsis corallina*, *Billardiera longiflora*, *Sollya heterophylla* and *Eccremocarpus scaber* can all be allowed to scramble over other wall shrubs, or be trained up bare walls with wire or trellis in the milder districts, and do not overrun either the shrubs or the house. Others should be treated with caution if they are not to smother everything within reach. Most of the actinidias come into this category, particularly *Actinidia deliciosa* (*A. chinensis*), the Chinese gooseberry or kiwi fruit. When male and female plants are grown, fruits can be obtained in warmer areas, but they require at least a two-storey wall or massive poles and strong wire in the open. The least aggressive is the unusual *A. kolomikta*, which has green, pink and white leaves when growing on a wall in full sunshine. Two climbing members of the potato family, *Solanum crispum* and *S. jasminoides* make quite long growth, but can be kept in check without curtailing flowering too much (see p. 63).

Palms and succulents

In addition to the reasonably hardy yuccas (p. 31), other palm-like plants bring variety to the outline of a garden and a sense of the warmer nature of seaside gardens. *Cordyline australis* and *C. indivisa*, often known as dracaena, are among the hardiest, but even they have been killed to ground-level once or twice in living memory in the mildest parts. They have then grown again from below ground and the only problem, after removing the rather stringy dead stumps, is to make sure that the many new shoots are thinned to one, or at most three, in order to preserve their distinctive outlines. They will soon reach sufficient height to allow the large bunches of creamy white, scented flowers to appear early each summer. A similar tree, the Chusan palm, *Trachycarpus fortunei*, has survived where the cordyline has been cut back. It is a true palm, with characteristic leaves clustered at the top of rather thin stems that are covered with the remains of the old leaf stalks. It also carries bunches of flowers each summer. *Chamaerops humilis*, the dwarf fan palm, is the only European native palm, but less hardy than the Chusan. It has similar leaves and flowers and an even

Above: Billardiera longiflora is a distinctive climber for a partly shaded wall
Below: The dwarf fan palm, *Chamaerops humilis*, does best in a sheltered sunny place

slower-growing stem. Not everyone approves of the shape and often bedraggled appearance of the cordylines and palms, but they certainly make distinctive features in many seaside gardens.

In the mildest gardens, one or two agaves may be planted to provide different shapes with their rosettes of sharp-pointed, tough, succulent leaves. *Agave parryi* is the hardiest and *A. americana* the largest and most exciting. Each grows the rosette for many years and then sends up a single stem, up to 10 ft (3 m) or more tall, with numerous cream-coloured flowers. *Agave americana* is known, rather extravagantly, as the century plant, but although many years elapse before flowering, it is seldom as tardy as implied by the name. After flowering, the original plant dies, usually leaving a cluster of small rosettes which can either remain or be transplanted to fresh sites. More tender and even more striking is the Mexican *Beschorneria yuccoides*, which grows with similar rosettes of pointed leaves. It is perennial and not very frost- or wind-hardy but, in a sheltered spot facing south, it throws rapidly growing, rose pink stems upwards to 8 ft (2.4 m) in early summer every year. The bracts on these striking stems are also pink, while the tiny flowers are bright green.

Scented plants

Many a garden can be improved by the addition of a few plants that contribute scent, either from their foliage in the warmth of the day or when touched in passing, or from their flowers. A tender shrub that does this well is the lemon-scented verbena, *Aloysia triphylla* (*Lippia citriodora*), which will grow into a rather straggling bush when there is not too much frost but is best against a south-facing wall. *Choisya ternata*, a much hardier evergreen, has two very distinct scents – that of the crushed leaves, which is difficult to describe and is not liked by all, and the extremely sweet perfume of the white flowers, which fully justifies the common name of Mexican orange blossom. Several oleasters (pp. 17 and 20) have insignificant white or cream flowers that fill the air with sweet scent in the late summer and autumn. Most of the pittosporums (p. 23) are heavily scented and are particularly noticeable on warm early summer evenings. The commonest, *Pittosporum tenuifolium*, has dark purple, fragrant flowers. The attractive *P. eugenioides* and its variegated form, together with *P. tobira*, are worth their places for their perfume, even if the occasional sharp frost deals harshly with them.

Most of the large number of escallonias so strongly recommended for their wind-hardiness (p. 28) produce a pleasant scent

44

from their foliage on warm summer days. All the myrtles are equally valuable for the fragrance of their flowers. Some, such as *Myrtus communis* and its varieties, are unharmed in all but the coldest winters, but others are less hardy. The least hardy is probably *M. ugni*, with pink flowers and – when sufficient plants are grown – dark red fruits, from which a full flavoured conserve can be made. Between them, the several species available can provide scented flowers for most of the summer. Also fragrant are most of the jasmines. *Jasminum nudiflorum*, the hardy winter species, can be grown almost anywhere but, because of the nature

The succulent *Agave americana* 'Variegata' lends an exotic air to the garden

Buddleia alternifolia makes a graceful shrub or small tree with arching branches

of its growth, looks best on a wall. Some of the others, such as *J. angulare, J. mesnyi* and *J. polyanthum,* are good climbers for a warm wall. The common buddleias, *Buddleia alternifolia* and *B. davidii,* are quite hardy and well known for their perfume. *Buddleia asiatica,* equally scented but less hardy, has the advantage of carrying its white flowers well into the autumn in the mildest climates.

Dwarf plants
Certain very low-growing plants, where they can be walked on, also give off scents. The thymes, particularly *Thymus serpyllum* with its many coloured varieties, are quite hardy and are useful in this respect on warmer sites. Less hardy but good in moist spots is the similar close-growing *Mentha requienii,* which will grow in a damp lawn if the grass is kept short. Another very dwarf plant, not scented but interesting in milder gardens, is *Polygonum capitatum,*

Osteospermum jucundum is a perennial in mild areas, with abundant flowers in late summer

which seeds itself to persist after the coldest winters and may come through without harm when frost is less severe. Two genera with daisy-like flowers provide very suitable dwarf plants for seaside gardens – the gazanias, especially the spreading types, and osteo-spermums, once known as *Dimorphotheca*. Both have given rise to many cultivars from several species, the former with a colour range among the yellows and orange, and the latter from white through pinks to deep purple. They survive mild winters, but are killed by sharp frosts. All strike very easily from cuttings and it is wise to make use of this to carry the plants over the coldest winters.

The ability to propagate vegetatively should really be a feature of any seaside garden where the gardener is tempted to have something of the unusual or, perhaps, to boast a little of the tender plants that he or she is able to grow. Winters in which cherished plants have been killed or cut to the ground leave gaps that have to be filled, either by replacing them with similar plants, or by retreating to the commoner hardy kinds that can be grown anywhere in the country. Although most local nurserymen maintain and propagate stocks of tender plants, many gardeners propagate a few every year as a precaution for their own gardens. Such gardeners tend to put in a few more cuttings than they need and the surpluses are often passed on when the gardens are open or at local plant sales.

THE ORTHODOX GARDEN

So far we have described the two special types of gardening that are available to seaside gardeners – the limited garden of wind-hardy plants and the more exciting but often frustrating garden of half-hardy plants. The two are not exclusive and can be merged into each other. But what of the gardener who does not wish to change?

For those who would garden in the ways that are so common all over the country, there are always limitations wherever they are. Temperatures and humidity vary from the cold of the high hills or high latitudes to the damp of the valleys; rainfall varies from Essex to the Highlands and the Lake District; soils vary, not least in degree of acidity or alkalinity. All have to be taken into account and plants chosen to suit the conditions, unless there is an overriding desire to grow something with a continual battle against the odds. In addition to these general restrictions, there are the effects of the wind and usually the increased moisture that occurs by the sea, which is intensified by the creation of shelter and reduction in wind speeds. Let us look at these problems as they affect the many aspects of gardening in Britain.

Trees and shrubs

Where trees and shrubs are concerned, there is little that can be done to improve their chances. We have discussed those that thrive. Others survive, but some are never really healthy, among them the flowering crabs and cherries and their relatives in the genera *Malus*, *Pyrus* and *Prunus*. Not only are they easily shaped and damaged by wind, but all suffer from fungal and bacterial diseases that are very difficult to keep in check. Few conifers, except those mentioned (p. 14), merit a place unless shelter is ample. Many of them, such as the cypresses, are used to provide the contrast of erect green spires among trees and shrubs, while the spruces and firs are attractive with their Christmas-tree shapes. However, strong winds soon spoil their outline and salt-laden gales brown their foliage.

Roses

There are many shrubby roses that will survive and produce satisfactory flowers and hips, some even in quite exposed sites, but the modern hybrids and their relatives are rarely happy unless they receive constant attention. The mild damp atmosphere encourages black spot and mildew is quite prevalent. Fungal diseases can be controlled by regular spraying, but mildewed buds, which are common, are difficult to avoid. Another problem with roses is the length of time that they will remain in growth. They are best lightly pruned in the autumn to reduce the top growth and thus prevent wind-rocking, and then finally pruned rather earlier than usual in the spring. Even so, in many years growth will continue throughout the winter, with the result that the plants need even more generous feeding than usual. Liquid feeding combined with fungal sprays can supplement any farmyard manure and powdered fertilizer that are used.

Roses *can* be grown by the sea, as at Compton Acres, overlooking Poole Harbour in Dorset, where skilled attention is given

Herbaceous plants

Most herbaceous plants are liable to be blown over unless well sheltered and may tend to be drawn up too high if over-sheltered. Staking the plants is a time-consuming job anyway and is even more difficult in windy situations. Some plants, such as delphiniums, lupins and hollyhocks, are almost impossible. In addition, they are so susceptible to the slugs and snails that proliferate in moist conditions as to make their survival very problematical. The popular hostas also look far from happy with their leaves eaten by these difficult pests. The most likely herbaceous plants to succeed where wind may reach them are those that need no staking, either because they are dwarf and sturdy, or because, like the various forms of astilbe, geum, bergenia, hemerocallis, heuchera and many more, they grow a mat of leaves close the the ground and then send up stiff flower stems for a short while in the summer. The ornamental grasses from among the fescues, holcus and poas may also do well.

Show flowers

The many carnations and pinks, *Dianthus*, rarely thrive unless the soil is alkaline, with a high pH, as on chalk, limestone and calcareous sea sand. Many irises also prefer such conditions to the more acid soils. Of the other common 'show' flowers, good chrysanthemums and dahlias can be grown if there is ample shelter, but with a little more care than may be needed elsewhere, since the moister atmosphere tends to produce more frequent attacks of grey mould (botrytis) on buds and petals. In the mildest districts, dahlias for garden and household decoration can be left in the ground for many years. When they are lifted for winter storage, they should be carefully dried to prevent them rotting in store. Sweet peas are liable to be blown down sometime during the season and the petals damaged unless they are very well sheltered. Daffodils, also a popular show flower, are widely grown around the coasts of Britain. Being quite short and thus easily protected, they are less likely to be damaged by wind and, anyway, can be picked in bud before the flowers can be battered. However, if too well sheltered, the bulbs are more vulnerable to attack by grubs of the large narcissus fly, since the fly enjoys still wind-free conditions in which to fly and lay the eggs which produce the grubs.

Above: dwarf garden hybrids of astilbe, such as 'Atrorosea', grow no more than 18 in. (45 cm) tall
Below: day lilies, *Hemerocallis*, are robust perennials in a wide range of colours

Annuals

In choosing annuals to sow in odd corners or special beds or borders, it will be obvious that shelter must be provided and, in any case, the short low-growing kinds will be preferable to the taller ones. In the sunny conditions that prevail in some coastal districts, many of the dwarf annuals with daisy-like flowers that open more completely in full sunshine are at a great advantage.

Lawns

A lawn is an essential feature of almost every type of garden. There is a modern view that any more or less green mown sward will serve the purpose, or may even be desirable in preserving some native weeds. There is no doubt, however, that a uniform covering of a single grass or similar grasses provides a more satisfactory foil to surrounding plants. Broad-leaved weeds, such as dandelions, daisies and docks, and plants like speedwell, oxalis and wild white clover that flower beneath the level of cutting distract the eye and spoil the appearance of the lawn as a background or foreground. Even variations in grass species, such as Yorkshire fog and annual meadow grass, can be distracting.

In the mild moist conditions of most seaside areas, several aspects of lawn management will need additional attention. Mowing will often have to be continued throughout the year and consequently, with the more frequent removal of the grass, extra fertilizer will be required if a good green sward is to be maintained. Weeds are just as prevalent in seaside lawns and moss tends to grow even more strongly, except on the very sandy soils that sometimes occur. Still windless days on which to apply herbicides are less common. On the other hand, leaf-sweeping is rarely necessary as strong winds regularly bustle the leaves into odd corners, where they can be left or moved to the compost heap.

Tree fruit

Many of the most valuable fruits that can be grown in English gardens are not at their best in seaside gardens. They can be grown – nothing is impossible in gardening – but they often cause more trouble than they are worth or they produce lower-quality crops than can be expected farther inland. New fruit trees, as with all other trees, should be planted as young as possible. Older and larger trees will have great difficulty in producing an adequate root

Sun-loving gazanias are ideal bedding plants for the seaside

system to hold the head of branches, leaves and fruit in windy conditions. Whatever the age, adequate staking is essential in the first years, and the stem or trunk and the stake must be wrapped to prevent chafing.

Apple trees, bushes or trained cordons and espaliers are best pruned by the gardener and not by the wind! Wind-shaped trees will produce fruit of sorts but, unless shelter is provided, the growing of tree fruits is hardly worth contemplating. If flowering coincides with strong winds, the flight of pollinating insects will be reduced and less fruit will result. If autumn gales come before ripening or picking times, as they nearly always do with the later apples and pears, windfalls will be more plentiful and storable crops will be diminished. Even earlier in the summer, the growing fruits may be bruised by being banged against each other and the rasp of leaves can damage the skins of the fruits. Worst of all, the atmosphere near the sea is usually more humid and this encourages

Actinidia deliciosa can be grown for its kiwi fruits in warm parts of Britain, but needs plenty of wall space

scab and canker. The former disease attacks leaves and twigs and spoils the appearance of the fruit, while canker kills twigs, branches and even whole trees. Both diseases can be controlled by spraying, but it must be thorough and generally has to be more frequent in moist conditions than where it is drier, where six or more applications each year are common. Brown rot also seems to be more troublesome in damp conditions, unless the necessary steps are taken to prevent or reduce it. These consist of carefully removing and destroying every affected fruit at the time of picking and removing all fallen fruits from the vicinity of the trees.

Pears present similar problems to apples and really need even more attention almost everywhere in Britain if good-quality fruit is to be grown. They are at their best in warmer climates, as the magnificent fruit we receive from countries farther south demonstrates. Cherries and plums are equally liable to damage by wind and have somewhat similar diseases to those that attack the apple and pear when growing in moist conditions. Heavy rain or a damp atmosphere at ripening time will also encourage fruits to split.

If the seaside gardener is prepared to do without the ornamental shrubs and climbers already recommended for the walls of the house, all these fruit trees will do better there than in the open. Peaches and nectarines, in particular, must have the protection of a wall with a southerly aspect and they also need extra care as regards spraying and shelter from wind. The young shoots due to bear next year's fruit may be broken by the wind if not tied in as they grow. In very mild districts, winter temperatures may not be low enough to break winter dormancy.

Dessert grapes of not very high quality may be grown on south-facing walls in the south and can contribute to a Mediterranean appearance. There are a number of vineyards along the south coast, but they must have shelter and conditions for them are usually better away from the sea breezes which reduce morning and evening temperatures. High temperatures in summer and, particularly, autumn are really essential for production of good wine grapes. The strong climber, *Actinidia deliciosa* (p. 54), will fruit in the milder areas. The New Zealand cultivars 'Bruno' and 'Hayward' are much larger than the species and even more recent ones may be further improvements when they are available. They must have ample length or height of strong wire for the very long vines that they produce.

The common hazel and its cultivated cousins, the cob nut and filbert, need protection from wind, especially at flowering time. If not sheltered, the pollen from the catkins will be blown into the next

parish and will not drop onto the tiny red female flowers that produce the nuts after pollination.

So, it is not an encouraging outlook for orchard fruit by the sea. Those who feel they must grow their own top fruit may either struggle to give all the attention necessary to produce the best possible, or they may provide what shelter they can, plant their orchard and let it grow as it will. In this way, they will provide a good environment for bulbs and other flowers in the grass, and some fruit will arrive in due time. It will not be saleable nor fit for shows, but it may still be better than the 'Golden Delicious' apples or unripe 'Conference' pears from the shops.

Soft fruit

The soft, bush and cane fruits are more feasible given some shelter although, as with tree fruits, the greater dampness of the seaside garden can be a problem. Raspberries and redcurrants are particularly susceptible to wind damage, blackberries, loganberries and hybrid berries, gooseberries and blackcurrants rather less so, but all grow best within good shelter. In all but the most exposed conditions, strawberries are close enough to the ground to avoid serious damage. The uprights and wire on which fruits are trained need to be stronger in windy situations, as does the fruit cage, which is essential if full crops of fruit are to be picked.

Strawberries, raspberries and loganberries are particularly prone to botrytis or grey mould on their fruits in damp seaside conditions and the disease is also likely to increase in the shade cast by the hedges or screens needed for shelter. Spraying can help to reduce damage and the selection of suitable cultivars is useful. Strawberries with smaller leaves and their fruits standing above them, such as 'Pantagruella', and less vigorous raspberries, such as 'Malling Jewel', tend to be less affected than the stronger-growing ones. The autumn-fruiting raspberries are often very successful, but too much rain in September and beyond will cause a complete loss as the grey mould attacks. However, the cultivar 'September' starts to fruit a little earlier than its name implies and than some other autumn croppers, and this usually allows some fruits to be picked before the damp autumn days make the grey mould so tiresome.

Above: the autumn-fruiting raspberry 'September' is worth trying in coastal gardens
Below: bamboos can form an outer screen to protect a vegetable plot

Cassia corymbosa is one of the more tender shrubs for a favoured seaside garden

If loganberries are chosen, the thornless clone is much easier to handle than others and is a heavy cropper. Some of the newer hybrids, particularly 'Tayberry', are far too difficult to deal with, especially in a high wind; this seems to have the prickles of the worst blackberries and the spines of a raspberry. The alternate training system, where blackberry, loganberry and similar canes are tied to one side of the plant as they grow, is better than allowing them to grow over the fruiting canes, as the fruit is left uncovered and therefore drier. Blueberries, from the several American cultivars of *Vaccinium corymbosum*, need really acid soil containing ample peat and the fruit must be protected from birds as well as from strong winds. (For further information, see *The Fruit Garden Displayed*).

Vegetables

The pleasures of eating fresh home-grown vegetables and salads and even of stocking the deep freeze or other stores are not diminished by the seaside. Almost all that is said in *The Vegetable Garden Displayed* applies to gardening by the sea. We will consider the special needs of the seaside garden.

On many coasts, valuable organic matter is there for the taking, and there is no doubt that liberal use of bulky manures is an essential feature of all vegetable gardening. Seaweed carried from the high-tide mark or cut from the rocks has been used for generations to manure near-by farms and gardens. It is heavy, unless allowed to dry, which is difficult on public beaches. It now so often contains unwanted plastics and other undesirable and indestructable debris that it is best sorted as it is collected to avoid cluttering the garden with rubbish. An added disadvantage of seaweed is its attraction for flies that will invade the house and other buildings. For this reason, it is best hauled in winter, when there are fewer flies and the seaweed itself is more plentiful. It can then be spread on uncropped land to be dug in when partially dried, or it can be added to the compost heap, mixed with weeds, hedge trimmings and leaves, and then covered with lawn mowings to encourage decay without encouraging the flies.

On many shores, seaweed is mixed with broken shells that contain much calcium, thus raising the pH of the mixture and making it unsuitable for application to acid-loving plants. It is, however, very welcome in the vegetable garden where the pH is always dropping as calcium is leached from the soil. In some parts of the country, the sea sand comprises a high proportion of finely broken shells and this is regularly used in place of lime or powdered chalk to maintain the best alkalinity for the vegetable crops that need it. Such sand can also improve the physical condition of heavier soils.

Wind has already been mentioned – some may say too often – but it is an ever-present problem, not least in several vegetable garden practices. Unless the vegetable garden is fully sheltered, runner beans will be difficult to keep erect on the usual tall sticks and the field method, of allowing suitable cultivars to run along the ground with their tips removed regularly, may be a better system. It does not produce such long straight pods, but the crop can be just as heavy. Similarly, dwarf peas growing on the ground may be better than tall ones on sticks or string. If sticks are to be used, they must be strong and have a few extra cross bracings to hold the rows together, or pea boughs may be supported on wires strained to strong poles at the ends of the rows.

It is often desirable to earth up the taller winter brassicas, such as brussels sprouts and sprouting and winter broccoli. Planted in shallow drills drawn with a hoe, they are first supported as the earth is levelled in hoeing and then supported by earthing up, almost as for potatoes. The mildest districts allow regular cropping of winter cauliflower or broccoli from November to May, and most other winter brassicas can be relied on to survive and continue in growth throughout the winter, when the shallow ridge and furrow thus created not only supports the stems but provides a certain amount of drainage.

It is rare that frost is so hard beside the sea that the usual early-sown vegetables will not overwinter. However, broad beans, sown in the late autumn, can be so battered by wind and swirled around in muddy little holes that they die of drowning instead of frost. Later sowing in boxes or pots under glass, for planting in early spring, may often be better, but even then protection is required. Winter lettuce, winter spinach and spring onions can all be blown to pieces where strong winds sweep across exposed gardens. While ripe onions need to be lifted and thoroughly dried for hanging in a dry shed for the winter, other root vegetables such as beet and parsnips can be left, as they are unlikely to be frozen into the ground.

Although the milder conditions allow many crops to survive the winter and others to be sown and planted earlier, all but the lightest soils are difficult to prepare in the heavier rainfall and fewer drying days that prevail. There is also very little frost to break up the surface after autumn digging. Early digging or merely clearing and levelling and no digging, to leave the minimum of large clods on heavy soils, may be the answer. If, when the time comes for early sowing or planting, the surface is too wet and difficult to work, the use of boards on which to walk beside the proposed line of sowing will avoid damaging the tilth; the spread of the weight on the boards does much less damage than the feet direct on the soil. Another way to prepare for sowing is to place a line of cloches over the intended row a week or two before sowing. This will dry the surface slightly and many crops will benefit from further cover if the cloches are replaced after sowing. Early potatoes, broad beans, peas, summer cabbage and cauliflower, carrots, turnips, green onions and beet-root can all be obtained much earlier from January to February sowings in this way. Some of them may be harvested even earlier from greenhouse sowing in pots or boxes, followed by early planting.

Cloches, frames and plastic tunnels are useful aids to early production of vegetables and salads in any garden. In exposed situations, they are at risk and special precautions are necessary, using strong cords to hold down frames and plastics, or providing local shelter to protect them. The older glass cloches usually remain firm once they have settled in, except in the teeth of the worst gales. It is a good plan, however, to draw a light drill on each side of the line of cloches when they are moved, so they can settle in more quickly and remain firm. Tunnels or cloches of pliable plastic are not usually damaged unless there is an opening or tear where the wind can enter and blow away the whole row. In the same way, an open door or ventilator on the windward side of a greenhouse will allow pressure to build up and blow out glass on the other side. Even the overlapping glass admits some air and produces similar pressure and it has been found worthwhile to open ventilators on the lee side to reduce the pressure and the risk of damage.

The damp atmosphere in seaside gardens encourages potato blight disease earlier in the season and more regularly than in drier districts. (It also affects tomatoes.) Spraying to prevent attacks, whenever moist mild conditions arrive, is essential if potatoes have not reached lifting time, and for tomatoes – even under glass – if potatoes are growing nearby. Spraying will also be necessary for mid-season and maincrop potatoes, if they are grown, although it is doubtful if they are worth it in small gardens. Earlies can, as we have mentioned, be planted earlier and have their haulms cut off before blight begins to appear because, unless spraying is thorough and frequent, it is of little use in the mild wet days of a seaside summer.

CONCLUSION

Almost any plant can be grown in nearly any situation with the necessary time, skills and money to provide the right conditions. To go to extremes, such as the commonly stated example of bananas at the North Pole, is to invite continuous struggle, frustration and expenditure. The number of specialist societies and books about individual plants indicates that there are many who must concentrate on their own speciality, and it is hoped that these notes will help them to overcome the problems if they insist on bringing their hobby to the seaside. Others may wish to create all the features of a

former garden. For them, the reduction of wind-damage and related difficulties may be of assistance, but it is suggested that the two main variations – the wind-hardy garden and the half-hardy garden – may have greater attractions.

The seaside garden, of whatever size, can be as varied as any other with the planned aid of ample protection from wind, salt and driven sand. In addition, it is possible to experiment with the many varied and truly exotic plants that can only be admired in foreign parts or heated greenhouses and are impossible to grow in colder gardens.

Opposite: *Solanum jasminoides*, a beautiful summer-flowering climber for the half-hardy garden

Below: Glendurgan, a sheltered garden on the Helford estuary in Cornwall

Cymru

Gardens to Visit

The following is a selection of gardens situated on or near the coast. Many seaside resorts also have interesting gardens on the edge of the sea, and useful ideas can be gleaned from both. (NT = National Trust; NGS = National Gardens Scheme; NTS = National Trust for Scotland).

England
Abbotsbury Gardens, Abbotsbury, Dorset (NGS)
Compton Acres, Poole, Dorset (NGS)
Glendurgan, Mawnan Smith, Cornwall (NT)
Headland, Battery Lane, Polruan, Cornwall (NGS)
Liverpool University Botanic Gardens, Ness, Neston, S Wirral
Overbecks Museum & Garden, Sharpitor, Salcombe, Devon (NT)
St Michael's Mount, Marazion, Cornwall (NT, NGS)
Trebah, Mawnan Smith, Cornwall (NGS)
Trengwainton, Penzance, Cornwall (NT)

Channel Islands
La Colline, Jersey

Isles of Scilly
Tresco Abbey, Tresco

Wales
Plas Newydd, Isle of Anglesey, Gwynedd (NT)

Scotland
Achamore Gardens, Isle of Ghiga, Strathclyde
Brodick Castle, Isle of Arran, Strathclyde (NTS)
Dunrobin Castle, Golspie, Highlands
Inverewe, Poolewe, Highlands (NTS)
Kiloran, Isle of Colonsay, Strathclyde
Logan Botanic Garden, Port Logan, Dumfries & Galloway (Royal Botanic Garden, Edinburgh)